THE UNDERTAKERS
LAST SIEGE OF HAVEN

TY DRAGO

Month9Books

THE UNDERTAKERS — LAST SIEGE OF HAVEN by Ty Drago
All rights reserved. Published in the United States of America by Month9Books, LLC.
No part of this book may be used or reproduced in any manner whatsoever without written permission of the publisher, except in the case of brief quotations embodied in critical articles and reviews.

Published by Month9Books, LLC.
Illustration by Zachary Schoenbaum
Title design by Victoria Faye of Whit&Ware
Cover design by Najla Qamber Designs
Cover Copyright © 2015 Month9Books

Month9Books

"Victory is a commodity. It has a cost. Always."
—*Anonymous*

This book is dedicated in friendship and gratitude to film producer Andrew van den Houten and screenwriter Jeffrey Reddick for their brilliant and tireless efforts to bring The Undertakers *to the silver screen.*

Gentlemen, you do me proud!

TY DRAGO

CHAPTER 1
BACK IN SCHOOL

The last day of the war started with two eleven-year-old girls clutching at me in terror, while a third girl stood protectively between us and a half-dozen of the walking dead, who closed in like lions around a wounded wildebeest.

Oh, and did I mention the Zombie Prince?

Um ... maybe I'd better dial things back about ten minutes.

Let's start with the snarling teacher.

"*Mister* Kessler," the teacher snarled. "Why don't you list for us three things that Walter Raleigh, or people in his employ, brought back to England from the New World?"

I don't much like teachers. But I *hate* teachers who call you by your last name, especially when it *isn't* your last name. And I really hate it when the teacher who's calling you by a last name that isn't yours is—well—*dead*.

Okay, that probably hasn't happened to you. But, trust me, it stinks on ice.

My name's Will Ritter. I'm an Undertaker. That means I spend my days battling Corpses, invaders from another planet, or dimension, or *something*. We're not quite sure. These beings, who call themselves the *Malum,* are actually super-scary ten-legged monsters on their homeworld. But they arrive on *ours* with no bodies at all—just man-sized lumps of dark energy that wouldn't last ten seconds in our atmosphere if they didn't immediately possess and inhabit dead bodies. These they wear like suits of clothing until the cadavers literally fall apart around them. Then they abandon them and find another, and so on.

Thing is: most people can't see them. To every adult on the planet—and most kids—Corpses look like regular folks: policemen, neighbors, bus drivers.

Teachers.

End of info dump. You'll pick up the rest as we go along. For now, just get this: my history teacher, Ms. McKinney, was a Corpse. And if she wised up to the fact that I *knew* she was a Corpse, she'd kill me.

But at least that was a familiar kind of fear. This "getting called on" thing was something else entirely.

Before this gig, it'd been a while since I'd gone to school.

"Well, Mr. Kessler?"

That was my cover name: Ryan Kessler. The Hackers, the Undertakers' computer crew, gave it to me when I first took this Schooler gig almost a month ago. Since then, I'd been Ryan, not Will. It had taken some getting used to, but eventually the lie had become second nature.

"Um … tobacco," I said.

"Yes. That's one." She'd left the backboard, and was shuffling down the aisle toward me.

She smelled *awful* and, whenever she moved, flies

as big as marbles flew in and out of holes in her neck and face. She was an early Type Three. That's the one-to-five measuring system we use to describe how ripe a Corpse is getting. Threes are *bloating*, their tissues filling up with gases as they decompose. In the next week or so, unless she traded up to a fresher cadaver, Ms. Marcy McKinney—her name and history as fake as my own—would swell like an overripe melon, filling her budget pantsuit until her eyes popped out of her head.

The kids around me, of course, saw none of it. They weren't Seers. To them, Ms. McKinney was simply a short, skinny redhead in her fifties, alive and, to their eyes, completely normal.

We call it their Mask. It's the face Corpses show to the world, and only Seers—a few, select kids like me—can recognize the stomach-emptying truth behind it. It's not an ability anybody asks for; it just happens to us one day. "Getting your Eyes," we call it.

"Two more, Mr. Kessler," she said, coming to stand by my desk. Her voice sounded thick, as if she were drowning. As if she *could*. The dead—no big surprise—are really hard to kill. Ms. McKinney's voice box was just rotting, that's all.

I racked my brain. I'd studied this last night, sort of. Well, *you* try to study by the light of a kerosene lamp while huddled in a tent in the woods outside of Allentown, Pennsylvania! True, it was June, with only one more day of school left, and, yeah, that *did* mean it was warmer than, say, February. But it also meant that I shared the small tent with a fistful of mosquitoes.

And one big roommate—who snored.

"Potatoes," I said.

"That's two." She kept glowering. "And the third?"

"I ..." But the final answer wouldn't come. A blank.

Nothing. Whatever the third thing was the old British dude had snagged in the Americas, I couldn't remember it.

Every school kid knows, in such a situation, there's only one kind of miracle to hope for.

And I got it.

The bell rang.

You could almost hear the room exhale. Suddenly, forty eighth-graders were in motion—collecting books, pencils, and paper, as they began spilling out through the hallway door.

Ms. McKinney eyed me dangerously. Then she straightened and shouted in her sticky voice, "Final test tomorrow! Everything we've studied all year will be on it! I don't care if it's the last day of school! It's fifty percent of your grade, so be prepared!"

Groans.

Only a Corpse calls a test for the last day of school.

Pure evil.

I'd gotten up with the others, a little more slowly maybe, given my close call. I wasn't the last one out the door, but I was close to it, when the teacher suddenly said, "Stay a minute, Mr. Kessler."

Crap.

I paused and turned, hoping I hadn't heard her right. She waggled a purple, lifeless finger at me and pointed to the guest chair beside her desk.

My heart sinking, I took a seat.

As she settled into her own chair, her knees popped loudly. Tendons had just torn, I supposed.

"I'm worried about you." She sounded almost kindly.

Leaning forward, Ms. McKinney clasped her hands in front of her on the desktop. As she did, maggots squeezed out through cracks in the flesh of her wrists. They were tiny, like little squirming grains of rice. The sight of them would have grossed out almost anybody else. But I'd seen bigger maggots than these.

Much bigger.

That's another story.

"Why?" I asked.

"You seem tired today. In fact, you've seemed tired all week. How are you sleeping?"

"Okay, I guess." I wasn't about to tell her about the tent, its mosquitoes, or my snoring roommate.

"Everything okay at home? You and your folks settling into your new house?"

"Sure." There was, of course, no new house and no "folks." My mom and sister were back in Haven, the Undertakers' HQ, thirty miles away in Center City, Philadelphia. I hadn't seen either of them in a month, though we talked on the phone two or three times a week. Mom's idea.

As far as Merriweather Intermediate School was concerned, I had a mom and a dad, and we all lived in the suburban house we'd just bought, the details falsified with practiced ease by the Hackers.

"I know how hard it can be to come into a new school, especially at the end of the year," Ms. McKinney told me gently. "And I want you to know: if there's anything I can do to help, just say so."

"Um ... thanks."

"Ryan?"

"Yes, Ma'am?"

"*Is* there anything I can do to help?"

"Don't think so."

"I've noticed how you look at me."

I involuntarily swallowed. Nerves. She noticed.

"What do you mean?" I asked.

She tilted her head. As she did, flakes of skin and wisps of dead hair sprinkled the shoulder of her suit. "You know what I mean."

So, either she suspects I just got my Eyes ... or she thinks I have a crush on her.

I hope it's the Eyes thing.

I glanced over my shoulder at the open hallway door. Through it, I could see swarms of kids moving back and forth in that funny kind of reluctant haste that's reserved for the five minute break between classes.

"Want to leave, Ryan?" Ms. McKinney asked, and though she tried to hide it, I caught the edge of menace in her voice.

Sure, I wanted to leave. But not quite the way she meant. In truth, even if I'd escaped with the rest of the history class, I'd have hung around in the hallway, waiting until the last possible second to head for my fifth period lunch. Watching.

Watching for Julie.

I had Ms. McKinney for fourth period eighth grade history. Julie had her for fifth period sixth grade history.

That was no accident.

Julie was the reason I'd come to Merriweather.

Watch Julie. Monitor Julie. Protect Julie.

My mission: Guard a little girl until the end of the school year. And do it without her knowledge.

That's me. Will Ritter. Guardian Angel.

"I asked you a question, Mr. Kessler," the teacher snarled. Her "Come to Me with Your Problems" bit was apparently over. She'd sucked at it, anyway.

"No, ma'am." I kept my eyes focused on the door.

Any second now.

Ms. McKinney said, "Look at me."

I looked.

She leaned *way* over the desk, her dead face—putrid and bug infested—inches from my own. Then she hissed, "What do you *See*, Mr. Kessler?"

Yep. It's the Eyes thing.

"I … um … see the next class coming in."

And they were. Sixth graders had started slogging in from the hallway, backpacks over their shoulders, weary expressions on their faces—expressions that turned curious when they saw Ms. McKinney and myself.

The teacher sat back and smiled, showing me her hideous toothless maw. The other kids, I knew, saw only a friendly, welcoming grin. After all, they were her adored pupils, and Marcy McKinney was teacher of the year.

Corpses are, above all else, completely full of crap.

"Go to your next class, Ryan. We'll talk again."

I stood up with my own backpack, turned toward to doorway to leave—

—and *froze*.

Julie Boettcher, small and brunette, stood at the classroom's threshold. Her thin, eleven-year-old body had gone statue still, her expressive brown eyes locked on Ms. McKinney. Her face, usually slightly darker in complexion than her sister's, had gone pasty white—and, as I watched her, her bottom lip began to tremble.

She just got her Eyes!

Every Undertaker remembers all too well that moment when they started Seeing Corpses, and got their first glimpse of the real world and the monsters that inhabit it. All the shock and horror and confusion of that initial moment shone like a beacon on this girl's face.

I glanced back at Ms. McKinney, but the history teacher hadn't noticed Julie yet. Her eyes—dead and seeming sightless—remained fixed on me.

Reactions are different for everyone. Some new Seers

faint. Others run. Others curse or scream.

Julie did none of those things. She was a Boettcher. Like her big sister, Helene, fellow Undertaker and—let's just get this out of the way now, okay?—my girlfriend, Julie had liquid steel running through her veins. On some level, she'd sensed the danger in revealing her newly discovered Seer talent. So, again as I watched, she steadied herself, took a deep breath, and stepped into the classroom.

Wow, I thought. *Sixth-graders are tougher than I remember.*

But then two more girls, a blond and a redhead, walked through the door, took one look at Ms. McKinney, and started screaming.

CHAPTER 2
AFTER THE BELL

*F*antastic.

Ms. McKinney didn't jump to her feet when the girls started pointing at her, shouting "zombie" accusations and hugging each other. Instead, she seemed to uncoil in her chair and rise like a panther poised for the pounce.

Julie stood off to one side, halfway to her desk. She'd paled all over again, her attention—as well as the attention of all the other kids in the room—locked on the bizarre confrontation at the front of the class.

"Girls," Ms. McKinney said coldly. "Stop this foolishness right now. I'd like to see you both out in the hallway."

I'll bet you would, I thought.

Then I pulled out my gun and shot her.

Okay, it wasn't a *real* gun. Just a water pistol. But the saltwater inside was way more effective on the Corpse teacher than a bullet would have been.

McKinney recoiled as my shot caught her full in the face. She slammed against the smart board and went into spasms, dropping to the floor and convulsing wildly as the saltwater messed with her ability to control her stolen body.

Now *all* the kids started screaming.

"I'll get help!" I shouted.

Then I grabbed Julie's hand, brought my mouth close to her ear, and whispered, "My name's Will. Your sister sent me. We're going. Now."

I pulled her toward the door. She hesitated, but only for a second. Then, with a final frightened glance at her flipping and flopping history teacher, she followed me.

"Come on, you two!" I called to the blond and redhead, who were still screaming.

They looked at me, wild-eyed with hysteria.

So, I shot them too.

Just one squirt each in the face. The screams stopped instantly and they snapped "Hey!" in perfect unison.

Girls hate it when you squirt them in the face with a water pistol. Every boy learns that one pretty early on.

"Come on!" I said again, still holding Julie by the hand. "Now!"

The "start of class" bell rang—had it *really* been just five minutes since Ms. McKinney had been grilling me on Walter Raleigh?—and the hallway stood mostly empty as the four of us broke into a run.

I led the girls away from the school's front entrance, strategizing with every step. Angel training. That's the crew I belong to, the Undertakers' squad most often in combat with deaders. True, this past month I'd been playing Schooler, which is more about infiltration than fighting. But after what I'd done to my teacher, something told me the whole Ryan Kessler thing was over.

McKinney would recover fast. When she did, she'd be on the horn with the other Corpses stationed here in Merriweather. There were seven that I knew of, including the principal, who called himself Robert Dillin. The trick would be to get Julie and the other two Seers safely off school grounds before Dillin and his cronies came looking for us.

"Where ... are ... we ... going?" the redhead asked breathlessly as we ran.

"Who ... are ... you?" the blond added, just as breathlessly

"Hang on," I told them both, pulling out my sat phone and hitting the right speed dial.

Three long rings later, my roommate's voice answered, *"Yo, dude!"*

"I'm blown," I told him. "I've got three Seers with me."

"Oh, crap. What about Julie?"

"She's one of them."

"Oh, crap."

"Where are you?"

"Yard work."

"Front or back?

"Side. We're laying mulch."

"Meet me behind the building."

"On my way. Hey, Will?"

"Yeah?"

"Does this mean we're done with that tiny tent in the woods?"

"Guess so."

"Good. I ain't into cuddlin', man."

"Funny," I told him. Then I shut the phone—grinning, despite myself.

Jerk.

The long hallway ended in a T-junction. I looked left and right. Right was clear. Left wasn't.

A Corpse, dressed like a science teacher, stood about thirty feet away. He was a Type Five, way far gone, with no hair left, and limbs made thin and brittle by loss of moisture and muscle tissue. He regarded us with sunken eyes, his lipless mouth working.

"Just be cool," I told the girls.

"Just be cool," Julie echoed from beside me.

Blond and Redhead started screaming.

Fantastic.

The deader made a dry, raspy noise that was probably supposed to be a growl. Then he came after us. He didn't run; I doubted if that withered old body of his *could* run. Instead he staggered, his skinny arms reaching, his bony fingers like claws.

They *really* look like zombies when they do that.

"This way," I said, grabbing Julie's hand and leading the girls to the right, two of them still screaming.

Doors began opening up and down the hallway as the noise attracted the attention of the various teachers in their various classrooms.

"Stop them!" the Corpse rasped from behind us, a sound that I knew all too well would be heard as normal speech by the Un-Seeing faculty members. Sure enough, a stout gym teacher reached for me. He was a big guy, probably a college football player, clearly used to getting physical with kids when the situation called for it.

"Now just hold up, son," he said in a voice as deep as the ocean.

"I'm not your son," I replied.

Then I Tased him.

Oh, didn't I mention my Taser?

It's actually a pocketknife—a weird, tricked-out

pocketknife with a bunch of buttons and all sorts of gadgets that really have no business being in a pocketknife. How did I get it? I found it under my pillow, left there by a mysterious woman who I used to think was an angel. What *do* I think she is, if not an angel? That's a long story, and we'll get there.

Anyway, Gym Teacher Dude went as stiff as a board when my Taser hit the meat of his big bicep. Then he toppled over with a crash that drew cries of alarm and shocked gasps from the gathering crowd.

"Head for the exit!" I told the girls, pointing at the fire door at the end of the corridor.

For a second, the three of them just stood there, rooted in place, their eyes moving from me, to the zapped gym teacher, and then to the thing that was still shuffling toward us.

"Julie!" I snapped. "Helene's waiting! Go!"

She went, grabbing the blond and redhead by their hands and pulling them along behind her. I kept up the rear, brandishing the Taser. The teachers all stared at me. One of them, a pretty woman in her twenties whose name I didn't know, came toward me, her hands outstretched.

"Listen to me," she begged. "Whatever's going on, let me help you!"

I shook my head.

"I promise you," she pressed. "It's not as terrible as you think it is."

"I only wish that was true," I replied.

I turned and followed the girls at a full run.

Julie pushed the heavy door open, letting in a bright splash of sunlight. I caught up just as the door swung closed and slammed the panic bar with one hand, leaving the school behind me—sort of.

We were in a blind alley that ran between the

auditorium and the gymnasium, a three-story windowless canyon of orange brick. In one direction, a green commercial dumpster stood against a blank wall. In the other direction, the alley opened onto the school's rear grounds. I could see the soccer field standing empty beyond the parking lot.

"Help me!" I yelled to the girls, who stood blinking in the sunshine. The blond and brunette didn't move. Julie *did*. She followed me to the dumpster, which wasn't particularly big or—thankfully—particularly heavy. Between the two of us, we managed to drag it up against the fire door. And just in time, too. Moments later, the door shook, though whether it was the Type Five deader or some well-meaning but totally useless teacher hammering on it, I didn't know.

I didn't care, either.

"Who *are* you?" Julie asked me. She still looked pale. She still looked scared. But she'd kept her wits, unlike the other two, who clutched at each other and cried.

"Will Ritter. I'm an Undertaker."

She nodded. "Like my sister."

"Just like her."

"Where is she?" the girl asked.

Good question. The easy answer was Haven. But if Dave "the Burgermeister" Burger had followed the Rules and Regs, then he'd called in the situation and Helene, who was monitoring our mission, might have already split for Allentown. Frankly, I hoped not. It would take her a long time to get here, and we couldn't exactly wait.

No point trying to explain all that, though. So I just said, "I'm taking you to her."

Julie nodded, unhappy but momentarily satisfied.

"Follow me," I said. "All of you!"

We headed down the alley toward the rear parking lot.

That's when a figure stepped in front of us, blocking our exit.

A Corpse. But not just *any* Corpse.

The principal.

Robert Dillin.

"Mr. Kessler," he said. He was a Type One. Very fresh and very strong, his stolen body probably dead less than a week. I didn't see too many Type Ones. The Corpses found them hard to come by. The fact that Dillin wore one suggested that he ranked high among the *Malum*.

Leader caste.

I held up my Taser and readied myself for his attack.

It didn't come.

"No need for that, young man," the deader remarked. Then he said something that I would never in a million years have imagined coming out of a Corpse's mouth.

"I'm here to help you."

CHAPTER 3

PARKING LOT WARS

"This way, quickly!" Dillin said, waggling a dead finger at us and hurrying along the rear of the school, skirting its outer wall. Then, after several steps, he stopped and looked back, seeming genuinely surprised that we hadn't moved.

Does he honestly expect us to follow him?

"Mr. Kessler," he said. "I know this has been a confusing and terrifying day for you and your friends. And I know what I look like, though I hope I don't look as bad as Marcy or some of the others you've seen. There's a reason for all of it. If you'll only come with me—"

Without taking my eyes off the dead principal, I said to Julie, "You and the girls head for the soccer field. On the way, you should run into a big guy in janitor's overalls. He's a friend of mine. Trust him."

"But … what about you?" she asked. Inwardly, I smiled. Helene's sister—no doubt about it.

"I'll be right behind you," I promised.

The girl nodded. Then she pulled Blond and Redhead across the parking lot and toward the open field.

Alarm flashed in Dillin's dead eyes. "It's not safe that way! Mr. Kessler, I know you're frightened. But you *have* to trust me!"

I held up my Taser. "My name's not Kessler. It's Will Ritter. I'm not a kid who just got his Eyes. I'm an Undertaker. And ... no, I *don't* have to trust you, deader."

Then, while his gaze was locked on my pocketknife, I whipped out my water pistol and shot him.

Except, I didn't.

It was a good move on my part: divert his attention with the Taser and then blindside him with saltwater.

Except my shot hit nothing but empty air.

With incredible agility, Dillin had leapt to one side, latching his feet and hands onto the school's brick wall. Then, as I stared, he *skittered* upward, as quickly as a spider, somehow driving the fingertips and toes of his stolen body into the mortar between the bricks.

That's when I noticed his shoes—brown tasseled loafers—sitting in the grass.

He'd jumped right out of them.

I'd only ever seen one other Corpse move like that. Just one. Her name was Lilith Cavanaugh, the Queen of the Dead. She wasn't just leader caste; she was royal caste, and that stature within the *Malum* class structure somehow made her faster, stronger, and way more agile than your average deader.

Whoever this *thing* was posing as the principal of Merriweather Middle School in Allentown, Pennsylvania, he *had* to be Corpse royalty.

A Zombie Prince!

I know: Don't call 'em zombies. What can I say? At that time and in that moment, this was the label that struck me. Robert Dillin: Zombie Prince.

Halfway to the roof, tucked between a standpipe and a big banner proclaiming the Merriweather Panthers, he looked balefully down at me. I expected to see anger in his expression. Heck, I expected to feel it radiate off of him like waves of heat.

But instead he just looked—well—sad.

In a loud, clear voice he called down to me, "We're not all monsters, Mr. Ritter!"

Then he leapt higher and disappeared over the lip of the roof.

I stood there for maybe a half-minute, trying to make sense of it.

I'd met a lot of Corpses. I mean a *lot* of them. I'd met the smart *mean* kind and the dumb *mean* kind. I'd met the polite *mean* kind and the downright rude *mean* kind. See where I'm going with this?

But the Zombie Prince was something—new.

At that moment, a loud crash caught my attention. I turned back down the alley toward the fire door, which had just smashed open, the dumpster in front of it knocked aside.

Three deaders came out. One was the Type Five we'd seen earlier, the *Night of the Living Dead* reject. The others were fresher. A pair of Threes. All of them took just a moment to scan the alley before their lifeless eyes settled on me.

Time to go.

I ran after Julie and the girls, who had reached the far edge of the parking lot—and stopped. After a moment, I saw why.

Two more Corpses blocked the gate that led onto the soccer field. One wore janitor's overalls. The other was the school nurse. Both smirked at the girls, two of whom—guess which ones—were screaming.

Julie had placed herself protectively between Blonde and Redhead and the Corpses, her small face set in a look of admirable, but completely useless, courage. As I got close, the crying girls noticed me and latched on like shipwrecked passengers to a life buoy.

Around us, the deaders closed in, taking their time about it.

Three at my back and two at my front. I'd faced longer odds, but not with fresh Seers in tow. I held the momentary hope that they wouldn't risk a direct attack, not within sight of the school. But then I remembered where we were, behind the auditorium and the gym. No windows. No witnesses.

I had my water pistol, with maybe two squirts left. I had my pocketknife. What I didn't have were any illusions.

But nobody ever beat any odds by giving up.

So, pushing the screaming girls behind me, I turned toward the three from the alley. They grinned savagely, unmoved when I pointed my water pistol at them.

"Undertaker," one of them, a dude in a ridiculous tweed suit, growled.

"Badly Dressed Dead Guy," I replied.

Then his head came off.

It's *amazing* how often I see that happen.

The two beside him looked over in surprise as Dave "The Burgermeister" Burger stepped from behind a nearby SUV. In his hands was a spaded shovel, one with a long wooden handle. Corpse juice dripped from its blade.

He grinned, and said in a truly awful Brooklyn accent, "You all lookin' for a pahty?"

The other two launched at him. I shot one in the ear

before whirling around and firing at the nurse, who was at that moment leaping at Julie. The saltwater caught her in the eye. She moaned, spun, and dropped, her purple hands opening and closing like crab claws.

Meanwhile, the Corpse janitor flanked Helene's little sister, whose attention had been fixed on Dead Nurse. But, as the big dude's purple fingers neared her throat, Julie did a surprising thing.

She yelped in fear, jumped up, and kicked him in the face.

Dead Janitor's head snapped back so hard that I actually heard his neck bones crunch. Then he staggered and fell against the chain link fence that surrounded the soccer field.

Disoriented, but not done.

So I lunged forward, past Dead Nurse's twitching form, and pressed my Taser against the fence's metal links.

Electricity raced along the chain links, causing Dead Janitor to convulse so hard, he fell over the fence and landed in a heap on the other side, his body doing a crazy horizontal dance.

I spun around, ready to help Dave.

But he didn't need it.

Three deader heads now lay separated from three deader bodies in the shadow of the SUV. In the fight, the Burgermeister had gotten hurt. He had fingernail gouges on his neck and what looked like an ugly swelling below one eye that would probably be an uglier bruise by morning.

Yet, despite it all, he was *grinning*.

"Where'd you get the shovel?" I asked him.

He shrugged. "Told yah: Yahdwork."

"What's with the Brooklyn accent?" I asked.

His grin vanished. "Brooklyn! That's *Boston*, dude!

We watched *The Departed* last night. I sound just like Jack Nicholson."

"Right," I said. "Sure. I can hear it now."

Off to the side, I saw Redhead faint.

A moment later, Blond threw up on her.

A moment after that, alarms sounded from inside the school.

"Fire?" Dave asked.

I shook my head. "Lockdown."

I'd Tased a teacher, which qualified by law as an act of domestic terrorism. That meant the school would go into immediate lockdown. By now, the cops had been called. Every kid would be literally locked, with their teachers, inside every classroom, with the shades pulled down at every door and every window. They'd stay there, huddled up against an interior wall, until the "proper authorities" arrived to scour the building and grounds before giving the "all clear" signal.

The upshot was that nobody else would be coming after us. At least, not until the cops arrived.

Julie went immediately to the blond girl, holding back her hair while she retched. On the ground at the girl's feet, Redhead lay in a heap on the curb, vomit on her jeans, her eyes closed, and her face twisted with terror.

I suddenly felt pretty crappy.

I'd been laughing at these girls—that is, when I wasn't irritated with them. Julie's courage and self-possession had impressed me from the moment she'd laid her eyes on Ms. McKinney's true face. In contrast, I'd labeled Blond and Redhead weak-willed and spineless.

But none of that had been fair.

Had I really forgotten what it felt like to start Seeing Corpses? The Zombie Prince had nailed it: confusing and terrifying at the same time. Everyone reacted differently.

And most first-time Seers didn't survive their reaction, not without a Schooler on hand to jump to their rescue, as Julie's older sister had jumped to *my* rescue the day I'd got *my* Eyes.

If Helene hadn't been there, I'd have screamed just as loud and long as these two poor girls.

And I'd have *died* screaming.

I pointed to Dead School Nurse, who was starting to recover from the saltwater eye wash I'd given her. Dave went to "take care of it," his shovel firmly in hand. Then I knelt beside Redhead and felt her pulse. It was slow but steady. At least she'd had the good sense to faint on grass instead of cement.

Meanwhile, Blond had finished retching and had let Julie sit her down on the curb. There, she quietly cried. I looked at them both. Julie looked back at me. There was so much behind her brown eyes.

"What happens now?" she asked.

Instead of answering, I pulled out my sat phone and dialed Haven.

Dan McDevitt, one of the Chatters, the crew that monitored communications, answered on the second ring. *"Main Street Auto Parts. This is Derek. Can I help you?"*

"This is Allentown One. We've got three Seers. We're coming in."

"Got you, Allentown One. Are things hot?"

I looked up in time to see the Burgermeister's shovel come down, blade first, across Dead School Nurse's neck. Her head rolled past the crying blond girl, who saw it and buried her face in Julie's shoulder.

Dave then turned his attention to Dead Janitor, who still twitched beyond the soccer field gate.

I heard police sirens in the distance.

"They're about to be," I said into the phone. "We could use an exit strategy."

"Hold on," Dan said. In the background, I could hear him tapping buttons on a keyboard. *"There's a bus into Philly. Allentown Bus Terminal."*

"They'll be watching that," I said.

"Not if you get there quick enough. I'll make sure tickets are waiting. How many? You, Dave, and three Seers. So, five?"

"Yeah," I said. Then after a moment's thought: "No. Make it four."

Nearby, I heard the Burgermeister say, "Will, what're you doing?"

"Four?" Dan asked. *"I thought—"*

"I'm not done here yet," I said. "Make it four. Thanks, Dan." Then I closed the phone and turned to Dave, who stood just beyond the soccer field fence, having made short work of the last Corpse.

Well ... not quite the last, huh?

To call Dave Burger a big kid is to say the Empire State Building is a tall building. He towers over pretty much everyone, and his upper arms are about as big around as my whole body. He's a fantastic fighter and my best friend.

But that doesn't mean he always agrees with me.

"You're an idiot," he said.

"I know."

"Why aren't you coming with us?"

Redhead was waking up and Blond had stopped puking, at least for now. Julie tended to them both, all the while looking at Dave and me as if we were Superman and Batman having a tiff.

And the police sirens were louder now. Closer.

"Go," I told him. "There's something I need to do."

"Not happening, dude."

"We need to get these girls out of here!" I snapped. "Look at them! You really think they can handle another Corpse encounter?"

"Is that what you call them?" Julie asked. "Corpses?"

It was the Burgermeister who answered. "That's what we call 'em. You're Helene's kid sister?"

Julie nodded.

"Then maybe *you* can talk some sense into my idiot roommate. Tell him he's coming with us if I gotta pick him up and carry him."

Julie looked from him to me, and back again.

"He's staying," she said.

Dave was stunned.

"And so am I," she said.

Now we were *both* stunned.

"No way!" I snapped.

"You want to talk to the principal again," she said. "The Corpse who was ... nice. Don't you?"

I looked at her. "Yeah."

"A *nice* Corpse?" the Burgermeister asked, staring at us as if we were both nuts. "Are you both nuts?" Called it.

"I don't understand it either," I admitted. "But my instincts are telling me to check it out." I turned to Julie. "But *you're* going with Dave."

The girl shook her head.

The sirens were at the school. I could hear police cruisers screeching into the driveway out front, on the other side of the big building.

Time's up.

Dave knew it too. With a final, desperate look at me, he picked up groggy, confused Redhead like she weighed next to nothing, took crying Blond by the hand and headed across the soccer field toward the woods. I noticed that he didn't ask Julie to follow him. The Burgermeister had long ago learned not to argue with crazy.

Julie came to stand beside me, her expression fearful but brave.

"You really ought to go with them," I told her.

"Yeah?" she replied. "You, too."

I thought, *Helene's gonna kill me.*

Then I grabbed Julie's small hand and pulled her at a run along the back edge of parking lot, putting as much distance as I could between us and the loose collection of headless Corpses. We had maybe *seconds* before those "proper authorities" I mentioned arrived on the scene.

Then the hunt would begin again.

CHAPTER 4

THE ZOMBIE PRINCE

A few facts:

One: The Corpses Dave had just decapitated weren't dead. By lopping their heads off with his shovel, all he'd done was trap the *Malum* inside their useless stolen bodies. They'd stay like that until more of their kind showed up and carried them off somewhere so that they could "Transfer" into fresh cadavers.

Two: In the meantime, to any Non-Seers, which includes the entire grown-up population of Planet Earth, these four deaders would appear as simply unconscious. No one would even notice that their heads were detached. The Corpses are masters of illusion. We don't understand *how* they get into people's brains and make them un-See their true rotting bodies, but they do it really well. Heck, you could take a picture of the headless bodies and a Non-Seer *still* wouldn't recognize what they actually were!

And Three: Corpses are evil—pure, bone-deep evil. No exceptions. None.

Except—

"I'm here to help you."

Julie and I huddled together, peering carefully around the corner of the school at the circle of activity going on in the rear parking lot.

Three cop cars had pulled up, their lights flashing. Uniformed police had gathered around the broken bodies sprawled near the soccer field entrance. No teachers yet. They were still inside, under lockdown. Once the cops had searched the school, *then* they'd all come out and start talking.

Still, I was a bit surprised that the Zombie Prince wasn't around somewhere. Even in a lockdown situation, you'd think the principal would be out and about, doing, you know, principal things.

"I don't see him," Julie remarked.

"Me, neither."

So far, none of the police on the scene were Corpses. But I knew that, sooner or later, some of the Queen's minions would show up to help their fallen buds. Maybe they'd arranged to be driving the ambulances.

We couldn't risk waiting around to find out.

"So ... what're we going to do?" Julie asked me.

"Find the Zombie Prince."

"Who?"

"Principal Dillin."

She looked curiously at me. "Why do you call him the Zombie Prince?"

"I ... kinda like labeling stuff."

"Why?"

I shrugged. "No clue. Let's see if we can get into the school. Maybe he's in his office."

I turned. Julie turned.

And Ms. McKinney grabbed us each by the throat.

Julie tried to scream, but all that came out was a low gurgle that would never have reached around the corner to the circle of cops. Still, she did better than me; I couldn't make any sound at all.

"Naughty children," the dead teacher hissed.

She'd come up on us quietly, and apparently downwind, because her rotting body stunk like a truckload of bad eggs. As she lifted us both off our feet, I tried to kick at her, but the angle was bad. I didn't dare Tase her. Doing that would zap all three of us, and I knew from experience how *that* felt.

My water pistol was in my back pocket but, struggling as I was, I couldn't seem to muster up the strength to go for it.

As it turned out, I didn't have to.

Julie swung up her legs and wrapped them around the teacher's arm, using the leverage to pry the dead fingers from her neck. Then, bending backward in a way that would've totally snapped my spine, she snatched the water pistol from my back pocket and, twisting, fired its last squirt into McKinney's face.

Air flooded my lungs as Dead History Teacher released me and collapsed, her arms and legs flailing. I dropped in a heap to the ground while Julie totally stuck the landing.

I looked at the girl.

She looked at me.

"Gymnastics," she said.

Helene's sister, I thought.

If Dave had been here, he could've snapped the Corpse's neck like a twig. Unfortunately, I'd never been able to manage that much upper body strength. So all we could do was leave McKinney where she lay and run along the school's outer wall to a door that led to the

Administrative Wing.

And the principal's office.

The door was locked, as middle school doors always are, especially during a Lockdown. Fortunately, my pocketknife has more going for it than just its Taser.

I pressed the **1** button, releasing the lock pick.

Thirty feet away, McKinney still convulsed. But, it wouldn't last.

I set to work on the lock.

Ten seconds passed. Dead History Teacher's spasms slowed. Then they stopped.

Fifteen seconds. Still sprawled on the grass at the edge of the building, McKinney craned her neck in a way that would have killed a living person. Her milky eyes found us.

"Naughty children," I heard her say.

Twenty seconds.

"How long does it take?" Julie asked me, fresh terror in her voice.

"Almost there." I worked my pocketknife deeper into the doorknob's keyhole.

McKinney leaped to her feet with super-human grace and spun around. She was snarling. This particular deader was *really* into snarling.

Twenty-five seconds.

Click!

"Go!" I cried to Julie.

I yanked the door open and we ran inside. The exit closed behind us, its lock re-engaging. That would buy us a little time.

But just a little.

The hallway stood empty, the classroom doors on either side shut, locked and shuttered. Beyond them, hundreds of kids and dozens of teachers huddled in careful silence, waiting for someone to announce the "all clear" on the school's PA system.

Lockdown.

I grabbed Julie's hand and together we ran toward the first corner, our feet hammering loudly on the tile floor. Behind us, I heard McKinney pull uselessly on the exit door and then howl in frustration.

I almost smiled.

Then we rounded the corner and ran straight into a cop.

He was human and in uniform—one of Allentown's finest doing his secure-the-school duty.

"Where are you two going?" he demanded.

I Tased him.

"Sorry," I said, as he gasped and dropped.

Two innocents in one day, I thought bitterly. *That's a record.*

We had to duck three more cops on our way to the Administration Wing, but we made it without getting spotted. Unfortunately, Marcy McKinney hit the school's main doors at pretty much the same time.

We saw her. She saw us.

I'd half-hoped these doors would be locked as well. But they weren't, probably because the cops had needed a way to get inside. Whatever the reason, Dead History Teacher snarled and charged in, rushing toward us as I pulled Julie past the Main Office and down the narrow Administration Wing corridor.

Like the rest of the school, this hallway stood deserted. The Guidance Office, Attendance Office, and even the Nurse's Office were all shut up tight—though I reminded myself that the school nurse currently lay, headless, in the back parking lot.

Julie and I skidded to a stop outside a big wooden

door with a plaque on it that read: Robert Dillin, Principal.

He's probably in there, I thought.

The dead principal.

The Zombie Prince.

I hesitated—but just for a second, because Ms. McKinney was already at the mouth of the Admin Wing, glowering at us. She looked kind of like a dead Bruce Banner just before the big green switch gets flipped.

I grabbed the doorknob.

You sure about this?

I was about to burst into a cramped, enclosed space—Dillin, I knew, had no outer office, and his inner office was pretty small. Even if he *was* in there, what did I hope to accomplish? With one alien invader in a stolen cadaver on my six, did I really think another alien invader in a stolen cadaver was going to answer my questions, much less help me?

Why was I doing such a stupid thing?

Because there'd been "something" about the way he'd said they weren't all monsters.

But, no. I'm not sure about this at all.

I pushed Julie and myself into the office as Dead History Teacher came at us—fast.

"Hello, Mr. Ritter."

He sat behind his desk. No secretary or assistant for Bob Dillin. He was a hands-on kind of principal. Students were always welcome to stop by between classes if they had some concern. At least, that was what he said at the monthly assemblies. I'd always thought that promise grimly funny, given what I knew him to be.

But, right now, I was counting on it.

Julie and I looked at the "man." I felt the girl's tiny hand slide into mine. I gave it a squeeze, conveying a confidence that I sure as heck didn't feel. I pressed my back to the door and, with my free hand, felt for the lock and turned it.

A second later, Ms. McKinney slammed into the other side, shaking the whole frame.

I considered playing it cool, but I just didn't have the energy.

So I said, "You gonna kill us, or what?"

Dillin stood. "No, I'm not going to kill you. Who's that behind the door?"

"McKinney."

He nodded. "Ah, Marcy." Then he smiled—actually smiled. I'd seen them grin hungrily and leer smugly. But this was the first time I'd ever seen a genuine, bemused smile cross a Corpse's face.

It was—jarring.

"Well, we'd better let her in before she bashes the door down," he said, coming around the desk.

Instinctively, I pulled Julie to one side, keeping as much space between us and him as possible. My pocketknife was in my hand, its Taser ready. Julie still held my water pistol, but I knew it was probably empty. But both, of course, weapons would be next to useless on this guy; Royals were too fast.

Except, he didn't attack. Instead he went to the door and, to my horror, unlocked and opened it.

Dead History Teacher leaped inside, her purplish fingers twisted into savage-looking claws, her dead eyes wild, her rotting teeth bared.

"Hello, Marcy," Dillin said. "Why don't you come in?"

She ignored him, scanned the office and, spotting us, readied to pounce.

Then the principal clamped his hands on either side

of her head from behind—and twisted it right off her shoulders.

Julie didn't scream.

I *did*—well, just a little.

The headless body stiffened and then dropped to the carpeted floor, twitching slightly. Her host cadaver had been embalmed, so there was very little blood. For a long moment, Dillin studied the face in his hands thoughtfully. "This must be terribly confusing for you, Marcy," he said.

"*Traitor!*" the head replied in Deadspeak.

Julie jumped a little at that. I gave her hand another squeeze.

"Well now," the Zombie Prince replied. "That depends on your point of view, doesn't it?"

Then, pressing with both his palms, he squeezed the severed head until it—well—popped. Eyeballs fell out. Brains squirted.

I'll be seein' that one in my dreams tonight.

He dropped what was left and looked at us. "We should go someplace else to talk. Even in this state, she can hear us."

"How?" Julie asked.

"Long story," Dillin and I answered together.

I'd just jinxed a Corpse. Okay, that was really freaky!

"Follow me, both of you," he said. Then, after a pause, "Unless you still don't trust me?"

I held up my Taser. "I wouldn't call it 'trust'."

He considered that. "No, I don't suppose you would."

Leaving what was left of Marcy McKinney staining his rug, he stepped out into the Admin. Wing, turned right and disappeared, apparently convinced that we'd follow.

We did.

He didn't lead us far, just to an empty teachers lounge a few doors down from his office. Once inside, I immediately pulled Julie over to a window that looked out over the front of the school. Everything seemed pretty quiet out there, even serene. It was easy to forget the headless bodies and cop cars in the back. The window was partly open to let in a late spring breeze.

We can go through it if we have to.

"We're keeping the goings-on in the back of the school as low key as possible," Dillin explained. "Five of my staff are down. Six, if you count Marcy. Is this a typical day for you, Mr. Ritter?"

"I've had worse." I shrugged. And I had.

"So I've heard." He crossed his arms and tilted his head. The gesture seemed really—human, but all it did was freak me out a little more. "You've become something of a legend amongst my people, did you know that? Well, no. 'Legend' isn't the right word. Your culture *does* have a term for it, though. Let me think ..."

He thought.

We watched him.

"Boogeyman." He snapped his fingers—another really human gesture. "*That's* it! You've become the *Malum* boogeyman!"

"Great," I muttered, not sure how I felt about that.

Julie blinked and looked at me, either with newfound respect or hardcore skepticism; believe it or not, it's the same expression.

"What do you want?" I asked, glowering at him.

"I told you," the Zombie Prince replied. "I want to help."

"Okay ... *why* do you want to help?"

He considered the question. "Yes, I imagine my demeanor must confuse you."

Julie said, "Ms. McKinney called you a traitor."

"In her eyes, I am. The term on my world is *Oreth Oreg*. The closest English translation would probably be 'betrayer,' but that doesn't quite say it. *Organized betrayer*. That's closer."

"I don't get it," I said.

He took a step toward us.

I pulled Julie a step closer to the window.

"Between us," he remarked. "You and I have effectively dispatched ... dispatched but not *destroyed* ... all of the *Malum* who were stationed in this school. But others are coming. Many others."

I shrugged. "No kidding. What's your point?"

"That you need to leave and, after what I just did to Marcy on your behalf, *I* need to leave. My wife will be none too pleased. She'll be hunting for me ... and it would be very unwise to let myself be found."

At least, that was what I *think* he said. To be honest, I stopped listening after "my wife."

"Hold up!" I snapped. "Who's your wife?"

The Zombie Prince met my eyes. Dead gaze on living gaze. Then he did something that struck me as especially human.

He swallowed.

And I thought: *So why would a dead guy with no saliva ... swallow?*

For that matter, what *does he swallow?*

"My wife is the *Malum* ruler, Mr. Ritter," he finally replied. "You know her as Lilith Cavanaugh ... the Queen of the Dead."

CHAPTER 5
EVENT HORIZON

Tom

"He's my boyfriend! She's my sister! How can I *not* go?"

Tom Jefferson, Chief of the Undertakers, stood in one of Haven's many narrow, crumbling corridors. They were deep below Philly's gargantuan City Hall, in a sub-basement that no one even remembered, much less used. It wasn't a particularly comfortable place—always dark, always dank—but it was safe enough.

And, in Tom's mind at least, it was home.

Except, right now, "home" was where three girls were yelling at him.

No, that wasn't fair. Helene Boettcher was yelling. Jillian, and Tom's twin sister Sharyn, were just watching.

His sister looked amused.

"It's a two hour trip by train," Tom said. "By the time you get there, whatever Will's got himself into will probably be over."

"He hasn't called!" she complained.

"I know."

"And he's not answering when the Chatters call him!" she exclaimed.

"I know."

"And that doesn't *worry* you?"

Tom glanced at Sharyn, who shrugged. Then he glanced at Jillian, a girl from his past, a girl only recently back in his life. There were feelings there, complicated ones. She met his eyes. Jill had great eyes.

Tom turned back to Helene. "Will Ritter's come back from the dead," he told her. "He's tamed monsters. I stopped worrying about him months back. You oughta do the same."

Helene gave him a look that should have scorched his nose hairs. Tom faced it down. Tom faced down a lot of things in his job and, so far, not one of them had killed him.

Of course, the day is young.

Wordlessly, the girl stalked off.

Sharyn waited until Helene was safely out of earshot. Then she asked, "How many and how soon, bro?"

"Take Chuck and Katie," Tom told her. "And go now."

She grinned and nodded. Then, without sparing even a look at Jillian—the two of them had never gotten along all that great—she, too, hurried off. Sharyn was the Boss of the Angels crew, the same crew that Will, Helene and Dave belonged to. She'd find Will and Julie and bring them both safely back to Haven. What's more, she'd do it smart and detached, without the desperate urgency that the elder Boettcher girl would have brought to the mission.

"Why'd you lie to Helene?" Jillian asked him, once the two of them were alone.

"I didn't." Tom replied. "I never said I wasn't sending a rescue team."

"So you *are* worried about Will."

"I'm always worried about Will."

The satellite phone on his belt chirped.

Tom unclipped and opened it. These were new—gadgets donated courtesy of F.B.I. Special Agent Hugo Ramirez, the Undertakers' "inside man" in the U.S. Government. Ramirez was one of the few adults who knew that Corpses even existed, much less about the hidden war they waged against humanity. Convincing the F.B.I agent had been difficult, and painful in more ways than one. But Tom secretly considered it one of his best moves as chief.

"Yeah," he said into the phone.

"Got time to come down to the Factory?" Steve Moscova asked.

The Brain Factory was Haven's scientific chop shop. Steve, the Brain Boss, ran the crew responsible for the majority of Undertakers' combat and tactical arsenal—fancy encrypted satellite phones notwithstanding. Lately, however, most of Steve's attention had been focused on a single project. And when Steve Moscova focused, he focused like a laser beam. This was the first time Tom had heard from him in more than a month, having relied on Steve's younger brother Burt to keep the chief updated on the Brain Boss' progress—and state of health.

It worried Tom. Obsession, even for a good cause, was still obsession.

"On my way," he replied. Then he shut the phone and said to Jillian, "Steve's poking his head out of his shell."

"Want company?" Jill asked.

"Sure." Tom took three calculated steps along the

corridor. Then he stopped, squared his shoulders, and turned back. "Actually ... how 'bout you go make sure Helene's cool, instead."

"You're afraid she might leave Haven without permission?"

"Wouldn't be the first time. But it ain't just that. She's scared. Scared for Will. Scared for Julie. Scared for her parents, who just lost their *second* daughter. I know you two've gotten tight. Go to her."

She studied him with those amazing eyes. "What's going on?"

He faked just the right amount of ignorance—he hoped. "'Bout what?"

"I dunno. I guess ..." She shrugged. Her gaze remained rock steady. "You've been weird toward me."

"I have?"

Jillian frowned. "Feels like it."

"I'm *tired*, Jill." His shoulders slumped. "Something's coming. I ain't sure what it is yet, but my gut tells me it's big. A game-changer. I guess it's got me ... distracted."

She seemed to consider this. "So ... I haven't done anything wrong?"

"You? Course not."

The girl nodded, apparently satisfied. "Okay, Chief. I'll go babysit Will's significant other."

"Thanks."

"No problem. Just make sure Steve doesn't blow the place up."

She went the same way the other two girls had, disappearing around the corner. Tom stood where he was for a few moments, looking after her, his thoughts churning.

The walk to the Brain Factory was a short one. But, as usual, he got stopped along the way.

Somebody always needed something.

"Hold up, Chief!" Alex Bobson called to him.

Tom faced the boy. Alex was the Monkey Boss, head of the Undertakers crew that built and maintained machinery and equipment. Alex's people kept the lights on, the water running, and the heat going. But lately, that wasn't all they'd been up to.

"Yeah, Alex?" Tom tried not to sound as weary as he felt. Alex was good at his job. No, check that, *great* at his job. But he could be—abrasive.

"I wanna talk about those new security improvements you asked for," the Monkey Boss said, barked really.

Dude, I'm kinda surprised it took you this long.

"What about 'em?"

"Sixty feet of piping at the northern entrance, camouflaged openings at the southern entrance, *piped*-in music and … I don't know *what* they are … cages? In the ceiling of the western entrance. It's been a lot of work, and we still don't got any real idea why we're doin' it!"

Tom said, "Beefing up security, like I told you."

"Chief, those pipes ain't for water. And what's with the air cannons?"

"Alex—"

But the boy rolled right over him. "And those cages! What've you got in mind? Why won't you tell me?"

To anyone else, Tom might have been able to say, "I ain't ready yet. I'll tell you when I am." And anyone else might have taken that as enough. But not Alex. Or Will, either, now that he thought about it. Those two had more in common than either one of them would ever admit.

"Okay." Tom took the boy's arm and led him into the nearest unoccupied room.

Then he told him.

Alex's eyes went wide. "Jeez. Are you *sure*?"

"I'm nothin' *like* sure. Which is why I ain't told nobody. I'm tellin' you 'cause your crew's the one doin' most of the work. So, you got a right to know."

"Yeah." The Monkey Boss sounded stunned. "Okay."

"Don't share it, Alex. Not yet. Soon, maybe. But not yet."

"I won't. I swear it. Jeez, I hope you're wrong."

"So do I, dude," Tom told him, meaning it. "So ... we're good?"

"We're good," Alex replied.

And Tom went on his way.

The Brain Factory was a long narrow room near the center of Haven, one of the few rooms with a door, a big heavy custom-made wooden barrier. This always stood closed—a pretty recent addition to the Rules and Regs that Tom had implemented after something had, as Jillian put it, "blown up."

Tom opened the door.

The room was, as usual, a hive of activity. Brains, members of Steve's crew, moved from table to table, doing this or that, taking notes or conferring. All were busy. All were serious. All were focused on their tasks. These were kids, yet none of them ever discussed video games, or the Phillies, or *Game of Thrones*.

The Undertakers.

Sometimes, and always privately, Tom thought of these children as *his* children. It was a tendency he'd picked up, as with so many things, from Karl Ritter, the founder of Haven. Every single Undertaker came into this life confused and terrified. Every single one had cried, or screamed, or sunk into a sullen depression at having to give up everything they'd known and loved—all because one day they'd started Seeing things that didn't want to be Seen.

But then every single one, with very few exceptions, had come around. Every one had found their place—some way that they could aid the war effort. Not all of them were soldiers. Some were scientists or spies, craftsmen or hackers. Some were even cooks or janitors.

But *all* of them were Undertakers.

I'll get you home, he silently promised them for the thousandth time. *I swear it.*

And, as always, he wondered if it was a promise he'd be able to keep.

Today, however, wasn't a typical day in the Factory. Today, instead of doing their own separate work, the crew's collective attention seemed focused on the goings-on at the far end of the long room. Tom caught snippets of conversation from kids who hadn't noticed him yet.

They were buzzing about a "hole," whatever that meant.

"Steve!" Tom called.

"Chief!" The Brain Boss waved him over.

As he approached, Tom noticed that the brightly-painted sawhorses set up around "ground zero" had been pulled back several feet.

"Ground zero" was what some of the kids had started calling the empty spot at the far end of the Factory—the place where one of Steve's experiments had gone wrong, and where Ian MacDonald, Haven's former medic, had lost his life. The sawhorses had been placed to mark the limits of the blast radius.

If what had happened that day, now almost two months ago, could really be called a "blast."

"Whatcha got?" he asked Steve, who stood with Burt, his younger brother.

"I'm about to test a theory," Steve said. He looked a little giddy. It always worried Tom whenever Steve

Moscova looked giddy.

"And I'm about to try to keep him from killing us all," Burt added.

Tom looked from one to the other. "Okay. Let's see what you've got."

Steve announced, "Brains! Clear the room!"

As his crew complied, grumbling about "missing out on the action," their boss handed Tom a heavy smock.

"This is lead-lined." Steve pulled one just like it over his head. "This stuff's probably safe enough, but there's nothing wrong with taking precautions. And *this*," he said, holding up a strange, full-face visor, "is a welder's mask. The light can hurt your eyes."

Once just the three of them remained in the Factory, Steve and Burt donned their own masks. Then the elder brother stepped into the barren circle at the rear of the room, where a heavy metal screen had been set up. Struggling a little with the weight, he moved it aside, revealing a rolling metal table, maybe a foot across.

Mounted atop the table was a car battery. And, beside that, held in place with steel clamps, lay the Anchor Shard.

Captured during a raid on a Corpse stronghold, the shard was a jagged piece of green crystal, maybe seven inches long. It was alien in origin—a rare piece of *Malum* technology that had some pretty bizarre properties. For one, just touching it to an injury healed that injury, whether it was a broken bone or internal bleeding. For another, running an electrical current through it seemed to do freakish, and deadly, things to organic matter.

Right now the Anchor Shard was *glowing*, and casting that glow toward the back of the room, a bit like pointing a flashlight.

Just looking at it made Tom's skin crawl.

"You sure about this?" he asked them both.

Steve nodded. Burt shrugged.

"I've done the math," the Brain Boss insisted. "Everything's fine. The stand's grounded and the shard's clamped down tight. No more accidents."

He sounded sure. But Tom's skin kept crawling anyway.

Steve added, "As far as I can tell, it's completely stable."

"*What's* completely stable?" Tom asked.

"Shard Energy ... that's what I'm calling it ... is only dangerous at two different times: when you first run an electrical current through it, and when you disconnect that current. But, once the current is running, it stabilizes."

Tom looked at Burt who said, "Yeah, I don't get it, either."

His older brother groaned. "Think of it like a lamp, only the switch is broken, so just touching the switch can electrocute you. That means turning the lamp on can kill you, and turning it off can kill you. But once it's either on or off, you've got nothing to worry about."

He said this confidently. Yet, to Tom's ears, it sounded like playing with matches.

"But, once you *do* turn the lamp on," Steve continued, grinning. "Something really interesting happens. Watch."

Steve picked up a rusty old horseshoe that had a length of clothesline tied to it. He handed the other end of the clothesline to Tom. Then he turned and tossed the horseshoe out over the Anchor Shard, toward the Factory's rear wall.

It vanished.

Tom gasped as the clothesline in his hands went taut.

Startled, he studied the rear wall. He could *see* where

the rope just *stopped*, as if cut by a laser beam, except that the sliced off end remained somehow suspended in mid-air.

Tom Jefferson took pride in rarely being surprised. *This* surprised him.

"What am I lookin' at?" he exclaimed.

"It's just Steve, wasting another horseshoe." Burt replied with a sigh.

"In the name of science!" his brother snapped.

Tom, still clutching one end of a clothesline that didn't have another end, said, "Listen, I dig the whole drama thing. But will one of you please tell me what *happened* to the horseshoe?"

"Nothing." The Brain Boss flashed another look at Burt before grinning from ear to ear. "It's just not on Earth anymore! It's in the Ether between worlds!"

Tom said, "I don't even know what that *means*!"

"Neither does he," remarked Burt.

Steve's glare should have melted the other boy's shoes and, despite the weirdness of the situation, Tom spared a moment to worry over it. Since Ian's death, the elder Moscova brother had become moody. Will's mom, Susan Ritter, a registered nurse who had taken over Haven's Infirmary, suggested that the Brain Boss might be bipolar, an unfamiliar term that Tom had researched on the internet.

What he'd found there had made him really hope his main science dude was *not* bipolar!

Steve took a deep breath. Then he said to Tom, "Remember when Ian ... um ... when we first ran an electrical current through the shard? Remember the hole in the floor I almost fell through?"

Tom nodded.

"Well, my legs were in the Ether! I'll admit it's not a

scientific term. For this, I don't think there *is* a scientific term. But it's definitely a place outside our universe."

"How can anything be *outside* the universe?" Tom asked.

Burt threw up his hands. "That's what *I've* been saying!"

"Hold up," Tom said. "Are you tellin' me the horseshoe is still at the other end of this rope?"

"Sure!" said Steve. "You just can't see it because it's ... elsewhere."

"The Ether between worlds," Tom echoed.

"Exactly! When you run electricity through the Anchor Shard, it opens a hole to someplace else, kind of like a tear in the fabric of spacetime. Matter can pass through this hole without damage. Go ahead, pull on the rope."

Tom hesitated. Then he pulled. It came easily enough, lengths of it appearing from out of the nothing at the back of the room.

Then, suddenly, it stopped.

He tugged. "I think it's stuck."

Frowning, Steve helped him. The clothesline wouldn't budge.

"Looks like we're out another horseshoe," Burt remarked.

"Shut up!" Steve snapped. Then, to Tom, sounding annoyed: "It must be ... caught on something."

"Yeah? What *kinda* something?"

The Brain Boss shrugged. "I've tried putting a webcam through there, but the event horizon fries electronics."

"Event horizon?" Tom asked.

"The limit of the singularity."

"English, Steve," Tom said, still pulling on the clothesline. He wasn't sure why, but not being able to retrieve that piece-of-junk horseshoe really bothered him.

"The limit of the tear," the Brain Boss explained. "The spot where our world ends and *whatever* is in there begins. That's the event horizon. Tom ... why don't you let go of the rope."

"You sure?"

"It's just a horseshoe. Besides, I want to see what happens."

Tom loosened his grip.

The clothesline danced away between his fingers, the end of it darting free and flying the length of the room, before vanishing into Steve's "tear."

"Gravity," the Brain Boss said, marveling. "Whatever's beyond that horizon ... it has gravity."

"Fantastic," Burt muttered. "So, whoever steps through there is going to plummet to his death."

"Hold up!" Tom snapped. "Whoever does *what*?"

Steve lifted his chin. It was his way of looking defiant. "We need to find out what's through that tear, Chief!"

The hell we do!

Out loud, Tom asked, "Why?"

The question seemed to take the Brain Boss by surprise. "Well ... because we *do*! Science demands it!"

His brother groaned, "Oh, Jeez ..."

Tom shook his head. "Sorry, Steve. Right now, I ain't worried about whatever science 'demands.' Nobody ... get this ... *nobody* is goin' through that whatever-it-is. I won't risk an Undertaker's life to satisfy your curiosity."

"But, Chief —"

"I mean it! Gimme your word or gimme that crystal. Your call."

The boy's face turned all kinds of red. As Tom watched, Steve glared Burt's way, as if his younger brother had ratted him out. Finally, his thin shoulders fell and he nodded. "You got my word."

Tom nodded back. "Good."

He stepped back and studied the rear of the Factory. Now that he knew where to look, he could clearly see the "tear."

Except it looked more like a hole. A black hole. A round spot of nothing, maybe six feet across, floating in mid-air and faintly shimmering.

His skin crawled.

"Steve … you said you could use this … thing … to help the war effort?"

The Brain Boss looked like he'd bitten into something sour, but he answered, "Yeah."

"How?"

"I'll show you."

Steve went up and replaced the metal screen around the Anchor Shard.

"Now step well back," he told them, pulling down his visor.

They all stepped well back.

"On three," the Brain Boss announced, his finger on a small switch mounted to a worktable. "One … two … *three!*"

Behind the metal screen there was a blinding flash of light. Tom got the crazy, unsettling feeling that, if the screens hadn't been in place, that light might have swallowed the room.

Then it was gone.

"Okay, we're good," Steve announced.

Tentatively, Tom lifted his visor.

"Last time that happened," he said, "this whole room looked like a twister had trashed it."

"The metal screen blocks the shockwave," Steve explained. "Most of the light, too. The vest and visor are just precautions."

He went up and moved the screen again.

The metal table, the battery, and the Anchor Shard were still there, untouched. But the ground around them seemed different—deeper. It was as if someone had taken a shovel and dug out maybe an inch of earth in a circle around the table.

It had been the same way when Ian had died.

"I ain't gettin' it," Tom said.

"Feeding electricity through the Anchor Shard does more than open the tear," Steve told him. "The crystal somehow stores up its energy. The longer it's plugged into power, the more power it collects. If you suddenly *cut off* the electricity ... in this case, I just flipped this remote kill switch that I'd rigged up to the battery ... the shard instantly closes the tear and releases its stores. The released energy forms a wave that utterly destroys all organic matter within its range."

"So you figure this could be turned into a weapon to use on deaders?"

"Well, maybe ... *if* you could somehow get a bunch of Corpses together inside the blast radius and then get *yourself* out before you killed the power. But that wasn't my point."

"Then what *is* your point, Steve?" Tom asked.

"That the tear *closes*. Don't you get it? *This* is how the Corpses are getting here! They've got another one of these, hidden somewhere in the city, and they've been using it ... all along ... to enter our world. Somehow, they've learned how to cross the Ether!"

Tom absorbed this. "Steve ... you *sure*?"

"Of course he's not sure!" his brother snapped. "How could he be?"

For a second, Tom thought the older Moscova was going to haul off and punch the younger one. He didn't, though his face went cherry-red. "It's a *theory!*" he was almost spitting the words. "And it fits the facts. We *know* this thing is *Malum*. We *know* it can open holes in spacetime. We *know* that, once those holes are stable, things can move in and out through them. Doesn't it make sense that this is how Cavanaugh's people do it? How they've been doing it all along?"

And it *did* make sense, sort of.

Tom said, "Just so I'm straight on this. You're sayin' … if we find this other Anchor Shard and unplug it …"

"Then the door between their world and ours shuts," Steve finished for him. "You'd have to watch out for the blast radius, which could be *huge*, depending on where the shard is and how long it's been attached to its electrical source. But once you managed it, then … no more Corpses."

CHAPTER 6
PARKER AND COLE

Lilith

The *thing* that called itself Lilith Cavanaugh stepped over the bodies of three of her underlings.

Their pieces lay scattered across her spacious parlor—legs here, arms there, heads over there. Moving slowly, taking her time about it, the Queen stepped to each arm and leg in turn, placed one fashionable pump on them, and pressed down, crushing them into pulp. Then, one by one, she did the same thing to the heads, applying pressure until all three skulls crunched like eggshells.

Then she watched as the Self of each *Malum*—the inner essence, or "soul," to use the human term—escaped its now destroyed host. Each hung in the air for a few seconds, desperately seeking a fresh body in which to hide. But Lilith had seen to it that none were available.

Finally, exposed and helpless before Earth's unforgiving environment, each was finally and forever destroyed.

It was *delicious*.

"There's a human saying..." she remarked, glancing at the only other two beings who remained standing in the lavishly furnished penthouse apartment.

One was called Parker, the other, Cole, and they were new to this world, having crossed the Void together that very morning.

Their host bodies were Type Ones, the freshest and strongest Lilith had been able to find. Their covers described them as seasoned, experienced, law enforcement officers. Each wore the uniform of the Philadelphia Police Department. Parker was the taller of the two. His cover showed a man nearing fifty with dark hair, dark skin, and a full face partially hidden by a thick beard. Cole's cover was shorter, but thicker in the shoulders, blond, light-skinned and clean-shaven.

Any human who met them, with their silent, unsmiling demeanors and underlying hint of barely-contained violence, would find them off-putting, even frightening. For this reason, their particular breed was ill-suited for infiltration missions. The Queen had never intended to use them on Earth.

But things had changed.

"What saying is that, Ms. Cavanaugh?" Parker asked. If the destruction of their fellow *Malum* distressed either of them, it didn't show. Lilith liked that.

"'Don't kill the messenger,'" the Queen replied. "The trouble is, killing messengers can be quite gratifying. Take these three for example. They came here to report the betrayal and escape of my consort, Robert Dillin. Betrayal irritates me. Now, had they been able to capture Dillin and bring him before me, they would have lived. But without him, my irritation ... well, it had to go *somewhere*, didn't it?"

Parker and Cole nodded in unison, looking as if she'd

just told them the square root of nine.

"Yes, Ms. Cavanaugh," Cole said.

The Queen went to her desk and pressed the intercom button on the phone. "Send someone in to clean up a mess. And bring me this morning's shipment." Then she broke the connection before her latest assistant, whose name was Stanley, or Stuart, or Something, could even respond.

She burned through so many assistants, it became hard to keep track.

"Parker, why are you and Cole here?" she asked.

"To serve you, Ms. Cavanaugh." Parker answered at once.

"Correct. Cole, *how* will you both serve me?"

"As commanders of your assault force, Ms. Cavanaugh," Cole answered.

"Correct. Parker, why do I *have* an assault force rather than an invasion force?"

"Because the *Malum* invasion of Earth is failing."

"Correct. Cole, *why* is the invasion failing?"

"Because of the Undertakers."

Lilith nodded. "Correct."

At that moment, the door opened, and two minions dressed as custodians came in. They didn't speak. They didn't even make eye contact. They simply went to work, as ordered, cleaning up the remains of the messengers.

The Queen ignored them.

"The Undertakers," she said to Parker and Cole. "In all the worlds we've unmade through all the long centuries that our people have devoted to this art, no one has ever defied us as they do. Children ... just children ... and yet everything we build, they tear down. Every victory turns out to be defeat in disguise. Everywhere I turn, whatever I do, there they are. It's *maddening*!"

"Yes, ma'am," Parker replied.

She said, "For the past six weeks, I've been trapped in this apartment. Parker, do you know why?"

"No, Ms. Cavanaugh."

"I'm here because Lilith Cavanaugh is dead. I was 'killed' ..." The Queen punctuated the word with air quotes, an embarrassingly human gesture. "... when Tom Jefferson, the leader of the Undertakers, kicked me out of my office window on the sixth floor of City Hall."

She'd suffered no physical pain in the fall, of course. But the indignity had been agonizing. The humiliation of that defeat still hurt each time Lilith thought about it.

"Too many humans saw me fall. Too many witnesses. There was no way to preserve my cover. Lilith Cavanaugh had died very publically."

She paced the room, seized by sudden, nervous energy.

"Now, I must live in secret. I don't dare go outside these few rooms. As you both know, I'm unable to manufacture a new cover, and I can't risk any humans seeing the face of *this* one. So here I stay. Minions tend to my needs, bring me fresh cadavers to occupy, and provide me with the information required to continue our efforts. But, in a real sense, I am a *prisoner*." The last word passed her rotting lips, laced with outrage.

Cole offered, "I'm sorry, ma'am."

She glared at him. "I'm not looking for sympathy, fool!"

He didn't flinch. "No, Ms. Cavanaugh."

"I'm telling you both this," she said, "because I want you to understand, truly *understand*, why you were summoned to Earth. The Undertakers have ruined this unmaking. They have defiled our art and our way of life. And they must be made to suffer for it. That will be *your* task."

Both men replied, "Understood."

"I've spent the last month amassing an attack force, fifteen hundred strong. Most wear the covers of Philadelphia policemen. All are warrior caste *Malum* who will live or die by your command. The two of you will lead this army into Haven, the Undertakers' hidden headquarters. You will block any and all exits. You will prevent their escape. Then you will slaughter everyone inside."

"Yes, Ms. Cavanaugh," Parker said.

"But first, I need one of you to spend part of today on a simple but important errand."

The two minions regarded her impassively. Neither volunteered. That wasn't their nature. From a logical standpoint, the two were virtually identical, so she picked at random.

"Parker, you'll do it."

"Yes, Ms. Cavanaugh," Parker replied.

Standing beside him, Cole displayed neither disappointment nor relief. In fact, he displayed nothing at all.

"As I've told you, my consort has betrayed us … betrayed *me!*"

"Yes," Cole said.

"He has disgraced his noble purpose as my mate and revealed himself to be *Oreth Oreg*. He has fled his post as principal of some ridiculous school in Allentown. He is believed to have done so in the company of two children: a brunette girl and a redheaded boy."

"Yes, Ms. Cavanaugh," Parker said.

"The boy has been identified as Will Ritter. The girl is apparently the younger sister of Helene Boettcher, another Undertaker whelp. The three of them are headed here, to Philadelphia. Parker, you are to find them before they reach Haven, kill all three, and bring me their heads as trophies. Clear?"

"Clear," Parker said. "But if they are already en route …"

"The Allentown train station and bus terminals are being watched. I don't know how they plan to get into Philadelphia, but it won't be by public transit. Dillin has not returned to his home, and his car is still in the school parking lot. Perhaps he'll steal another. Or buy one. Your cover identity puts the entire Philadelphia Police Department, human and *Malum* alike, at your disposal. Set up roadblocks. Do whatever you must. But trap them."

"Yes, ma'am," said Parker.

"Also, I've arranged for you to have extra help."

Lilith went to the desk and hit the intercom button a second time. "The shipment!" she snapped. "Where it is?"

Stuart or Stanley or Whoever replied nervously, "It's just arrived, Mistress. I'm sending it in."

Mistress. That proper *Malum* term was forbidden on Earth. Whatever her latest assistant's name was, he'd just sealed his fate.

A moment later, the door opened and two minions came in, each carrying a red metal toolbox. At Lilith's instruction, they placed their burdens side-by-side on the throw rug at Parker's feet.

"Do you know what *those* are?" the Queen asked Parker, motioning with one purple, shriveled hand at the two red toolboxes.

"Yes, ma'am," he replied. "May I ask a question?"

"You may."

"How were you able to bring *two* of them across the Void?"

"With considerable difficulty and cost of *Malum* life," Lilith replied. "I had intended them for the assault on Haven, and I'm confident we'll be making good use of their peculiar talents for that very task ... later on. But for now, Parker, you may employ them in your hunt for Dillin and the children. Their Selves, such as they are, will be keyed to your command."

"Yes, ma'am," Parker said.

"May I ask a question, Ms. Cavanaugh?" This time it was Cole who spoke.

She studied him. "You may."

"If Haven is truly so secret, how will you discover its location?"

The Queen of the Dead smiled a smile that, had there been any humans present, would have caused their hearts to burst with fear. "Why, I already know it, Cole," she replied. "I know *exactly* where those brats are hiding!"

CHAPTER 7

ON THE ROAD WITH A DEAD GUY

I glared at Dillin. "No, I won't 'Take you to my leader!' Why would you even ask a lame question like that?"

We were in a stolen airport limo, heading along the Pennsylvania Turnpike toward Philly. The Zombie Prince was driving. I was riding shotgun. Julie had somehow managed to fall asleep in the back. Traffic was light and it looked like pretty smooth sailing from here to Philly.

I had to admit it. This "alternative mode of transport" as Dillin had put it, was a solid idea.

While in the faculty lounge at Merriweather Intermediate, we'd heard more sirens coming. Ambulances, this time. "They'll be driven by my wife's minions," the principal had explained. "And they won't be alone. By now, Marcy's distress call ... which is like a bell ringing in my head ... has been heard by other *Malum*. Before long, my treachery will be common knowledge. The Queen will have people watching the bus and train stations. We can't get out of town that way."

"We?" I exclaimed. "There's no 'we'!"

He looked at me, this strange Corpse, with his patient expression and absolute lack of menace. "Mr. Ritter, you're a capable young man. You and the Undertakers have conducted yourselves astonishingly well. I don't think you really comprehend the level of your success. But things are 'coming to a head,' as the human saying goes, and I have information that you desperately need."

"So tell me."

His dead head shook. "We get out of here ... together. *Then* I tell you."

I looked at Julie. But there was no help there. For all her courage, Helene's sister was still a rookie. So I decided to call Haven. But, as I reached for my sat phone, the sirens suddenly got louder. Vehicles squealed into the school's front entrance. Not three or four of them, either. I counted at least eight.

"We're out of time," Dillin said urgently. "I need to run. I have a method for getting us safely to Philadelphia. An alternative means of transportation, if you will. Now, if you and Miss Boettcher prefer to make your own way, that's fine. But I need an answer from you. Now."

"I don't trust you," I said.

"I don't blame you," he replied. "Coming or staying?"

"You've got a way out of Allentown without running into deaders?"

"Deaders. That's cute. And, yes, I do. Last chance, Mr. Ritter."

I looked again at Julie. She shrugged.

Finally, I said. "Coming."

He offered up what *seemed* a sincere smile. I decided then and there that I really didn't like sincere smiles on dead guys. "Glad to hear it! Let's go."

So we did. Out through the faculty lounge door and down the hall to a basement stairwell. From there, he led us along a series of passages that smelled so much of mold and rat crap that I got nostalgic for Haven. At last, we came to a locked gate that looked as if it had been there for a hundred years.

The Zombie Prince explained, "This old conduit connects the school to the sewer system. From here, we go straight to an abandoned gas station at the edge of town. I've already arranged for an airport limo to meet us there." He checked his watch, a weirdly human thing for an animated cadaver to do. "Let's hurry."

My every instinct kept telling me to zap this dude, take Julie, and run. But if Dillin was even half-right about how many Corpses would be on the streets looking for us, we wouldn't last ten minutes. By now, they'd probably be bringing in the local cops to help in the search for "students who assaulted some teachers."

But the first time you go squirrelly on us, I'm taking you down, deader!

As promised, the abandoned gas station *was* there, boarded up and completely deserted. The airport limo was there too, a gray van with the service's name and phone number stenciled on its side.

Seeing it, Dillin waved and marched over.

I took Julie's hand and followed cautiously.

"Here's the situation," Dead Principal said to the driver. "My friends and I aren't going to the airport. We're going someplace else entirely, and I'm willing to pay you three hundred dollars to take us there. You can't ask any questions and you can't use your radio at all."

The driver, a stocky dude in his fifties with more hair on his chin than atop his head, scowled at Dillin, and then looked past him at Julie and me. His scowl deepened.

"You takin' those kids somewhere you shouldn't?" he demanded.

"Absolutely not!" Dillin actually looked offended.

The driver opened his door and climbed out of the van. He was big.

"I'm not liking this," he said. "My dispatcher sent me here … to the middle of nowhere … to pick up a lone man. That's freaky enough. But now you show up with two kids and want to make some kind of *deal* with me?"

"That's about it," Dead Principal told him pleasantly.

"What's say I call the cops?" the driver said, reaching back into the van for his radio.

"No!" Dillin yelped. Yep, the Corpse actually yelped. "Wait! Please! You don't—"

The driver ignored him.

So I let go of Julie's hand, ran up and Tased the guy with my pocketknife.

"Sorry," I muttered.

"Mr. Ritter!" the principal exclaimed in a tone that made him sound like—well—a principal.

"We'll tie him up," I said, pulling the big dude out of the van as he convulsed. "Leave him in that old gas station. Then, when we get far enough away, we'll call the cops and have them come rescue him."

Dillin stared at me. He looked—I guess "uncomfortable" is the best word for it. "But he's … innocent!"

"I know," I said. "Third one I've zapped today. Sucks, huh?"

We dragged the poor guy over to the closed gas station, where I picked the lock. Once inside, I trussed him up pretty good with his own shoelaces. I didn't gag him. Gags are more dangerous than you'd think. People choke and die on gags. So instead, I just left him on the floor with an apology. Being still pretty zapped, he didn't respond—though the look in his eyes made me question his forgiving nature.

Julie said, "Is he gonna be okay?"

"Yeah," I told her. And it was true. Almost certainly.

War sucks, I thought.

Dillin said he'd drive. I didn't mind. It's easier to defend yourself when your hands are free. So I got Julie settled in the van's back seat. As I did, she looked up at me with those huge brown eyes of hers and said, "I wanna go home."

"Um … I'm taking you to your sister," I replied, hoping that would end it.

It didn't. "My mom and dad are getting divorced."

"I know."

"Dad moved out. He wants to take me with him."

"I know."

"Did Helene tell you?" she asked.

I nodded.

"Were you at my school to protect me?"

"That was part of it."

"What was the other part?" she asked.

"You're the right age to start Seeing deaders, and the Sight usually runs in families. But your sister was worried about more'n that. She also wanted me to … watch over you … until the end of the school year, when your dad was gonna take you out of the area. Away from … them."

"Helene's been gone a long time." She sounded sad.

"I know."

"Years."

"I know."

"She's been fighting … them." Her eyes flicked over to the Zombie Prince, who was settling himself behind the steering wheel.

"Yeah," I said.

"If I go where she went, I won't be able to go home either," Julie added. Her gaze locked on mine, and there was a quality in them—a kind of steel—that would brook no lies. "Will I?"

"No," I replied. "Not until we beat them. Not until it's safe."

"When will *that* be?"

"Soon, I hope," I told the girl. "You tired?"

"No."

"Well, why don't you lie down anyway? It's been a scary day."

She considered that. "Yeah, it has." Then she stretched out across the seat and closed her eyes.

And, just like that, we were off.

"I need to call Haven," I told Dillin, pulling my sat phone out of my pocket.

The Corpse moved fast. Seriously fast. The kind of fast I'd only ever seen in Royals. One instant the phone was in my hand and the next it was out the open window, sailing deep into a passing treeline.

"Hey!" I snapped, instinctively readying my pocketknife.

"I'm sorry!" he said quickly, holding up his hand in an "I come in peace" gesture.

"Pull over!" I told him, holding up the Taser. "Now!"

"Mr. Ritter—"

"What'd you *do* that for?"

"Will—"

"Tell me!"

He took his gaze off the road and gave me a hard look with his dead eyes. "What do you think would happen if you called Haven and told them about *me*? What do you think your chief, the infamous Tom Jefferson, would say?

What would he tell you to do?"

The only reason I gave him the answer he expected was because it also happened to be the true one. "Waste you."

"Right. So, no phone calls ... not until we can set something up, a meeting in a public place where there can be a free, *safe* exchange of ideas."

Exchange of ideas. Dude even talks like a principal!

"You told me you had information." I tried not to think about my sat phone, lost back there in the woods. Haven had probably already sent the Angels out looking for us. When I didn't check in, they'd freak. Helene, especially. She'd figure the deaders had gotten me and her sister, both.

"I do," Dillin replied.

"And you said you'd tell me on the way."

He considered this. Then he replied, "Take me to your leader."

Which catches us up.

"What's wrong with 'Take me to your leader'?" he asked, looking perplexed when, in my generally poopy mood, I'd called his line lame. "You *have* a leader. *Take* me to him! Then I'll tell you both everything I know."

I squirmed in the passenger seat, trying to settle myself down. I was on edge—and most of what was honing that edge had nothing to do with the Corpses hunting us. I'd been hunted by so many dead people for so long that it had gotten to be second nature. No, what had me so wired was the idea of *cooperating* with one!

"I'm not taking you to Haven!" I snapped.

He looked confused. "I don't expect you to. I told you: a public place where there can be a free, safe exchange—"

"Yeah, I heard that part. But how am I supposed to set up a meeting without my phone?"

"Once we're in Philly, we'll … I don't know … buy you one of those throw-away cell phones. You can contact Mr. Jefferson using that."

I sat back in the passenger seat and regarded him. He wasn't making a lot of sense. First he throws my phone out the window and then turns right around and offers to buy me another one. He doesn't want me to contact Haven because he's afraid Tom'll order me to kill him. But then he says I *can* phone home as soon as we're in Philly, as if he thinks the chief's attitude will have changed in the next hour?

This dead dude's all over the map. It's almost as if he's not just running, but running …

"Scared," I remarked aloud. "You're scared."

He didn't reply. He didn't have to. I'd nailed it.

A scared Corpse. I'd encountered them before, of course. When cornered, helpless, and faced with their own death—*real* death—deaders tended to blubber like the cowards they really were. But this wasn't that kind of scared. This was much closer to the fear that Undertakers carry with them every minute of every day: a slow burn kind of scared, born from the knowledge that any moment might be your last.

This was *dread*.

Trust me. I know dread when I see it.

"Is Cavanaugh really your wife?" I asked him.

"She is," he replied. Then, more pointedly: "I'll never lie to you, Will. That's a promise. Never."

Uh huh.

"But you're scared of her."

"Aren't *you?*" he asked.

"Sure," I admitted. "But I'm not married to her. What happened to 'love, honor and cherish'?"

"It's not the same where I come from. Love isn't …

that is, we don't ..." His words trailed off, and he gripped the wheel tighter. I actually heard the bones in his dead fingers crack.

"What's she going to do if she catches you?" I asked him.

For half-a-minute, he didn't answer. Then, in a very small voice, he said, "Have you ever been in a 'No Win' situation?"

"Answer the question," I said.

"I *am* answering the question. Have you or haven't you?"

I thought about it. "No."

"Well, they exist. I'm in one now. I've been on your world for about four months. My wife and mistress, the Queen of the *Malum*, summoned me. Do you know why?" Then, without waiting for me to reply, he said, "So that I may give her children."

All kinds of *ewwww.*

"Okay ..." I muttered. "That's not—"

But there was no stopping him now. "I'm of royal blood, Will. The Queen may only mate with royal blood. That rule is absolute in my culture. So, when she desires to, she selects her mate from among the royals. The male ... me ... is not offered a choice."

His already pale face looked somehow paler, which was weird, since blood can't drain from your cheeks when it's not pumping in the first place. He said, "It's considered a great honor to be chosen, and my family was suitably compensated. As for me, I was put on 'standby.' Our mistress would call me when she was ready."

"And now she's ready?"

He nodded.

He was dead. She was dead. Picturing that was bad enough. But I'd seen up close what the *Malum* actually looked like. And picturing *that* was the kind of thing that put you in therapy for the rest of your life.

"Um …" I said. Mr. Articulate, that's me. "I'm not sure I want to know—"

"Immediately after mating," the Zombie Prince said, "she'll kill me."

I blinked. "Kill you?"

"Kill me and consume me. That's also my culture. I'm supposed to be further 'honored' by becoming nourishment for my own offspring."

Praying mantises did that, didn't they? Black widow spiders, too. "Sounds like a pretty crappy honor," I told him.

He nodded. "That's what I mean when I describe my situation as 'No Win.' If I betray her, my wife kills me. If I *don't* betray her, she still kills me. No way out."

"Sorry, dude," I said, and I was astonished to find that I meant it. Since when had I started feeling sorry for Corpses? "But that still doesn't explain why you picked 'betray' over 'don't betray.'"

"Will," he replied, "do you know what a 'Fifth Column' is?"

By then we'd left the turnpike, taking Exit 326 toward Valley Forge and Philadelphia.

Smooth sailing—up until now.

Ahead, all traffic braked to a stop. And, in the distance, I spotted something that looked a lot like a police roadblock.

Crap, I thought.

CHAPTER 8

THE SURE-KILL

The Schuylkill Expressway has made somebody's list as one of the top ten most dangerous roads in America. For that reason, locals sometimes call it the "Sure-Kill."

From end to end, it's only ten miles long. But they're ten *tough* miles, running from the burbs northwest of the city, down along the steeply-cliffed western bank of the Schuylkill River, and eventually into Philly. There, it slices right through the middle of town, almost all the way down to the stadiums.

At rush hour, it's a sight to behold. Wall-to-wall cars. At such times, those ten miles can cost you two hours.

And, trust me, it's even worse when there is a roadblock.

They were Philly cops. This was weird, since technically the Sure-Kill is a state-owned road. The cops had stationed themselves right at Philly's northern border—the City Avenue exit, it's called—with a total of eight cruisers working the site, some parked to the side and the rest blocking the eastbound lanes and checking drivers. All their lights were flashing.

It was just past one in the afternoon, so the expressway wasn't anywhere near as bad as it would be in three hours. But that still left a *lot* of cars on the road, all of which had piled up behind the barricade, forming a line of braked traffic at least half-a-mile long.

"Think your ... wife ... is behind this?" I asked Dillin. It was still weird to picture Lilith Cavanaugh married to anybody, though, if I added on the notion of her *eating* her husband—well, that helped.

"I don't know," the Zombie Prince admitted. "Do *you* think so?"

"Yeah, I do."

He braked smoothly to the back of the right-hand line of cars. "Why?"

"Because, otherwise they'd be state troopers, not Philly cops. This has got Cavanaugh's stench all over it."

"You're a smart young man." He looked around. "Plenty of exits coming up. Lincoln Avenue. City Avenue. Roosevelt Boulevard. But they're all blocked."

They would be, wouldn't they? The Queen of the Dead wouldn't want her flies slipping out of the web.

For several minutes, we just sat there, gazing sullenly out at the wall of red and blue between us and Philly. There was no way to turn around. The Sure-Kill wasn't about turning around. At this particular point along its ten-mile length, the east and west bound lanes were split up, separated by a wide, sloping median that would rip the bottom out of this van if we drove across it, never mind the cops who would drop on us like vultures the moment we tried.

I glanced back at Julie, hoping to find her still asleep. She wasn't. Her dark eyes were open, her face half-covered by thick strands of dark brown hair. She regarded me pensively. Then she asked, "What's wrong?"

"Quite a bit," Dillin said.

"Nothing," I said. "Try to sleep."

"Not tired," the girl replied, sitting up.

"They might not be here for us," the principal suggested.

"I could check," I said sourly. "Haven monitors police scanners. If I only had my satellite phone ..."

He made a sound very much like a sigh, which is weirder than you'd think, considering the dude didn't breathe. Then he reached into the pocket of his sportcoat and pulled out an iPhone. "I'm sorry. I acted ... hastily. You're right. I was scared. Here, use mine."

I took it from him—hesitantly, but I took it. As I did, it occurred to me that I'd never actually been handed anything by a Corpse before. Attacked, sure. Chased, all the time. But the simple act of one person handing something to another person? Nope. This was a first.

His screen saver showed—

I blinked.

"*South Park*? Really?"

He shrugged. "It makes me laugh."

I called Haven. Dillin's iPhone wasn't encrypted, of course, so I had to use one of the "safe" numbers. These were phone numbers that the Chatters changed constantly, to make them harder to monitor. Even so, they were only ever used in emergencies.

Dan McDevitt, Chatter Extraordinaire, picked up. *"Grant's Pest Control. We live to kill. How can I help you?"*

"It's Will," I said.

"Oh, Jeez. You're not on your sat phone."

"I kinda know that, Dan."

"Right. Hold on. I got orders to pipe you right through."

The line clicked and, when another voice came on the line, I expected it to be Tom's.

It wasn't.

"Where are you?" Helene demanded.

"Helene?" I asked, momentarily startled, while in the back seat, Julie suddenly perked up. "Where's Tom?"

"Where's Tom? You drop off the grid for two hours, and the first thing out of your mouth is 'Where's Tom?' Where's my sister?"

"She's here," I said quickly. "She's safe."

Then I glanced over at the dead guy who drove the van, and wondered if that was really true.

"Lemme talk to her!"

I handed the cell phone to Julie, who snatched it eagerly. "Helene?"

She listened.

"I'm okay."

She listened.

"In the back of this big van headed into Philly."

She listened.

"Uh-uh."

She listened.

"Uh-uh."

She listened.

"Yeah, kinda. But Will took care of me."

And I thought: *Whew! That ought to score me some points. Unless she—*

"Well, him and Mr. Dillin."

I felt my stomach jump up through my neck and try to squeeze out my ears.

In the driver's seat, I saw the Zombie Prince smile thinly with his bloodless lips and mutter, "Uh-oh ..."

Julie listened.

"Huh? Oh yes, he's one of them ... but he's nice!"

She listened some more.

"Sure, I'm sure. They were all over the school. Will and the Burpmister fought them. But then Will sent Megan and Bridget off with the Burpmister and he and I went to find Mr. Dillin."

Still more listening.

"Well … 'cause he was nice."

A final bout of listening, very short this time.

Then she held the phone out to me. "My sister wants to talk to you."

Despite whatever he was feeling, Dillin managed a lopsided grin. Dead guys should avoid lopsided grins; their faces can't quite pull them off. "Woman trouble?" he asked slyly.

"Look who's talking," I grumbled as I took the phone.

"Point taken," he replied.

In my ear, Helene exclaimed, *"Who are you talking to?"*

"Oh … um …" I stammered. "That's … just …"

"Please just tell me that my sister's got it wrong! Tell me you're not in that van with a deader!"

"He's different," I said defensively, wondering if I believed it myself.

"What are you talking about? What's the matter with you?" Then, after a long pause, she asked, *"Will … my God … were you … compromised?"*

Compromised. A fancy word for brainwashed. Deaders could do that. In fact, they *had* done it to Helene once upon a time. They used these little creatures from their home world called *Pelligog*. Once one of them burrowed into you, it made you very—cooperative— where the Corpses were concerned. It wasn't something we'd seen them try for a while; we'd gotten too good at spotting it. But, given the circumstances, I supposed I couldn't really blame Helene for running down that particular street.

"No, I haven't been brainwashed," I told her.

"Yeah? That's just what a brainwashed person would say, isn't it?"

I sighed. "How do I prove I'm not brainwashed?"

"You can't!" she snapped. *"If you were me, you'd be thinking exactly what I'm thinking!"*

"I know."

"And you've got my little sister!"

I felt like a fool. I felt like a traitor. Somehow I'd allowed myself to be led along by this walking cadaver, this Zombie Prince. Stupid. Really stupid. Why had I done such a thing?

Then I looked up at Dillin, who met my eyes with a look of—well, "desperate sincerity" is the only way I can describe it. No Corpse had *ever* looked at me that way before. Until now, I wouldn't have imagined it was even possible!

I did it because my instincts told me to trust him.

They're still *telling me to trust him.*

This is crazy!

"Helene," I said into the phone.

"What, Will?" she demanded. *"Go on! Tell me! What do you want to say?"*

"I'll die."

There was silence on the line. If my girlfriend—still weird to think of her that way—was breathing, I couldn't hear it. Then: *"What?"*

"I'll die," I said, "before I let anything happen to Julie."

More silence. Finally, reluctantly, she replied, *"I know."*

"Helene, I'm not compromised. But I *am* in trouble.

All of us are." Then, deliberately, I added, "All *three* of us."

"Where are you?"

"On the Schuylkill, coming up on City Avenue. But the cops have set up a roadblock. They're checking cars."

"Are they deaders?"

"Can't tell. We're still too far back. But, if they are ... and it's a good bet ... then we've got maybe twenty minutes before we're made."

"You need to talk to Tom."

"I know. That's who I *wanted* to talk to. But Dan put me through to you, instead."

"I ... asked him to." She actually sounded a little sheepish. *"I was worried about you both."*

"I get that," I told her.

As I said this, I looked through the windshield at the roadblock. We were maybe ten cars back in the right lane—close enough to see that at least half the PPD on hand were, in fact, Corpses. Twos and Threes, mostly.

Except one.

He was in a fresh host body, tall and lean and hardcore scary-looking. Like the others, he wore a police uniform. Except, while the others were moving from car to car—both the Corpse cops and their Unseeing human partners—the tall guy stood back and watched.

No, not watched—*supervised.*

I saw Dillin stiffen. He muttered something that I didn't catch.

"Will?" Helene asked. *"You're quiet all of a sudden. What's happening?"*

I told her, "We just got close enough to see that some of the cops at the roadblock *are* deaders. But we're still a ways back, just sitting in line." Except that wasn't entirely true, was it? Something else had happened, too. I didn't know what exactly, but I could read it on Dillin's slack-featured, lifeless face.

Helene's voice, tinny but clear, rose up through the phone, which I'd lowered a little from my ear. *"Listen … I'm on my way to Tom's office. You can tell him what's going on."*

"No time," the Zombie Prince muttered. Then he looked at me—hard at me. "We need to get out of this car. *Now!*"

I looked through the windows at the mass of traffic. To our right stood the expressway shoulder and then a wall of solid Pennsylvania granite rising at least fifty feet straight up. To our left was another lane of stopped traffic, followed by that sloping median I mentioned earlier. Then came two lanes of roaring westbound cars, a steep drop to a series of commuter railroad tracks, and finally, the river.

"Go *where?*" I asked him.

"Anywhere!" Dillin said, shouting now. Behind us, Julie kind of squeaked with fear. "Away from here. Away from *him!*" He pointed one gray, trembling finger at the tall Corpse who was evidently running the roadblock.

"Who is he?" I started to say.

Instead of answering, the Zombie Prince shifted the van into park and, to my horror, opened the driver's side door.

"Will … we have to go. Please trust me!" Then he climbed out.

"Bro?" said the voice on the phone. This time, it wasn't Helene. It was Tom.

"Call you back, Chief," I said quickly. "Gotta situation here."

Then I ended the call and looked at Julie.

"Do you trust him?" I asked her.

"Do you?" she replied. Her face was as pale as the moon.

I allowed myself two seconds to think about it. Then I said, "Yeah, I do."

The two of us climbed out of the idling van and followed the Zombie Prince.

CHAPTER 9
A RIVER RUNS THROUGH IT

"You there!" one of the cops yelled. I think he was human. "Stop!"

If we'd still been twenty car lengths back, ditching the van might not have been noticed, at least not until the drivers behind us started honking. But nine or ten car lengths was too close, and three people weaving through idling traffic on a highway that doesn't see too many pedestrians—well, that tends to get noticed.

"Keep going!" I called to Julie.

"No kidding!" she yelled back. Definitely Helene's sister. No doubt about it.

Dillin reached the far shoulder of the Sure-Kill. He hesitated there, looking back at us.

This is it. The Corpse'll ditch us to save his own neck.

But he didn't, and I was surprised by how not surprised I was by that.

As we caught up with him, I spared a moment to look over my shoulder. A half-dozen police were coming our way, the Corpses moving faster than their human counterparts.

"Where are we *going*?" I demanded.

"Follow me!" Dillin yelled. Then he led us at a run down the hill and across the grassy median.

Traffic ripped along the westbound lanes, great deadly blurs of colored metal.

Crossing that'll kill us all!

Well, except for the dead guy.

Then Julie screamed.

I turned in horror to see that the Zombie Prince had grabbed her around the waist, scooping her off her feet with one sweep of his arm. Then, before I could even begin to react, he reached for me and did the same thing.

"What are you—" I exclaimed, struggling. But the guy wasn't just a Corpse, he was a *royal* Corpse, which meant he was way too strong for me.

"Hold on," he said.

He jumped.

Suddenly, the ground receded. Wind filled my ears and tossed my hair around. Below us, I saw the two westbound lanes of the Sure-Kill pass in a rush of gray asphalt, some of its travelers slamming on their brakes and staring up at us in astonishment. The other travelers, of course, immediately rear-ended them amidst shrieks of metal.

"You kids are heavy," Dillin complained as we descended. He didn't quite clear the expressway, landing instead on the roof of a BMW, denting it badly, before launching himself again. This time we passed right over the far shoulder and dropped down the steep slope toward the railroad tracks, leaving in our wake a junkyard of damaged cars, honking horns, and screaming people.

I could only pray no one had been killed.

I half expected the Zombie Prince to stumble and fall, landing as we did halfway down the bush and thistle-laden slope. But instead he touched down perfectly, and with the agility of a mountain goat.

Ahead lay a half-dozen railroad tracks. To my right, I spotted the shimmering shape of an approaching train. Big. Fast. Unstoppable.

Oh Jeez!

"Listen," I gasped, still hanging uncomfortably under one of Dillin's impossibly strong arms. "You might want to wait until this thing goes—"

"No," he said.

Then he jumped again, this time right over the train.

I don't know what its operator saw, much less, its passengers, but whatever it was made him blow the whistle—a high, shrill sound, way louder than the car horns.

We landed on the far side of the tracks, where Dillin immediately dropped us both onto our feet. As he did, the train roared past behind us.

"Sorry," he said. "But you move too slow."

I groaned, trying to catch my breath. "At … least … we lost the cops."

"Probably," he agreed. "But we haven't lost *him*."

"Him … who?" I demanded.

"His name's Parker. He's a *shavvik*."

Julie asked, "What's a—"

"Later." Dillin cut her off. "For now, we run."

I groaned. "Run *where?*"

"Honestly, Mr. Ritter. At this point, I was rather hoping *you'd* tell *me*."

We stood in a broad alley behind a big, nameless building. Around the corner, I could see the gray water of the Schuylkill River running beyond a line of trees that fenced the riverbank. No handy speedboats around. Not even a kayak. The Zombie Prince had "jumped" us across two lanes of traffic, down a hill, and over a train just to trap us against the water.

"Great," I muttered.

The nearest bridge was City Avenue, maybe a quarter mile away and at least a hundred feet over our heads. Even with Dead Hoppity Guy doing his thing, I doubted we'd make it that far. Besides, doing so would only drop us back in the traffic jam, and right in the middle of all those cops.

No, Dillin's instincts—if that was what they were— might have been right: we needed to be down here, away from traffic, away from people.

Julie said, "Will, I'm scared." It was the first time during this long, terrifying day that she'd admitted it to me out loud. When I looked at her, I saw her small round face screw up. "You told my sister you'd die before you let anything happen to me."

"I know I did," I replied. "And I meant it."

Tears filled her eyes. "But ... I don't *want* you to die before you let anything happen to me."

I started to go to her, but the Zombie Prince beat me to it. He knelt down in front of the girl and asked, "Ms. Boettcher, can I tell you something?"

She looked warily at him, but nodded.

Get away from her! I wanted to say. But, for some reason, I didn't—though, for the umpteenth time since I'd gotten up that morning, my hand went reflexively to my pocketknife.

"Will Ritter's pretty famous among my people. Do you know what for?"

Julie nodded again. "You told us. He's your 'boogeyman.'"

The principal laughed, a weird gurgling sound. *Voice box starting to rot,* I supposed. "Indeed he is, but there's a reason *why*. It's because he wins, Julie. He beats us, over and over again. Every time we go up against the Undertakers, we lose. In all our history, that's never happened before. And it's largely because of Will. He frightens us. He frightens us like nothing we've ever encountered before."

"Then why are you helping us?" she asked him. It was a frank question. A fair question.

"Because not all of us are monsters," he repeated. He glanced at me, and then up at the embankment. So far, there was no one in sight. The *shavvik*, whatever that was, hadn't shown up yet.

He turned back to Julie. "Do *I* scare you?" he asked her.

"A little," the girl admitted. Yet I noticed that she looked right at Dillin's dead face, not flinching at the sight of his gray skin or bloodless lips.

"That's because of what I look like," he said. "Not the way I act, right?"

She nodded. "I guess so."

"Well, Julie, I can't help what I look like. But I can promise you this: I will never hurt you or Will, or anyone else if I can help it. I'd like to be your friend, if you'll let me. But either way, I'm not your enemy. Do you believe that?"

Her eyes searched his face, again without flinching. "I think so ..." she said.

Dillin smiled. "That'll do for now."

"The Falls Bridge," I said suddenly.

Julie looked at me. "Where's that?"

I pointed southeast along the riverbank. "That way, about a mile. These railroad tracks run right by it. There's no highway access, so the cops'll have to go around the long way to cover it. If we hurry, maybe we can make it across to Kelly Avenue, which will lead us into Center City."

"Are you sure?" Dillin asked.

"It's near Manayunk, where I live ... or used to." For the first time in a long while, I thought about the house I'd grown up in. It stood empty now, abandoned. These days, my mom and sister lived in Haven—war refugees.

The principal looked at Julie. "Does that sound like a good idea to you?" he asked.

She shrugged. Then, after a moment's thought, she nodded.

"Then it certainly works for me!" he announced brightly.

He straightened and turned around. As he did, his smile died—no pun intended.

Suddenly wary, I followed his gaze across the railroad tracks behind us, where the *shavvik*—the tall dead cop—stood at the base of the steep embankment, eyeing us. The moment he spotted us spotting *him*, he dropped the two red toolboxes he carried. Both of them popped open the minute they hit the uneven ground.

The Zombie Prince uttered an inhuman cry of pure, animal terror. Then, without warning, he scooped us both up under his arms again and exploded into motion, moving around the building, into the trees and southeast along the Schuylkill.

CHAPTER 10
TROUBLED CROWN

Tom

Tom closed the satellite phone and handed it back to Helene, who immediately demanded, "What happened?"

"I don't know," he told her.

Then he pulled out his own sat phone, pressed a speed dial button and waited until Sharyn answered. "Where you at?" he asked.

"Just picked up Hot Dog and two Seers. No sign o' little bro, though ..."

"Just heard from him. He's got Helene's sister, but things are hot." He looked up at Helene, who stood there looking pale and frightened. "Where did he say he was?"

"A Corpse roadblock on the Schuylkill. Up near City Avenue. Tom ... he's with a *deader*!"

"What's that mean? With a deader?"

"I mean *with* him! Teamed up with him. He said he's ... nice."

Tom didn't let the alarm show on his face. It was

a knack he'd mastered so long ago that it had become second nature—as thoughtless as breathing. "Nice," he echoed with deliberate calm. "Well, now ... that'd be a first."

"A first!" Helene exclaimed, gaping at him incredulously. "He's either crazy or brainwashed!"

He studied her from across his desk, Karl's old desk. They'd found it in a Goodwill store. Karl had paid twenty bucks for it. It was small and scratched and so far from level that you couldn't place a pencil on it without it rolling off the edge. Only two of the four drawers still worked. More than once, Sharyn had suggested that he replace it, insisting that they *had* the money.

And they did. The Undertakers had been smart with Karl's life insurance policy and could certainly afford a second-hand desk for their chief.

Except he didn't need one.

Or, more to the point, he didn't *want* one.

"Bro?" Sharyn asked over the phone. The same word he'd said to Will right before Karl Ritter's only son had hung up.

"I'm here," Tom said. "Seems Will and Julie Boettcher are hangin' with a ... friendly ... Corpse."

"Say what now?"

"A good guy deader," Tom replied. "Yeah, I can't figure it, either. But it's Will, sis."

"'Course it is. Who else would it be?"

That gave Tom his first genuine smile of the day. "Right now, they're either stuck in a Corpse roadblock around City Avenue ... or on foot. I thought I heard a car door open just before he hung up. If they're on foot, they'll be heading into the city ... and there are only so many ways to do that. Call him. Here's the number he's using." Tom rattled off the digits. "If he don't answer, *keep* calling. In the meantime, send Chuck and Katie back here with those two Seers. Have 'em use public transit. Then you and Dave get your butts to the Schuylkill River. Sooner or later, Will's gotta cross it."

"On our way. Tell Helene we'll find 'em and bring 'em both home."

"Straight up. What about the deader?"

There was a long pause on the line. Then his sister said in a glacial tone, *"I'll give him five seconds to be 'friendly' to me. Then I'll waste him."*

She hung up.

Tom lowered the phone and looked at Helene. "He ain't brainwashed."

"What makes you so sure?" the girl demanded.

"'Cause, if he had been, he wouldn't have told you about his 'nice' Corpse friend. He would've said it was all cool and then led this deader, whoever he is, right to us."

Helene considered this. "So ... we're going with crazy?"

Tom grinned. He liked Helene. He liked Will and Helene being together. Haven wasn't a happy place, and a little happiness was always welcome. "He knows what he's doing. And Sharyn'll find him."

The girl scowled. "I should be out there."

Tom shook his head. "You know why that ain't true."

"If it was me, *Will* would be out there!"

Fair point.

He said, "There *is* something you can do for me ... while we wait to hear, I mean."

Helene's scowl deepened. "Busy work."

"Might seem like that at first, but it ain't."

"Okay. Fine. What?"

"Take a camera, go up to Penn Centre Plaza, and take some pictures."

She blinked. "Pictures? Of what?"

"People."

"Live people or dead people?"

"Both. Random as you can."

She looked at him. He looked back at her, giving her nothing. Not yet. Soon, but not yet.

"What for?" she asked.

Tom said, "Take about twenty pictures. Then run 'em over to the Hackers and get Sammy to print 'em out for me."

Helene put her hands on her hips. "Why, Tom?"

"When you come back with the pics, I want you to bring Jillian ... and Susan."

"Will's mom?" Helene blinked again. Tom watched her sort through it. "This is a test, isn't it? You think Susan Ritter might have the Sight?"

Again, Tom gave her nothing.

"Why would she hide that?" the girl pressed.

She was smart. And she was close.

He said, "She wouldn't and this ain't about her. But you'll find out when you get back. Half-an-hour. Cool?"

She paused again, considering him. "Cool ... I guess."

"Thanks, Helene."

After she'd left him alone in his tiny office, Tom opened one of the two drawers in the desk that still worked. From it he took a photograph.

In it, a younger version of himself stood beside a tall redheaded man wearing a Philly cop uniform. Both Karl Ritter and the young Tom Jefferson were mugging for the camera. Sharyn had taken the photo, long before Karl's death, long before the war.

All the other pictures of Karl had gone into the Shrine, the room in Haven that had been forever dedicated to its founder's memory. But this one, Tom kept for himself. A rare bit of sentimentality, he supposed. At certain times, bad times, times like this, there was some comfort in being able to pull it out and gaze at the only father he'd ever known.

Your son's a lot like you. Your real son, I mean. He's smart and brave ... probably smarter and braver than is good for him. He's out there right now, playin' it scary, walkin' the line, 'cause that's what he does. That's what you did, too. And it got you killed. Don't think I don't know that. Don't think I don't fret over it every single day. But while Will's like you, he ain't you. He's got this way of makin' miracles happen that I don't get and probably never will.

But I ain't here today to talk 'bout him. Sharyn'll find him. And Dave. The two o' them are an item these days. They think I don't know, but I do. Same as Will and Helene. It's cool, seeing 'em make these connections. I only wish ...

Karl, somethin's coming. I've been feelin' it for a while now ... in my gut, the gut you taught me to always trust. I could wait for it to happen and then take it for what it is. Until Will came along, that was pretty much my style. But no more. Now my gut's tellin' me I gotta do something about it. That "something" is risky, maybe even flat out stupid, but I gotta do it.

I gotta take a page from your son's playbook.

I gotta walk the line.

Helene returned almost exactly thirty minutes later. The girl was nothing if not prompt. With her came Jillian and Susan Ritter, the latter looking confused and more than a little irritated. Apparently, Tom's request had pulled her away from something important in the Infirmary.

Susan was the only adult in Haven, and the only adult Undertaker since the Corpses had murdered her husband Karl, two-and-a-half years before. Her recruitment had been—challenging. She and her six-year-old daughter Emily, Will's little sister, had been rescued and brought in as refugees. At first, the woman had balked at the Undertakers' way of life. But, eventually, she'd come around.

Still, you could take the grown-up out of the adult world, but you couldn't take the adult out of the grown-up. Even now, having proven herself a true Undertaker, and having taken over as Haven's medic, she remained the only person, other than Sharyn, willing to challenge Tom's leadership and decisions. Not that he minded being challenged occasionally. Actually, it tended to be a good thing.

But it could also cause—problems.

"Hey, y'all," Tom said, coming around his desk to the small conference table.

Everyone sat.

"What's going on?" Jillian asked.

In answer, Tom turned to Helene. "Got the pics?"

She nodded, holding up a small stack of white photo paper. "Hot off Sammy's printer."

"Lay 'em out across the table. Face up."

Helene did so.

People. It was a sunny, late spring day topside, and men and women in suits were busy going about their business. From the look of it, Helene had found herself a choice spot near the "clothespin," a big modern sculpture of—well—a giant clothespin, that stood at 16th and Market Streets.

Helene had been subtle with the camera, maybe holding it in the palm of her hand while turning in a slow circle. Most of the shots were at an upward angle.

Smart.

Dozens of faces, all wearing different expressions, all

clueless that their image had just been digitally captured.

"Susan," Tom said, turning to Will's mother. "Look at these pics."

Obviously perplexed, the woman did so. "What am I looking for?"

He asked her, "How many are Corpses?"

To her credit, she actually tried. She even picked up a few of the shots and held them closer to her face, as if that would help. Finally, with a sigh, she put the last one down and said, "I don't know. Are *any* of them?"

Tom looked from her to Jillian.

"Are any of them Corpses?"

Now it was Jill's turn to look perplexed. Her gaze moved from Tom to the pictures, to Helene, to the pictures again. "Three," she said.

"Which ones?"

She picked up three shots, two women and one man.

"Give 'em here," Tom said.

Jillian handed them to him and, for half-a-minute, Tom studied them.

"What's going on, Chief?" Helene asked.

Tom Jefferson lowered the pictures and regarded each of them in turn. He would have preferred to have Will and Sharyn here, but that wasn't possible. Things were happening, and he simply couldn't wait.

So he told them, "I wanted to be absolutely sure before I said anything."

"About what?" Susan asked.

He replied in a calm, matter-of-fact voice. "I've lost the Sight. I can't see Corpses anymore."

CHAPTER 11

FALLS BRIDGE

Falls Bridge looks kind of like a birdcage with a tunnel running through it. It crosses the Schuylkill River just at Philadelphia's northwestern border, connecting Martin Luther King Drive with Kelly Drive. Martin Luther King Drive *used* to be called West River Drive, while Kelly Drive *used* to be called East River Drive, but they got renamed because—

Oh, who cares?

For the last ten minutes we'd been carried by the Zombie Prince, who'd traced the western edge of the river, following the railroad tracks in leaps and bounds. No subtlety at all in this guy. Any normal person who saw us—and while there weren't many, there had to be *some*—would, at best, have found it deeply strange and, at worst, called 911 or maybe even caught the whole thing on a cell phone and uploaded it to YouTube.

Robert Dillin wasn't behaving like a Corpse at all. There was nothing sly or sneaky about him. Corpses were all about protecting their Masks, about hiding their true nature.

This guy was just scared.

Falls Bridge has two roads coming into it from the west. Martin Luther King Drive comes from the city. The other's called, naturally enough, Falls Bridge Road. It runs in from the west, actually passing under the Schuylkill Expressway without connecting with it. Right where these streets meet there's a busy, lighted intersection.

That's where the Zombie Prince finally stopped and let us go.

Julie immediately vomited.

Trust me: being carried under someone's arm and then bouncing along while they run for about a mile and a half will do that to you.

I rubbed the girl's back while she retched in the bushes. My own stomach and I weren't exactly on speaking terms either—though, for now at least, the cold Pop Tart I'd had for breakfast seemed to be staying put.

I'd been living this crazy life for most of a year. This was Julie's *first* day. Regardless of her strength and courage, I needed to remember that.

I also needed to call Haven.

I went to pull Dillin's cell phone out of my pocket—only to discover it wasn't there anymore.

Oh, you've got to be kidding me!

I fished through my other pockets. Nothing. Zilch. I must have lost it while riding underarm on the Zombie Prince.

Two phones in one day. That was a record, even for me.

Glancing over at Dillin, I saw him looking back the way we'd come, his dead eyes wide and watchful. I craned my neck, but saw nothing behind us along the tracks, not even a train.

"Who *was* that?" I asked him.

"I told you," he said. "His name is Parker." I noticed he wasn't breathing hard. Then, of course, I remembered that he was dead, and so didn't breathe at all.

I'm starting to forget what he is.

"Yeah, I know," I said. "And he's a *shavvik*. But what the heck is a *shavvik*?"

At first, he just shook his head. But, after a hesitation, he answered. "The nearest English translation is probably 'special.' He's ... well, you know how my people have a caste system?"

"Royal. Leader. Warrior," I said.

"Those are the top three. But there are others. There's a Merchant Caste, a Worker Caste and a Builder Caste. When we're born, it's into one of those castes, and that's where we stay until we die. No chance of advancement. No hope of improving your lot in life. You just do what you were born to do and shut up about it."

"Sounds sucky," I said.

"It *is* sucky, Mr. Ritter," Dillin replied, sounding like a principal again. "But it's the way the *Malum* have lived for far longer than anyone can remember. That said, there *are* exceptions ... individuals bred for very specific functions that are outside the normal caste system. We call these *shavvik*. Specials."

"Parker's a Special," I said.

"Yes."

"What's his function?"

The Zombie Prince's eyes continued scanning our trail. I looked again, but there was still no movement.

"Did we lose him?" I asked.

"We *can't* lose him," Dillin said. "He'll keep coming. And, worse, he's not alone."

I remembered the two red toolboxes—the ones

Parker had dropped to the ground at the sight of us.

But, before I could ask about them, Dillin said, "Specials have a lot of different functions, depending on what's required. Parker, in particular, is a 'commander.' You see, among my people, the Royal Caste is supreme. We never let anyone challenge our control. Leader Castes are bread to be ambitious, to a point. But, while we put them in charge of off-world missions—"

"Like Kenny Booth," I pointed out.

He nodded. "I hated that guy."

"That makes two of us."

At that he almost smiled. "—we don't give them armies. We don't let them lead in battle. If we find ourselves in a situation where deception, infiltration, and deceit don't work ... our so-called *art*." He said the last word almost like a curse. "When we decide we need to wage true and honest war, that's when we produce a Special ... a commander."

"Parker's a commander?"

Dillin nodded. "He's one of two, actually. The other one's called Cole."

"How do you know that?" I asked him. "Did Cavanaugh tell you about them?"

"Certainly not! I'm just her mate, not her confidant! No, I picked it up through the grapevine. Specials are rarely used. And when *two* of them pop up, it's noticed. *Malum* gossip, just like any other race."

"Why *are* two of them here?"

"That's obvious," he said. "They're *both* Specials, and *both* are here to lead an army."

"A *Malum* army?"

"Yes."

"Against us?"

"Yes."

"Earth?"

He looked at me. "Well, no. Not the whole Earth. We aren't ready for such a thing. No, Parker's here to wage war against *you*. Well, not you, specifically. The Undertakers."

An icy chill rolled down my back.

"Will?"

The small voice made me turn. Julie stood near a row of bushes. She looked pale and tired.

"I'm here," I told her. "It's okay."

She asked, "When do we get to see my sister?"

"We're on our way." Then I faced Dillin. "Once we cross the bridge, we can follow Kelly Drive along the river all the way into Center City. That's when we'll split up."

"I need to talk to Tom Jefferson," he reminded me.

"I know. But *my* priority is to get Julie safely to Haven. Once we're there, I'll ask Tom about meeting with you."

He seemed to consider this. Then, with a nod, he regarded Falls Bridge. Traffic rumbled across it in both directions. "I can carry you over there, but it's going to be ... conspicuous."

"I know," I said, partially because I agreed with him, and partially because I didn't think my stomach could handle another underarm ride.

The Zombie Prince said, "Maybe out best bet would be to—"

That's when something sliced his arm off.

Whatever it was, it was *fast!* I'm talking "faster than a speeding bullet" fast. A blur of motion, nothing more. Then Dillin's arm fell off just above the elbow and landed in the grass at the shoulder of Falls Bridge Road. Since he was a dead guy, he felt no pain. Also, his host body had evidently been embalmed, so there was no blood— just some juices that I won't describe, which dribbled out of the stump and onto the fallen limb like gravy on a seriously messed-up pot roast.

For a split second, he looked down at it in bewilderment.

Then he moved.

At that same instant, whatever had dismembered the principal sheared past my face, so close that I felt its breeze. I caught a glimpse of something small and furry—like a bat maybe, though if it was a bat, then it was Superbat.

Behind me, Julie screamed.

I whirled, my heart jumping up into my throat. If Superbat had done to her what it had done to Dillin—

But the girl seemed intact, though her face had gone white with terror.

She'd seen it too.

I grabbed her hand. "Let's go!" I told her sharply, though, at the moment, I didn't have the slightest idea what that meant. Go where? Across the bridge? This thing, whatever it was, was *way* faster than we were. If it meant to kill us, we wouldn't make it a dozen steps.

Then the Zombie Prince answered my question for me.

He leapt at an SUV that was trundling over the bridge from the opposite bank, appearing in front of it so that its driver—a guy in a suit—screeched to a halt. Then he bounded around to the driver's side and yanked the door open. "Sorry," he said conversationally. "I really am."

Before the dude could utter anything besides a curse word that didn't go well with the suit, Dillin yanked him out of the SUV and dumped him unceremoniously onto the street at the mouth of the bridge. Then he climbed behind the wheel, slammed the door and gunned it our direction.

I glanced around for some sign of the flying *thing*.

Nothing. Just trees and the steel superstructure of the nearby bridge. Lots of hiding places, though.

Dillin called to me. "Get in!"

I grabbed Julie and made for the SUV, which the Zombie Prince had braked in front of us. As we had in the airport van, Julie climbed in the back while I took shotgun.

By now, three or four cars had stopped around us, their drivers wising up to some of what was going down. Meanwhile, the owner of the SUV had managed to get to his feet. He started yelling and pointing wildly at us.

"Buckle up," Dillin commanded.

We buckled up.

As he pulled the big car in a tight turn that headed us back across the bridge, I glimpsed something flash by the side window, small and indistinct.

We rumbled past the guy in the suit, who made a crazy grab for my door, which I hastily locked.

Then the Zombie Prince's dead foot mashed the accelerator and we charged forward, leaving behind the SUV's foul-mouthed owner.

"What *is* that thing?" I yelled at Dillin.

"A *Malite*," he replied, which didn't help me even one little bit.

"What's the heck's a *Malite*?"

I got my answer seconds later when, as we reached the halfway point across the bridge, whatever was chasing us slammed hard into the windshield.

That's when I got my first good look at it.

It was a rat.

But no. Calling this thing a rat is like calling a werewolf a puppy.

It looked as if someone started with a rat—and not

a cute pet-store rat, but a big city rat the size of a cocker spaniel—grafted on huge leathery wings, and added about six hundred teeth. Its head was huge and bulbous, really nothing more than a pile of fangs with eyes.

Those eyes, black as coal, glared at us through the windshield.

Then its teeth—those impossible teeth—bit *into* the glass.

"Holy crap!" I yelled, instinctively pulling myself as far back into my seat as I could go.

Behind me, Julie started screaming again.

The *Malite* chowed down, crunching away at the thick windshield like it was peanut brittle, sending long spider lines running in every direction.

We've got maybe five seconds before that thing's in here with us.

Then the Zombie Prince turned on the wipers. Seriously. He did.

They didn't help. As the first one slammed into the little creature's flank, it hissed, grabbed it with its front claw, and ripped it off.

But the pause had given me the time I needed.

Pulling out my pocketknife, I hit the **2** button and slammed my Taser into the fresh hole in the glass.

Teeth met electricity.

Electricity won.

The thing seemed to explode away from the SUV as if fired from a cannon. It bounced off one of the big steel struts that lined the bridge before disappearing from view—either behind us or off the bridge and into the river, I couldn't tell which.

"Nicely done, Mr. Ritter," Dillin said.

"That … *Malite* … was in one of Parker's toolboxes," I said. Not a question.

"In a manner of speaking," he replied. He looked shaken but calm, though his remaining hand had clamped so tightly around the wheel that I wondered how it didn't just snap off.

"This guy's playing it pretty loud and large, isn't he?" I asked. "You Corps— ... um ... *Malum* are usually more careful than this."

He glanced at me as we reached the far side of the bridge.

"As of today, the rules have changed," he said. "You should know. *You* changed them."

CHAPTER 12

MALITE

We turned off the Falls Bridge and onto Kelly Drive, heading into Center City.

Kelly Drive is no Schuylkill Expressway. For one, it's narrower, only one or two lanes headed southeast, into the city, and one or two lanes headed northwest, out of the city. For another, it's *way* prettier, with the shops and neighborhoods on our left giving way to towering, rough cut granite cliffs as Philly got ever closer. To our right, the river followed us like an old friend, with a wide grass park between it and us.

Fairmount Park.

There were plenty of cars, but even more joggers and cyclists—just innocent civilians enjoying a sunny June day, blissfully ignorant. To these folks, mostly college age or older, there *were* no Corpses, there *was* no war, and the things—*Malites*—chasing us were only figments from nightmares.

At that moment, *in* that moment, I hated them.

From the backseat, Julie's cries had changed into wracking sobs.

I turned around in my seat, drawing a sharp, disapproving—and very dead—look from Dillin for unhooking my seatbelt.

"Julie?" I said.

She sobbed.

"Julie. Look at me."

She looked at me, her eyes red from crying, her small round face ghostly pale. "I'm ... scared ..." she stammered.

"It's gonna be fine," I promised. "I'll get you to your sister, don't you worry."

She stared hard at me, wanting to believe. *Needing* to believe. Then, gulping air, she nodded. I nodded back, did my best to smile, and then turned forward again.

It suddenly felt like an awful burden. I'd told the girl what I had to, the same thing I'd been telling myself.

But Parker's out there. And that thing. No, those *things. Parker had* two *of those toolboxes!*

"Are they still after us?" I asked Dillin, who kept one dead eye on the mirrors. Of course, he was also driving with only one hand, as his other was back on the bridge.

"Unless Parker calls them off, yes. But he *won't* call them off." He switched lanes, cutting left around a panel truck that was moving too slow for him. "That said ... they're new to Earth. They don't know the environment. Its strangeness probably frightens them."

I blinked. "Frightens them?"

He nodded. "Children get frightened. You should know that better than most."

For a second, an offended reply about *everyone* getting frightened, child or otherwise, sat on my tongue. But then his real point sunk in.

"Children?" I asked.

Another nod. "*Malites* are our children."

"The monster that took your arm off and almost chewed its way through our windshield was a *Malum* kid?"

"Yes."

"But it looked like a *rat*! A *flying rat*!"

"That was just the host body it found when Parker released it."

I admit processing this took longer than it should have. It'd been a hard day. "You mean *Malites* ... possess animal dead bodies?"

"Not exactly."

"What's *that* mean?"

"It means that they *do* use animal bodies for hosts ... but they don't necessarily have to be dead."

More processing.

"But it had *wings*!"

"*Malites* like to alter their host bodies at the genetic level. That's why they take living hosts. Dead hosts can't be altered."

Nope. Not getting it. "But how can they—"

That's when Dillin cursed.

Three cop cars were blocking the road just around the next bend. Another roadblock.

Double crap.

"Your wife's pulled out all the stops," I said.

"She's nothing if not thorough," he replied.

Then he cut the wheel hard to the right, pulling us into a parking lot that ran beside the river. There were already a bunch of cars there, probably belonging to bikers and joggers. June days were like that.

How far are we from Center City?

Then I spotted the building at the far end of the parking lot and knew.

It was a boathouse.

Boathouse Row.

Philly's a big crew town. I mean a *big* crew town. One of the biggest in the country, maybe in the world. Just to give you an idea, remember when I told you Kelly Drive used to be East River Drive? Well, it got renamed for John Brendan "Jack" Kelly, Jr., an Olympic rowing champion from the 1920s. Don't believe me? Look it up.

Today, there are a whole bunch of boathouses lining the eastern banks of the Schuylkill River—big, colorful, two or three-story wooden buildings, all with direct river access. Each is owned by a group that sponsors a rowing crew. Some are new and fancy enough to get rented out for parties or weddings. Others are old, like 1860's old. And a few are condemned.

This was one of the condemned ones.

As we climbed out of our stolen car with the hole in the windshield, Julie immediately took my hand. She'd recovered somewhat, but I could feel her trembling, and her dark eyes seemed to look everywhere at once. Then they settled on Dillin's missing arm and she asked nervously, "Does … it hurt?"

"No," he replied. Then, having to turn awkwardly to shut the car door, he added, "But it *is* inconvenient."

"What if people … see it?" she asked.

"They won't," he said.

"Why not? How come Will and I can see what you really look like? How come those other two girls could … but not anybody else?"

"It's called his Mask," I replied.

"It's called my cover," he said at the same time.

We looked at each other.

Dillin said, "We need to get out of the open. Any ideas?"

I pointed at the boathouse. "In there."

He looked at it, seeing the same signs splashed across it as I had.

CONDEMNED BY ORDER OF THE CITY OF PHILADELPHIA! DANGER! ASBESTOS!

"Okay," he said.

That's when a *Malite* took off his other arm.

He'd been just turning away from the car when it happened, otherwise the *thing* might have nailed him in the chest.

As it was, his newly detached arm went flying, spinning up and over the nearest cars, where it clobbered a big bald guy, knocking him over.

The guy's wife, or girlfriend, or whatever, screamed.

Julie gasped.

The *Malite* kept going, whipping out across the river in a long arc, getting ready for another attack run. Here, where there were fewer trees and much more open ground, I was able to follow it more easily.

This one wasn't a rat with wings.

This one looked more like—

—a duck.

Except its bill was more than a foot long, with serrated teeth along both edges that seemed to be moving back and forth, like the blades of a tree trimmer.

Jeez.

"Come on!" I cried, grabbing Julie's hand and pulling her toward the relative safety of the condemned boathouse. I could only hope the Zombie Prince was following. I mean, it wasn't like I could grab *his* hand too, now was it?

We'd gotten maybe twenty feet when the rest of the

people in the parking lot registered at least some of what was going on. Nobody had panicked yet. Instead, they just stood, staring at the bald guy who'd been knocked down by Dillin's arm. He'd found his feet again and was rubbing angrily at a bloody lip and looking around. "Who hit me?" he exclaimed, tacking on a couple of a words that, if I copied them down here, would probably get the book banned from most school libraries.

The severed arm lay at his feet but, of course, he couldn't see it. Dillin's Mask remained in effect.

"Will! It's coming!"

This came from Julie, and a glance over my shoulder proved her right. The *Malite* was gaining speed, and this time it seemed to be coming after *us*.

"That car!" I exclaimed, pointing to a big pickup truck with lots of undercarriage space. "Get under it! Go!"

The girl didn't argue. As she ran for the pickup. I went toward the bald guy, who scowled at me as if maybe I was the one who'd knocked him flat and had now returned to pop him a second time.

"Don't try nothing, kid!" he growled.

I ignored him, bent down, and picked up the severed arm he couldn't see.

For just a moment, because a moment was all I had, I watched the guy's eyes. To him, I wasn't carrying anything in my arms. But I could read the confusion in his expression, as if his eyes and his mind were telling him two different things.

"You're blind!" I snapped, suddenly angry at him without really knowing why. "Just like all the rest!"

Oddly, that seemed to offend him and he actually made a grab for me, but I jumped clear and turned—just in time.

The *Malite* lanced down at me.

I swung the severed arm up to meet it.

Dead flesh connected with flying monster. The little stolen body bounced away, slamming into the side window of bald guy's car so hard that I heard its bones crunch.

Home run, I thought.

"What's going on?" the bald guy demanded, and there was an edge of menace in his voice that I didn't much care for. "What *is* that?" He stared down at the *Malite's* broken body.

Then he pulled a gun.

The confusion was gone from his expression. Panic had replaced it.

"It's okay!" I told him. "Put that down!"

He ignored me, waving the weapon around. "What *is* that thing? Are there more of them?"

That's when I heard a scream at my back.

Turning, I spotted a woman on the jogging path that ran past the far side of the parking lot. From the look of things, her leashed dachshund had suddenly leaped up and ripped out its owner's throat.

Then, as the poor woman collapsed, the creature spouted bat wings and leapt into the air.

It just Transferred.

As the reborn *Malite* approached, cruising maybe four feet above the gravel lot, I readied Dillin's arm a second time.

Then I heard a gunshot. A bullet whizzed past my ear. "Hey!" I yelled.

An instant later, the flying dachshund was swatted out of the air as if by an invisible hand.

An instant after that, a guy in bicycle pants riding along the jogging path, right behind where the *Malite* had been, toppled over, shot through the chest.

Oh, God …

"I got it!" the bald guy yelled. "Did ya see that, Jess? I got it!"

His wife, or girlfriend, or whatever seemed *not* to have seen it. Her eyes had gone glassy with shock.

I glared at the dude. He looked back on me, his face flushed with animal triumph. "Did ya see that shot, kid?"

"I saw it," I said.

Then I hit him upside the head with Dillin's arm—hard.

He went down a second time. And stayed down.

Finally, though no more than a minute had passed since Dillin and his arm had parted company, the folks in the parking lot started panicking. Most raced for the safety of their cars. Others took off on foot, some south and some north, scattering like frightened deer.

"Julie!" I called.

"I'm okay!" she called back, though her voice sounded like she'd been crying again.

Girl's gonna have nightmares for the rest of her life!

"Come on!" I told her, looking around for Dillin.

The Zombie Prince was nowhere to be seen.

Had he split on us? Probably. I mean, he *was* a Corpse, after all. But still, from what I'd seen of the guy, it didn't feel right. He'd had plenty of opportunities to ditch Julie and me. Why do it now, especially with no arms?

But I didn't have time to find out. The *Malite* had transferred once already. It would do it again.

We needed to get into the boathouse, if only to buy time to plan our next move.

Julie scrambled out from under the pickup and the two of us ran the length of the parking lot, reaching a padlocked door that had once been painted red.

"Hold on," I said, fumbling for my pocketknife.

"Will!" she screamed.

I looked where she was pointing.

A rabbit was bounding across the parking lot toward us. Except this was no happy park bunny. This rabbit's ears had been turned into razor-tipped horns and its mouth was a symphony of fangs. Instead of front paws, it had talons as long and savage as an eagle's.

I swear ... I'm gonna have nightmares for the rest of my life, too!

My only hope was to use my pocketknife to either pick or, more likely, slice the lock open.

But who was I kidding? I didn't have time to do either one. That thing was coming way too fast.

"Julie," I said.

"What?" she asked, pressing close to me.

"I'm sorry."

Then someone appeared in front of us, a figure in skin-tight blue.

"Out of the way!" the gunshot biker yelled.

We got out of the way.

He kicked the door in with such force that it almost blew off its hinges. Then, as the *Malite* leaped, he spun and caught it midair, his grab lightning-quick. "Not this time, little one," he said, crushing it in his fist.

"Dillin?" I asked.

He actually smiled at me. His teeth were white. But then, this new host body hadn't been dead more than a minute. About as fresh as they get. Hardcore Type One.

"Inside," he said.

The three of us ran into the boathouse, slamming the door behind us.

CHAPTER 13
THE BOATHOUSE

It was dark inside, the windows boarded up. Despite that, as I shone my pocketknife's flashlight along the walls, colorful graffiti told tales of years, maybe decades, of visitors.

Dillin found an old bench and used it to wedge the door shut.

"Will that keep 'em out?" Julie asked tearfully.

"Not at all," he replied. "But the *Malite* will first have to find a new host and then figure out where we've gone. That should buy us some time."

I asked, "What if Parker and the *other Malite* show up?"

"No 'if' about it. They *will* show up. And the boathouse is a pretty obvious place to search. But, by then, the parking lot out there will be a crime scene, with plenty of police around ... most of them likely human. Parker won't want to just burst in here and kill us with so many potential witnesses. Things *have* changed in this war, as I told you ... but they haven't changed *that* much."

A nice pep talk, though I wondered how much of it he really believed.

Then the Zombie Prince did a strange thing. He marched over to me and, moving with that uncanny speed Royal Corpses have, snatched the pocketknife out of my hand and shone its flashlight beam on something in his own.

A thin wallet.

"Raymond Exler," he said solemnly.

"Who?"

"The man who was killed on the bike just now. His name was Raymond Exler."

"Oh," I said, perplexed.

Then the Zombie Prince did an even stranger thing. He closed his eyes—his new eyes—and said, "Ray, I'm sorry you died. I'm sorry I've had to borrow your body. I will do everything in my power to respect it, and I vow to keep it not one moment longer than I must."

His eyes opened again. He handed back the pocketknife.

"Thank you."

"You're the weirdest dead guy I ever met," I said.

"I'll take that as a compliment. Now, let's explore, shall we?"

The boathouse was basically one big room, with a vaulted ceiling and a half-rotted wooden floor. There were two other doors, both padlocked from the outside, and a wide boat ramp that was also tightly closed–though river water, loaded with trash, lapped underneath its doors, slapping noisily against old pilings.

I found a brass plaque, tarnished almost to the point of being unreadable.

THE ORDER OF SAINT JEREMY
BOATHOUSE
DEDICATED ON THE
EIGHTH OF MAY IN THE YEAR
EIGHTEEN HUNDRED AND SEVENTY

"That's about the time we started watching," Dillin remarked.

I shone my light on him. "What?"

"1870. That's about the time my people started watching your people."

"That's almost a hundred and fifty years ago," I said, unable to keep the accusation out of my voice.

"I know."

Out of the corner of my eye, I saw Julie watching us. The girl was still shaking, but she seemed alert. That was good. I'd been half afraid she'd go into shock. A lot of new Seers did.

Boettcher girls, it seemed, were made of tougher stuff.

"Is that how Corpses know how to act so … human?" I asked.

He nodded. "We're forced to study each target world for a long time … decades … before an invasion begins. Your language. Your culture. Your history."

History.

"So when Ms. McKinney was teaching us history, she was just parroting back the facts she'd memorized while learning how best to destroy us?"

He looked at me. "That's an interesting way of putting it. But, yes."

I looked back at him. "We should focus on finding a way out of here."

"Agreed," he said. "But there are already police cars

approaching."

"How do you know?"

"I can hear them. Can't you?"

I listened, but didn't hear anything. Then, distantly, I did. Sirens.

Royals have good hearing.

"Let's give it about ten minutes," he said. "Let the parking lot fill up with lots of activity. Lots of witnesses. Then we'll decide on our next move."

Ten minutes.

It can be an eternity when you've got nothing to do but count the seconds and hope not to die. Best to fill the time somehow, even if it's with stuff that doesn't matter.

So I said to him, "Name me three things that Walter Raleigh or one of his reps brought to Europe from the New World."

He regarded me thoughtfully. Then, with a flash of white teeth, he answered, "Potatoes."

"That's one," I said.

"Tobacco."

"That's two," I said, ticking them off on my fingers.

"And curare."

I groaned. "Curare! Right! *That's* the one I forgot! That South American tribe who learned how to dip their darts in poison."

"A number of tribes, in fact," he said. "My personal favorite was called 'calabash curare' and was used in the eastern Amazon regions. Those clever people found a way to mix the poison with other plant ingredients to make the curare glutinous, so it would stick to their darts and arrows."

"Calabash?" I echoed.

"Yes."

"Glutinous?" Julie echoed.

He grinned. "To make it stickier. By the way, Raleigh didn't really bring back curare. He just wrote about it."

"Teachers," I muttered, shaking my head.

He laughed.

Then, more somberly, he said, "You could learn a thing or two from those ancient tribes, Mr. Ritter. Take, for instance, the salt you employ to destroy us. Your so-called 'Ritters.' It takes far less of that substance than you would imagine to generate the necessary effect. A little goes a long way. Your delivery system, while ingenious, is actually rather inefficient."

Why would he tell me that?

Out loud, I asked, "Why would you tell me that?"

Yeah. I know.

"To help earn your trust," he replied, looking pointedly at me. "To try to convince you that, unlike the others of my kind, I really *am* on your side."

Then Julie asked, "Why?"

The Zombie Prince turned to her. "Why what, Ms. Boettcher?"

"Why'd you pick *us*?" I asked. "The Earth, I mean. Why'd you pick the Earth to invade?"

He shrugged. "Luck of the draw. The Eternity Stone found you."

"The Eternity Stone?"

"It's a crystal, huge and ancient. Nobody remembers where it came from or how long it took our people to learn to use it. But there isn't a *Malum* who doesn't know what it does."

Julie asked, "What *does* it do?"

"It scours the universe. Constantly. Searching the cosmos for worlds that resonate a certain way."

She blinked at him in the bad light. "Resonate?"

"All matter vibrates. From grains of sand to entire

planets. In that resonance, one can read much about a world ... including, most importantly for my people, the presence of intelligent life."

"So," I said. "You look for planets with people on them."

"The Eternity Stone does, yes. And when it finds one, our entire civilization ... or nearly so ... drops everything and devotes itself, as though with one mind, to the single purpose of studying that intelligent life ... and snuffing it out."

I'd known this. Not the details maybe, but the gist.

Julie, however, let out a gasp. "You kill whole planets?"

Dillin seemed to flinch at her tone. "We do," he admitted.

"How many?" I asked. "How many worlds have you un-made?"

"Too many, Mr. Ritter. More than you can imagine. More than I can count."

My God.

"Why?" Julie asked, sounding somewhere between anger and tears. "Why do you hate everybody?"

"I don't know," he said. "It's just what we do ... as a people." Then, after a pause, he added, "But not *all* of us."

I'd been fighting Corpses for a long time—so long that, often, I couldn't really remember what it was like when I hadn't been. I'd seen victories and defeats. I'd watched friends die. Yet, through all those battles, I hadn't truly understood my enemy. Sure, I'd had hints, but precious few answers.

Well, *here* were the answers, standing in front of me.

"What's a ... fifth column?" Julie asked.

I'd completely forgotten Dillin mentioning that term. The Zombie Prince said, "A 'Fifth Column' is a group that works to undermine a larger group from within. It's an Earth term that my rebel colleagues have sort of adopted. It dates back to your Spanish Civil War."

"You work against your own people?" I asked.

"I do. There aren't many of us. Nowhere near enough. We hide ourselves carefully within our castes and communities. Sedition isn't well tolerated amongst the *Malum*. At the first hint of it, the traitor is destroyed. No trial. No appeal. Many of us have been lost that way. Friends. In some cases, siblings."

A crappy way to live. As it happened, I knew a little something about crappy ways to live.

"So how does a member of the Fifth Column end up married to Cavanaugh?" I asked.

He laughed. It sounded very human—the advantage of a fresh body.

"Not by choice," he replied. "I told you: the Queen has to marry a Royal. My brood is Royal. I drew the 'lucky' straw, as humans say."

"But she doesn't know you're Fifth Column?"

"If she did, we wouldn't be having this conversation," he snarked. Then, more somberly, he added, "But it was … an opportunity. We all knew that the Queen's consort would be provided a rare chance, one that no other Fifth Column had ever before been given."

"What chance?" Julie asked.

"The chance to come *here* … to Earth. The chance to do some real good."

"Is that what you're trying to do?" I asked him, unable to entirely remove the suspicion from my voice. What can I say? Old habits die hard. "Good?"

"Yes," he said, meeting my eyes in the dark. I noticed he was still holding Ray Exler's wallet in his hand, as if dropping it or even pocketing it would be disrespectful.

"Though I admit I didn't know exactly what kind of 'good' I could do. I mean, one *Malum*, however well intentioned, can't stop an invasion, can he?"

"One *Malum* could kill Cavanaugh," I said. "I've seen how you move. You're fast and crazy strong … like her."

He nodded. "It's a Royal trait, bred into us. And, yes, I suppose that … before today … I could have arranged to destroy my wife. Of course, scheduling an audience would be difficult. The consort does not summon the Queen. The Queen summons the consort and, aside from a brief meeting when I first came through the Rift four months ago and was *told* who I would be and where I would work, she hasn't so much as contacted me."

"Doesn't sound like a great way to … breed," I said.

"True. But *that* aspect of my role is at the Queen's behest, whenever … if ever … she's ready."

"TMI!" I groaned.

"But you see my situation. Despite my 'elevated' position as the Queen's husband, I couldn't just knock on her door and assassinate her … however much I might want to. Besides, doing so wouldn't end the invasion. You know that better than anyone."

"Me?"

"The killer of Kenny Booth. That single act made you infamous on my world, and your exploits since have only enhanced your reputation. So, imagine my wonder when I suddenly encountered you … of all the Undertakers … and in my own school. We *Malum* don't subscribe to the concept of fate, but we know good fortune when we see it."

"And so your plan became … what?" I asked. "To help us? How?"

"I have information you need."

"So tell me."

"Not yet."

"Why not?"

He looked hard at me. "Because I don't completely trust you, Mr. Ritter."

I admit that one stunned me, though it shouldn't have. After all, I sure didn't completely trust *him*. "What? Why not?"

"'Cause you're *you*," Julie said. "You're their boogeyman. And nobody trusts the boogeyman."

Dillin didn't agree with this, though I noticed he didn't deny it either.

"So then what *is* your plan?" I asked.

"Arrange a meeting with your chief, the esteemed Tom Jefferson, whose reputation is only slightly less infamous than your own. But he's the leader of the Undertakers and, by all accounts, an honorable young man."

"So ... you're saying you'd trust Tom to not waste you the instant you gave him your 'information,' but not me."

"I'm sorry if that offends you."

And the thing is: it *did* offend me. There'd been a time when I'd struggled with the idea of actually killing a Corpse, once and for all, despite their evil. These days I did it—well—a lot. But did that mean I'd become so callous that I'd really betray a man—

Not a man!

—a being who'd been nothing but nice to me? Had this war really turned me into someone who would give his word and then break it, violently, the minute he had what he wanted?

Offended? That wasn't the word for it, exactly.

I felt—demoralized.

Look it up.

"Okay," I said. "Let's get to Philly."

"Soon," he told me. "Things are happening out there."

And they were. As we'd been talking, maybe a half-dozen police cars had rolled into the parking lot. It'd been hard to miss their arrival—all sirens and tires on gravel. Plus, there were voices out there. Lots of them. Cops investigating a murder scene. Right away, they'd have found two bodies: the old armless one that Dillin had been wearing, and the poor lady who'd been killed when her dog had gotten possessed.

I figured, that, by itself, would keep the police busy for a while.

The other side of the coin was that Parker would almost certainly be among them, which meant his toolbox monsters would be nearby.

And, sooner or later, the boathouse was going to get searched.

"I wish I could call Haven," I said.

Dillin tossed something to me. Instinctively, I snatched it out of the air, though it wasn't until I held it in my hand that, given the bad light, I knew what it was.

A cell phone.

"Compliments of Ray Exler," the Zombie Prince said, his white teeth visible in the gloom. "Let's see how long you can hang onto *this* one!"

CHAPTER 14

BLIND MAN'S BLUFF

Tom

"Don't look so surprised," Tom told the two girls and one woman around his conference table. "You tellin' me you ain't never wondered what'd happen to my Sight when I went adult?"

"But ... you're not eighteen yet!" Helene protested.

"Maybe it ain't about a number." Tom shrugged. "Maybe it's about other things."

"Physiological changes happen when a body reaches full maturity," Susan suggested.

Sure, Tom thought. *Let's go with that.*

Jillian said, "But ... Sharyn's the same age as you. Exactly the same. You're twins! Has she lost it too?"

Tom shook his head. "Not so far. Just me."

As he said this, he watched them. Helene had gone quiet, her slender face drawn and pale, as if he'd just told her Santa Claus had opened fire in a shopping mall. Susan Ritter wore a troubled frown, as though he'd posed a math problem that needed solving.

Jillian seemed fidgety. "What are you going to do?" she asked.

Tom replied. "Step down as chief."

"What?" exclaimed Helene. "You can't!"

"Gotta. I can't run the Undertakers without the Sight."

"You could just stay in Haven!" the girl insisted, even going as far as slapping the tabletop. "Not having Eyes only becomes a prob when you're topside ... when you've got to know who's a danger and who isn't. But you can still run things from down here!"

"No," Tom replied.

"Tom!"

"No."

Susan placed a cool hand over his. "She's right. We need you. You're still chief. No matter what."

"Thanks," he replied, meaning it.

He couldn't tell them what he really thought: *It ain't so simple. We got Rules and Regs, even for this. Ain't never needed 'em before today, but Karl wrote 'em up with the rest. The Chief of the Undertakers has to be an Undertaker. And, despite the one exception we made for you, Mrs. Ritter, all Undertakers are Seers. Doin' it another way means anyone could be chief, even an adult. And not having my Eyes makes me, at least by the Undertakers' dictionary, an adult. No way am I handin' Haven over to an adult. Not even if that adult is me. Not ever. Period.*

Out loud, he said, "Maybe somebody could run this place without the Sight. But I ain't that somebody. No, my mind's made up. I'm steppin' down."

"Then ... who takes over?" Helene sounded defeated.

"Sharyn, in the short term. Then we'll probably have an election."

Susan sat back in her chair. "Who else knows?"

"Just you three. And, for now, let's keep it that way.

Once Sharyn and the others get back, I'll pull her and Will in here and tell 'em what's happened. Then we'll figure out the best way to explain things to the rest."

"Then why tell us at all?" Jillian asked.

A smart question.

No flies on her.

This was the part he'd been dreading. The truth wasn't an option, at least not yet. That old saying, "the truth shall set you free," was straight up—except when it wasn't. Except for those times when the truth could get you and everyone you loved killed.

The truth is two of you are just cover. There's only one of you I'm really talking to right now.

Out loud, he delivered a long, measured sigh. "Because ... I had to tell somebody."

Susan's hand found his again, giving it a gentle squeeze. Helene slowly nodded. Jillian looked thoughtful.

"What do you need us to do, Chief?" Will's mom asked.

You've turned into a helluva Undertaker, lady. Karl would be proud.

"There's more," he said. Then he twisted around in his chair, took a folder of papers from his desk and dropped it on the countertop, where it mixed with the pictures Helene had taken.

The three of them looked perplexed.

"What are these?" Jillian asked.

"Printouts from online worm searches. Articles and press releases from the last couple o' weeks."

Helene sifted through the pages. "They're all about ... police training?"

He nodded. "I've had the Chatters monitorin' 'em for me."

"Why?" Susan asked.

"Because I started gettin' the feeling that something's

comin'. Had that feeling ever since I kicked Cavanaugh out that window. Philly took her 'suicide' hard."

"If they only knew," Will's mother replied.

"Yeah. But ever since then, *stuff's* been happenin'." He held up one paper. "Two hundred new cops hired. New 'urban peacekeeping' training exercises planned around City Hall. New police procedures put into place. Then, just this morning, two new 'interim' co-police chiefs get hired: Griffin Parker and Spencer Cole. Today's their first day."

"Pretty boring," Helene noted, scanning the pages.

"Yeah," Tom agreed. "In fact, the way it's laid out, it almost comes off as a little *too* boring. Maybe … deliberately boring."

Jillian said, "Like they're doing something they can't cover up, but that they don't want anyone to really … notice."

"Straight up," Tom told her.

"You think Cavanaugh's behind this," Susan said.

"I think it's possible. Her people basically run this city. Oh, the mayor *thinks* he's in charge, but the Corpses play him like an old song."

Helene asked, "But what do you think she's doing?"

"Ain't sure," Tom told her. "Like I said, most of this is feelin'. But it needs checkin' out … quietly. I can't do it myself. So, Jill and Helene, you're both Angels. I'm gonna ask you to hit the streets. Go to the places they talk about in these papers, the training sites for Philly cops. See what you can find out. So far, there ain't no published pics o' these new co-police chiefs, Cole and Parker. Try to snatch a peek at 'em. Tell me if they're deaders."

"On it," Helene said brightly. This, at least, was familiar territory for her.

"No prob," Jillian added.

"And me?" Susan asked.

"Go back to the Infirmary and, soon as you're able, empty it out. I don't even want Amy in there. Then I'll come down and have you give my eyes a good looking at. Maybe we can find … I dunno … *something* that'll tell us more about how the Sight works. Or doesn't work, in my case."

Haven's medic looked skeptical. But she nodded.

"Okay," Tom said, standing up. "That's it for now. There'll be more once Sharyn and Will get back. Thanks."

They all watched as he stood up and turned away. He pretended to study a report on his desk, something about monies spent last month by the Moms on foodstuffs, while he listened to them rise uneasily and, just as uneasily, leave the room. His news had shaken them up, and he felt bad about that.

But, of course, shaking them up had also been the whole point.

Single file, the three of them slipped through the tattered curtain that hung across his office entrance. As they did, Tom counted the rustles.

One.

Two.

Silence.

One of them's still in the room. One of them needs to talk to me some more. I only hope it's not who I think it is. I've already "lost my Eyes." Ain't that enough for one day?

Someone shuffled their feet. Someone cleared their throat.

"Tom?" a female voice asked.

He turned.

Jillian said, "There's … um … something I need to tell you."

I know.

CHAPTER 15

RESOURCE IN ACTION

"*Tell me that's you, little bro.*"

"It's me," I said into the phone.

"*Thank God.*"

In the background, I heard the Burgermeister exclaim, "*Well, it's about time!*"

"Sorry," I said. "I lost my sat phone."

"*That much we knew,*" Sharyn told me. "*But ain't you been talkin' to Haven on another phone? A borrowed phone?*"

"Yeah. I … um … lost that, too."

She laughed, though there was an unmistakable edge of worry in it. "*Well, ain't you had a morning! Where you at?*"

"We're hiding out in an old condemned boathouse on Kelly Drive."

"*Boathouse Row?*" Sharyn groaned. "*Hot Dog, we're on the wrong side of the river!*"

"Dave's with you?"

"Yeah."

"What about those two Seers he was bringing in. The girls?"

"Chuck and Katie took 'em back. Hot Dog stayed with me."

"Why?"

"Well, he—" There was the sound of muffled disagreement, followed by the clatter of a cell phone being passed from one person to another.

Then the Burgermeister's voice: *"'Cause I'm sick of you getting into trouble and I'm not there to bail you out, that's why!"*

Despite myself, I smiled. "Is it just of two of you?"

"Whatcha mean, 'just'? Me and Sharyn are like a two-person army!"

That won a chuckle out of me, mainly because it was true.

"You okay?" he asked, more serious now.

"Yeah," I said.

"Julie okay?"

I glanced at the girl sitting beside me on the dirty floor. "She's better than okay. She's actually pretty cool."

Julie smiled at this.

"Great," Dave said. *"Now ... what's this crap about you traveling with a deader?"*

I looked over at the Zombie Prince, who crouched near the far wall. He seemed to be listening, his body impossibly still. Corpses don't fidget like living people do. Instead, when they're motionless, they're *completely* motionless—almost like statues or, well, dead bodies.

It's creepy.

"Long story."

"You really trust this dude?"

"Yeah. I do."

"Why?"

A good question. Yes, he'd stuck with us, even saved our lives on at least two occasions. But all that could have been just smoke and mirrors. He *said* he didn't expect me to take him to Haven. But maybe that was just crap to keep us happy until he picked the right moment to turn on me and make me talk. Or maybe his scheme was subtler than that. Maybe he wanted to meet Tom in some public place just so he could kill him. True, the Corpses usually didn't risk open confrontation in view of normal people.

But, like Dillin kept saying: the rules had changed.

I've *changed them.*

So, given all that, why did I trust the Zombie Prince?

"My gut," I finally said.

"Your gut," Dave echoed.

"My gut."

"You're nuts."

"I know."

He made a sound halfway between a laugh and a grunt. Then there came another clatter, and Sharyn said, *"Listen, little bro. Can you get to the Water Works?"*

"I dunno. Maybe. Listen, there's this particular Corpse chasing us. Name's Parker. He's some kind of special commander that the Queen brought over to come after us. And, even worse, he's got these ... things with him."

"Things?"

"They're called *Malites.* They actually *Malum* kids, freaky as that sounds. Except they can possess the bodies of living animals and ... morph them."

"Morph 'em? Into what?"

"Little killing machines."

This time, when Sharyn said it, it was without a trace of humor. *"Ain't you had a morning."*

"Yeah."

"Got a car?"

"Not anymore."

"So you'll have to hoof it. Keep off the streets. Stay close to the river. Hot Dog and I'll meet ya at the Water Works."

"Okay," I said.

"Stay ahead of these Malite things. Stay alive."

"I'll try. Um ... Sharyn?"

"Yeah, little bro."

"Sorry about this."

The Angels Boss had such a musical laugh. *"Will Ritter, apologizing for causin' trouble? That's a new one!"*

Then she broke the connection.

I lowered the phone and rested my head against the cold, half-rotted wood.

"Everything ... okay?" Julie asked.

I sighed. "We've got a plan."

"Good," she said, sounding pleased. Then, after a pause: "Are you my sister's boyfriend?"

My throat went suddenly dry. Must have been the abrupt change of topic. "Huh?"

Her gaze remained steady, almost challenging. "Are you my sister's boyfriend?"

"Um ..." My mouth felt suddenly dry. "I guess so."

"Oh," she said. Then after a thoughtful pause, she added, "Because if you weren't, I was gonna ask you to be mine."

I gaped at her like an idiot.

Okay, so what was the rule for *this* one? How do you respond to getting hit on by an eleven-year-old girl who also happens to be your girlfriend's sister?

Me being me, I played it smooth.

"Um ... sorry."

Crushed it.

After a full minute of uncomfortable silence, I finally got up, dusted myself off, and walked over to the Zombie Prince, who still hadn't moved. Julie watched me, but said nothing.

As I approached him, Dillin whispered, "She'll be fine."

"What?"

"Ms. Boettcher. She'll be fine. It's just hero worship."

"Great." The *last* thing I needed right now was relationship advice from a Corpse. "Ten minutes are up. What do you think's going on out there?"

"I know exactly what's going on," he replied. "The police are canvassing witnesses. They've arrested the fellow with the gun. So far everyone's saying he opened fire, though that doesn't explain the woman who was savaged by her dog, or my former, armless host. So things are pretty confused. Fortunately, no one's reported seeing us run in here. At least not yet."

"You can hear all that?" I asked, astonished.

He nodded. "One of cops even tried the door while you were on the phone. Thankfully, the brace held. He thinks it's jammed from age."

"Jeez! Why didn't you tell me?"

"You were busy."

"How about the *Malites*?" I asked.

"I can't hear them. If they're out there, they're staying quiet and out of sight. Probably at Parker's direction."

"Is Parker out there?" I asked.

"Oh, yes. He's conferring with the other policemen. They seem to be calling Parker 'chief.'"

"Chief? As in chief of police?"

"I assume so."

Parker was the new chief of police? News to me. But it meant the cops on the scene, both human and deader, would obey his every command.

Not good.

I said, "Sooner or later, they're coming in here."

"Yes," Dillin said.

"We need to leave."

"Yes," he said.

"The Undertakers want to meet us at the Water Works."

"So I heard …"

"It's only a mile or so down the road," I pressed.

The Zombie Prince looked at me in the darkness. "Might as well be a hundred. We're not going to get past those *Malites*, never mind the dozen or so police out there."

"Then … what?" I said in disgust. "We just wait here until Parker comes in and kills us?"

He said, "I've been trying to come up with a way to get us out of here unseen."

"Any luck?"

"None," he said. Then, after a pause, he added, "My people are afraid of you."

"Huh?"

"My people are afraid of you," he repeated.

"So I hear." I wondered where this was going.

"But … we also *admire* you."

"I'm touched."

"Don't you want to know what we admire you *for*?"

Nope. I just want *to get Julie safely out of here, like I promised Helene I would. I couldn't care less what a bunch of ten-legged monsters, who'd kill me as soon as look at me, "admire me for."*

But out loud, I replied, "Sure."

The Zombie Prince said, "Because you're resourceful, Mr. Ritter. You have no idea how rare a thing that really is. I come from a world where, with few exceptions, each of us does as we're told. As a people, we are *not* resourceful. In fact, we are taught from an early age that any sort of independent thinking is dangerous. As a result, we both fear and admire that trait in our enemies.

"What's your point?" I asked.

"Oh, I think you know my point," Dillin said. "I'll be sitting here listening. If it sounds like we've run out of time, I'll let you know."

Then he turned away and went statue still again.

I watched him for a bit. Then I looked over at Julie. In the dim light, I could tell she was looking back at me, though I couldn't read her expression. But something told me she'd heard at least some of my conversation with Dillin—and that she, too, was waiting for me to save the day.

No pressure.

I switched on my flashlight and scanned the walls again. Three doors. Two padlocked from the outside and the third wedged shut from the inside. The walls were old but solid. The floor was partially rotted away, but there didn't seem to be anything below it, at least not anything useful. The boat doors were closed tight and, even if they weren't, how far would we get trying to swim the Schuylkill River?

Then I shone my light up at the ceiling.

And that's when I saw it.

I hadn't noticed it before because, well, I hadn't been looking for it.

"Hey, Dillin," I said.

He was at my side in a heartbeat—mine, of course, not his.

I gestured up at the ceiling, and at the ancient *something* that hung there.

"Think *that* might still float?" I asked the principal.

CHAPTER 16
SCULL

Know what a double scull is?

Well, one of them was hanging from the ceiling of this forgotten boathouse, its long, lean shape lost in the shadows between the rafters—until I'd shone my pocketknife's flashlight directly up at it.

One of my dad's best friends had been heavy into crew. Once, my family had actually come down to Boathouse Row to watch him compete in one of the twenty or so rowing races that Philly hosts each spring and summer. I remember thinking that the boats seemed barely wide enough to sit on, and even asked my dad why they didn't just fall out.

He'd laughed and replied, "That's why they row so fast, Will … so they can make it to shore before they capsize!"

Believe it or not, at least five years passed before I realized he'd been kidding.

Basically, a double scull is a boat built for competitive

rowing. It seats two rowers, one behind the other, and is designed to cut through the water fast—*really* fast.

But could it get three of us downriver to the Water Works before Parker and his *Malites* wised to the trick?

"Float?" the Zombie Prince remarked. "I'm not sure that old thing won't fall apart the minute we get it down here."

"Except, I don't see how we *can* get it down here," I told him. "It's gotta be ... what? ... twenty feet up?"

Dillin looked thoughtful. "I could possibly make the jump. But given the chains holding it, I'd be as likely to break the boat as free it."

Then a voice said, "How'd they get it up there?"

We both looked at Julie, who'd come to stand beside me.

It was actually a solid question. So I traded my pocketknife's flashlight for its telescope, which had a night-vision feature. With it, I zoomed in and studied the chains holding up the dusty old boat. Then, moving slowly, I followed those chains. There were four of them, and they came together at a spot somewhere above the scull, where I couldn't see. But I *could* see a single chain, all but lost in shadow, that ran away from the boat to a nearby pillar and then disappeared into a hole.

"Hang on," I said, going to the pillar. There were a half-dozen just like it in the boathouse, all of them holding up the old roof. But this one, I noticed for the first time, seemed to include a little door, set right at eye level.

I used my knife blade to pry it open.

And there it was.

A crank.

"Julie, you'd make your sister proud!"

The girl grinned.

To Dillin, I said, "This thing might be rusted solid, or it might fall apart the second I touch it."

"Do it," the Zombie Prince replied. Then he positioned himself right under the hanging scull.

I gave the ancient crank a tug. It didn't move. I tugged harder. A creak and then a shudder ran through the pillar.

The chain moved an inch. Then two inches.

Then it broke.

A loud, rolling rattle ran up through the pillar and across the ceiling. The scull came suddenly free in an explosion of dust and slackened chains.

Instinctively, I spun Julie around and put my body between her and the falling boat. I tensed, waiting for a crash that might just bring this whole place down around our ears.

It never came.

I opened one eye. The boathouse was choked with dust.

"Cover your mouth," I told Julie.

Then I straightened and turned.

Bob Dillin stood with his legs apart, cradling twenty-five feet of scull, easily supporting its weight with Royal strength—and with poor Ray Exler's dead arms.

"Now what, Mr. Resourceful?" He smiled at me.

"Cute," I told him. "Think they heard that outside?"

"Maybe. Let's move quickly."

We examined the boat. It had just two cramped seats and absolutely no cargo space. There was only one set of oars.

"If we can get the boat doors open," Dillin said, "do you think you can handle this thing? Get yourself and Julie to the Water Works?"

"How hard can it be?" I asked with more confidence than I felt. "But what about you?"

"I'll meet you there. I can go on foot, draw Parker and the police away from you."

"We should stay together," I said automatically.

He gave me a pointed look. "Should we? Surprising talk from an Undertaker ... to a Corpse."

Can't argue with that.

"If they catch you, you're toast," I told him.

"True. But first they have to catch me."

It sounded like something I would say.

Julie came forward, moving with her gentle, silent step. She spent several long moments just looking up at Dillin—or, more accurately, at Ray Exler's dead body possessed by Dillin.

Then she did something neither of us anticipated.

She hugged him.

Her thin arms wrapped around his waist, the side of her face pressed against his flat, biker's stomach. For a moment, I thought the Zombie Prince might balk at the contact, struggle even. But he didn't. Instead, he placed his dead hands on the top of the girl's head, his pale fingers gently stroking her short dark hair.

"Thank you, Mr. Dillin," Julie whispered.

"You're ... welcome, Ms. Boettcher," he replied awkwardly. Given what I knew about *Malum* and *Malites*, I doubted too many hugs got thrown around on their world.

When Julie pulled back, there were tears in her eyes. The girl was young. And green, at least in the Undertakers' world. But she was no fool. She knew our chances of seeing the Zombie Prince again, even if she and I made it to the Water Works, were slim to none.

I knew it, too.

Except I wouldn't be hugging him.

No way.

"Um ..." I said. "Is there something you want me to tell Tom?"

He regarded me with Ray Exler's eyes. "You have a soldier's practicality, Mr. Ritter."

I didn't reply. I mean, "thanks" didn't seem like the right thing to say.

"But don't be too quick to count me out," he added. "The odds may be long, but they've been against me since the moment the Queen chose me as her consort. We may yet meet up at the Water Works."

"I hope so," I replied. "But ... just in case?"

"Just in case," he echoed. His eyes slid from me to Julie, and from Julie to the scull, and from the scull to the boat doors. "All right. But while I talk, let's get this thing in the water and see if it doesn't, in fact, sink."

So we did.

He talked. Julie and I listened, and—miraculously—neither the police nor the *Malites* burst in.

We didn't interrupt him. Yet, every word he said seemed to drill itself into my brain. I moved in a fog of mental overload as the Zombie Prince told me more about the *Malum* than I'd ever known—or ever *wanted* to know. He described his world, his life as a privileged Royal, his commitment to the Fifth Column, his selection as Cavanaugh's consort, and his eventual determined sacrifice: to come to Earth, find the leader of the Undertakers, and tell him—

—this.

By the time he got to the end of it, the scull floated in the dirty, waist-deep water that filled the bottom of the boat ramp. All three of us were soaked, which made both Julie and me shiver, while Dillin simply shrugged it off with a grim smile and the observation, "At least it isn't seawater."

Along the way, I'd figured out how to open the boat doors. Unlike the others around the boathouse, these river-facing doors had been padlocked from the inside. I'd spotted the lock—heavy with rust—dangling just below the surface. Then I'd simply sliced it open with my pocketknife.

"That's *nagganum*," Dillian said.

"Huh?"

"Your knife blade. The whole knife in fact. It's made of *nagganum*."

I looked at my faithful gadget. It had been my constant companion for so long that I couldn't imagine not having it. But I'd never really known—no one had known—what it was made of.

"What's … *nagganum*?" Julie asked.

"It's hard to explain," the principal replied. "And we don't have the time. Suffice it to say that we have plenty of it where I come from. More of it, in fact, than any other single substance. Metal, yet not metal. Stone, yet not stone. It's stronger than any known material though, of course, the *Malum* don't use it in the creation of weapons."

"You don't use weapons," I remarked.

"No, we don't. Doing so is considered the height of cowardice. But let me ask you, Will … where did you get that?"

I felt myself waffling. This dude—no, this *Corpse*—had been dropping secrets on me like presents at my birthday party for the last ten minutes. Now, he wanted one of *mine*, and my every nerve ending was screaming to lie to him. "Um …" I said.

"Military secret?" he asked, smiling.

"No. Well, yeah." I looked at him, struggling to decide what to say.

Then I noticed Julie standing nearby, soaked to the skin and studying me.

There was no judgment in her gaze. No anger. Just the kind of simple, uncomplicated expression that you sometimes get from a younger kid who looks up to you. She wasn't any more clued into my pocketknife's origins than Dillin was. This meant that I could whip up some story about finding it in a park or something and neither of them would be the wiser.

Except I didn't *want* to whip up some story.

So I said, "A woman gave it to me."

"A woman?" Julie asked.

"A woman in a white room. I see her every so often, usually when I've been hurt or something. She heals me … sort of. Maybe. Anyway, she gave it to me."

"Did she?" the Zombie Prince remarked thoughtfully. "And you don't know who she is?"

"Nope."

Dillin studied the knife in my hand. Then, as if reaching some internal decision, he said, "Well, perhaps you'll find out one day. For now, I think you two had better get going. I can hear Parker and his underlings out there. It sounds like they're ready to come in."

"Let's do it," I said.

Getting onto a scull isn't easy, especially when you're soaked and standing in waist-deep water. Finally, the Zombie Prince had to help us, lifting first Julie into the back seat and then me into the front seat. Once there, drenched and cold, I struggled to figure out how the oars fit into their—well—*fittings*.

"I'll open the doors," Dillin told us, turning the front—*bow*—of our long skinny boat toward the boathouse's water exit. "Then I'll give you a push. But don't start rowing right away. Give me half-a-minute to get their attention."

"You sure about this?" I asked the walking, talking dead man.

He grinned. "I've just broken my own rule and told you everything I came here to say. Not the way I'd intended to do it, but the circumstances seemed to demand some flexibility on my part. Just promise me you'll make something of the information."

"I promise," I said.

He nodded. Then, after a pause: "Will, when I came across the Void, I knew it was going to be a one-way trip. Either the Queen would use me and then kill me, or I'd meet up with an Undertaker and eventually die for treason. I'm pleased it was the latter. Sometimes, dying well can be its own reward."

Then, after a pause, he added, "I'm very glad *you're* the Undertaker I met."

"Me, too!" Julie added. "I'm an Undertaker, too."

I almost told her she wasn't. That she would need training and commitment before she could call herself that.

But it would have been a crock.

Julie had faced down deaders. She'd fought. She'd survived.

If that wasn't being an Undertaker, I didn't know what was.

So I glanced over my shoulder and said, "Yeah. You are." And then, to the Zombie Prince: "See you at the Water Works."

"Of course," he replied.

I wondered if either one of us believed it.

He went to the big boathouse door and heaved it open. Beyond, the waters of the Schuylkill River looked gray, cold and scary. Behind me, I heard Julie gasp.

"Ready?" Dillin asked.

"Ready," I said.

"Ready," Julie said.

"Straight out," he said. "Head to the middle of the river. It'll be safer. Then turn toward the Water Works."

"Since when are you an expert on crew?" I asked him.

He looked momentarily startled. "I'm not. In fact, I don't really know anything about it. It's just, you're children … that is … and I'm …"

I hadn't thought it was possible for a Corpse to look embarrassed. After all, it's not like they can blush or anything. But the Zombie Prince managed it.

So I threw him a bone. "Thanks, Principal Dillin," I said with a grin.

With a final smile, he pushed us out onto the water.

CHAPTER 17
ON THE RIVER

Thirty seconds goes by *fast*.

Especially when you're on a boat that's like an inch wider than your butt—which, by the way, is perched on a seat that's sliding forward and back on a rusted track. I wrestled with the moving seat until I thought I might topple over the side.

Then Julie said from behind me, "I think it's *supposed* to move."

She was right. Once I found the correct angles for my arms and legs, I started to understand how the sliding seat came into play when rowing. It still felt weird, though.

A crash from somewhere inside the darkened boathouse stole my attention, telling me that Dillin had made his move. Our thirty seconds were up.

So I planted my soaked sneakers against the scull's angled braces, centered my butt on its shifting seat, squared my shoulders between the long oars, and gave the river a clumsy stroke.

We moved.

Behind me, Julie uttered a nervous squeak. Remember, I was rowing a boat, which means I was faced backwards and couldn't see where I was going.

"You okay back there?" I asked her.

"It's just … faster than I thought it would be."

Again, she was right. The old scull sliced through the river like a hot knife through butter. Two strokes later and we'd completely cleared the boathouse. Two strokes after that and we were in the middle of the wide Schuylkill.

Time to turn.

So I did what seemed to make sense: I lifted one oar clear of the water and rowed with the other. That *did* turn us, though on such a wide arc that, if I didn't do something, we'd slam into the west bank before our bow was facing downriver.

"Will …?" Julie said warily.

"I know! I'm working on it!"

"Not that," she said, and something in her tone told me that not crashing into the opposite bank had suddenly gotten demoted on our ever-changing list of priorities. From out of the corner of my eye, I saw her point across the water, in the direction of the now distant boathouse.

The riverbank on either side of the condemned building was alive with activity. Police had cordoned off Kelly Drive, the lights of maybe a dozen cruisers splashing the granite cliff face on the road's far side. Men and women in uniform—too far away to tell if they were human—seemed to be everywhere, some in the boathouse parking lot, working the crime scene, others stationed up and down the park, shooing bystanders away.

In the city, tragedy always draws a crowd. I'd seen it before. Folks run from trouble—they do. But, depending on the nature of the trouble, they only run *so far* before turning and gawking. Tom calls it the There-but-for-the-Grace-of-God Syndrome, a way to come to grips with your own troubles by witnessing other people's worse troubles.

But I think he's being too generous.

I think some people just *like* to see carnage, so long as it's from a safe distance.

A couple of ambulances were arriving, lights and sirens off. Ambulances only use sirens when they're transporting injured but living people. The two in the parking lot didn't need rushing to the hospital. Just the morgue.

Where's Parker?

Then I saw him. Dead Police Chief watched us from just inside the boathouse's river door, standing in the very spot we'd launched from. His fists were on his hips, as if impatient to get something done—that "something," I supposed, being *our* deaths.

But he wasn't the problem.

The problem was the flying Doberman.

One of the *Malites*—I didn't know if it was the rat from the bridge or the rabbit from the parking lot—had found a new host. The thing coming at us looked as sleek and graceful as a miniature dragon. I wondered vaguely if it could breathe fire. Seemed unlikely—but, let's face it, it had been that kind of day.

Then I spotted the Zombie Prince. He'd split the boathouse by the eastern door and was bounding across the grassy riverbank in the general direction of the Water Works, dodging both cops and bystanders. As he moved, people started screaming and running in a wave of panic that widened like the ripples in the pond. For a second, I wondered at their reaction. I mean, a guy running through Fairmount Park, even rudely, wasn't exactly front-page news.

But then I spotted the thing that was *chasing* Dillin, and I understood.

The second *Malite*, of course.

This one had "possessed" what looked like a squirrel, and it was darting through the air after the fleeing deader like a heat-seeking missile.

And it was doing it within full sight of everyone.

The rules have changed.

The Zombie Prince was in big trouble.

But, right then, so were we.

"Stay as low as you can!" I called to Julie, and I heard her shifting in the seat behind me.

I rowed with all I had.

The scull exploded forward, this time *deliberately* heading toward the opposite bank. A few strokes later we were moving quickly enough for the breeze to tousle my hair.

But I could tell we wouldn't make it.

Dober-Dragon closed on us. It was close enough now for me to see the vicious talons that had once been its paws and the crazy number of teeth filling its pointed snout. With an arsenal like that, this freak-show reject could tear us to pieces, or sink the boat and *then* tear us to pieces.

"Can you swim?" I asked Julie.

"Huh?" she stammered. Then: "Yeah."

"Get in the water, dive down and make for the riverbank!" I told her. "I'll hold it off!" I had some crazy idea of using an oar like a baseball bat, the way I had with Dillin's arm.

"What about you?"

Twenty-five yards. Teeth and claws.

"Go!" I exclaimed. "Please!"

But, as the girl struggled to throw one leg off the scull without dunking us both, I knew we were out of time. The Dober-Dragon bore down, its wings hammering the air, its toothy mouth wide for the kill. I pulled out my pocketknife. I was *way* too wet for the Taser, so I popped its blade.

That's right: a five-inch blade against a dragon-shaped alien buzz saw.

Maybe if I can slice its wing…?

Who am I kidding?

Something long and slender cut the air, coming from the Schuylkill's western bank. It nailed the *Malite* when it was only yards away, knocking the creature sideways. Uttering an unnatural shriek, Dober-Dragon struggled to remain airborne while its claws tugged at the thing that now protruded from its small, but weirdly muscular, chest.

A Ritterbolt.

"Hey, little bro!" Sharyn called from the riverbank. "Keepin' your usual low profile, I see!"

But before I could reply, the *Malite* exploded, the saltwater inside the shaft of the custom-made crossbow bolt having done its work.

Monster guts splashed over me. Not the first time.

I heard Julie scream, first in disgust and then in alarm.

I twisted around in time to see that she'd risen into an unsteady crouch, ready to abandon ship, when a baseball-sized lump of Dober-Dragon caught her in the temple. Before I could so much as reach for her, the girl's body toppled sideways. Her head struck the edge of the scull with a loud, scary *thunk*.

And then she fell into the water—and disappeared.

Oh God!

Without thinking, I threw myself in after her.

Somewhere behind me, Sharyn yelled my name.

The water was cold. I mean *really* cold. So cold that it almost shut me down right away. It took all I had to push through the shock and start diving, my eyes scanning the murky water.

I got a glimpse—just a glimpse—of dark hair sinking into the depths, and I went for it, kicking my feet and fighting the icy current.

I reached for the girl, but a sudden sideways eddy yanked me away before I could get a hold of her arm. With a curse that exploded out of me in a rush of bubbles, I went after her again, ignoring the fiery ache that had already started to burn in my lungs.

Drawing on a well of desperate strength, I kicked my legs hard and managed to swim toward Julie, who hung in the depths like a puppet with her strings cut, a thin wispy trail of blood rising from her forehead where she'd struck the boat.

Please … let me get to her!

I gave another kick, more feeble this time. My lungs felt like they were about to explode, and my vision had begun to turn gray at the edges. I wanted to breathe—*needed* to breathe, despite the terrible knowledge that the moment I did, I'd drown.

My hand touched something soft. It was the girl's upper arm, and my fingers, already half-numb from cold, closed reflexively around it. But as I turned upward, making for the surface, dragging the unconscious girl behind me, I felt awareness sliding away. I fought with all I had, but that well of strength was dry. My limbs stopped working and my vision went from gray to graveyard black.

Helene, I'm sorry.

My lungs reflexively heaved, and the water poured in.

CHAPTER 18
CONFESSION

Tom

It struck Tom that Jillian Birmelin was beautiful.

Nothing new there; he'd always thought so. But right now, with her straight back and raised chin making a sharp contrast to the guilty cast of her eyes, she looked especially beautiful—heartbreakingly so.

"What's up, Jill?" He kept his tone level. Of course, he knew what was up. Until now, it had only been suspicion. But suspicion had turned to certainty the second she'd cleared her throat.

The girl said, "Tom, I've ..." Her words trailed off as the blood drained from her face.

"Just say it." He put the right mixture of command and comfort behind his words.

She swallowed, regrouped, and tried again. "Tom, I've been talking to some people ... about the Undertakers."

"Some people," Tom echoed. He made it a statement, not a question.

"Agent Ramirez," she said.

"That right? I didn't know you even *knew* Hugo Ramirez."

Jillian said, "We met because of Senator Mitchum."

"Jim Mitchum," Tom remarked. "Top senator from Pennsylvania. The dude who got Will and Sharyn into the page program a few months back."

She nodded slowly. "Maybe we should ... I dunno ... sit down for this?"

"If you want."

Jillian dropped gratefully into a chair at the conference table. Tom took a seat beside her, studying her silently. She flinched a little under his gaze.

"Senator Mitchum," he prompted.

"After my friend Keith died," she said. "I mean ... after the Corpses killed him, I told you, I started poking around, trying to find out what happened. But what I didn't tell you was, during that time, I was approached by Senator Mitchum. He pulled me right out of the Capitol hallway and told me that he knew about Keith's death ... and that he knew what it was that had killed him, too."

Tom kept his face carefully neutral when he said, "So ... Mitchum knows about the Corpses?"

"Agent Ramirez had told him," Jillian explained. "The two of them have known each other for a long time."

"Even so ... I can't figure why the senator believed him."

"I don't know. But he did, though he told me he knew there wasn't much he could do about it without the Sight. Instead, he asked me if *I* would do some digging for him."

"But you didn't have your Eyes either," Tom reminded her. "The first time you saw a deader was when you hid out in the fake Lindsay Micha's office."

The girl fidgeted. Her gaze fell. "That's ... not quite

true. The senator showed me some photos of a few of Micha's staffers. Most were normal … I mean *alive*. But one of them wasn't. At first, I almost thought it was a joke. But this was James Mitchum … and he wasn't smiling." Her gaze rose to meet Tom's again. "But, when I pointed out what I saw, the senator seemed pleased."

"Straight up. It meant you had Eyes."

So, Mitchum's known for months. That means when Will and Sharyn went to his D.C. office undercover, trying to get gigs as Senate pages, he knew full well who he was talkin' to. The dude's played this cool. Gotta give him that much.

Jillian said, "He started … helping me. He got me Micha's schedule, which was why I went up to her office when I did. Only, she broke her routine that night and almost caught me. You know the rest."

"I know you split D.C. and came to Philly, lookin' for us," Tom said. "Something tells me maybe that wasn't necessarily *your* idea."

Jillian swallowed, but didn't reply.

"Come on, Jill," he prompted. "You told me this much. Spill the rest."

After several beats, she said, "Once I escaped Micha's office, I called the senator and told him what I'd seen. *He* suggested I leave town, head up to Philly. He told me to try to find you and, if I did, to …" Her words trailed off.

"Spy on us for him?"

"No! That came later. Tom … he wants to *help*."

"Then why not just be straight with me from the get go?"

"He … didn't feel you were ready to know that you had … allies … in the adult world."

Tom's anger flared. Carefully, he suppressed it. "So what've you been doin' for him?

"Keeping him up to speed on what goes on around here," Jill said. "He gave me a special cell phone to use. Dedicated. Encrypted."

"Cool of him," Tom remarked dryly. "And how often you been usin' it?"

Another long pause.

"Jill? How often?"

"Everyday ... pretty much."

"What does he know?" Tom asked her.

"Everything."

"Haven?"

"Yeah."

"Our numbers?"

"Yeah."

Now it was Tom's turn to hesitate. Then he asked, "Where we're at?"

Jill looked squarely at him. "You can *trust* the senator!"

"Does he know where Haven's at?"

"Yeah."

Tom felt a cold knot of terrible certainty tighten in his gut. "The layout? The exits?"

"I drew a map," Jillian said. "Then I took of a picture of it with the cell phone and texted it to him."

Tom Jefferson jumped to his feet, his self-control momentarily shattered. "Why? Why in God's name would you do somethin' like that?"

"Because he's a powerful man!" the girl shot back. "Someone who's great to have on your side. He's not a Corpse, Tom! I swear it! He's human and he wants to help us! We're just kids!"

And there it was.

How many times had Tom listened to that endless song? *Just kids.* Kids are only good for watching TV and playing video games. Kids can't fight a war. Kids can't die with honor.

Kids can't save the world.

Just kids.

Tom asked, "Why tell me all this now?"

Jill considered before answering. "Well, for one: I don't like lying to you and I didn't want to do it anymore. For another ... you lost your Sight."

"So?"

"So, you're thinking of stepping down as chief. I figured you had to be pretty messed up about that. I thought you might be cool with someone else taking the reins."

"Someone else?" Tom asked.

"Someone powerful," Jillian replied.

"Like Jim Mitchum?" Tom asked.

"Exactly like Senator Mitchum," Jillian replied.

Tom said, "Gimme your special cell phone."

The girl blinked. "Why?"

"Because I'm *still* chief, and I'm *asking* you for it."

Jillian stared at him, a lot of things in her eyes. Then she pulled a blue clamshell cell phone out of her pocket and handed it to him. It was a satellite phone, much like the ones Ramirez had gotten for the Undertakers. Opening it, however, Tom noticed that it started dialing immediately.

As Jillian watched him, he put the phone to his ear—and waited.

On the fifth ring, a deep voice said, *"Hello, Jill."*

"This is Tom Jefferson, Senator."

There was a long pause. Then: *"Is Jillian all right?"*

Okay, Tom thought. *You get points for that one.*

"She's totally fine," he replied. "And she's right here. We've been ... talkin'."

"I see. It wasn't my intention that you find out this way.

I'd thought I'd made that clear to Ms. Birmelin."

"The situation's changed," Tom said.

"How so?"

Tom silently counted off the seconds. He got to twelve before the Senator said, *"Mr. Jefferson, you called me."*

Tom kept counting. This time he got as far as twenty-two.

"Young man ... I can appreciate your reticence, but —"

"I've lost my Eyes," Tom said with a sigh.

"Excuse me?"

"I can't See Corpses no more."

This time it was Mitchum's turn to be silent. Tom waited. Finally: *"I see. And what are the repercussions of that, in your opinion?"*

Reticence. Repercussions. Dude's a walkin' dictionary.

"I can't run the Undertakers without the Sight."

"Really. Why not?"

"For the same reason a blind man can't fire a gun."

"I'm sorry?"

"He *can*," Tom said. "But ain't nobody gonna thank him for it."

"Ah. Yes. But none of that explains why you're calling me."

"No, I guess it don't," Tom said, going for sheepish. "I'm calling 'cause you been on our side, Senator. You ain't been able to help us outright 'cause you ain't got Eyes, and you figured we'd never accept anyone in our ranks who couldn't See."

Tom didn't mention Susan Ritter. Neither, he noticed, did Mitchum.

Tom continued, "Thing is: I'm where you're at now. As Sightless as any grown-up. And when that gets out, I'll be done 'round here. Oh, they'll rally around me and all, but 'fore long, someone'll start talkin' about needing a *real* chief. After that, I get to be the Undertakers' very first veteran."

He paused a beat. Then, as if steeling his nerves, he said, "What I'm looking for, Senator Mitchum ... is a job."

CHAPTER 19

WHITE

"*William.*"

Figures, I thought.

I opened my eyes to find myself on a hospital bed in a white, featureless room. No surprise there. I'd lost count of how many times I'd woken up in this strange place.

Light seemed to come from everywhere at once. The only sound was the voice of the "angel," the vaguely familiar stranger who always called me "William."

Still, something felt different, though it took me a few moments to figure out what it was.

There was a second bed in the room.

I looked over at Julie Boettcher, who lay on her back, tucked under a blanket. For a split second I thought she might be dead, but then I heard the whisper-soft rhythm of her breathing and relief warmed me like sunshine.

"Is she okay?" I asked the woman.

"*She's fine. Thanks to you.*"

"All I did was dive into the river after her and almost

drown myself."

"Not 'almost,' William."

"Huh?" I started to sit up on the bed but then flopped back down. My arms and legs felt like their bones had been surgically replaced with molded Jell-O.

"Relax," she told me, offering a gentle smile. *"We were able to reach you both in time."*

"We?"

Her smile flickered for a moment, as if she'd said something she hadn't meant to.

My clothes were gone, replaced with one of those hospital gowns that ties in the back. My hair felt slightly damp, as if I'd just had a bath, but at least it didn't smell like river water. I asked, "How long have we been here?"

Her delicate features, framed by waves of blond hair, tilted in a particular way, as if curious or intrigued. *"Why would you ask that?"*

"Because I've figured out that sometimes you keep me here for a long while. Weeks or even months."

Not quite true. Actually, it was Tom who'd figured it out. But, at the moment, I didn't see any reason to cloud the issue with facts.

At first, I didn't think she'd answer. Finally: *"We keep you as long as we need to."*

Which, as was her M.O., didn't really answer my question.

"How long *this* time?" I pressed.

"Just long enough to drain the fluid from your lungs, treat Julie's head wound, bathe you both, and let you both rest. You've been through a lot today. Julie's still asleep, but it's a safe, natural sleep. She's out of danger."

That, right there, represented the most solid information I'd ever gotten out of her. Compared to her usual answers, it was practically a Wikipedia entry.

Of course, the idea that I'd been *bathed* by this person, or *any* person, totally creeped me out.

Nevertheless, I managed to say, "Thanks."

"You're welcome."

"Are you going to send us back now?"

"Yes."

"Into the river?"

"Yes."

"With Julie still asleep?"

"She'll awaken as soon as the cold water hits her."

That much I believed. "Do I get my one question this time?"

She hesitated again. Then she said carefully, as if picking through her words, *"The next time we meet … I'll tell you everything."* Then, after a pause, she added, *"Almost everything."*

"Great," I said sourly. "But no question *this* time?"

"Are you going to ask me if you can trust Robert Dillin?"

I looked hard at her. "No."

I noticed that she didn't seem surprised. Nevertheless, she asked, *"Why not?"*

"Because I already know the answer. He's helped us every step of the way. And he's told me what we need to know to … maybe … end the war."

"He could have lied to you."

"He could have. But he didn't."

"How can you be sure of that?"

I shrugged. "My gut says so."

Something about this statement made her laugh with what seemed to be genuine delight. *"William the Conqueror,"* she said. *"Trusting your gut is a rare gift."*

"Thanks," I replied, only because I couldn't think of anything else.

"All right then. What's your one question?"

"Are you an Undertaker?"

This time, she clearly *was* surprised, her expression a mix of astonishment and a weird sort of admiration.

She didn't answer right away.

"Well?" I said.

"Yes," she replied. *"I'm an Undertaker."*

Then the world went white and I knew our visit was over. In moments, Julie and I would be back in the Schuylkill, back in the water, back in the fight. But at least, finally, I had something real to take back with me. True, this woman had given me my pocketknife, and *that* was real. And, true, this woman had offered me intel that had saved lives, including my own, and *that* was real, too.

But this piece of real seemed somehow realer than those.

I know who she is!

CHAPTER 20
EXTENSION CORD

When I opened my eyes, I found myself cold, wet, and to my surprise, no longer exhausted.

Well she did say she'd let us rest, didn't she?

But for how long? Did I just get eight hours' sleep?

It sure felt like it.

Nice.

I was back in the river, as promised. Back in my clothes too, I noticed, which meant she—I couldn't think of her as an "angel" anymore—must have changed me *again*.

I'm gonna have to have a talk with her about that.

I was clinging to a rusted length of chain that hung over a barrier wall along the river's edge. I couldn't tell whether it was the east or west bank, but at least I wasn't floundering in the stronger currents anymore.

A small voice said, "Will?"

I turned and saw Julie. The girl wore an orange lifejacket, and she bobbed easily in the water only a couple of feet away. Her forehead had a small cut and the beginnings of a nasty bruise. But, aside from that, she seemed all right.

Still, it was worth asking. "You all right?"

She nodded. "You saved me."

Not exactly.

But out loud, I said, "Um ... no problem."

"Will?"

"Yeah?"

"Where'd you get this lifejacket?"

I struggled for an answer. There hadn't been any in the scull. There hadn't even been a place for any; it wasn't that kind of boat. Obviously, White Room Woman— couldn't quite bring myself to use her *name* either, at least not yet—had put Julie in the floatation vest as a precaution.

I noticed that she hadn't done the same for *me*.

But, trying to explain any of that to Julie would only confuse her.

"You find all kinds of crazy stuff in this river," I said. "I guess, when you think about it, a lifejacket is pretty far from the craziest."

She considered this. "I guess."

I took stock. I still had my knife; I could feel the weight of it in my pocket. I knew from experience that it was waterproof, as long as I didn't try the Taser.

But the scull was missing.

Then I spotted it.

The old boat still floated in the middle of the Schuylkill, maybe a hundred yards away. The current spun it in slow circles, and it was headed downriver at a pretty good clip. Somewhere close by, I heard the rush of falling water.

The dam.

The Schuylkill has this man-made waterfall that kind of cuts the river in half, with the boathouses being on the high side of the falls and Center City on the low side. The scull was heading straight for that waterfall, which wasn't all that tall, but might be tall enough to smash it up. When we'd first launched on the river, I'd forgotten all about that particular hazard.

I was suddenly grateful Julie and I wouldn't be on the darned thing when scull met dam.

We might have drowned! I thought, and the idea almost made me laugh. But I squelched the impulse, afraid of how the laughter might sound.

Rough day.

Suddenly a voice, a *loud* voice, boomed from somewhere above us.

"Attention! By order of the Philadelphia Police Department, Kelly Drive northwest of the Water Works is closed to any and all vehicular and pedestrian traffic! Again, until further notice, no pedestrians or vehicles, whether motorized or not, will be permitted on the Kelly Drive northwest of the Water Works. This is for your safety. The Police Department thanks you for your cooperation."

A bullhorn. Or maybe a cop car's loudspeaker.

"What's going on?" Julie asked fearfully.

"They've closed off everything around the crime scene," I told her. "Makes sense, especially if they think there's still a killer on loose."

What *didn't* make sense was the size of it. The Water Works were more than a mile downriver from the condemned boathouse. That's a pretty big crime scene, especially in the city. Maybe Parker was spreading a wide net, trying to box either us or Dillin in, trap us in a big stretch of empty park so he could hunt us down.

We had to get out of here.

But first I had to figure out where *here* was.

I pulled myself higher along the rusted chain and craned my neck upward. What I saw put a smile on my face.

The Parthenon.

Okay, not the *real* Parthenon. That's in Greece. You all know it. It's that ancient crumbling building with all the columns that shows up on pretty much every postcard that's mailed out of Athens.

But this particular building had been designed to look like it. In fact, so had *all* of the buildings in the immediate area. What put the smile on my face was the certain knowledge that only *one* place in Philly looked like something out of a Hercules movie.

The Philadelphia Water Works.

A hundred years ago, the Water Works was exactly what it sounds like: the place where Philly got its water. These days, all that was handled more—well—modernly, and what was once the Water Works was now a museum below ground and a fancy restaurant above ground.

It was the restaurant that hid inside those Parthenon-ish buildings.

Anyway, the *point* was that Julie and I had been deposited in just the right spot.

A break at last, I thought.

The chain I hung onto reached up to a tangle of branches about three feet below the lip of a cement walkway that edged the Water Works' river view. There were people up there; I could hear them. Some had come to the railing to peer curiously at the doomed scull as it neared the waterfall. None of them, as far as I could tell, had spotted us. The angle was wrong.

That was both good and bad since, on one hand, keeping a low profile was kind of the Undertakers' motto.

On the other hand, we weren't going to get from down here to up there without some kind of help.

"What do we do?" Julie asked.

I was wondering the same thing.

"Will!"

I looked straight up at the walkway. A big, round face looked down at me.

The Burgermeister grinned and called, "You okay?"

So much for a low profile.

Still, I'd take it.

"Yeah! We're okay!"

"Hang on!" he yelled. "We'll find a way to get you up!"

"Julie first!" I called back.

Tom's twin sister poked her head over. Sharyn's hair, which had been shaved bald some months ago, had grown back in a bit since I'd last seen her. She was starting to look more like the girl who had literally ridden to Helene's and my rescue in Center City back when I'd first gotten the Sight.

"Hey, little bro! Last we saw you two, you both went under the river!"

"I *told* her you'd make it to the Water Works!" Dave added. "She didn't believe me, but I said, 'Will does what he says he'll do ... every time!'" He turned to Sharyn. "Didn't I say that?"

She smiled and kissed his cheek. "Yeah, you did. Now shut up."

These two were an item.

I yelled, "Um ... guys? This water's way colder than it looks."

"Hear ya!" the Boss Angel called down. "Hang tight."

She disappeared for a minute, returning with one of those long orange extension cords. You know, the ones they use for electric hedge trimmers or leaf blowers. I didn't bother to ask her where she got it.

But the Burgermeister did. "Where'd you get that?"

"Spotted it when we were parking. It was in the back of one of those landscapin' trucks. Catch!" She dropped the heavy coil down to me.

It hit the water with a loud splash.

I suddenly wondered what the Non-Seer people up there were making of this half-ass rescue?

"Julie?"

The girl still bobbed in the water, her dark hair soaked and her lips blue. She didn't say anything, just shivered. So I grabbed the extension cord and wrapped it twice around her waist, knotting it securely.

"It's okay," I said. "You already met Dave. And Sharyn's one of the leaders of the Undertakers."

"What about you?" she asked, looking a little panicky.

"I'll be right behind you," I promised. Then, I yelled upward, "Do it!"

Julie didn't rise out of the water—she practically rocketed. Dave Burger didn't mess around when he rescued somebody. Within a few seconds the girl was up and over the railing. Half a minute after that the extension cord came down again, splashing a second time in the dirty river water.

That was when people started screaming.

CHAPTER 21

WATER WORKS

"Dave!" I called. "Sharyn!"

But neither of their heads appeared over the railing. I took hold of one end of the extension cord and tugged on it. It didn't budge, but it didn't feel like Dave's enormous hands were holding the other end of it either. Could he have tied it off on something?

I couldn't see anything that was going on above me, but I heard more screams, followed by the sound of running feet.

So I grabbed the orange cord with my wet, half-numb hands and braced my sneakers against the slimy cement surface of the barrier wall. Taking a moment to find my balance, I started "walking" up the wall. This isn't as easy as it sounds. In fact, it's pretty freakin' hard. But it was also part of my Angel's training.

One hand at a time. One foot at a time. Slow but steady. *Too* slow, given what I was afraid was going on up there. As I went, I considered calling up again, but decided not to waste my energy. If either Sharyn or Dave could have answered, they already would have.

Had White Room Woman saved Julie and me, just to have Helene's little sister get killed ten minutes later? That seemed crazy!

And yet there *was* another *Malite* around somewhere!

I kept climbing, trying to focus on what I was doing. Worry is your enemy in dangerous situations. Worry can distract you. Worry can kill you. The best thing you can do is keep steady and keep moving. Or, as Sharyn puts it, "What is, *is*. And what *might* be ain't the same as *is*."

Okay, it sounds better when she says it.

I reached the upper edge, my arms and shoulders burning and my heart trip-hammering. Keeping both feet wedged against the wall, I pulled myself high enough to grab the lower railing and peek over the lip.

I saw a dead body.

Oh no.

It took all I had to get myself high enough to grab the railing and climb over it. My arms felt like a lead weights, their muscles like shifting sand. For a few precious seconds, I simply lay there on the concrete, which had been warmed by the early afternoon sun. Finally, painfully, I climbed to my feet.

The body belonged to a woman, maybe forty.

It wasn't pretty. *Malite*-work, by the look of it.

There was no sign of my friends.

I could almost picture the scene. The two Undertakers had just managed to get Helene's little sister up onto the walkway when the monster attacked. Probably Sharyn had spotted it first and gone immediately into combat mode. Either Aunt Sally, her crossbow, or Vader, her faithful wakizashi sword, would have come out.

For his part, Dave would've shielded Julie, at the

same time hastily tying the extension cord to the rail and tossing it over. Then, because they had no other choice, the three of them had run for it, somehow managing to stay ahead of the *thing* that chased them.

The woman at my feet had probably been standing in the wrong place at the wrong time—and she'd died for it.

Tomorrow's "top stories" would make the national news. A lot of attention. A *ton* of attention, yet Parker didn't seem to care.

The rules have changed, Mr. Ritter.

You changed them.

Dillin ... where are you?

I scanned the grounds. In front of me stood the fake Greek buildings, all white columns and phony marble: the Water Works' fancy restaurant.

The place was the kind of *empty* that only panic can create. Soda cups and purses lay scattered where folks had dropped them after the *thing* had shown up and the poor woman had died. I could imagine the horror of it, the mothers grabbing their kids and running, the fathers shielding their families from what must have seemed like a waking nightmare.

There *were* some people still around. A lot had fled as far as the nearby restaurant parking lot, where their cars had gotten jammed up in their hurry to escape. Others had taken off on foot, heading further down the road toward Center City, or up a staircase that climbed the granite cliff face across the street from the Water Works. Atop that cliff, the Philadelphia Art Museum glowed red in the afternoon sun.

A few folks—either brave or too terrified to run— had apparently hunkered down in a nearby gazebo. One of them, a thirty-something dude in cargo shorts and an "I LUV PHILLY" T-shirt, stood up and hastily beckoned me, motioning with his arm as if to say, "Come here, kid! It's dangerous out there." His eyes kept scanning the sky.

He was taking a risk showing himself and he knew it.

There are good people in the world.

That's when I heard footsteps approaching at a run from my left and, for some reason, I thought: *Dillin!*

I actually had a smile on my face when I turned in that direction—

—and Parker grabbed me by the collar of my soaking shirt.

The Corpse was fast, Royal fast, which was probably what had made me think Dillin, instead of trouble. I was off my feet in a heartbeat and out over the railing again a heartbeat after that.

I expected him to drop me. In fact, my Undertaker's mind was already calculating how I might be able to kick off the barrier wall, land in deeper water, and *maybe* survive. But he didn't. Instead, he held me there, dangling helplessly.

"Where is he?" he hissed in the dry voice that I generally associate with Type Ones. He was fresh and very strong.

"Who?" I gasped.

"Dillin! Speak or die!"

These guys are always so freakin' melodramatic. I mean, "Speak or die!" Who talks like that?

"Hey!" someone yelled. "What the hell are you doing?"

The guy from the gazebo suddenly appeared, grabbing Parker's arm and reaching for me at the same time.

"He's just a kid!" the guy exclaimed. "He didn't do this!"

Parker growled and struck the man with his free hand, knocking him off his feet. In the process, he twisted his upper body, which pulled me closer to the railing.

I took the opportunity to pull my out my pocketknife, hit the **3** button, and jab its blade deep into just the right spot in the Corpse's triceps.

His arm went limp and dropped.

I grabbed the railing and vaulted over it.

Parker spun toward me, his seemingly sightless eyes ablaze with fury. He tried to reach for me again, but his right arm hung at his side as if its bones had melted. Thing is: strong as he was, his stolen body remained human. I'd cut the nerve that ran from his shoulder to his elbow, and all the murderous rage in the world couldn't help him move that arm. Not anymore.

Of course, the dude had *another* arm.

He came at me, moving fast. But I was ready. I ducked under his left arm and, as he went by, jabbed my knife into the tendons behind his right knee. Then, as he lost his balance, I rammed my shoulder into his side and sent him over the railing and down into the river.

"Let's see how *you* like it," I muttered.

The dude on the ground—my hero—looked blearily up at me. Blood from a broken nose covered the lower half of his face, his expression a mixture of pain and confusion. Parker wore a cop uniform, after all. First, this "policeman" had inexplicably assaulted me, and then *I'd* inexplicably stabbed and assaulted *him*, all in the aftermath of a flying monster attack.

I started reaching for the guy—you know, to help him to his feet or something. But then a voice roared from somewhere below the railing. "Ritter! I will tear your limbs from your body and drink your filthy human blood!"

"Get out of here," I told the hero. "Run. Hide. He doesn't want you." Then, after a moment, I added, "And … thanks."

I ran.

CHAPTER 22
JOB INTERVIEW

Tom

"*A job, young man?*" Senator James Mitchum asked. "*What kind of job?*"

"First of all," Tom said into Jillian's phone, "don't call me 'young man.' I don't like it. I'm the Chief of the Undertakers, at least for now."

A pause. "*Of course. I apologize, Mr. Jefferson. Please forgive an old man's prejudices.*" It was a politician's answer, humble and just "fake sincere" enough to be condescending. "*You're looking for employment?*"

"I'm looking for a new place in this war, a way to help the fight even though I can't See the enemy anymore."

"*And you think I'm the person to talk to about that?*"

"We both know you're the *only* person," Tom said. "You been runnin' an operation all your own against Cavanaugh and the Corpses. Mostly, I'm guessin', that op's been about collecting intel ... on them and on us. That sound 'bout right?"

Another pause. "*That's an accurate assessment.*"

"Well, Senator, I *am* intel. I know more 'bout the war and the enemy than anybody else in this city. Anybody on this planet. More'n I've told Jill. More'n I've told even my sister. And certainly way more'n *you*."

"I see," Mitchum repeated, though now his tone had gone from condescending to thoughtful. *"You make some very good points, young … Mr. Jefferson. I could use someone with your particular expertise. What's our next step?"*

"We meet," Tom said. "But not just you and me. I want Ramirez there, too. And anybody else on your staff who knows about the Corpses and the Undertakers."

"That's a small group. Agent Ramirez, of course, was the one who came to me with this terrible knowledge. I've only shared it with one or two of my most trusted staff members, and only because circumstances demanded it."

"Which is it?" Tom asked flatly.

"Excuse me?"

"You said 'one or two.' That ain't good enough. Not with info like this, not with so many lives at stake. Is it one or is it two?"

"It's two."

"Then I need to meet with all four of you."

"When?"

Tom took a long, measured breath. "Now."

The senator surprised him. *"I'll cancel my appointments for the remainder of the day. Fortunately for both of us, I'm not in Washington. Congress is currently out of session so, as is my custom, I've moved to my offices here in Philly. I can accommodate you very easily."*

"How 'bout Ramirez?" Tom asked. "He in town, too?"

"He is. In fact, he's on his way here for a meeting as we speak. So your timing is quite fortuitous. Now, my offices are located at—"

"Not your offices," Tom interrupted. "A neutral place."

A third pause. *Forgive me, Mr. Jefferson, but we're all friends here, aren't we? I don't see any need for cloak and dagger—*

"My whole life for the past three-and-a-half years has been cloak and dagger. Watchin' my back is like breathing to me. The last time I met somebody in their office, I ended up fightin' for my life. I want a neutral place."

"That sounds a bit paranoid. If you don't trust me—"

"I don't know you, Senator. Given that, how can I even *start* to trust you?"

A fourth pause. *"Well, in your situation, I suppose paranoia might be considered a reasoned response."*

Tom waited.

Finally: *"All right, Mr. Jefferson. We'll play this your way. Where would you like to meet?"*

Tom told him.

"When?"

"In exactly one hour. Just me and the four o' you."

"I'll make it happen."

"Good. See you in an hour."

Tom closed the phone. He looked down at Jillian, who sat at the conference table, appearing small and guilty. "I'll hang onto this for a while, if that's okay," he told her. "Might need to call him again."

"Sure," she said. "I'm ... sorry, Tom."

"Yeah, I know."

"I messed up. I should've told you about the thing with Senator Mitchum right away. I know that. But ... it'd been so long since I'd seen you! Years! And, at first, the Undertakers just seemed like ..." Her voice trailed off.

"Kids playing soldier?"

Jillian lowered her eyes—her beautiful eyes—and nodded. "Yeah."

"Still think that?"

Her gaze met his. "Maybe a little. Even so, I *wanted* to tell you. By the time I'd been here a week, I started practically begging the senator to let me tell you everything! But he wouldn't let me."

"You could have told me anyway."

"I thought about it," she said. "I thought about it a lot. But—"

"But by then, you'd painted yourself into this corner: you couldn't come clean without lookin' like a liar and a spy."

She nodded. A tear traced a lazy path down her cheek. "Except now, you gotta see how much we can use his help! Without your Eyes, you're as blind as he is! You have to *get* that! Isn't that why you called him just now?"

Tom didn't reply.

After half-a-minute of silence passed, she asked, "You want me to leave?"

Leave, Jill? Tom thought in quiet misery. *You were never really here.*

"What I *want* is to trust you," he said. "But you're a wildcard in the deck. A loose cannon."

This time, it was her turn not to reply.

Finally, Tom told her, "I need to meet Mitchum and his crew in less than an hour. That means I got stuff to do."

She stood up. "You're going alone?"

He offered her a shrug. "They're on our side, Jill. Why wouldn't I?"

CHAPTER 23

THEIR FIRST FIGHT

Lilith

"You betrayed me," said the Queen of the Dead, seething.

"I'd make a poor traitor if I didn't," her former consort replied.

They were in the *Szash.*

It was a sort of psychic neutral zone, a place only Royals could visit. Here, they could talk without interruption—and without fear. For here, in this featureless world of the mind, Robert Dillin remained outside her reach.

Lilith was somewhat surprised that he'd agreed to meet, even in this "neutral" place. After all, what did it benefit the prey to "discuss" things with his hunter?

Especially when the hunter is me, she thought.

"You know, of course, that your life is over," she told him.

"My life was over the moment you chose me as your consort."

"You bring shame to your family."

"Better than bringing your *children into the world … honey."*

The Queen of the Dead seethed again.

"Tell me where you are. Where Ritter and the girl are. Do that and I'll be merciful."

"No."

"Then I'll tell Parker to end your existence slowly."

"You mean you haven't already? You must be getting soft."

"You're a fool! You could have fathered rulers! Queens! Kings! Now you'll die as valueless as the humans you defend!"

"Valueless?" he said, as if tasting the word. *"I'm aiding the Undertakers, and that has value. They've bested you every time you've faced them. You know it. I know it. Our people know it. You're less queen these days and more public joke."*

"How *dare* you?"

"I dare because we both know I have nothing to lose."

"I could take revenge on your family."

"That's human thinking … honey. Family doesn't mean to us what it means to them. It's one of the ways in which they're superior."

"Superior!"

"Oh, far from perfect. But yes, superior to us."

"You're a fool!"

"And you're repeating yourself. Anyway, I only accepted your Szash invitation because I wanted the satisfaction of throwing what I've done in your self-important face. Now that I've done that, I'm afraid I have things that require my attention."

"You will be found, Dillin! You will die. And then Ritter and his gang of street rats will join you by this time tomorrow!"

No response.

"Dillin!"

No response.

"Dillin!"

Nothing.

With a savage curse, the Queen closed the *Szash*.

Around her, the penthouse apartment reappeared. As did Cole, who stood on the carpet near her desk, looking as calm and composed as ever, despite the continuing failure of his fellow Special.

Worse: one of the *Malites* had been destroyed.

The Queen of the Dead seethed some more.

"Cole," she said.

"Yes, Ms. Cavanaugh?"

"I've just met with my former consort. He still lives. So do Ritter and the Boettcher girl."

"Yes, Ms. Cavanaugh."

She eyed him from inside her withering, rotting body. An hour ago, one of her fingers had broken off—the forefinger of her left hand. She'd foolishly caught it in a drawer and it had snapped like a pretzel stick. The sight had infuriated her.

I am the Queen of the Malum, and yet circumstances force me to wear this—

With an effort, Cavanaugh steadied herself. Her situation would be improving soon.

Very soon.

"I wish someone would tell me," she said. "What is it about Will Ritter that inspires such incompetence?"

Cole replied, "Perhaps he is as formidable as his reputation suggests."

Lilith looked at him. She was surprised that he'd answered at all, though she shouldn't have been. He was a Special, and, when a Special heard a question being posed, he answered it. It was simply how they were "wired" or "programmed" or whatever the Earth term would be.

She glowered. "I know what our people say about the Undertakers. That Will Ritter is invulnerable. That Tom Jefferson is unbeatable."

"Jefferson beat *you*, Ma'am."

That sort of honesty would have cost any other *Malum* his life on the spot. But Cole wasn't any other *Malum*. Besides, she needed him.

"He did," the Queen admitted.

"Most would have called that impossible."

"He beat me," Lilith told him. "But he didn't defeat me. I still live. I still rule."

"Yes, Ma'am."

She stepped up to her minion, bringing her face very close to his. His host was a good deal fresher than her own, only a day dead. She envied him the strength and vitality of that body.

By this time tomorrow, I'll have my pick of hosts. I'll never again have to slink around wrapped in such a festering cocoon.

"You will be facing Jefferson in battle very soon," she told the Special. "Tell me ... do you fear him?"

"No, Ma'am," Cole replied at once.

"Do you fear *me?*"

No hesitation. "Yes, Ma'am."

And the Queen believed him. Specials were incapable of lying. Another factor in their "programming."

Her cell phone rang.

She answered it, careful not to press the small device too hard against her ear. The last time she'd done so, the tissues had torn and the ear had slid off her face like a stick of butter down a pane of hot glass.

Stuart or Stanley or Whoever said, *"Mistress, Greg*

Gardener is on the line for you."

"Remind me of your name," Lilith said.

A pause. *"Stephen, Mistress."*

Oh yes. That's right. Stephen.

"Call me 'Mistress' one more time, Stephen ... and I'll tear you limb from limb."

Another, longer pause. *"Yes ... Ma'am."*

"Put Gardner through."

She waited while Stephen did as he was told. Gardner's voice filled her ear. *"Hello, Ms. Cavanaugh. How's the Bellevue Hotel treating you?"*

Always so flippant, this one. From the night he'd first called her, almost two months ago, she'd been struck by this leader caste's overabundance of both intellect and confidence. He'd been a servant of Lilith's traitorous sister, a role that would normally have cost Gardner his life. But he'd been spared because of what he'd offered her.

The location of Haven.

And he continued to exist because of his position as a trusted member of Senator James Mitchum's staff.

"I've no patience for your usual games, Gregory," Lilith said into the phone. "You called for a reason. What is it?"

"I have news you may find ... welcome."

"I'm listening."

"Tom Jefferson has lost the Sight."

"Has he?" Lilith asked. "And how do you know this?"

"Jillian Birmelin, Mitchum's mole inside the Undertakers, apparently reported it. Jefferson and the senator have already spoken."

"About?"

"Jefferson feels that, without the Sight, he can no longer command the Undertakers. So he's asked to join Mitchum's staff."

The Queen said, "This is all somewhat interesting, I

admit. But I don't see—"

Gardner interrupted her. That, by itself, would have sealed his fate, if his next words hadn't wiped all such thoughts from her mind. *"He's requested a personal meeting with the senator ... in a public place."*

"Where?" Lilith demanded.

Gardner told her.

"Can you arrange to be there?"

"I've already been asked to attend, along with two others, including Hugo Ramirez."

"When is this happening?"

"In about forty-five minutes."

"Listen to me very carefully, Gregory. I will *not* accept excuses for failure ... not in this case. You are to attend that meeting and, when Jefferson shows himself, you are to pick an opportune moment to *kill* him. Let him relax. Lower his guard. Then strike. No warning. Just break his neck."

A pause. *"I can try, Ms. Cavanaugh, of course. But this is Tom Jefferson we're talking about. As you well know, he's not easy to—"*

This time *she* cut *him* off. "Without the Sight, you'll have the element of surprise. Strike quickly, before he even knows it's coming, and you'll succeed. Do it!"

"I will. But—"

She broke the connection and whirled on Cole. "In less than forty-five minutes, Tom Jefferson will attend a meeting with Senator James Mitchum in a very public place. I want you to select two of your very best warrior caste. I want you to send them there and have them kill Jefferson on sight."

"Yes, Ma'am," the Special replied.

"Afterward, I want them to kill Senator Mitchum and his entire entourage ... *including* Gregory Gardner."

"Yes, Ma'am."

The Queen noticed that Cole didn't bother to ask why she wanted Gardner destroyed. But if he had, she might have said something like, "He's displeased me," or "He's condescending," or even "He irritates me." Any of these would have been acceptable reasons from Lilith's point of view.

Instead, the Special asked, "What about the humans in the vicinity? How should I hide the carnage?"

"Don't bother," she replied. "The rules have changed. After you dispatch the warriors to kill Jefferson and the rest, I want you to rally my attack force. I will personally address them before combat begins."

Cole nodded stiffly. "Yes, Ma'am."

"Get out," she said.

The Special turned on his heels and left the suite.

For several long minutes, Lilith Cavanaugh stood in the midst of her penthouse prison, fuming.

The entire invasion of Earth had led to *this*.

Soon, she would perpetrate something upon the "good" people of Philadelphia that could only be called an atrocity. A war crime. And it *was* a crime of sorts, since there would be no subtlety in it, no artistry.

The Undertakers had forced her hand.

Now it was simply about *killing*.

Someone knocked on her door. At her command, Stephen entered, looking cowed and fearful—as he should.

"What is it?" the Queen demanded.

"Mistress, we've received reports that the mayor has become ... concerned ... about the incidents in Fairmount Park this afternoon. In light of the human deaths, he's begun questioning the police exercises you've ordered. Apparently, he's challenging the need to remove so many officers from active duty for the purposes of urban training, especially when acting police chiefs Cole and Parker are so new to their jobs. According to our people in the mayor's office, he's planning to launch a special investigation into what he's calling a 'misappropriation' of city resources."

So, that fool of a mayor is finally beginning to wonder who really runs this city!

Lilith almost smiled.

"Very well," she told her assistant. "Tell our people that I will be paying the mayor a visit this evening … personally."

"You?" Stephen exclaimed in apparent horror. "But 'Lilith Cavanaugh' is dead! What will the mayor say when you walk into his office?"

"I expect *I'll* do most of the talking." Then she approached the minion, who trembled as she neared. "On second thought, I'll notify our people myself. You needn't bother."

He opened his mouth to say something, but the only sound that emerged was a terrified moan.

The Queen remarked, "I told you what would happen the next time you called me 'Mistress.'"

She tore him limb from limb, as promised.

CHAPTER 24
KITCHEN CAPERS

The Water Works Restaurant and Lounge had been in the middle of its lunchtime rush when the crap hit the fan, if you know what I mean. Its front doors stood wide open, and the foyer looked like it had been evacuated in a big hurry. Menus lay scattered on the floor and the pedestal thing that the greeter stands behind looked like someone had cleaved it in two.

Almost as if a *really* sharp sword had been brought down on it.

To the left was the dining room entrance. To the right stood a small bar that looked as deserted as the foyer. Then I heard something coming from that direction.

A frightened whimper.

Frowning, my knife still in hand, I stepped inside and peeked over the bar.

A woman in a tight black waitress uniform huddled there, sitting on the floor with her knees pulled up. When she saw me, or maybe when she saw my knife blade, she let out a little squeak of terror.

I put it away and said, "Sorry. It's okay. I'm not gonna hurt you."

She stared at me with wide brown eyes, her dark skin ashen.

"You all right?" I asked her.

"You're ..." Then, she swallowed, regrouped, and tried again. "You're a kid."

Inwardly, I sighed.

"What happened here?"

"There's a ... a monster."

I said, "Did you see three other kids come in? A tall girl, a big strapping boy, and a smaller girl?"

She blinked at me. "The girl with the sword?"

"Yes! Do you know where they went?"

The woman stammered "She came running in through the front entrance, screaming for everyone to get out. At first everybody ... you know ... just looked at her, like it was a joke. But she had this sword in her hands and she used it to ... *cut* ... the lectern in half!"

Lectern, I thought. *That's what it's called.*

She went on. "Then this ... this thing ... followed her through the open doors. A monster! It looked a little like a pigeon, but it had this awful *mouth*!" She hugged her knees tighter to her chest. "Everybody started screaming and running. I came in here and hid. I ... didn't know what else to do."

"Did you see where the girl with the sword went?" I asked.

She pointed toward a door that led to a canopied porch crammed with tables and chairs. "The ... flying thing ... chased them out there."

"Thanks," I told her. "You should leave."

"I'm waiting for the cops."

Might be a long wait. Parker will have called them off. Now that he knows we're all here, he won't want any humans getting in the way of his hunt.

"Be safer if you took off," I told her. "Seriously."

But she shook her head. "You should hide. You should go hide someplace else."

I left her where she was.

On the canopied porch, half-eaten meals and half-drunk beverages covered the tables. Most of the seats had been pushed back or toppled over.

Still no sign of Dave, Sharyn, or Julie.

I found my way to the restaurant's big kitchen. It stood empty—lots of gleaming counters, cutlery, frying pans, pots, and stainless steel cabinets. A door into the dining room stood against the side wall, and—

Oh crap …

There was blood on the floor; a trail of it ran to a body sprawled against a big commercial refrigerator. It was a dude in one of those mushroom-shaped chef's hats. The side of his neck had been torn open—with such force that the guy's lower jaw had been completely chopped off. Clearly, the *Malite* had taken him. Like the woman down by the river, he'd had probably just gotten in the way—a perfect example of "wrong place, wrong time."

A really lousy reason to be dead.

There came a scream from somewhere behind me, high-pitched and terrified.

I whirled around, my grip on my knife instinctively tightening.

The girl behind the bar!

Thirty seconds of heavy silence followed. Then a voice sounded, deep and half-choked with anger.

"Ritter!"

Parker.

That girl had been waiting for the cops. And so, when he'd come in there looking for me …

Should have thought of that.

Had he killed her in his rage? Or just questioned her to find out where I'd gone, hurting her in the process? Either way, it was *my* fault.

And now the Special was coming.

I whirled around, scanning the kitchen for a weapon bigger and better than my puny pocketknife. Pots. Pans. Skillets. Even butcher knives and meat cleavers.

Then my gaze raked the dead man on the floor, settling on something clutched in his right hand. I knelt down and picked it up, the man's limp fingers falling off of it.

It was a small, black bottle.

Bingo.

"Thanks, man," I muttered. "I'm … sorry."

Heavy footsteps sounded from the porch behind me, sending my heart into my throat.

I ducked behind the nearest counter.

Moments later, Parker crashed into the kitchen, all power and fury. "Boy!"

After very little debate, I decided against saying something back—like, "Yo!"

The Corpse staggered around the kitchen, tearing open random cupboards and cabinets. From the way he moved, I could tell he was dragging one leg. When I'd stabbed him behind the knee, I'd cut some of the tendons, but not enough to cripple his stolen body.

Too bad.

"Where are you?" he demanded.

After some more thought, I decided against yelling, "Over here, moron!"

There came a creaking sound, followed by another

voice, maybe coming from the door to the dining room. "Um … I don't think yer supposed to be in here."

Parker was silent for several long seconds. Then he growled, "I'm looking for a boy. Where is he?"

"What's the mattah with your arm?" the voice said. Guy had a weird accent. "You huht?"

"It's nothing," Parker snapped "Tell me where the boy went. Now."

"You're ah cop," the voice replied, sounding snarky. "You gotta be niceh to me!"

What *was* that accent? Brooklyn?

Double crap …

Parker started toward the voice, dragging his wounded leg. As he did, he snarled, low and dangerous. Apparently, the dead dude was done talking.

Screwing the cap off the bottle in my hand, I jumped to my feet. "Hey!"

Parker turned and looked at me, astonishment showing in his slack, dead face.

"Boy!" he growled.

I hated it when Corpses called me "boy."

Then, from the dining room doorway, an enormous figure said, "Stand back, Will! I'll take care of this guy!"

The Burgermeister grinned and waved.

Jack Nicholson, I thought miserably.

"I'll kill you both!" Parker declared. "I crush your skulls in my fist!"

I also hated it when Corpses narrated themselves. It happened more often than you'd think and it always made them sound like villains in a bad cop show.

Then he leaped at me, his dead body vaulting over the wide counter between us.

"Watch it, Will!" Dave bellowed, coming forward fast.

He managed to snatch the deader's ankle just as it cleared his side of the barrier. Then, with a single great heave of his insanely thick shoulders, he swung Parker sideways, smashing his face into the business end of a commercial deli slicer.

I heard the Corpse's cheekbones crunch.

But then the deader kicked the Burgermeister with his other foot and knocked the big kid off his feet, sending him crashing into a wall of ovens.

By now, I was coming around the nearest corner, my bottle open and ready.

Parker righted himself and faced me, his already ugly mug now a ruined mass of drooping and mangled facial features. I swear, both his eyes were on the same side of his nose.

Dude looked like a Picasso painting.

Google it and you'll see what I mean.

He opened his mouth to say something, but Dave's blow had broken his jaw. So the only sound that escaped him was a crackle, like popping bubble wrap. No idea what made it.

"Know what?" I told him. "I think we've found your 'look'!"

Then I threw the contents of the bottle right into his face.

The soy sauce—yeah, soy sauce—caught Parker in his mis-positioned eyes. The thing about soy sauce: it's salty.

Really salty.

The Corpse groaned and spun around, clawing at his face with his remaining hand. Again, this wasn't pain so much as panic. What I'd just done had blinded him—temporarily.

I ducked around him and ran to Dave, who lay

sprawled beside the ovens, a trickle of blood running down from under his mop of yellow hair. "You okay?"

He looked blearily up at me. "Ice cream," he replied.

"Fantastic," I said.

Then I did my best to help him to his feet. This wasn't easy; the Burgermeister's got nine inches and a hundred pounds on me. But it wasn't the first time I'd had to get him out of a danger zone, and I'd gotten pretty good at playing his crutch.

Parker, reacting to the sound of our voices, tried to stagger toward us, but he misjudged, bounced off the edge of a counter, lost his balance, and crashed to the floor.

I leaned over and Tased him. I mean, *really* Tased him—held my pocketknife against the flesh of his thigh for half-a-minute or more, until his stolen body convulsed in a way that told me I'd trashed its nervous system.

Parker wouldn't be coming after us anymore. Not without a new body.

"You okay?" I asked Dave a second time.

"Think so," he muttered. Then, sounding miserable: "Blew it again."

"No, you didn't," I told him, meaning it. "You just saved my butt."

But he shook his head, a move that seemed to hurt him, because he groaned. "Tried to ... blew it."

I used my shoulder to push open the dining room door.

It was important to keep the Burgermeister conscious and talking. Head injuries could be scary, and he'd gotten clobbered pretty good. "I liked the Brooklyn accent," I said.

"Boston!" He blinked. "I told you! It's a *Boston* accent!"

"Sure. That's what I meant. Where are Sharyn and Julie?"

Then, as we staggered into the dining room, I got my answer.

Sharyn and Julie were both there. The Angel Boss had her sword out. Julie huddled behind her, looking small and scared, but holding Sharyn's crossbow, Aunt Sally, in her tiny hands.

Unfortunately, the second *Malite* was also there.

I mean *right there*—buzzing in mid-air about six inches from the end of my nose.

"Crap," Dave muttered. "*That* wasn't in here a second ago …"

CHAPTER 25
FINE DINING

The girl in the bar had been right; it looked like a pigeon.

Except it was something like twice the size, had *four* wings that beat so fast they buzzed like a hummingbird's, and instead of a beak it had a maw filled with tiny spinning drills where its teeth should have been.

As I stood there, dumbfounded by the sight of it, its dark eyes—like doll's eyes—turned toward me.

Okay, I'm dead.

I knew how fast these things moved. In a second, this twisted monstrosity would come at me like a bullet and burrow its way straight through my forehead.

"Look out!" the Burgermeister cried.

Then he shouldered me aside, throwing one beefy hand up, just as the *Malite* darted forward.

It cut my friend's hand off at the wrist.

As I watched in horror, Dave's hand spun in the air. Then, opening its huge maw, the Pigeon-Thing snapped it up and swallowed it whole.

"No!" I screamed.

"Hot Dog!" Sharon screamed.

"Will!" Julie screamed.

In fact, the only one who didn't scream was the Burgermeister, who stared at the empty space where his right hand had been with a kind of foggy astonishment. Blood gushed from the stump, almost hitting the ceiling.

For its part, the *Malite* buzzed in a tight circle around the boy. After all, it wasn't really after *him*.

"Red!" Sharyn cried. "Run!"

But standing there, gaping at my maimed friend as the horror of what had happened to him sunk in, I realized something.

I was *done* running.

So, as the Pigeon from Hell came for me, I made a move that will probably seem a little—well—stupid.

I grabbed it.

You need to understand that I had two things going for me. First, the *Malite* hadn't had time to really come up to full velocity. If it had, I wouldn't have stood a chance. But, as it was, I clocked its speed as about as fast as a tossed baseball.

Second, I was seriously pissed.

I can be really quick when I'm seriously pissed.

So, as it made a literal beeline for my face, I sidestepped and snatched it out of the air, wrapping one hand around its hard, quad-winged body.

It was *strong*. Stronger than I would have thought, given its size. Making a sound like a boiling teapot, it struggled wildly in my grasp, at one point nearly pulling me off my feet.

"Help Dave!" I exclaimed to the others. "Now!"

Then the Pigeon from Hell *did* pull me off my feet.

Its wings, only one of which I'd managed to trap inside my fist, beat furiously at the air, managing to yank me off balance. I slammed against one of the nearby dining tables, knocking over two chairs, before sprawling painfully across the tablecloth and place settings.

Still, I held onto that disgusting creature like grim death—because grim death was *exactly* what waited for me if I let go.

It twisted and writhed, trying to reach me with those insane drill teeth. But the young *Malum* had picked a form that was big on offense but bad on defense. It couldn't reach me.

As I fought with it, trying to right myself, I saw Sharyn out of the corner of my eye. She was at the Burgermeister's side, and spoke soothingly as she wrapped the stump of his right wrist with a cloth napkin, twisting its corners tight around a spoon, both of which she'd filched from another tabletop.

A tourniquet.

Feeling the *Malite's* struggles increase, I gave up trying to stand and instead rolled purposefully across the table and crashed to the floor, making sure to land on top of the creature. I tried to get my other hand on it, but its drill-like teeth dug savagely into the skin of my palm. I yelled and pulled back.

Then, looking around frantically for something that would answer the nagging question of "Okay, *now* what do I do?" I spotted Julie.

Helene's little sister huddled nearby, gaping in mute terror at all the blood and chaos, Aunt Sally still balanced in her small hands.

"Julie!" I called.

At the sound of her name, a little bit of awareness seemed to return to her eyes.

"Julie!" I repeated. "Come here! Quick!"

And the girl came—slowly, fearfully—but she came.

I was on my knees now, holding down the creature in my fist with every ounce of my fading strength. "Listen to me," I told the girl. "I want you to point Aunt Sally at the monster."

"I ... can't ..." She sounded frightened almost beyond reason. And how could I blame her? This morning she'd woken up in her own bed, in her own home, with her own mom there to make her breakfast. Now, just half-a-day later, the world she thought she'd always known had become a realm of walking dead people and flying monsters. Up until now, she'd held things together beautifully. But even *this* girl's courage had its limits.

"You *can*," I told her, gritting my teeth as the *Malite* managed to slice off a piece of skin between my thumb and forefinger. "Just point the tip down. It's easy."

She nodded. But she didn't move.

"Julie. I know you're scared. But I *need* you to do this!"

She nodded again. Then, at last, the business end of the crossbow focused down at the creature in my grasp.

"I ... can't hit it," the girl wailed. "Your hand—"

"Julie," I said, slowly and deliberately, "I want you to shoot *through* my hand."

"What? No!"

"It'll be okay!" I told her, yelping as the drill teeth slashed me a second time. Blood was starting to fill my palm, making it harder to keep a firm grip. In a second, this thing would be free again—and seconds after that, we'd both be dead. "I'll be fine. We have something at Haven that can fix it."

I tried not to think about Dave. Could the Anchor Shard, for all its miraculous healing ability, replace a missing hand?

"No," she said again.

"Julie," I pleaded. "If you don't do it now, this thing is going to kill us both!" Then, after a moment's pause, I added, "Then you'll never see Helene!"

Something in her heart-shaped face changed. Hardened.

She took aim with the crossbow.

And fired.

The Ritterbolt slammed into the back of my hand. Pain, like lightning, lanced up my arm and into my shoulder, almost blinding me. But, as I'd hoped, the power behind the short-range shot was enough to drive the syringe all the way through and into the body of the *Malite*.

I felt more than saw the plunger *plunge*.

I heard myself say, through gritted teeth, "Pop goes the weasel."

Then the thing in my fist exploded.

More pain, like a hundred simultaneous needle pricks.

With a final cry, I fell back onto my butt, clutching at my wrist and staring at the ruin that used to be my right palm. Bone fragments, leftovers from the *Malite's* destruction, had turned the skin to bloody shreds.

But at least *my* hand was still there.

"It's okay," Sharyn said. "It's gonna be okay."

It took me a couple of seconds to realize she wasn't talking to me.

Dave lay on his side in a puddle of his own blood. He was vampire pale, and his breath came in deep, painful heaves.

Kneeling over him, Sharyn's panicked eyes found mine. "We gotta get him to Haven!" If she'd noticed my own situation—which wasn't good—she gave no sign.

I understood.

Dave was *her* Hot Dog, after all.

I tried to get up and flopped back down. I tried to get up again and flopped back down again. Finally, Julie got herself under my good arm and, together, we managed to find my feet.

The room swayed.

It's mostly shock. You're hurt, but you haven't lost all that much blood. You gotta keep it together for Dave's sake.

"Sat phone?" I asked Sharyn.

She nodded and tossed it to Julie, who handed it to me. It was my fourth phone of the day and I could only hope it would last longer than the others had. With a sigh, I opened it and, using my left hand, clumsily pressed the number for Haven.

That's when the dead chef with the white mushroom hat came crashing through the kitchen door.

Sure, I remember thinking. *Why not?*

CHAPTER 26
CLASH OF THE TITANS

Some days kick your ass.

One thing after another. Bang. Bang. Bang. And no matter how many times you tell yourself the worst is over—it's not.

I'd trashed Parker's old body, the one with the useless arm and the bum leg. So he'd done what Corpses *always* do: he'd jumped into the nearest available cadaver. And, in my worry over Dave and my eagerness to find Sharyn and Julie, I'd missed the danger.

I stared down the *new* Parker, gripped by this weird sense of calm. I mean, the day had been a long series of near-death experiences, culminating with me here, in this spot, and him there, in that spot.

Enough.

Win or lose, this was ending *now*.

I only wished my hand didn't feel like I'd stuck it into a garbage disposal.

Not that Parker looked any better. The chef's lower

jaw was completely missing. That left just the top half of his face along with an awful black tongue, which flipped and flopped this way and that, hanging down almost to the dead dude's neck.

Yet he glared at me with eyes still fresh enough to almost look alive.

Then he raised both his arms, his hands like claws.

Sharyn, who'd still been crouching at Dave's side, jumped to her feet, drawing Vader from its sheath on her back with a single, smooth, lightning-quick movement.

Yet, quick as she was, the Special proved quicker.

Ducking her sword slash, he savagely backhanded her with the speed and force of a Major League batter. Vader flew from Sharyn's grasp, burying itself halfway in the drywall near a big silver coffee urn. The Angel Boss crashed down hard, landing beside the unconscious Burgermeister.

Julie grabbed my good hand and pulled frantically. "We gotta run!"

"You run," I told her. "I'm done with that."

Parker's grotesque head turned my way. His face did something that *might* have been a smile—but try smiling when your chin and lower teeth are gone.

"Will—"

"Go!" I told her.

She went, but only as far as the foyer archway. There she stopped, looking back at me in helpless horror.

The deader didn't come at me fast. He seemed to sense that I wasn't going anywhere.

Have. Orders. To. Kill. You. Boy.

This was said in Deadspeak, not English, since Deadspeak is more about telepathy and doesn't require—well—a mouth.

I pulled out my pocketknife and popped its Taser.

Was I being brave? Even now, I'm not sure. I'd been running all day and I was tired of it. *Malum* and their offspring, they're *evil*. Homicidal, pitiless, and thoroughly savage. And you know what? Sooner or later, you have to stand up to evil. Then, you have to take what comes next, comforted maybe in the knowledge that, live or die, at least you stood up.

Or maybe I'm just stupid.

Your call.

He came within five feet. Four feet.

I didn't wait for the attack, I lunged with the Taser. Problem One: the Taser was in my left hand, since my right one was in no position to be holding anything. Problem Two: he saw it coming; he saw it coming from like a mile away.

Seizing my wrist, he pulled me close to the ruin of what he probably still considered a face. He tried to speak. Corpse smack talk, probably. But all he did was wheeze, his long black tongue twisting like a dying eel in the space where his jaw used to be.

Then he squeezed my hand—hard.

I yelled and dropped the pocketknife.

He threw me into a table. I actually heard my head connect with the edge of it. For a few seconds, flashes of light danced in front of my eyes. Then it was like a shroud had been draped over me.

Everything went black.

I'm not sure if I actually passed out or if I just kind of fell into a fog of disorienting pain. Either way, the next thing I knew I lay sprawled on the carpet, while the deader turned his attention on Julie.

"Your. Turn. Girl."

I tried to move. I really did. But my body wasn't going for it. Blearily, I could see my pocketknife about five feet away. Close, though right now it might as well have been on the moon.

Me down. Sharyn down. Dave *hardcore* down. I supposed that I'd been in deeper trouble than this since becoming an Undertaker; I was just having a hard time remembering when.

I focused on Julie. She remained in the foyer archway, her attention seemingly fixed on something off to one side, something that I could see. She looked so small and helpless. Aunt Sally was still in her hands. But she'd fired its bolt already, and it would require a reload before it would be of any use.

"Run!" I groaned.

But she didn't. Instead, trembling, she turned toward the dining room. Toward me. Toward Parker. Maybe the sight of his hideous form had frozen her, like an animal in traffic. Or maybe she was simply too brave for her own good and wouldn't abandon us. Either way, she was going to die now, and there wasn't a thing I could do about it.

As he had with me, Parker took his time, savoring the kill. He approached until he came within two feet of her, until his twisted, grotesque body loomed over the girl. Then he paused and did that *thing* with his upper lip again—the thing that kind of looked like smiling.

That's when Julie did a funny thing, too.

She smiled back.

Then she said, "Now."

The floor at Parker's feet exploded upward. Two pale hands emerged, seized the Corpse's ankles, and pulled him straight down.

For a moment, the dining room filled with the sounds of splintered wood as the Special disappeared through the floor. Then everything went quiet.

Julie hadn't moved. Her eyes met mine. There was

still fear there, and concern—mostly for me. But there was something else there, too. Something new.

Triumph.

The girl is *an Undertaker.*

That's when the Zombie Prince came flying out through the jagged hole in the floor between us, the imprint of one of Parker's boots on his cyclist's forehead.

Dillin landed hard enough to flatten one of the tables, but immediately jumped to his feet with all the speed and poise of a jungle cat. And good thing too, because an instant later Parker followed him, emerging through the gap in the floor like a demon from the Pit.

The two Corpses faced off with maybe a dozen feet between them.

Oreth Oreg! Parker said in Deadspeak, his tongue twitching and bobbing, as if he were trying to repeat the word in English.

"Whatever," Dillin replied.

Parker lunged, his big hands like claws.

Then it was the Zombie Prince's turn to do a strange thing.

He tossed me something.

It landed on the floor about three feet from where I lay.

An instant later, the Special grabbed the Royal and hurled him the length of the room. Dillin hit the wall beside the kitchen door so hard that the floor shook. That kind of blow would have killed a living man.

But he wasn't a living man.

Parker closed on him again, muttering in Deadspeak. *Destroy. You.*

This time, the Zombie Prince replied, "Calabash!"

As smack talk went, it sucked. Yet the word was vaguely familiar and, my instincts told me, really *really* important.

This time, as Parker neared, Dillin dodged to his right, sidestepping the Special before pivoting and body-slamming him. Parker toppled over, crashing against one of the tables. He landed hard, splintering the wood, before rolling and regaining his feet.

Dillin said, "Glutinous."

Another vaguely familiar word, though between my pounding head and throbbing right hand, I couldn't manage the brain power to remember why.

Meanwhile, Parker shoved the Royal hard against another table, before scooping up a chair and smashing it over the principal's head, reducing the hard wood to splinters.

Dillin dropped to his knees.

But then he came back up—fast.

The principal's fist would have nailed Parker in the chin, if he still had one. Instead, it slammed into the roof of his mouth, smashing that bizarre, floppy tongue of his to pulp and driving the Special off his feet. He flipped head over heels before hitting the carpet, almost right on top of me.

For scant seconds, his half-face was inches from mine.

I almost expected him to take the opportunity to kill me, which wouldn't have been hard. But he didn't seem to even notice I was there. All of his attention remained on the principal, who came after him with a glint in his dead eyes that I'd never seen before.

Well, I'd *seen* it; Corpses wore it a lot.

But never on Bob Dillin's face.

Seething hatred.

"Lots of ingredients in the cellar," he told the Special.

Why is he saying these weird things?

Then, like a bolt of lightning, comprehension hit me. My right hand was a useless knot of pain. But the left one worked and, with it, I managed to get first to my elbows and then my knees. The world threatened to spin. I firmly told it not to—and it listened, mostly.

Walking was out of the question, at least for now, so I crawled. And since I still couldn't use my right hand, it kind of went like this: left hand, right knee, right elbow, left knee.

Slow going. But I managed to reach the thing that Dillin had tossed my way.

A pouch, one of those clear plastic freezer bags.

And inside it was what looked like a big glob of hastily mixed white paste.

The Zombie Prince seized Parker's collar and yanked him to his feet. Parker, in turn, grabbed Dillin's bicycle shirt. Then the two of them started spinning around, fighting for advantage, slamming each other into everything and anything handy.

"Julie," I said, surprised at how weak my voice sounded.

The girl still stood on the other side of the jagged hole in the floor. She looked at me. She didn't speak.

I said, "Help me."

She didn't hesitate. She didn't stop to consider the dead men who so ferociously fought only a dozen feet away. She just came.

And, between the two of us, we got me standing again.

She led me over to the side wall. I leaned against it, trying to ignore the pain and dizziness, *willing* my vision to clear.

"How'd you know Dillin was going to do that?" I asked her.

"I saw him in the foyer," she replied in a whisper, "standing at the top of the stairs that lead down to the cellar. He shushed me and then made one of those 'I'm gonna reach up through the floor and grab him' gestures."

What in the world does an "I'm gonna reach up through the floor and grab him" gesture even look like?

But that was a question for another time.

"Hide," I told her.

"You okay?"

"I'm fine. I know what to do. Hide."

She nodded and ducked under the nearest table. I would have preferred it if she'd left the dining room—heck, the *restaurant*—but she was too much of an Undertaker for that.

The two Corpses finally broke apart. Warily, they circled one another, eyes locked. Both deaders had suffered a truckload of damage.

The principal lunged.

But Parker was ready.

He caught Dillin's arm and swung him in a wide arc, yanking his sneakers off the floor, and ramming him face first into a wooden archway.

The Zombie Prince crashed to the floor. As he did, his gazed locked on my mine, full of silent message.

I forced my legs to move.

But not toward him, not toward the fighting. Instead, I staggered over to Sharyn and the Burgermeister, who lay almost side by side on the carpet near the kitchen door. Sharyn had a lump the size of an egg on her forehead. But her pulse, when I checked it, was strong. Dave was in worse shape. His makeshift tourniquet had held so far, keeping any more of his blood from gushing out of the stump left behind by the last *Malite*. But his face was ghostly, and his pulse felt slow and thin.

If we didn't get him out of here, he was going to die.

That awareness fueled me. It's amazing what you can

do when a friend's life is at stake.

I went to the wall behind him and took hold of Vader. The sword was still buried deep in the sheetrock and, given my condition, it took a *lot* of effort to yank it free. But I managed it.

Behind me I heard the crash of glass. Turning, I saw that Parker had managed to hurl Dillin through one of the windows and out onto the porch. But the Zombie Prince recovered almost at once and leaped back through, his face and clothes shredded by the shards of glass.

I opened the freezer bag. Sniffed its contents.

Salt.

Of course.

Salt mixed with water and what? Flour? Corn starch? Whatever had been handy in the storerooms below the restaurant, I supposed.

Whatever would make it glutinous.

Sticky.

Awkwardly tucking Vader under my right arm, I used my left hand to scoop out a fistful of the stuff and smear it along the length of the blade.

Dipping my arrow in the poison.

Dillin must have spotted what I was doing because when I looked up at him, he was smiling—at least insofar as he could, since his own face wasn't much to look at anymore. Then he grabbed for Parker, pulling him into what boxers might call a "clutch."

They grappled like that, face-to-face, spinning in angry circles and crashing into everything.

"Do it!" he yelled to me.

"Get clear!" I yelled back.

Balancing myself as best I could, I started toward them.

Parker craned his head, finally interested in what I

was doing. When he saw what I'd done to the sword, he must have put two and two together, because he started struggling harder against Dillin's grip, repeatedly butting the Zombie Prince in the face with his forehead.

He'd do this, I knew, until both their stolen skulls cracked.

He'd pull out *all* the stops.

Because if he didn't, he would die. Really, permanently die. And Corpses feared that more than anything. All of them.

Except one.

"Will! Please!" Dillin yelled. "I can't hold him!"

I could see what had to be done. If Parker got free, then he'd be on me in a second. No slow approach this time. He'd pounce like a lion and rip me apart before I could even begin to defend myself.

I came within three feet of the struggling dead men.

This was all about aim. I'd skewer Parker, while missing my friend—yes, my *friend*. But my head was pounding, and my strength hung by a thread. I'd have to be careful.

Really careful.

As I neared the two of them, still locked in their clutch, I drew back Vader, ready to thrust.

"Get clear!" I told Dillin again.

But instead, the Royal shoved the Special up against the nearest wall, pinning him. Parker gurgled and squirmed, struggling like a panicked animal. Holding him there was taking everything the Zombie Prince had.

He looked back at me, his eyes—stolen eyes, dead eyes—filled with *stuff*. So much stuff. There was desperation there. And fear. And courage. And something else. Something that looked completely out of place on a Corpse's face.

Nobility.

"Dying well is its own reward," he said.

I stared at him, unable to move. But then Parker rallied, nearly pushing off the wall, nearly breaking free.

And I knew I was out of time.

"I'm so sorry," I said to Dillin.

Then I drove the poisoned blade hard into his back, pushing it in. All the way. All the way through.

And into Parker.

"No!" the Special wailed in Deadspeak.

But the Zombie Prince just said, in the same weird language, *"Dying. Well."*

Then the two of them exploded.

The force of it knocked me off my feet yet again, bits of flesh and bone raining down around me. For a second or two, I thought I actually *would* pass out. But I didn't. Instead, I simply lay there, my mind reeling, my heart pounding—

—and feeling sick to my very soul.

CHAPTER 27
CONTROL

Tom

Ten feet away, a homeless woman was playing "giant chess" against nobody.

Tom watched her with half an eye. She was stooped over, draped in a heavy hooded coat that didn't work with the warm afternoon. Beside her sat a plastic basket, probably stolen from a supermarket, into which the woman had piled a collection of junk and scavenged food—most likely everything she owned in the world.

Philadelphia had so many people like her. Ignored. Abandoned. Invisible.

The "giant chess" she played was just that: giant chess, a huge chessboard painted onto the cement in the midst of this large, concrete public park. It had even been populated with three-foot plastic chess pieces. The homeless lady was currently playing both black and white, cackling to herself as she moved one piece, and then ran around the board and moved an opposing piece.

"Do you think she's winning?" Senator James

Mitchum asked.

Tom regarded the man. He was in his fifties, hefty, and dressed for success in a dark blue suit and power tie. He had an American flag pin on his lapel. Tom had heard that everyone in Washington wore one of those.

"She probably hasn't eaten in two days, man," Tom told him. "So ... what do *you* think?"

Mitchum's smile faltered. "I didn't mean it that way."

"Whatever."

The senator occupied one of the five metal chairs that they'd squeezed around one of the round metal tables that the city maintained in this crowded public area nestled between the inbound and outbound lanes of the Ben Franklin Parkway. Around them, people moved and talked and laughed in the afternoon sunshine. Nearby, vendors sold everything from hotdogs to Chinese food.

To the southeast, skyscrapers dominated the horizon, with William Penn's statue atop City Hall sitting smack dab in the middle.

In the opposite direction, much closer, the Philadelphia Art Museum shimmered like red gold. A huge, columned building, it sat atop broad tiered steps, up which Sly Stallone, as Rocky Balboa, had gone running more than once. There was actually a statue of the movie boxer on the museum grounds.

As Tom watched, three police cruisers made their way up the Ben Franklin Parkway, heading in the direction of Kelly Drive. Their lights were flashing and their sirens bleated.

Something big's goin' down at the river.

Will and Sharyn. Gotta be.

But he'd have to let them handle whatever it was—for now.

Tom had his own agenda.

"What's happening?" Mitchum turned in his chair to watch the cop cars disappear behind the art museum.

"There were some killings in Fairmount Park," Ramirez replied. "I heard it on the radio. The entire area's been closed off."

"Tragic," the senator remarked.

F.B.I. Special Agent Hugo Ramirez sat beside Mitchum. Unlike the senator, he showed the good grace to look uncomfortable, even a bit guilty. Ramirez had *been* to Haven, had *seen* firsthand how the Undertakers lived and what they had to do. Yet, he'd brought that secret to Mitchum and had approved, or at least cooperated, when the senator had introduced Jillian as a spy.

After meeting Tom's gaze for a few seconds, Ramirez looked away.

The fourth chair at this crowded table had a woman in it. Mitchum had introduced her as Millie, his confidential secretary. "Privy to all my secrets," he'd said.

All ours, too, Tom had thought.

The last dude was Greg Gardner.

To all outward appearances, he was kind of a Mini-Me for Mitchum. Same sort of suit. Same sort of tie. Same vaguely condescending air. And he'd been all smiles from the get-go, shaking Tom's hand with a firm politician's grip, all the while telling him what an honor this was, and how he'd so looked forward to meeting him.

"Thanks," Tom had replied.

And so the "job interview" had begun.

Mitchum said, "Let me start by asking you a few questions."

"Okay," Tom told him.

"Do you have a college education?"

"You know the answer to that, Senator."

"Do you even have a high school diploma?"

Tom said, "You know the answer to that one, too."

"So you dropped out of high school? When?"

"When it felt like the right time."

Mitchum seemed to consider this. Tom's answer had been truthful, and yet just a bit defiant.

Finally, the senator said, "Those are both obstacles to any employment in my office."

"I ain't lookin' for employment in your office," replied Tom.

Mitchum blinked. "Then I'm not sure what—"

"Let me ask *you* a couple o' questions," Tom said.

The senator glanced at Ramirez before shifting a little in his chair. "Go ahead."

"When you offered to help Jillian find out 'bout the Corpses in D.C., had you already figured on using her as a mole in Haven? Or was it more of a 'spur o' the moment' thing?"

"Senator, I don't think you should answer that!" Millie snapped.

"Mr. Jefferson," Gardner said. "I suggest you remember who you're talking to."

"Tom ..." Ramirez began in a warning tone.

Tom ignored them all, keeping his attention focused on Mitchum, who looked back at him as if sizing him up. "A man in my position," the senator said, "needs to recognize a potential opportunity when one presents itself."

"Sorry," Tom said flatly. "I ain't got my diploma. Care to talk a little plainer than that?"

"Hugo came to me with what he knew about the Corpse War ... and about you and your ... organization. Obviously, he didn't know enough. At first, I had difficulty believing what he had to say, despite our long association and his sterling reputation with the Bureau. But some of what he described applied to Senator Lindsay Micha ... the sudden lack of public appearances, her odd bout of camera shyness, very uncommon on Hill."

"Straight up," Tom said.

"So, after that first page went missing and was eventually found dead, I started looking at the others. After all, if one of them had 'gotten his Eyes,' as Hugo put it, then it didn't seem impossible that another would as well. That's how I found Jillian."

"You just walked up to every Senate page and said, 'Hey, you see dead people or what?' to them?"

Mitchum scoffed. "I was subtler than that ... finding different pretexts for showing each child an assortment of photos of Micha's staff."

"How did you know any of the pics were of Corpses?" Tom asked.

"Obviously, I didn't," the older man replied. "I didn't even know for certain, at the time, that Senator Micha had been compromised. It was what we in Washington call a 'fishing expedition'.

"In any case, that's how I happened upon Jillian. She was trying to discover what had happened to her friend, the dead page. Once I confirmed she could actually *See* these creatures, I offered to help her.

"Later, when she found out who ... *what* ... the late senator really was, she called me. She mentioned overhearing your name. I suggested that she go straight to Philly, to find you. As she did."

Tom asked, "Did she know you knew about the Undertakers? About the war? Or did you leave her in the dark on that?"

Greg Gardner said, "I'm starting not to like your tone."

But Mitchum held up a hand. "I *chose* to withhold that at first, Mr. Jefferson. I wanted to see how resourceful

Ms. Birmelin could be. There'd have been little point in placing someone in your organization if I couldn't count on her to keep her head and maintain her cover."

"Yeah," Tom said bitterly. "'Cept she started lookin' for us in our old hood, down South Street, and Cavanaugh sent every Corpse in the world after her. She was lucky to get out alive."

The senator nodded. "Extremely lucky. *And* it proved her worth. So I contacted her and told her exactly what I … what her country … needed her to do."

"Wrapped yourself in the flag, huh?" Tom remarked.

Millie said sharply, "Senator, this man isn't here looking for a job. He's here to … interrogate you!"

"No," Tom said. "That *ain't* why I'm here."

Millie pressed. "Senator, I strongly suggest we leave."

But Mitchum didn't move. Neither did Ramirez or Gardner. Finally Millie, with an exasperated sigh, fell into a sullen silence.

"When did you bring these two into it?" Tom asked, nodding to Millie and Gardner.

"From the beginning. Greg was there when Ramirez first came to me, and Millie's been my secretary for many years. You can trust them both, Mr. Jefferson."

Tom didn't reply.

A couple of Philly cops had arrived on the scene, the only ones Tom had spotted so far. Both were in uniform, and both were a little ways off, standing at the edge of the park.

But they were clearly watching this little gathering.

"Check!" the homeless woman announced from the chessboard, cackling.

Then she hurried over to the other side of the board to make the countermove.

Countermoves, Tom thought.

He said, "We been fightin' this war on our own for three years, Senator."

Mitchum nodded. "And you've conducted yourselves with distinction."

"But you figured you'd better ... what? Keep an eye on us? That's why you planted Jill as a spy?"

"I don't think I'd use the word 'spy,'" Mitchum replied flatly.

"Tom ..." Ramirez said. "It wasn't like that."

Millie said, "The senator knows what he's doing, young man."

Gardner leaned forward. "He's been looking out for you, Tom. We *all* have."

But, again, Tom's eyes remained fixed on Mitchum, who regarded him coolly. Finally, flatly, the big man said, "I see what we have here."

"I doubt it," Tom replied.

"No, I see quite clearly. For these past three years, you've been the king of your hill. But now you've discovered ... lo and behold ... that authorities had an eye on what you've been doing. You don't like that. It threatens your position. It threatens your sense of control."

Tom's eyes flicked over to the two cops, who were approaching them slowly from across the patch of grass separating the park from the parkway. Their hands were at their sides, expressions grim.

To the senator, he said, "You want to talk about control?"

Tom reached into his coat pocket and placed a water pistol on the tabletop.

Gardner sat back.

"What's that?" Mitchum asked.

Tom didn't reply. Instead, he reached into his coat

pocket a second time, and placed a Ritter on the table beside the pistol. The big syringe, loaded with saltwater, glistened in the sunshine.

"Let me tell you about control, Senator," Tom said. "Control, in my mind, ain't somethin' you hold over other folks. It's 'bout controlling your own self. It's about gettin' ... really *gettin'* ... what you *can* do and what you *can't* do. In my case, I know that, without the Sight, I can't chief the Undertakers. I also know that *you*, without the Sight, can't chief 'em either."

Mitchum began, "Now, just a moment. I think you —"

But Tom talked right over him. "Your people are right. I didn't meet with y'all today 'cause I want a job. I came 'cause I found out that you had a spy ... and yeah, that's the word: *spy* ... in Haven, and I needed to find out who knew about what and how much."

"It's just the four of us," Mitchum said defensively. "I wouldn't risk a larger circle. I know the stakes are high."

"Do you?" Tom asked.

Then he moved.

With one hand, he grabbed the Ritter off the tabletop.

With the other, he grabbed Gardner.

He snaked an arm around the man's neck and yanked him out of his chair, throwing him over the table and pressing the side of his face against its metal top. Then, before anyone could react, he jabbed the point of the syringe against Gardner's lower back.

The others jumped to their feet in horror. Around them, strangers and bystanders looked over in alarm. Only the homeless woman ignored them, playing her game of chess. "Check!" she yelled again, cackling and changing sides.

The two cops stopped at the edge of the concrete that

marked the limits of the park. Their eyes were fixed on Tom. But he noticed they still didn't go for their guns.

Well, they wouldn't, would they? he thought.

"What are you doing?" the senator demanded.

"Tom! For God's sake!" Ramirez exclaimed.

Millie didn't say anything. Her face had gone pale, her hands flying to her mouth.

Tom ignored them all, speaking instead to Gardner, who'd struggled at first but then had gone still when the point of the Ritter touched his spine. "You know what this is, don't you?"

"You're insane!" Gardner snapped.

"And you know what happens if I inject you ... right?"

"Help me!" Gardner screamed.

"You put on a solid act. I'll give ya that much. Here's the thing, though: if you're human and I stick you, it'll hurt. But that'll be as far as it goes. Then again, if you *ain't* human ... well, then you get to pop like a balloon and die. Permanent die. You get that, right?"

"Senator!" Gardner exclaimed, his eyes wide with terror. "Help me!"

"Jefferson! I'm ordering you to put that ... weapon ... down! I don't know what you think you're doing, but—"

This time it was Ramirez who cut him off.

To Tom, he exclaimed, "You *can* See!"

CHAPTER 28
ON THE STEPS

Tom

Tom said to Gardner. "Here's how this is gonna go. You got a five-count to start talkin'. If you don't, I stick you. If you don't tell the straight up truth, I stick you. We clear?"

"I'm human!" Gardner screamed.

"Then you got nothin' to worry about," Tom told him, pressing the point of the Ritter syringe just into the man's skin, about where his right kidney would be. "One."

"Jefferson," Mitchum said. "Listen to me. I don't know what—"

"Two," Tom said.

"Hugo!" the senator exclaimed. "Talk to him!"

But Ramirez didn't say a word. His gaze was fixed on Tom, his face pale.

You thought you knew how the world really worked, Tom thought. *But you didn't learn the lesson quite good enough, huh?*

"Three."

"Help me!" Gardner yelled again, only this time the plea wasn't directed at the senator or Ramirez or Millie. It was directed instead at the two cops who watched from the park's edge.

Mitchum saw them too. "Officers, I think we need a little help here."

The cops started forward.

About time, Tom thought.

"Four," he said.

"All right!" Gardner screamed. "Don't do it! Please don't do it!"

"Then talk," Tom told him.

Gardner's face suddenly twisted into an expression of hatred and defiance. "You old fool!" he said to Mitchum. "You think yourself so clever, so in command. But you're as blind as the rest of your pathetic species! How easy it was to stroke your ego, earn your trust. I should thank you! Being your 'confidant' kept me alive when the Queen wished me destroyed!"

Why do they always talk like super-villains when their Masks drop? Tom wondered.

Gardner was a Type Two, and a fairly fresh one. His host had once been dark-haired, but that hair was now falling out in clumps. His skin, also dark, had turned a sickly gray with death, the flesh slackened and purple in places where the blood had pooled.

Ten days gone. Maybe two weeks, tops.

Mitchum went pale. Ramirez drew a gun from inside his jacket, as if *that* would do any good. Millie just looked confused.

"How much does Cavanaugh know?" Tom demanded of the deader, jabbing him a little deeper with the syringe.

Gardner, of course, felt no pain. But he *should* have felt fear.

Instead, he laughed.

"It doesn't matter, Jefferson. You and your band of brats are *done*! In a minute, you'll be dead. You too, Mitchum! The Queen has ordered it!"

Gardner turned his head in the direction of the two cops, who had stopped right behind Millie.

A pair of early Type Threes, they'd started to bloat inside their stolen uniforms. Both glowered menacingly.

Mitchum exclaimed, "What's going on? I don't understand."

"They're Corpses," Tom told him. "Both of them. Just like Greg here."

The senator looked like he might vomit. "What? No!"

Ramirez trained his gun on the cops. Again: pointless.

"Kill them!" Gardner commanded.

Tom said calmly, "Now."

The chess-playing homeless lady pulled a Super Soaker out from under her unseasonably heavy coat.

She sprayed both cops in the back. Instantly, they stiffened as the saltwater did its work. One fell backward, his body twitching as if electrified. The other fell forward, knocking Millie over and slamming into the side of their little table. Tom, who was still leaning over Gardner, was knocked off-balance. For a moment—just a moment— his grip on the Corpse slackened.

Gardner, seizing his chance, jumped to his feet, the Ritter in his back falling to the cement.

At the same instant, the homeless lady pulled back her hood.

"Tom!" Helene called. "You okay?"

"Shoot him!" Tom ordered.

She leveled her soaker and fired, but Gardner was just a little too quick. He darted around Mitchum, ignoring Ramirez and his "Freeze!" order, stiff-armed Helene, and pushed her to the ground.

Then he ran.

Tom snatched up the fallen Ritter and went after him. As he passed Helene, who was already righting herself, he said sharply, "Keep 'em safe! Get 'em outta here if you can!"

"Okay, Chief."

Gardner charged into the crowd, most of whom had been watching the drama with a mixture of excitement and confusion. Those who blocked his path were thrown aside. But the effort slowed him, allowing Tom to gain a little ground.

The Corpse left the park, tearing across the grass and around the statue of George Washington high on his horse, which marked the northwestern end of the Ben Franklin Parkway. Ahead lay a wide traffic circle, and beyond that, the Art Museum steps.

Tom pursued, wondering when he'd last run as hard as this. He kept trying to remember the Parisi lessons he'd learned as a kid: lean forward, keep your toes up, run on the balls of your feet. It had been a long time since he'd needed those skills.

But he needed them now, and there they were.

Gardner leapt into the traffic circle, apparently unconcerned about the near constant rush of cars. A tour bus hit him almost immediately, spinning him around and bouncing him off the fender of a passing Hyundai. Tom didn't slow his stride, but instead shifted his center of gravity at a key moment, slipping behind the bus and through a gap between two honking cars.

Barely a dozen feet ahead, the deader made another bad move and got slammed by a Ford pickup, his stolen body tossed over the hood and against the windshield, which cracked with the impact. Uttering an oddly human curse, he pushed off and kept going, though Tom noticed he was moving slower than before.

Dude's clumsy for a Corpse. He's trashin' his host.

Then Tom jumped and slid across the same pickup's roof, drawing swear words from the driver.

Gardner hit the curb and crossed the sidewalk, darting between two food vendors before launching himself up the Art Museum's famous staircase. Every time someone got in his way, they were bowled over, sending flailing bodies tumbling down the steps in the deader's frantic wake. Tom kept after him, more than once having to jump over a falling tourist as he climbed the stairs.

Halfway up, the Corpse spun around and grabbed the nearest innocent—a dude in a Phillies T-shirt. The guy struggled, even threw a punch or two that Gardner didn't feel, before the dead man pinned him in a chokehold and glared down at Tom.

"One more step, Undertaker, and he *dies*!"

Tom stopped.

Around them, people were screaming and pointing, much as they had done in the park.

And, as in the park, a *lot* of them had camera phones.

"Look around you," Tom told Gardner. "Look at the witnesses."

"They can't See," the deader sneered.

"No, but they can *think*. Your picture's gonna be all over Twitter in the next ten seconds, and all over the news minutes after that. Your days of spyin' for Cavanaugh are done!"

At first, the prospect seemed to upset the dead man, and he glanced left and right, looking very much like the trapped animal he was. But then a slow, savage smile settled on his blackened lips. "What does any of that matter now?"

Tom took a step forward, but Gardner saw this and clutched his hostage tighter.

The dude in the T-shirt cried out in pain.

"Okay!" Tom exclaimed. "Take it easy. Nobody else has gotta die."

"That's where you're wrong, Jefferson!" Gardner cried. In fact, he practically *sang* it. "Lots of people have to die! *All* of you have to die! And you ..." he added, pointing a finger at Tom. "You and your little Peter Pan Club are going to be *first*!"

Tom said, "That's what brought me out today. That's why I did all this. Reports have been comin' at me for weeks ... reports of cops, a lot of cops, all comin' together at different spots around City Hall, all at kinda the same time. By themselves, each one don't seem like much. But take 'em together and ... well, it made me wonder."

"Wonder what?" the Corpse demanded, his grin as terrible as the slash of the knife. "Wonder if the Queen might have finally found your hideout? Might have decided to take you all down, once and for all?"

"Yeah," Tom replied, his throat suddenly dry.

"Well, you've got only yourself to blame," Gardner hissed from behind his hostage. "You pushed us too far. Your constant meddling. Your endless interference in our glorious work. The Queen's abandoned the true, artistic destruction of the Earth, and has decided on a more ... direct approach. The siege on Haven is only the beginning. What's the old Earth cliché? Today, Philadelphia. Tomorrow, the world!"

He threw back his head and laughed.

And that's when two other tourists grabbed him.

They'd come from further up the museum's wide steps, moving in slowly and carefully. Tom had noticed them at once, and had considered waving them off. But, given the situation, their help might be the only way to save the dude in the T-shirt. So he'd kept Gardner talking.

The Corpse snarled as one of the men, a big guy in a polo shirt, grabbed his shoulder. Meanwhile, an older dude in sweats reached around and tried to pry Gardner's forearm from around the hostage's throat.

The deader flailed his free arm with terrible strength, knocking the first Good Samaritan away. But in doing so, he'd given the other man the leverage he needed to release the dude in the T-shirt.

What came next was a wild, violent sort of dance as four men—well, three men and a monster—grappled on the steps. As the crowd watched, cameras clicking, Gardner kept trying to push past them, but his attackers closed in, landing punch after punch. The Corpse, of course, felt none of it, but that didn't mean the blows didn't do further damage to his stolen body.

Tom had to wonder what these good folks were seeing. They didn't have Eyes, obviously, so how did Gardner's Mask reflect all of the "injuries" that he must be suffering? For a moment, Tom adjusted his vision and checked it out.

Nothing.

No bruises or cuts. The deader's projected illusion showed no sign at all that he had been repeatedly hammered by human fists.

That's gotta be raisin' some eyebrows.

Suddenly, with an animalistic roar, the dead man threw his attackers off him. The man in the polo shirt stumbled and went down on the steps. The older man staggered back. And the dude in the T-shirt, seeing himself one-on-one again, decided it was time to split.

By then, though, Tom was already moving.

As Gardner turned to run, his true face a ruin of

ripped tissue, Tom blindsided him. He knocked the Corpse off his feet and slammed him, face first, into the edge of the next step. Bones crunched, sounding like egg shells underfoot.

Gardner lashed out with a forearm like a baseball bat, but Tom ducked under it and then pinned it across the deader's back. It was a move that would have agonized a human being.

But this was no human being.

"You will *die*, Undertaker!" Gardner shrieked, his voice choked with rage and hatred and terror.

Tom, straddling the monster, leaned close and whispered, "You, first."

He rammed the Ritter into Gardner's lower back, emptying its syringe.

Then he stood up and walked back down the steps.

A hundred gazes followed him. He ignored them all.

He even ignored the screams that came a few seconds later, when the thing that had called itself Greg Gardner exploded on the Philadelphia Art Museum's stairs.

No one challenged Tom as he made his way back to the park. There weren't even any cops around, which seemed odd at first, since you'd figure *one* of the witnesses would have called 911 by now.

But then he remembered that a big percentage of the city police force was *Malum*, and they were busy elsewhere.

Ramirez had taken charge of the scene. The two dead cops that Helene had doused lay handcuffed on the ground. The F.B.I. Guy had gone into full professional mode, flashing his ID and announcing, "Move along! Nothing to see here!"

Helene stood over the deader cops, who continued to convulse as she re-sprayed them with her Super Soaker.

As Tom approached, she said, "I've got a couple of Ritters. But there's so many people around."

Tom told her, "I ain't sure that matters anymore." Then, with a wan smile, he added, "Solid work. You nailed the whole chess-playing bag lady thing."

The girl didn't smile back. "Thanks. Now how about telling me why you lied to me in the first place about losing your Eyes?"

Tom shook his head. "I wasn't lyin' to *you*. I was 'lyin' to *Jillian*. I'd been suspectin' for a while that she'd been turned. I didn't think it was the Corpses, at least not directly. But I needed to put her in a mind to come clean about it. She had to think I was leavin' Haven, givin' up my gig as chief. And the only way to do that was to convince her that I'd 'outgrown' the Sight."

"So why bring me and Mrs. Ritter into it at all?" Helene asked.

"To help sell it."

"But you didn't trust either of us enough to tell us the truth?" the girl demanded, looking hurt.

Tom put his hands on her shoulders. "Helene, I trust you with my life. Proved that right here and now, didn't I? But Jill ain't a fool. She'd have seen through an act. Your reaction and Susan's reaction had to be solid. Had to be *real*. That's why I waited until after I set up this meeting and Jillian split my office before I called you in. Sorry I didn't leave myself time for a real explanation, but we had to get out here fast."

Helene considered this. "I'm still mad at you."

"I can dig that."

"Mrs. Ritter's gonna have a cow."

"I know."

"And then there's Jillian …"

Tom sighed. "I wish that was my *only* problem today."

He stepped around her, going up to Ramirez.

Mitchum and Millie occupied chairs nearby. Both looked like they were in shock.

"I'm surprised they're still here," Tom told the agent.

"So am I," Ramirez said. "Helene tried to get us all to leave, but the senator wouldn't hear of it. He insists on talking to you."

"That right?"

"Tom ..." Ramirez swallowed. "I'm sorry."

"I know, Hugo," Tom told him. Which wasn't, when you got right down to it, the same as forgiving him.

"Where's Greg?" Millie asked as Tom approached their chairs.

"Where he belongs," Tom told her.

Mitchum rose on shaky legs. "Mr. Jefferson. I can't begin to —"

But Tom held up a hand. "No speeches. I ain't in the mood. How much did Gardner know about Haven?"

The senator blanched. "As much as I did."

"The layout of the place? Jillian told me she drew a map."

"Yes."

"Entrances and exits?"

"Yes."

Tom nodded. "They're gonna hit us tonight. They're gonna hit us with everything they got. Helene and me gotta get back to Haven while we still can. Once Cavanaugh hears that Gardner's blown, she'll bottle up all the ways in and out."

He turned to leave, but Mitchum grabbed his arm. "I was trying to help!"

Tom whirled on him. "You just don't *get* it! You *can't* help! No adult can help. You're blind! That by itself ain't your fault, but you're blind to the fact that you *are* blind!

All these months, you *knew* the Corpses were all around you. You *knew* you couldn't see them. You *knew* there was no one you could trust ... and yet one of 'em managed to cozy right up to you!"

The senator looked sick. "He was such a bright young man," he moaned. "I never imagined—"

"Take your hand off my arm."

"Son—"

Tom brought his face within inches of Mitchum's. Beside them, Millie gasped, maybe at what she saw in Tom's eyes.

"Don't," he said slowly, "*ever* call me 'son.'"

Then he turned, went back to Helene, and said, "Ritter 'em, and then let's go home."

But the girl replied, "Tom, Haven just called. They heard from Will. They're close ... and they need help."

CHAPTER 29

AFTERMATH

"Jules?" Helene said.

She'd just appeared in the doorway to the foyer, taking in the mess left behind by Dillin's last stand. For a moment, her gaze met mine. Then her eyes settled on her little sister, who been helping me tend to Dave and Sharyn.

The younger Boettcher girl took one look at the older Boettcher girl, and flew into her arms.

Unfortunately, battlefield reunions tend to be short.

Tom showed up an instant later, coming in through the kitchen door. "I dropped Helene off and parked 'round back. Cops are already on the scene. Not many, but more's comin'. Sis, you okay?"

Sharyn, who'd come around just after the fight was over, nodded through the tears in her eyes. "But Hot Dog's hurt, bro. He's hurt bad."

The chief came forward and silently assessed the stump at the end of Dave's arm. "Okay …" he said, his expression carefully calm. "Okay … it's a good field dressing. We can move him. Will, you solid? Your hand looks pretty bad."

Actually, my hand was screaming.

"Let's do it," I told him.

It took all of us, working together, to get Dave's unconscious bulk out through the kitchen and into the back of the van. As we did, I actually heard Philly's Finest enter the Water Works from the front, guns drawn. Fortunately, the blood and body parts littering the dining room stopped them in their tracks before they found us.

A near miss in a day that had seen too many of them.

Tom drove. I took shotgun. The girls stayed in the back with Dave, who still hadn't woken up.

That scared me.

We left Fairmount unchallenged and reached the underground garage below Love Park without any problems. Nobody said much during the drive. There'd be time to swap stories later.

We parked in the far corner of the lowest level and carried my handless friend through an old fire door and into Haven's northern entrance. Once there, my mom rushed us all into the Infirmary, where she and Amy Filewicz, her assistant, went to work at once. As Mom did triage—that's where you examine everyone quick to see who needs attention first—Amy made sure the beds were ready.

Then she fetched the Anchor Shard.

I watched the girl work, a million things running through my head. Amy had once tried to kill me while under Corpse control. Long story. Book One. Since then, she'd spent her every waking moment trying to make up for it. She was, for all intents and purposes, a nurse—a role that she took very seriously.

Amy.

I shook my head. Too much to deal with right now.

The Burgermeister remained unconscious.

His hand was forever gone. If the *Malite* hadn't eaten it, the Anchor Shard *might* have been able to reattach it. At least that was my mom's theory. "But now, all I can do is make sure the stump is closed up and doesn't get infected," she said, looking up at each of us, Sharyn in particular, and adding, "I'm so sorry."

Sharyn tried a snarky smile. "Well … dude was too big, anyhow."

But then, when her brother went to her, she fell against him, sobbing openly.

"Will he die?" I asked my mother.

"I don't think so," she said. "He's low on blood, but that's something the shard's good at: stimulating the generation of new blood."

I nodded, relieved.

My own hand throbbed. Amy had cleaned and bandaged it, but the *real* healing would have to wait until Dave was finished *and* then Sharyn, in case she had a concussion. It wouldn't have been her first. We only had one Anchor Shard.

My mom, who hadn't laid eyes on me since I'd left for Allentown a month ago, said, "I missed you."

"I missed you, too," I replied. And I had.

"Are you … okay?"

"No. But what difference does *that* make?"

Then, as tears filled her eyes, I gave her a quick, one-armed hug and went to check on Julie.

The little girl sat on the next gurney, her body trembling. Helene sat beside her, holding her close. When I joined them, both looked at me with glistening eyes.

Helene hopped off the gurney and put her arms around me.

Then she kissed me.

I'd been playing eighth-grader at Merriweather Intermediate for weeks. And, while I can't say I dreamed about kissing Helene every night, it was close enough. There'd been times, living in that tent in the woods behind the school, when I thought the loneliness would kill me. True, the Burgermeister had been there.

But the Burgermeister—thank God—wasn't my girlfriend.

So, even though I figured Tom and Sharyn, Julie and Amy, and even my mom were looking on, I took the kiss and gave it back. That's what you're supposed to do with kisses. A little something I learned recently.

After the kiss she hugged me again. Fiercely.

"I'm glad you're back," she whispered.

"Me, too," I said.

When we finally separated, I noticed Julie chewing her lower lip. Her attention seemed to be anywhere but on us. Then I glanced at my mom and saw her doing pretty much the same thing.

It would have been funny if I hadn't been so down.

"Thanks," Helene said to me, pulling me aside.

"For what?" I asked. Stupid, I know.

She rolled her eyes, "For getting my sister here, safe and sound, you idiot!"

"I didn't do it alone. Sharyn and Dave helped." Then, in a voice that cracked just a little bit, I added, "And Principal Dillin."

Tom and Sharyn approached. "How's the hand?" Sharyn asked.

"Hurts. How's the head?"

She smiled. "Hurts."

"But I'm still standing," I said.

"Me too, little bro. And that rocks." Then the Burgermeister groaned and, with a relieved sigh, Sharyn hurried over to his gurney.

That left Tom, Helene, and me alone in a corner of the Infirmary.

The Chief asked, "Up to a quick debrief?"

I nodded.

He nodded.

And we spent the next ten minutes swapping stories.

"Dillin died to save us," I told the chief when I'd finished. "He came to Earth knowing full well he wouldn't survive the trip, and he was okay with that. He was … one of the noblest people I've ever met."

Tom's reply surprised me. I'd expected skepticism, maybe outright dismissal of the idea of a "noble" Corpse. Instead, he said, "Sounds like the dude was an Undertaker."

And so he had been.

"But what's it all *mean*?" Helene asked. "What's going on?"

The chief replied, "Before I wasted him, Gardner told me that we'd pushed Cavanaugh too far. That she's gotten so pissed that she's decided to skip all that *Malum* subtlety and art crap and jump right to the 'unmaking.' The gloves are off. She knows where we're at and she's gonna hit us here… soon and *hard*."

Helene's face paled. "We gotta get ready."

"Already on it. But we'll get to that in a bit." He turned to me. "You say Dillin had something important to tell me. Since he ain't never gonna get the chance, I'm guessin' he told *you*. Yeah?"

"Yeah," I said. "But I'm not really sure I understand it."

"Spill," Tom said. "Then we'll figure it out together."

I thought back to those last moments in the restaurant. Trust had come slowly where the Zombie Prince was concerned, a fact that he seemed to take— as he took everything—in stride. But in the end, he'd proved himself a soldier, like me, except more fatalistic, or maybe more realistic.

He'd known he was going to die. He'd accepted it. Embraced it. His only concern had been making the death *mean* something—dying on his own terms.

Dying well is its own reward.

And, along the way, he'd become my friend.

"There's this door," I said.

They all looked at me, confused.

I explained, "The Corpses come to Earth ... all of them ... through this door they've made between their world and ours. Dillin called it the 'Rift.'"

"That's been Steve's theory," Tom said. "He thinks they got another Anchor Shard."

"They do," I told him. "And it's been hooked up and running for all these years, keeping that door open so that more Corpses can come in."

"He thinks if we can unplug the shard, it'll stop the invasion," the chief remarked.

"It'll do more than that," I said.

"So what?" Helene asked. "We don't know where it is!"

I looked at them both and replied, "*I* do."

CHAPTER 30

GIVING HIM A HAND

"Lilith Cavanaugh's been taking this slow," Tom told us. "And she's played it smart."

We were in the cafeteria, which was crammed with Undertakers, more than had ever before tried to fit into this crumbling chamber. Kids filled every seat. Kids lined the walls. Kids flooded the aisles. Kids spilled out into the hallway beyond the only door. I'd never seen anything like it.

It was really rare for *all* of us to be in the same place at the same time.

Tom had pulled a chair to the front of the room and climbed onto it. It was something he'd done before. It helped him to be seen by as many of the kids under his command and protection as possible. Well, seen and *heard*.

He said loudly, "She's been plannin' this for at least a month, scheduling three different police events all around City Hall, all around *us*, and all for this evening. The media's been callin' 'em 'urban peace-keeping simulations' or 'training exercises.' The Queen ain't been settin' them up herself, of course. Lilith Cavanaugh's dead as far as the world's concerned. She jumped out her sixth-floor office window almost two months ago." He managed a grin. "I know, 'cause I was there."

That actually earned him some laughs and applause.

Standing nearby, Helene and I swapped glances. We were thinking the same thing: those were likely to be the *last* laughs he got today.

I flexed my right hand. It felt good. The Anchor Shard had done its job.

I glanced over at Sharyn. She'd been healed up too, and now stood at her brother's side—though, from her expression, I could tell that, right now, she wanted to be somewhere else, *with* someone else.

The only Undertaker who wasn't here.

The chief continued, "But she's got cronies positioned in just the right spots in city government, and *they've* been settin' this up. Just today, she brought in two new Corpses to be co-police chiefs, since the last one got iced by Helene."

A few more cheers and applause. Helene blushed uncomfortably.

Tom said, "Both these chiefs are somethin' called 'Specials,' a particular breed o' *Malum* that's hardwired for combat. They're tough. Very tough. But they ain't unbeatable. Will already managed to waste one, the one called Parker, this afternoon at the Philly Water Works."

Still more cheers. I ignored them. I hadn't taken out Parker.

Dillin had.

"But that still leaves Cole, who's gonna be commandin' the *Malum* attack. Undertakers, they've gathered up at each of Haven's entrances ... and our best guess puts their numbers at close to fifteen hundred. They've already closed ranks and sealed off the exits, trapping us in here."

No applause this time. No laughter. Just graveyard silence.

"They've found us," the chief said. "It don't matter how. Cavanaugh's been biding her time, waitin' for the right moment to hit us. Well, that moment's here, 'cause school just got out. All through the area, the last middle schools've shut down for the summer. So every Schooler, more'n seventy of them, are back home. 'Course, in a week's time, some of y'all would've gone back out, taking up spots in summer camps and such, always on the lookout for more Seers. But for now, for this tiny window, all of us ... *all of us* ... are here. And the Queen of the Dead knows it.

"Bottom line, Undertakers. She's comin' for us. Tonight."

I watched the faces, at least as many as I could see. There was fear. Plenty of it. But mixed in with it was courage. And, mixed in with that: a terrible sense of acceptance. We'd all lived with death for so long. Was it really so surprising that, finally, it had literally come knocking at our door?

I spotted my mom. She was huddled in a corner of the cafeteria with my little sister, Emily, in her arms. Em, at six years old, might have been too young to make sense of everything going on around her. But I noticed she was sucking her thumb, something she only ever did when things got bad.

And that little girl knew more than her fair share about bad things.

As often happened, my mom's gaze found mine and held it. I could see that she was feeling what I was, what we all were. Only in her case, it was maybe worse, since she was a mother with kids to worry about.

We're not dead, yet, I silently told her.

Tom, reading the crowd, said, "I know that's the bad news. But, bad as it is, it don't mean there ain't no *good* news. Undertakers, we're not defenseless. Far from it."

He held up the Anchor Shard.

The kids who were crammed into the room had been shuffling nervously and murmuring to one another. But all that stopped when they saw the shard. Tom held it high, until the tip of the strange artifact almost touched the ceiling. As usual, it glowed, as if with its own light.

"This came from the *Malum* world, wherever that's at," the chief announced. "Turns out it's a kind of key. Run enough electricity through it, and this key opens a door 'tween worlds. The Corpses call that door the Rift, and it's how they been gettin' from there to here.

"Seems the *Malum* got this giant crystal called the Eternity Stone. They use it to find worlds with intelligent life, like ours. Then they chip off a tiny piece of it and make one of *these*, which they use to punch a hole into that world ... and invade. But chipping off an Anchor Shard from the Eternity Stone ain't easy. In fact, somethin' like ten thousand low-rankin' *Malum* gotta die to provide the necessary mojo. But they do it. And once they're here, they use the shard to keep that hole, that doorway, that *Rift*, open, so's they can keep bringin' more of their people into our world."

Again, the silence in the room was almost inhuman, as if the chief were addressing a horde of statues.

He said, "But here's the great secret, one that Will learned just today from someone he came to trust." He looked down at me and smiled.

I did my best to smile back.

Then he continued, "If we switch off the power to Cavanaugh's Anchor Shard, then we do more'n just close the Rift. We do more'n just keep more o' her people from coming into our world. We cut the connection between these invaders and the physical bodies they left behind. And without that constant connection running through a continually open door, the Corpses die.

"All of 'em!"

The news hit everyone hard. Heck, I'd known it since before going out onto the river and it still hit *me* hard.

Unplug Cavanaugh's Anchor Shard and win the war. Unplug Cavanaugh's Anchor Shard and win the war. Unplug Cavanaugh's Anchor Shard and win the war.

It kept repeating that way through my mind, like a song you can't seem to get out of your head.

Today, finally, we knew what to do.

And we knew *where* to do it.

Tom said, "Here's how it's gonna go down. Will was the last of the Schoolers, and now that he's back, Cavanaugh's put her people ... lots of 'em ... outside every exit to Haven. She thinks we're trapped, and she's both wrong and right. Her people are waitin' for her order to start the attack, and we're pretty sure that order won't come before nightfall ... at least nine o'clock tonight. The gloves may be off, but that don't mean she wants to draw *too* much attention to what she's doin'. After all, the Corpses may control the cops, but they don't control the Army or the National Guard, either or both of which might come rollin' in if it looks like Philly's turned into a war zone.

"So she'll wait just a few more hours, and then come at us when it's dark.

"That gives us time ... to get ready."

I checked my watch. It was four forty-five. We had a

little over four hours.

The chief went on. "As of now, everybody's duties get changed. Hackers, you're gonna leave your computers. Elisha and y'all will be settin' up defenses at the western entrance. See Chuck Binelli 'bout that. Sammy, one o' your Chatters is gonna stay on the police scanners, in case something comes in. The rest report to Burt Moscova, who's takin' the lead at the northern entrance. Schoolers, see Katie at the southern entrance. Those three are the captains for however long this fight lasts. Listen to 'em. They know what to do.

"Alex Bobson and the Monkeys will be supplyin' the raw materials y'all will need.

"The Brains'll be settin' up some special little tricks we got in mind. They're also workin' on a brand new weapon that Will brought back today ... somethin' that might give us a bit more of an edge. You'll get the info on that later from your captains.

"And the Moms, under Nick Rooney, are gonna make sure everybody's got food and water for the duration. Mrs. Ritter and Amy'll be on medic duty and might call on some of y'all to help with that, as necessary.

"Meanwhile, my sis is puttin' together a small team to sneak out of Haven. Their job is gonna be to reach Cavanaugh's Anchor Shard and unplug it. We just need to hold off the Corpses 'til then. Everybody clear?"

Everybody was clear.

"Cool," the chief said. "Then let's finally *end* this thing!"

There were cheers. We might all be scared. But we were soldiers.

And soldiers fight.

"I want Will," Sharyn said as the kids began filing out of the cafeteria.

"I'm coming, too," said Helene.

"You got your sister to worry over," Tom told her.

"Julie can help with the wounded. I'm coming." Then she looked at me as if she expected me to argue.

And smiled when I didn't.

"Anybody else?" Tom asked his sister.

Sharyn looked from him to me. Then she looked over at Alex Bobson.

The Monkey Boss wasn't my favorite guy in the world. But he always came through in a pinch.

This felt like a pinch to me.

The boy nodded grimly.

Sharyn said to her brother, "Maybe one more."

Five minutes later, Sharyn, Helene and I found Dave in the small bedroom he and I shared. He was sitting on his cot, staring at the wall and slowly stroking the healed rounded stump that used to be his right hand. Though his blood had been replenished, thanks to the Anchor Shard, he still looked pale.

I tried to tell myself it was the candlelight.

He looked up as the three of us came in.

"Hey, Hot Dog!" Sharyn said with a forced brightness that didn't fool anybody.

He didn't reply.

"Does it hurt?" Helene asked.

The Burgermeister shook his head.

I sat down on the cot across from him. He looked at me. Then he said, "I'm a cripple."

"No, you're not!" Helene snapped.

"No way!" Sharyn exclaimed.

"Yeah, you are," I said.

The girls glared at me like I'd just sprouted horns and a tail.

I ignored them, keeping my eyes on Dave and—

more importantly—*his* eyes on *mine*. It was a trick I'd learned from Tom. "You lost your hand," I told him. "It's gone and it's not coming back. It sucks, but it happened, and it means your life's not ever gonna be what it used to be. Your job now is to get right with that ... and find a way to keep going."

His eyes actually welled up. I could count on less than five fingers how many times I'd seen Dave Burger cry. The number was sure as heck a lot smaller than my own.

"I don't know if I can, Will," he muttered.

I leaned closer. I didn't touch him. No supportive hand on the shoulder. He wouldn't have liked it. "You don't *have* to know if you can," I said. "Not yet. For now, you just gotta believe that *I* know you can. So does Helene. So does Sharyn."

His gaze flicked up to the girls, who both nodded gravely. Then it came back to me. After several seconds, he said, "Know what the worst part is? I screwed up again. We'd set up this trap for Parker. Me, Sharyn, and Julie. We heard him trashing the kitchen, looking for you, so I went in there to lure him into the dining room. Then Sharyn was gonna do her thing with the sword. Sweet as you please."

"Solid plan," I said.

"Except I let him get the drop on me. If you hadn't been there, he'd have wasted me."

"That's ... not quite the way I remember it," I said.

But he wasn't listening. "Then, when you got me outta there and we ran into that stinkin' flying pigeon ... I wanted to bat it down, maybe stomp on it. But I blew *that*, too. And that's why *this* happened!" He held up his right stump.

"It happened," I said evenly. "'Cause you put your

hand up to keep that *Malite* from chewing my face off."

He didn't look convinced.

As I watched, he tried to bury his face in his hands. Except he no longer had hands, not two of them anyway, and all he managed to do was poke himself with the stump. His huge shoulders sagged.

Sharyn said, "We're gonna sneak out and get the Anchor Shard. We're gonna end the war."

He didn't reply.

"And we want you to come with."

That made him look up in surprise. "Me?"

"Yeah. You."

"But I can't fight. I can't even write my own name!"

Sharyn replied, "Well, maybe I got an idea 'bout that."

She motioned to someone in the corridor. After a moment, Alex appeared. The Monkey Boss looked as grim as ever, and in his hands was some kind of bundle, wrapped in an oily cloth. "Hey," he said to Dave.

"Hey," Dave said back.

"Sucks about the hand."

"Thanks," Dave said.

It was the warmest conversation the two of them had ever had.

Dave nodded at the bundle. "What's that?"

Alex squeezed past Helene and sat on the bunk beside the Burgermeister. "Sharyn had me put it together. At first, I thought it was nuts, but as I got into it … it turned out to be pretty simple."

"Show it to him," Sharyn said.

So Alex placed the bundle in his lap and opened the cloth.

It was a pickaxe.

Or, more accurately, it was the head of a pickaxe.

The blades were hard iron, the points sharp. One went one way and one went the other, both slightly curved. It looked a little like a funky letter "T", maybe eighteen inches across.

Except it had no handle. Instead, there were two thick leather straps and some kind of harness.

"What the hell am I supposed to do with that?" Dave asked, scowling.

"Hold your arm out straight," Alex told him.

The Burgermeister did so, the palm of his left hand facing the floor.

Sharyn sighed. "Your *other* arm, doofus."

Without comment, Dave lowered his left arm and raised his right. The stump caught the candlelight. It wasn't smooth or round, as you might expect, but puckered, almost like the face of a fish.

I'm sorry, Dave.

"Yeah?" he said sourly. "So?"

"Hold still," Alex remarked. Then, leaning close, he fitted the head of the pickaxe over the stump and ran the leather straps along the Burgermeister's thick forearm. Next, he fitted the harness just above the elbow and cinched it tight before sitting back to check his work.

Dave looked at it blankly.

Now, instead of a right hand, he had a wicked pickaxe.

"What am I supposed to do with this?" he asked.

Sharyn rolled her eyes. "Pick your nose."

Helene said, "We're thinking you should spend a few hours practicing with it. Then you should come with us tonight and see if you can plant it in the foreheads of a few deaders."

The Burgermeister hefted his new, weird appendage. "Feels a little heavy."

"A *little* heavy?" Alex remarked. "I can't think of

anyone else at Haven who could possibly use it!"

"He can," I said.

"Maybe," Dave added. Then he said it again, more thoughtfully, this time, "Maybe."

Was there just the tiniest hint of a smile? No, probably not. You don't lose a hand and then start smiling a couple hours later. But at least the despair seemed to be gone, for now.

"Thanks," he said to Alex.

"No sweat," the Monkey Boss replied. Then, as was his way, he left the room. No goodbyes. No "see you laters." Sharyn slapped him on the back as he passed, a gesture that he didn't even seem to notice.

Then she turned back to the Burgermeister. "I found a place for you to do some practicing. But somethin' tells me you're gonna take to that like a duck to water."

Dave considered, holding up the pickaxe and turning it slowly, so that its twin spikes caught the candlelight.

After a few seconds, he remarked, "Well, I guess the right thing to say in this situation would be … 'Groovy.'"

I think it's a movie reference.

CHAPTER 31
VISITOR FROM BEYOND

Lilith

City Hall emptied on weekdays after six o'clock. The nine-to-fivers all went home and the only people left in the mammoth building were janitors, a few security staff, a handful of late workers—

—and the mayor.

He hadn't been mayor long. His predecessor had resigned under a cloud of scandal, forcing the city to hold a special election to replace their disgraced leader. Originally, the Corpses had slated Kenny Booth to win Philadelphia's top seat. But that hadn't happened. Instead, Kenny Booth had exploded on camera, a mystery that the adult human world still hadn't solved.

And the mayor's office went to someone else.

A human.

A particularly foolish one.

Lilith Cavanaugh entered the building discreetly, dressed in a pantsuit, dark glasses, and a wide-brimmed hat that covered most of her face. Lilith didn't like hats.

The hair of her hosts fell out quickly enough as it was. But she needed to avoid being recognized.

None of her minions were with her. After all, what did she have to fear, really? The Undertakers were bottled up in their hole deep below this very building, every exit guarded. With them out of the picture, the city was, for all intents and purposes, *hers*.

Except Parker is destroyed.

Word had reached her only hours ago. Somehow, Dillin and the Ritter boy had managed to defeat a Special. That, by itself, was troubling. But even more disturbing, the *Malites* that she'd gone to such lengths to bring across the Void were destroyed as well. Her intention had been to use them as the vanguard of the attack on Haven, wedges to break through whatever defenses those whelps had managed to erect.

Now, that advantage was gone.

But I still have Cole. And, more importantly, I have might. We outnumber the Undertakers five to one.

And wars, the Queen knew, were *always* won by numbers.

Somewhat comforted, she climbed one the building's sweeping staircases to the second floor.

No one was around. Somewhere in the distance, she could hear the hum of a floor polisher, but otherwise all was quiet.

Lilith walked, her high heels clicking along the tile floor, to Room 215.

Double wooden doors greeted her with the words:

OFFICE OF THE MAYOR

She stepped inside.

"Excuse me," the woman behind the desk said, crisply

and with more than a little indignation. "Can I help you? It's after hours."

Her name was Sarah. She was a thirty-something brunette with a healthy, well-maintained body, and she had served as the mayor's personal assistant since he'd been just a city councilman. In a vague way, Lilith admired that level of loyalty. Each of her own assistants had failed her to some degree, and none had lasted more than a few months.

Or, in some cases, a few *hours*.

"Hello, Sarah," she said, shutting the door and removing her hat.

The woman's eyes went wide. "Ms. Cavanaugh?" she gasped. "But, you—"

That was as far as she got before the Queen pounced on her.

Two minutes later, now wearing Sarah's healthy, well-maintained cadaver as her new host, Lilith Cavanaugh opened the door to the mayor's private office.

It was larger than her own had been, and better furnished. Lots of dark wood furniture and high, sunlit windows. The desk looked big enough to land a plane on.

And the owner of that desk currently sat behind it.

"Hello, Frank," Lilith said.

The mayor looked up from his reading. He was a big man, with impeccably groomed pepper-gray hair crowning a square head set atop a thick neck and broad shoulders. His gut was substantial and his legs short and dense, like tree trunks. On his nose he wore a pair of reading glasses, which he now removed as he slowly rose to his feet.

"Wha ..." he began.

"Eloquent as always," the Queen remarked.

"Lilith?"

"That's right, Frank."

He scowled, stood, and came around his desk, stumbled really, since his attention was so fixated on the woman in his doorway that he didn't watch where he was going. "Lilith?" he said again.

She came a few steps into his office.

"You're dead," he told her, coming close.

"Yes, I am," she replied.

Then she backhanded him.

The blow knocked the mayor completely off his feet, up and then down. His big body hit the carpeted floor like a sack of flour. Groaning, he wiped at a trickle of blood near the corner of his mouth, his eyes wide with shock.

Lilith reached down, grabbed him by his thick upper arm, hauled him to his feet, and threw him into a nearby bookcase.

Unread titles rained down as the mayor once again collapsed in a heap.

"Sarah," he moaned. "Where's Sarah?"

She knelt in front of him. "Look at me, Frank." He looked at her. "You want to know where Sarah is?"

He blinked dully. Didn't nod. Didn't shake his head. Two hits and already the fight was out of him. Pathetic.

"She's right here, Frank," the Queen told him.

Then she dropped her cover.

Sarah hadn't been dead long. Only a few minutes, so Lilith supposed the wonderful impact of revealing herself to a human was—somewhat diminished. Still, the mayor gasped in horror, perhaps more from the fact that, to his eyes, one woman had just transformed into another, than from the realization that the transformee was no longer living.

"You find that interesting, Frank?" she asked. "Let

me show you something else."

Straightening, she went through the doorway into the outer office and returned moments later dragging a cadaver—her old host.

"Watch this," she told the fallen man.

Then she transferred from Sarah back into her old host.

As Sarah's now empty body collapsed to the floor, the rotting cadaver beside it sat up and grinned at the mayor.

"See me," Lilith said.

And, this time, the mayor *screamed*.

Yes. That's better.

"What are you?" he exclaimed, pulling himself up into a sitting position and scrambling away on his buttocks until his back pressed against the shelving. "What in God's name, are you?"

The Queen nodded, satisfied.

Standing, she fetched two of the leather guest chairs and set them up in front of the ruined bookcase, one facing the other. Then, ignoring his blubbering, she yanked the mayor off the floor and deposited his butt into one of the chairs. The other she took for herself.

"I am *Malum*," she told him conversationally. "A member of a conqueror race. Its absolute ruler, in fact."

"W—what?"

He was in a terrible state. His tailored suit had been torn in the struggle. His face was bruised, his lip swollen, and his perfect hair a sweaty tangle.

"Now, Frank," she said. "Try to keep up. I knocked you around a little bit specifically so we could get past the denial part as quickly as possible. I am *Malum*. I am not of this world. I am alien. Get over it."

He looked about to protest, maybe say something absurdly human like "You're crazy!" or "Is this some kind of a joke?" If he did, she would hurt him some more.

But he didn't.

Instead, he coughed, spit a little blood into his palm, looked at it, and wiped it on his pants. Then he asked, "What do you want?"

"Good. A sensible question," she told him. "What I want, in a nutshell, is your complete and utter obedience. And since we both know that obedience wouldn't be forthcoming based on friendship or professional courtesy, I've decided to go with fear. You *do* fear me now, don't you, Frank?"

He visibly paled. Then he nodded.

"I'm sorry, Frank," she said, leaning closer, giving him a really good look at her rotting face. "I didn't catch that."

"I ... fear ... you."

"One more time? This body's ears aren't what they once were." Then, just to drive home the point, she casually tore off her only remaining ear and tossed it into his lap.

For a second, she thought he might faint.

He didn't. He didn't even knock away the torn bit of flesh. He just stared at it as if it might catch fire. Then, more loudly: "I fear you!"

"I'm happy to hear it," the Queen said. "That fear might just keep you alive. However, now I have to ask you for a moment's patience. I don't like this old host."

She looked over at Sarah's dead body, which still lay on the floor where she'd left it. So strong and fresh, perfect for the evening's *activities*.

Lilith transferred back into it. Then, as the mayor watched, trembling and speechless, she stood and yanked her old host—slumped, rotted, and missing both ears— off the chair, dropping it to the carpet.

She sat back down. "There. Much better. Now, we

have a few things to discuss. But before we do, there's something I need you to grasp. No, more than grasp, I need you to accept it as absolute, unshakeable truth. Clear?"

"Clear," he said.

She nodded. "The truth is this: I am not alone, Frank. Quite the contrary. There are many thousands of us now. Even I couldn't tell you exactly how many ... more are coming in every day. Thousands, Frank. And every last one of them reports to me. At my command, they've taken positions throughout this city. They're policemen. They drive buses. They run shoe stores. They panhandle in the streets. Many work in this very building. You know quite a few of them, in fact."

The mayor shuddered. "I do? I've never—"

"Seen one?" she finished for him. "We disguise ourselves. We don't usually show Earth people what we really look like ... what we really are."

"Then why are you showing *me*?" he wailed, sounding like an angry toddler.

"Because the rules have changed. Until recently, we were about secrecy, about hiding in the shadows. My people are conquerors, but we prefer subtle, quiet conquest. Unfortunately, that's no longer possible. So I've decided it's time for conquest of a more direct and decisive nature. You're my first step toward making that happen."

The mayor looked smaller, as if the fear had shrunken him inside his expensive suit. Lilith loved the look on his face. Terror was so *delicious*. "I don't understand," he whimpered.

"Then I'll be more specific. To launch this new, more direct phase in the conquest of your world, my first task is to make absolutely sure of your compliance. Well, either that, or kill you—"

"No …" he begged.

She held up one of Sarah's fingers. "Interrupt me again, Frank … and I'll tear out your throat, much the way I did to Sarah. You can see my neck, can't you?" She tilted back her head to show him the damage. His secretary had died quietly, but she'd died *hard*.

"I see it," he said, sounding even smaller.

"Good. That gives me hope that my first task will be successful. Now, as for my second task, I want you to stop questioning the police exercises going on around City Hall this evening."

The mayor looked at her with watery eyes. "But…so many! I don't see the point—

She was out of her chair and on him in a blur, grabbing him by his thick neck and lifting him off his feet. "You don't *need* to see the point!" she hissed.

Then she carried him effortlessly to the nearest window and gazed out at the clueless humanity moving about in the courtyard below. "I went out a window like this two months ago," she said. "On that day, Lilith Cavanaugh died … but the Queen of the *Malum* lived on. However, if I throw *you* out, I don't think you'll be coming back. Would you agree with that, Frank?"

"Please …" he gasped, his face reddening.

"Of course, this is only two floors. I fell from six. To even things out, I'll have to throw you out and down, head first. Any witness might think you were trying to fly! Rather like that ridiculous comic book fellow in the red and blue pajamas. What's his name? Superman?"

He didn't reply. He just struggled uselessly.

"Yes, Superman," she said. "Are you Superman, Frank?"

"No …"

"So, you're just a normal human?"

"Y—yes …"

"Breakable? Fragile?"

"Yes … please …"

She threw him across the room, casually, using little more than a flick of her wrist.

The mayor hit the wall beside his office door and crumpled to the carpet. Lilith studied him for a long moment. Then she returned to her chair and sat down, her back to him. "Come and sit, Frank. Now."

He came. He had to crawl to do it, but he came. A stronger man might have run for it. A stronger man would have failed, of course, but he might have tried. The fact that the mayor didn't, proved to the Queen that she could use him, at least for a while.

He reached the chair and climbed feebly into it.

"Good, Frank," she told him. "Now, where were we? Oh yes. You're not going to question tonight's police exercises anymore, are you?"

"No."

"Instead, here's what you *are* going to do. You're going to call the governor and bring him to Philadelphia. You will tell him there's an emergency, one that you are unable to handle on your own, and one that requires state-level attention. I don't care what you say, but you *will* bring him here, to this office. Do you understand, Frank?"

"Yes?"

"Any questions or concerns?" She glared at him.

"No."

"Good. Make the phone call. Do exactly what I've told you and you'll survive the night. Betray me in even the slightest way, and I'll peel the skin from your bones. Clear?"

"Clear."

"Good. Do it now."

As he staggered to his desk to obey, Lilith stepped into the outer office and raised her own cell phone to her dead lips. Her new assistant picked up—Randell or Robert or something. *"Yes, Ms. Cavanaugh?"* he asked.

"Remind me of your name again?"

"Richard, ma'am."

Richard. Yes.

"Richard, the mayor is making the call. We'll have the governor here tonight. I want you to bring the *Pelligog* to me now. Do it personally. I'll remain on site to assure the mayor's continued cooperation."

"Yes, Ms. Cavanaugh. You asked to be reminded about your upcoming address to the attack force."

"I can do that from here."

"As you say, Ms. Cavanaugh. But may I ask a question?"

The Queen paused. "Be careful," she told him.

He said, *"Why not use the Pelligog on the mayor just now?"*

It was, she thought, a fair question. She could indeed have gone into the mayor's office, overpowered him, and then planted one of the mind-bending creatures at the base of his spine.

"Because, Richard, terrorizing him was much more fun."

She broke the connection.

Richard had some sense.

He might actually last a week or two.

CHAPTER 32
COMMUNION

Tom

Tom moved through Haven.

It was seven o'clock. Two hours before the earliest estimate for the Corpses' attack. Two hours since he'd given his speech in front of almost three hundred scared, brave teenagers, plus one terrified mom and one confused six-year-old.

His army.

Karl's army.

Except that it had all gotten so much—*bigger*—since Karl had died.

Now, Tom went from worksite to worksite, checking on progress, making suggestions, and, when necessary, bolstering courage. He hadn't fudged the numbers. His best guess *was* fifteen hundred deaders rapping on their doors as soon as it turned dark.

A big number.

Too *big*.

He stopped outside the Shrine, the room reserved for,

and dedicated to, the memory of Karl Ritter, founder of the Undertakers. Karl had been the first of them to die. Well, that wasn't quite true. Seers had been lost. Plenty of them. But they hadn't been Undertakers, at least not yet. Until Kenny Booth had murdered Will's father, no one calling themselves by the name "Undertaker" had been killed.

Ain't that way anymore, though.

Tom slipped through the tattered curtain. The room was dark. A candle and lighter sat on a nearby table, but he ignored them. He knew, down to the inch, where every stick of furniture stood and where every picture hung. He knew this place better than he knew his own bedroom.

After all, the only thing he ever did in his bedroom was sleep.

Here he—what? Prayed? No, that wasn't the right word. "Communed" might be better.

He *communed* with Karl or, more accurately, with his memory.

"Chief," Tom said in the darkness. Back in the day he'd called Karl by that title, so much so that it still secretly sounded a little odd when others used it on *him*. "We're at the end."

The darkness, of course, didn't reply.

Tom said, "They know where we are. And *we* know how to pull their plug. So it's come down to a race. And, like I always figured, it's come down to *Will*."

He stepped deeper into the darkness, sensing more than seeing Karl's old cot and the even older footlocker that the former chief had picked up at an Army/Navy surplus store. On the wall were photos, exactly twenty-three of them, all taken in the early days of the war—or before. Back then it had seemed like a crazy adventure, not quite real. Of course, back then, he and Sharyn had been fourteen instead of seventeen, and there'd been a "grown-up" to take care of things.

For a time, Tom had hated Karl for dying—a grim fact that he rarely admitted to himself, and *never* to anyone else. Part of the grief process, he supposed. But that hadn't made the feeling seem any less real, or any less poisonous.

It had taken him a long time to get past that.

"Your son. He's ..." Then he shrugged. "There ain't no words. He's the bravest man I ever knew, and that's sayin' somethin'. I don't figure he's had a selfish thought since he came to us. Everything he does, he does for someone else. Sometimes, it pisses me off, or used to, back when he first showed up. He does the kinda things *you* used to do, charges into trouble without thinking, without a plan. Except, somehow, he always gets out of it again. Maybe he's saved by somebody, or maybe he's visited by that lady in the white room, whoever *she* is. Or maybe he squeezes by on luck or brains. But, one way or another, he *always* survives.

"Which is why ... maybe ... we got hope tonight.

"Officially, it's Sharyn's show. She's the Angel Boss. She's in charge. But she knows as sure as I do that ... once again ... it'll come down to Will. And, when it does, I figure she's smart enough to get outta his way."

Tom rubbed his face with hands he could barely see.

"And all the while, I'll be here, in Haven, where I belong. Our only job is gonna be to buy time. To keep out the Corpses and stay alive long enough for Sharyn's crew to pull the plug and send every single one of those alien wormbags to wherever I sent Gardner this afternoon.

"Thing is: it ain't gonna be easy, and while we're doin' it, some kids are gonna die. Kids who shouldn't be here.

Kids who should be in school, or cuttin' school, or doin' chores, or ditchin' chores, or playin' ball, or sittin' in front of the tube with a video game controller in their hands. Courageous kids who only wanna go home.

"Some o' them are gonna die tonight … buyin' time.

"So, listen … I ain't never asked this before. But if you got any pull, any at all, with whatever Powers-That-Be … I could really use a break. It don't gotta be a *big* break. I ain't expectin' armies of winged angels to come swoopin' in with blazing swords. Just, you know, a *small* break, maybe a few minutes at the right time. That'd be enough. I could work with that."

He fell silent then, wondering if it would be appropriate to finish up with an "amen."

Probably not.

Someone said, "I'm sorry."

And Tom Jefferson, Chief of the Undertakers, almost jumped out of his skin.

He spun toward the cot, where one of the shadows *moved*.

Then a flame lit the darkness, making him wince.

The candle began to glow—

—and Jillian looked up at him.

Tom said, "I didn't know you were here."

"Yeah," she replied. "I kinda got that."

His heart was hammering. With an effort, he steadied it. For a few moments, bitter embarrassment filled the back of his throat like bile. But then he pushed the useless feeling away. He had more important things to worry over.

"Saw you at the briefing," Tom said. "But you split right after."

"I didn't belong there," the girl told him. From the way the flickering candlelight caught her eyes, he could see she'd been crying. "I'm not an Undertaker."

Tom didn't reply. At that moment, he didn't trust himself enough.

But his silence seemed to hurt her more than his words might have. "I was lying from almost the minute I came to this place."

Again, he didn't reply—this time because he honestly had no reply. What she'd said was true.

She added, "But I really am sorry."

He could have told her: "So what?" Because of what she'd done, the Corpses were out there, right now, waiting for the signal to attack. Because of what she'd done, kids were going to die. Who cared if she was "sorry?" What did that help, besides her conscience?

But, instead he said, "You made a bad call. You trusted Mitchum and he trusted the wrong people."

"It wasn't supposed to be like this," she said, sobbing between sentences. "He was supposed to *help* us. Save us. We're kids. He's an adult. Isn't that the way it's supposed to work?"

Tom sighed. Maybe it *was* the way things were supposed to work. But he'd been living with the Sight and its crazy rules for so long that he couldn't really imagine the world any other way.

She said, "Nice trick, pretending you'd lost your Eyes. It fooled me."

"That was kinda the point."

"How did you know that I was ... um ... wasn't ..." Her words trailed off.

"I didn't," he admitted. "Not at first. But the way y'all got outta D.C. made no sense. The Feds *had* you. They had you and Will and Helene and they just let you go. That don't happen. With all that went down in the Capitol that day, you three shoulda been interrogated for *weeks*! The only way it worked was if somebody down there, somebody *big*, decided to *let* you go. I didn't know who and I didn't know why, and the notion of a spy didn't hit me 'til later. But when it did, I figured ... of the three ... it had to be you."

"Why?"

"'Cause I've known Helene for years. And Will's ... Will. He'd cut off his own head before he'd turn traitor. But you were ... a stranger."

"A stranger! What about all that time growing up together in Mr. P's dojo?"

"Another life," Tom said. "A long time ago."

More tears.

He almost went to her. He almost dropped the whole "strong detached leader" thing, put his arms around the girl, and finally said all those things he'd wanted to say from the minute she'd come back into his life. He almost told her how his heartbeats would kick into high gear whenever she walked into a room, so much so that he'd actually gone to Susan about it, worried that something might be physically wrong with him. But Haven's medic had only smiled knowingly, and told him he was fine.

"Why are you here, Jillian? In this room, I mean. You never knew Karl. I get why you hid out, but why here?"

She shrugged. "It's quiet. Almost nobody comes in here but you, not even the Ritters. Besides, it made me feel ... I dunno ... closer."

"Closer to what?"

"Closer to you, I guess."

You betrayed us, he thought. *Maybe you did it innocently, but you did it.*

So ... given that ... how can I tell you what I'm feeling? I can't.

"Jill ..."

"I know you hate me!" she exclaimed. "And I don't blame you. I don't expect to be forgiven. But I want you to understand ... really understand ... how sorry I am. And I want you to believe that when the fighting starts, I'll be right there, in the middle of it. I'll die to defend Haven. I will!"

"I *do* believe that." He said.

She'd done what she thought was right. It hadn't been her decision to make, but she'd done it with what Karl used to call a "true heart." Problem was: plenty of the world's evils were committed by folks with "true hearts."

But I ain't in the judgment business. Leastwise, not tonight.

"Then get yourself over to the southern entrance and report to Katie. That's where your parkour will work best, I figure."

"Does Katie know about ... me?"

"No," Tom told her. "Just Helene and me. I ain't even told Sharyn or Will. They got enough to deal with."

She looked relieved—*very* relieved. "Thanks."

"I didn't do it for you."

"What about Sharyn and her team?" she asked. "How are you going to sneak them past the Corpses?"

Tom studied her, wondering if she should tell her.

Then he did. "There's an old maintenance door, one that leads up into City Hall. It would be hard ... very hard ... to get a lot of people out of Haven that way. But a small group can manage it."

"Maintenance door," Jillian echoed.

"Yeah."

"I didn't know about that," she said.

"Which means the Corpses don't know about it either," he replied. "Probably."

She studied him for a long moment. The silence

between them felt heavy—painful.

Wordlessly, Jillian stood up and left the Shrine.

Tom stayed where he was for a few minutes, now truly alone in the dark.

As he was about to leave, his satellite phone rang. Ramirez.

"What's up, Hugo?" Tom asked.

"I want to help."

"You can't. You know that."

"Mitchum's offered to contact the state police. Maybe the governor's office."

"And tell 'em ... what? No one's gonna believe him, leastwise not in time."

"Tom ... this is my fault."

"That's what Jillian just said. Thing is: it don't matter. Not now. It is what it is and we gotta deal with it."

"There has to be something I can do!"

Tom considered for a few moments. "Can you get your hands on some explosives?"

There was a long pause. *"What kind of explosives?"*

Tom told him what kind of explosives.

"Yes," the F.B.I. agent replied. *"I can manage that. Just tell me when and where."*

Tom did.

"It's a good idea."

"It's a stall. All of this ain't nothing but a stall. This kind of fightin' ain't about *beating* your enemy. It's 'bout *outlasting* him. Let me know when you're in position. I'll call you when it's time to push the button."

"Chief ... thanks. And good luck."

We'll need it, Tom thought.

CHAPTER 33
HAUNTED PLACES

We were in the brain factory, and Steve Moscova was showing us the impossible.

"Tell me again," Dave said. He tried to raise his right hand to point, but ended up pointing with the blunt head of his pickaxe since, of course, his right hand was gone. He flushed and lowered his arm again. "What is *that*?"

The "that" was a black, faintly shimmering hole, about four feet wide, which floated in midair near the Brain Factory's back wall. In front of it, maybe six feet away, the Anchor Shard sat clamped to a metal table and wired to a car battery. The light that pulsed inside the weird crystal seemed to be directed at the hole—like the beam of an alien flashlight.

Making the hole.

Steve looked impatient. "I *told* you! It's a bi-dimensional singularity!"

"Yeah," Helene replied. "But what the heck is *that*?"

The Brain Boss sighed. Steve had been more patient when I'd first met him. Ian's death had changed the kid, hardened him, left him angrier—but no less smart.

That last part was good. We needed smart right now.

"It's a doorway," he explained. "A tear in the fabric of spacetime."

"Which?" Dave asked.

"Which what?"

"Space *or* time?" the big kid exclaimed.

"Both, of course!" Steve snapped.

"That makes no sense!" Dave insisted.

Steve's face darkened. "It makes *perfect* sense! They're parts of the same thing!"

The Burgermeister glowered. "How can space and time be the same thing? There're satellites in orbit *and* I got a wristwatch. My wristwatch ain't in space and the satellites ain't wrapped around my arm!"

The Brain Boss looked as if he wanted to launch himself at the much larger boy. I stepped between them, trying to be casual about it. "A doorway to the *Malum* homeworld?" I asked Steve.

"No. Well, I don't know. Not for sure. This technology is *way* beyond us. But I *think* the Anchor Shard opens the door to an empty space between universes."

"Void," I said. "Dillin called it a 'Void.'"

"Good name for it," Steve replied.

"Can we go through it?" Sharyn asked.

Steve lowered his eyes. "I wanted to try that. But Tom wouldn't let me, even though, based on some test I've run, there *is* air ... and gravity ... beyond the doorway."

"Rift," I said. "The Corpses call it the Rift."

"Okay ... Rift. But, so far, there doesn't seem to be solid ground over there. At least none that I've been able to find without actually ... you know ... poking my head through and looking."

"*Don't* poke your head through and look," Sharyn told him firmly.

We could all see how much the Brain Boss wanted to.

"We can't lose you," Helene said. "Not now."

"Not ever," Sharyn added.

Steve frowned. Then he nodded.

"So, what's the bottom line?" I asked.

He said, "Bottom line: we might fall to our deaths … or fall forever … the minute we stepped through."

"Then how do the deaders cross it?" the Angel Boss asked.

"As energy," Helene said. "They come over as those person-sized lumps of hate we sometimes see when we kill one. That's why they need the dead bodies."

"But from where?" Sharyn pressed. "If all this crystal thingy does is open a Rift, then there's gotta be *another* Rift, right? On *their* side of the … Void … in-between?"

"It's a solid hypothesis," Steve told her. "But I have no idea how it works."

"Then it don't do us no good!" Dave growled.

I expected Steve to get pissed off again, but he didn't. "Well, that would be true … if going *through* the Rift was what we were after. But it's not."

"Yeah, I dig," Sharyn said. "All we gotta do is find this Rift and unplug the crystal that's juicin' it."

"We don't know where it is!" Dave complained.

"Yes, we do," I said. "The Zombie Prince told me."

They all threw blank stares my way.

I said, "Um … Bob Dillin, the principal at Meadowlark Intermediate."

"Oh," Sharyn said.

But the blank stares kept coming. Most of them knew my morning's story, parts of it, anyway. But the concept of a "friendly" Corpse just didn't compute. It was like trying to picture Santa Claus scuba diving.

Go on: try it.

"Where's it at, little bro?" Sharyn asked.

"Fort Mifflin," I replied.

"Mifflin!" the Burgermeister exclaimed. He sounded as if the very idea offended him.

"Kinda where it all started," added Helene. Of all of them, she was the only one present who'd already known; she'd been in the Infirmary when I'd told Tom.

"It *is* where it all started," I said. "According to Dillin, it's where the Corpses first punched through into our world. *Every* deader that's come across the Void since then, has come through Mifflin. Every single one!"

"Why there?" Sharyn asked. "What's so special about an old Revolutionary War Fort in a swamp? It makes no sense!"

"Actually," replied Steve. "It *does* ... in a weird way. You all remember where we found *this* Anchor Shard?"

"Eastern State Penitentiary," Dave replied. "And 'we' didn't find it. Will and Helene and me found it. *You* weren't there."

"What's your problem?" Steve demanded. "Why are you riding me?"

"'Cause you're doin' what you always do! Talkin' down to everybody!"

Steve's face turned purple. "Is it my fault that you've got the intellect of a pot-bellied pig?"

The Burgermeister started forward. Steve started forward. I still stood between them, and put a hand on each of their chests.

"What're you both doing?" I demanded. "We got a little over an hour before it gets dark." I whirled on Dave. "I know you're pissed at the world! I can't even pretend to get what you're dealing with right now. But you gotta remember who the enemy is!" I pointed at the Brain Boss. "We *need* this dude, alive and conscious!" The Burgermeister scowled, but he backed away. I whirled on Steve. "And *you*? What are you thinking? He's twice your size and he's got a pickaxe for a right hand!"

Steve also scowled.

But then he backed away, too.

For half-a-minute, nobody said anything. Everyone looked at the floor, except for Sharyn, who was looking at me with this strange little smile on her face. It made me uncomfortable, so I said, "Clock's ticking, guys."

The Burgermeister and Steve both raised their heads. They faced one another.

Dave grumbled, "I'm ... in a crappy mood."

"Yeah," the Brain Boss replied. "Me, too."

"At least you still got both your hands!" the bigger kid snapped.

I almost stepped forward again. But then Steve said, "Yeah. I just don't have my best friend."

Ian.

You know, it had never occurred to me that Steve and Ian were best friends. It had never occurred to me that either of them even *had* a best friend.

The Burgermeister's face went slack with surprise. Then he said in an uncharacteristically gentle voice, "Man, I'm sorry."

"So am I," Steve told him. "About Ian *and* about you."

"Um ... can we get back to it?" Helene asked, clearing her throat.

"Right," Steve said. He blew out a long sigh. "Mifflin and Eastern State have something common."

"What's that?" Sharyn asked.

"They're both associated with paranormal activity."

Dave blinked. "Paranormal—"

"Ghosts," Helene translated.

And they were right. Both places had been on *Ghost Hunters* at least once. Fort Mifflin and Eastern State Penitentiary were considered to be the two most haunted places in Philly. Both of them offered Halloween events. Mifflin led you on a tour and told you ghost stories, while Eastern State staged a huge, walk-through haunted house, complete with black lights and guys in horror makeup popping out and scaring you.

At least, they *used* to—before the deaders took over both landmarks and closed them to the public.

"Now, I'm not saying I believe in ghosts," Steve remarked. "I'm just saying that the Corpses seem drawn to places that have that reputation. Maybe ... well, maybe the fabric of spacetime is a little *thinner* there, making it easier to cross the Void. In fact, maybe *that's* why we can't actually link up with the *Malum* home world. Haven's spacetime walls are too thick."

I said, "Dillin told me the Anchor Shard at Fort Mifflin is inside something called the 'East Magazine.' It's where they used to keep the gunpowder back in the old days. It's mostly underground. I've been there ... during a school trip. It's like a brick cave, with a high curved ceiling. Used to be all one big room, but Dillin told me that by the time he came through the Rift, a cinderblock wall had been built, floor to ceiling, that cuts the room in two. He said the only way in or out is through a heavy steel door."

"Cavanaugh's locked down her crib," Sharyn said.

"Sounds like it," Helene agreed.

I continued, "The Corpse's Anchor Shard is inside that new room, hooked up to ... not one ... but *three* car batteries, which Dillin told me are constantly being changed. No matter what happens, the Queen can't let the Rift close. Ever."

Steve said, "Because, if it does, then the Corpses all die."

"So ... we pull the plug," I added. "And the war's over."

"Simple!" Sharyn said.

Then Steve remarked, "Except for one tiny problem: pulling the plug will kill you."

We all looked at him.

"Remember what happened to Ian? He pulled the plug on our Anchor Shard and the crystal immediately released all its stored up energy. I've since repeated the experiment more than once, *very* carefully. Tom was even in here the last time. It's always the same. The blast radius of the released energy increases exponentially based on the length of time that the crystal is hooked up to an electrical power source."

"Exponentially?" the Burgermeister asked.

"A lot," I told him. Honestly, it was a guess.

"Oh," he muttered.

"So ... even if we get near enough to this thing to unplug it," Sharyn said. "We'll get wasted doin' it?"

The Brain Boss nodded. "The wall and door will block the energy. But you'd never get out the door and close it behind you fast enough to outrun the wave. Everything organic in the room would be vaporized."

"And we're all organic," Helene muttered.

Then Steve said, "Unless, of course, you have a way to *delay* the unplugging ..."

Sharyn's grin was back. "What you got, genius?"

For the first time in a while, the boy smiled. Then he lifted a towel that had been draped over something on a nearby lab table. Under it stood a gadget, about a foot high, with a broad metal base and two tall metal posts with some kind of slanted blade wedged between them.

We all examined it.

"I call it a McDonald," Steve said proudly.

After Ian McDonald, I thought. *Nice.*

"Looks like a guillotine," remarked Helene.

"Basically, it *is*," Steve replied. "You fit it over the positive cable closest to the shard. Then you flip this switch here and the device waits exactly ten seconds before dropping the blade. It's spring-loaded, so it drops fast and hard enough to slice right through insulation and copper wiring. The blade is nonconductive, so cutting the cable breaks the circuit and kills all power to the crystal."

"And closes the Rift," I said.

"And kills the Corpses," Helene said. "All of them."

"We'll spend the next half-hour practicing with it using our own Anchor Shard," Steve said. "You'll need to know how to assemble it and how to hit the switch and then reach a safe distance before it activates. I've already tried it myself a half-dozen times. It works."

Sharyn laughed. "You've outdone yourself with this latest invention!"

But the Brain Boss wasn't laughing. He was looking at the machine he'd designed, and named after his dead best friend. "I hope so," he said in a small voice. "Because if it works … it's my *last* invention."

CHAPTER 34
FINAL PREP

I went to see my family before we left.

Haven was a lot more crowded now than it had been when we'd first moved here last October. The ranks of the Undertakers had doubled, and finding room for them had been keeping the Monkeys busy for months.

But now all that was over. No more shoring up unused corridors in this forgotten subbasement. No more trapping and relocating feral cats. No more worries about ceiling collapses or moldy walls.

Tonight, one way or another, would be everyone's last night in this place.

Tonight, the Undertakers either won—or they died.

So, yeah, I went to see my family.

Their new digs weren't far from mine, and looked pretty much the same—but they weren't there. Instead, I headed for the Infirmary, where my mom had taken a break in her medic chores to tuck Emily into a small cot that she'd set up in one of the big room's far corners. It was eight-thirty, which was my little sister's bedtime.

"Now it might get noisy in here in a little bit," my mother told her. "But I want you to try to sleep."

"Okay, Mommy." Then, looking past her, she cried, "Will!"

Mom offered me a weak smile. She seemed tired. Fear will do that to you.

"Leaving?" she asked.

I nodded. Then, as my mother stood, I squeezed around her and sat down on the edge of Emily's cot.

My little sister looked up at me with those big eyes of hers.

"I'm scared," she said.

"I know," I said.

"The bad people are coming."

"They won't get in. Tom'll stop them." Then, after a little internal debate, I added, "And tomorrow, we'll be able to go home."

That made her smile. "I miss my dolls."

"I miss your dolls, too," I said.

She giggled. "You don't play with dolls!"

No, I don't. I don't "play" at all. Not anymore. Children play.

Soldiers fight.

"I miss watching *you* play with them," I told her.

She nodded. Then she hugged me—hard. I hugged her back—hard.

One of three things was going to happen in the few hours. One: Sharyn, Helene, Dave, and I would get to Fort Mifflin and use Steve's "McDonald" on the Corpses' Anchor Shard. Two: We'd die trying, and Haven would fall. Three: We'd fail but survive, and return here to find everyone we loved dead, and the war lost.

It was the last one that *really* terrified me.

I left Emily and followed my mother out into the hallway. There, she stood, hugging herself in the dank corridor, silently looking at me. I understood. I had no idea what to say, either.

Finally, she asked, "Are you ready?"

"As ready as I can be."

She nodded. "I feel like telling you not to go. I feel like that's the 'mom' thing to do. But, we're past all that, aren't we? Besides, it's not going to be any safer here."

"No, it's not," I said. "Listen, I've talked to Tom. If things get real bad, he can try to get you and Emily out the same way we're going. It'll be risky, but it's better'n nothing."

"He told me about it. And *I* told *him* that he can get Emily out that way, if need be. But I'm staying."

"Mom—"

"Will, we've all got our jobs to do tonight. I'm Haven's medic. I'm staying."

"Even if it means Emily ends up an orphan?"

"Even if," she said. Her expression was determined, but her eyes were moist and I could see the way she trembled.

"I'll end this," I told her. "I promise."

"I know you will," she replied, trying a smile. "You know … I'm *incredibly* proud of you."

"I'm incredibly proud of you, too."

I opened my arms and she came to me. Not quite crying. Neither one of us was crying. That might come later. For now, there was too much to do, too much to think about. Want to know how you keep going when things are at their worst? Well, for my part, the answer's simple: because you have to.

I hugged my mom, maybe for the last time.

Then I went to meet up with the others.

Haven was quiet. All those kids in those tight quarters, yet there was very little sound. Almost everyone was busy working on the fortifications. If I made my way to one of the three exits, I supposed I'd find things *very* noisy. Sawing and digging. Yelled questions and yelled answers. But here, in the empty places between those exit worksites, everything seemed still and hushed.

Tomb-like.

I poked my head into Helene's room, expecting to see her. She wasn't there. Instead, I found Julie sitting on her sister's bunk, wrapped in a blanket. When she looked up at me, I saw tears in her eyes.

A lot of that going around today.

"Hey, Will," she said, wiping her face with one hand. "Sorry."

"For what?"

She shook her head and didn't reply.

"I'm looking for Helene," I said.

"I know," the girl replied with a sniffle. "She told me to tell you she went on ahead, and that she'll meet you there."

Did she? I wonder what for.

"Listen," Julie said. "Before you go … can I talk to you for a minute?"

"Sure," I replied, stepping into the tiny room.

She stood up and met me, the blanket still wrapped around her thin shoulders. "It's been so busy today … that I never got the chance to really thank you."

That's what for, I thought.

"Just doing my job," I said. A pat answer. Almost snarky.

"That's what Helene said you'd say. But it's stupid."

"Stupid?" I asked, smiling.

"Yeah. Stupid. You risked your life for me. That's

more'n a job."

"Julie—"

"Shut up," she said, sounding so much like her sister that I almost laughed out loud. But then she rose up onto her toes and planted a kiss on my cheek. Not much. Almost bird-like, there and gone in an instant. Now I understood why they called them "pecks."

"Thank you, Will. Thank you for saving my life."

"You're welcome."

"Now get out of here," she said with a grin. "And do it again."

So I got out of there.

The unmarked rusted metal door stood down a corridor that, even in these crowded times, remained little used. Tom and Sharyn were already there. So were Helene and the Burgermeister. The four people who, outside my family, were the most important to me. That seemed *right* somehow. Fitting.

"Hey, Dude," Dave said as I approached.

"Hey," I said.

"You ready?" the chief asked me.

"Yeah," I replied.

Helene took my hand. "You see your mom and sister?"

"Yep."

"Did you see Julie?"

I gave her a look. "Yep."

She grinned and kissed me on the cheek, just like her sister had. Except Helene's kiss felt like more than just a peck. Hers made my stomach flipflop.

It's funny how some kisses can do that.

I think it depends on the kisser.

"Listen up," Tom announced. "It's nine o'clock, which means things'll start happening 'round here anytime now. I wish we could've sent y'all out before this, but nighttime's as much your friend as it is our enemy's. You'll need the darkness to get down to Mifflin and do what you gotta do. Keep your sat phones on you." He looked at me. "And *try* not to lose them."

Okay. Fair point.

He said. "But don't use 'em any more than you gotta. Way I see it, either this'll work or it won't. Either we'll be able to hold off the deaders long enough ... or we won't. Checkin' in on each other every ten minutes won't help nobody."

"We got this, bro," Sharyn said, smiling.

"I know you do."

"We'll be back before you know it," Dave said.

"And then we'll *all* go home," Helene added, sounding wistful. "At last. Really go home."

Sharyn shrugged. "I *am* home. Always was. But that don't mean I wouldn't mind some better digs. Maybe something in the sunshine."

"The burbs?" Dave asked.

"No way! I'm a city girl. Ain't never gonna mow no lawn!" Then she laughed her musical laugh again—and took the Burgermeister's remaining hand in hers.

Tom said, "I could tell y'all 'good luck,' I s'pose. But that don't seem quite right. Instead, let's go with an old one." He looked at each of us in turn before adding, "Godspeed."

"Godspeed," I told him back.

And with that, Tom opened the big metal door and ushered us through to—well—whatever came next.

CHAPTER 35
DEEP BREATH BEFORE THE PLUNGE

Tom

Tom swung by the Infirmary first.

It stood empty, all its beds and gurneys made up with linens. Ready.

Susan Ritter was talking to Amy Filewicz and, to Tom's surprise, Julie Boettcher. The three of them huddled at the back of the room, near what Tom still thought of as "Ian's desk." After a few moments, Karl Ritter's widow spotted him and waved him over.

"Y'all set?" he asked. "Anything you need?"

"Tons," Susan replied. "Starting with the Anchor Shard. My guess is we'll be using it before the night's out."

"Steve's doin' somethin' with it. Some new 'idea,' But I'll get it to you."

She nodded. Then Haven's medic treated him to what he imagined to be a "mom" look. Never having had a mom, he couldn't be sure. "So ... I'm glad to hear you still have your Eyes, Chief."

"Sorry," he told her. "For whatever it's worth, I wasn't lying to *you*."

"Helene's already made your case for you," she replied. "It's all right."

Tom turned to Julie: "Volunteering?"

The little brunette, about the same age and size as blond Amy, shrugged. "I gotta do *something*. This seemed like a good idea."

Susan added, "I'm happy to have the help."

"Keep your phones handy," Tom said. "When ... if... we get some wounded folks, I'll make sure to clue y'all in."

"Thanks, Chief," the medic replied. Then she managed a smile. "Is Will gone?"

"Yeah."

"Think we'll see him again?"

He had no idea how to answer that question. So he dodged it. "You got Emily all settled in?"

Susan looked back at her daughter, who seemed to be asleep. "She's faking it."

"How can you tell?"

"A mother can *always* tell."

Tom said, "Listen, it's your call. But you should be ready to scoop her up and bounce if things head south."

Susan shook her head. "I told you. I'm not leaving Haven. No matter what happens."

She's tryin' to think like a soldier. But she ain't a soldier. Not yet.

Maybe not ever.

"Like I said: your call. But, if push comes to shove, having her here with you ... well, that might make you change your mind."

"Is that why you insisted on setting up a cot for her in here?"

"Pretty much."

"Well," Will's mother remarked dryly. "At least that's *honest* emotional manipulation."

"Honesty's the only promise I can make," Tom told her. Then, after a long pause, he said, "But … yeah. I do think we'll see Will again."

"Why?" She sounded a little desperate.

"'Cause we always do."

As he left, he pulled out his phone and called Steve, who picked up on the second ring. "Infirmary's gonna need the Anchor Shard."

"I know. But I'm on to something. Gimme a little more time."

"You got it. But Steve … if the Corpses get in and kids start gettin' hurt …"

"I know, Chief. If it comes to that, I'll take it down there myself. I promise."

"Good enough. You doin' okay?"

"Are you?" the Brain Boss asked.

"Nope."

"There you go." Then he broke the connection.

From there, Tom went to Haven's western entrance, which was the one closest to his own room. The usual, ancient door had already been replaced by the Monkeys, one of the chores he'd set Alex to last week, before he'd been *sure*. The new door was custom-built—heavy, solid wood banded with iron, with bolts that fit into the floor and ceiling. It even had what looked like a genuine gate bar leaning against the wall, waiting to be dropped into place. As Tom neared the door, it opened and Chuck appeared. He and another Undertaker—there were so many these days, Tom found it hard to keep track—were carefully running a thin black wire through the concrete sentry room that stood beyond Haven's exit.

As Tom watched, the boys carefully fastened the wire to the room's left-hand bottom edge, just where the floor met the wall.

"All good?" Tom asked Chuck.

"So far," Chuck replied, straightening. "Finish it up," he said to the boy, who ran off wordlessly, presumably to follow the order.

"I ain't sure I ever saw you without your sunglasses before," Tom remarked. Chuck Binelli *always* wore sunglasses, even indoors. They were like his trademark— so much so that Tom found himself noticing, for the first time, that Chuck's eyes were dark brown, like his own.

The kid shrugged. "I'm cool enough without 'em."

"Straight up. You got everything you need?"

"Yeah. Everything's flowing the way it should be. The trigger wire's the last of it. We're followin' Steve's map, or diagram, or whatever he calls it—"

"Schematic," Tom said.

"Yeah. That. We're followin' it to the letter. I've already sent most of the kids back to the cafeteria, where they're being armed. If the Corpses get past this point, they need to be ready to fight back."

The image of hundreds of deaders tearing through these crumbling hallways, killing everyone in their path, flashed through Tom's mind. It made him feel things that he didn't dare show.

"How much longer before you can close that door?" he asked.

"Ten minutes. Maybe less." Chuck glanced back through the sentry room, at the *other* door, the one leading into the parking garage. "They're out there, Chief. A *ton* of them. All still and quiet. I don't know what they're waitin' for."

"Better make it five minutes," Tom suggested.

"Heard that," Chuck said.

"Did your crew get issued enough knives?"

In answer, the boy drew a long bladed kitchen knife from his belt. Then he pulled a small plastic bag out of his pocket. Inside the bag was a clump of white goop the size of a large meatball.

"Steve says that Will insisted on calling this a 'Dillin Dagger,' though I guess that doesn't apply until the poison actually goes on the knife."

Tom nodded his approval. "Tell your crew to wait until the Corpses bust through before they treat their blades. Make sure they know that, at best, the stuff'll work two, maybe three times, 'fore it needs to be reapplied."

"They know, Chief," Chuck told him. "We're ready."

No, you ain't, Tom thought. *But you're as ready as you can be.*

He left Chuck to his work, making his way to the northern entrance—where the stink was *horrible.*

"Burt!" Tom called, pinching his nose shut.

Steve Moscova's younger brother appeared. He wore a long leather smock and what looked like welder's gloves. His face was covered by a clear acrylic safety plate.

"Checkin' up on us, Chief?"

"I'm just standin' here … thinkin'. Corpses can *smell* stuff, can't they?"

"Sure," the boy replied. "But … so what? It's a sewer out there. It's *supposed* to stink. I mean, why would they even wonder about it?"

Tom hoped he was right. "How many you got?"

Burt announced proudly, "A hundred and sixteen!"

"That many? Last I heard you only had fifty or so."

"Well, fear's a great motivator."

"Straight up. Need anything?"

"Nope. We're as ready as we can be. I've had close to sixty kids working down here for hours. The speakers are wired in and the door's been welded shut. Once they make it past that, there's this hallway, which we can close off tight on the other end. Then we can start the 'introductions.'"

"And the deaders?"

"Lined up outside, going all the way back to the old printing house basement, as far as we can tell. We're watching 'em close. If … *when* they make their move, we'll know."

"How many drops you figure you'll get?"

"Depends on how many Corpses can fit in the hallway. But I figure four, maybe five."

"Cool," Tom said. Though it wasn't. Nothing about tonight was going to be "cool."

"We got this, Chief," Burt told him.

"I know you do. Just pull those kids back in as soon as you can, and arm them."

"Just in case?" the boy asked. He looked at Tom with about a hundred things in his eyes—too many to name, though clearly courage topped the list.

And for the millionth time, Tom wondered how he could have gotten so lucky with so many of the kids under his command.

"Just in case, man," he replied.

Finally, he made his way to the southern entrance. Except for the old exit he'd ushered Sharyn and her crew through a few minutes ago, this way in and out of Haven was the least used. Kind of ironic, since it was also their *first* way in, back when Tom had scouted out this place out as a Plan B in case the original Haven needed to be abandoned.

Which, of course, it had.

The southern entrance consisted of an old service door that opened into a long-abandoned spur line of the Broad Street Subway. A "spur" meant a second, usually smaller subway line that got split from the main tunnel. Apparently, *this* spur had been started and then abandoned by the city maybe sixty or seventy years ago, for reasons unknown.

Tom had first found it while exploring down here, back in the war's early days. Then, six months ago, when they'd moved here from Haven's former site, all their equipment had been brought in this way.

There was space in the spur, a lot of it. Beyond the service door was a huge tunnel, large enough to admit— well—a subway train. It was about fifty feet wide, thirty feet high, and maybe a hundred feet long, with the broad mouth at its end having been long ago barricaded off, first by the city with wooden planks, and then later fortified by the Undertakers with corrugated metal and iron bars.

Katie and Jillian had been busy down here.

"Tom!"

Jillian approached. The girl held a shovel. She looked filthy, layered with mud.

"How's it going?" he asked.

"We're ready," she said. "Katie's pulling the kids back now. Though she's wondering if you're sure ... you know, about Ramirez."

"I'm sure," Tom said. "He'll come through when the time in right. He's makin' amends."

She nodded. "Me, too." Then, after a pause, she remarked, "All any of this is gonna do is slow them down."

"I know."

"I mean ... they're cute tricks and all, but ..." her words trailed off.

Tom knew what she'd meant to say. Tricks. Traps. Clever snares. In the end, they would only delay the inevitable.

Everything was riding on Sharyn, Dave, Helene.

And Will.

"Nice job," he told her.

"Um ... Tom?"

"Yeah, Jill?"

"Thanks."

He looked at her. "For what?"

"For not telling everyone this is my fault."

He nodded, though the truth was he hadn't done that for her. He'd done it for the others. Nothing killed morale quicker than knowing you'd been betrayed from within. And right now, they *needed* morale.

"It's okay," he said.

"No, it's not," she replied. "I'm not sure it ever will be. Kids are gonna die tonight, and I'll have to live with that for the rest of my life."

She was looking at him with earnest, almost desperate eyes, hoping for just the barest glimmer of—what? Forgiveness? Tom had barely had time today to explore what he felt where she was concerned. How could she expect him to shrug it off so soon? It wasn't fair.

Except, how you gonna feel tomorrow ... if she's dead?

He put his hands on her shoulders. "Listen up. You didn't *do* this. You trusted the wrong guy and *he* did this. Now, I ain't sayin' you played it right. I ain't never gonna say *that*. But I do get why you did what you did. Tomorrow, when all this is done, you and I are gonna have a long talk. A *real* talk. But, 'til then, I want you to do something for me."

"Anything," she said, tears in her eyes.

"Stay alive."

A voice yelled, "Chief!"

They both turned toward the spur, where kids, dozens of them, were already running toward the service door and the relative safety of Haven. Katie ushered them along before hurrying over to where Tom and Jillian stood.

"Something's happening beyond the barricade," she announced, a little breathlessly. "We could hear 'em over there, making noise. Getting restless. It's gonna start, Chief. Any minute now."

Showtime, Tom thought.

CHAPTER 36
THE YUCK FACTOR

The maintenance door led us up a flight of unused stairs to a forgotten records room in City Hall's huge basement. Then another door took us into City Hall itself. It was nearing nine o'clock and the place was pretty deserted, so slipping out onto the street on the south side of the insanely big building wasn't hard.

Not many cops around. The Corpses in uniform were mostly below us, waiting for the order to storm Haven. And their human counterparts were elsewhere in the city, probably trying to pick up the slack.

Sharyn said, "The parking garage is crammed with deaders. But my bro thought ahead, like he does, and kept one of our vans out on the streets. It's in a public lot off Broad, about two blocks down. Close as we could get. Let's hoof it."

We hoofed it, crossing Market Street and then Chestnut. Around us, the nighttime city was alive: cars, buses, and even few brave folks on bikes jockeyed their way either north or south along Philly's widest boulevard. Broad Street, get it? On the curbside stood restaurants and theaters, most of them lit up and crowded, even though this wasn't a weekend.

There were *lots* of people around.

It was a warm night, so we were all in short sleeves, except the Burgermeister, who had to wear a long jacket with one of its sleeves hanging loose. He held his right arm pressed tight against his chest as he walked, not wanting anybody seeing his—um—new "hand." He could have removed the pickaxe, of course, maybe carried it in his backpack, but we hadn't wanted to risk it damaging the MacDonald, which seemed pretty fragile.

Besides, Dave had insisted on doing it this way. "The longer I wear this thing," he'd said sourly, "the better the chance I'll get used to it, and not hate it so much."

Sucks, Dave. I'm sorry.

Anyway, it worked. Nobody paid us any mind. In return, we pretty much ignored everyone we passed.

Until we spotted the Corpse.

He was coming up on our side of the street, heading north on foot. A Type Two, maybe two weeks dead. He wore a nice suit and carried a duffel bag. At first sight of him, half a block away, Sharyn immediately herded us off the sidewalk and into the shadow of the Ritz-Carlton hotel, which sits on the corner of Chestnut and Broad. The front of the hotel has these Greek-style columns, which the four of us hid behind.

"How do you want to play it?" I whispered. "Let him pass?"

"Nope," she replied. "I know we're on the clock, but my gut's screamin' at me to see what's in that duffel. Somethin' tells me he ain't headin' for no gym. Number Eight."

"Got it," Helene said.

The Angel Boss stepped out into the middle of Chestnut Street just as the guy was passing along Broad.

"Yo, wormbag!" she called, drawing stares from passersby.

Dead Guy in Nice Suit glared at her. Normally, a public confrontation was something nobody wanted. But, as I'd learned today, the rules had changed, and I could tell this deader wanted to attack. He wanted it *bad*.

Still, he hesitated.

"I have no time for you, Undertaker," he snarled.

"Crap," I muttered.

I ducked quietly around my column and circled behind the dude. Then I rushed his flank, yanked the duffel out of his grasp, and kept going. As I passed Sharyn, she threw a mocking laugh at the Corpse and followed me.

"No!" the deader hissed.

Then he pursued.

We darted down an alley that ran behind the hotel. About halfway along, Sharyn and I stopped and turned to face him.

The Corpse stopped too, wary, maybe twenty feet away. His milky, seemingly sightless eyes scanned the darkness, looking for further threats. Then they settled back on us, and he snarled, baring loose, yellowed teeth.

"Return that."

"You didn't ask nice," Sharyn pouted.

"I didn't *ask* anything!" he snapped. "Return it, or die here in the filth."

"Know what?" I said. "I think maybe there's a third option."

His gray dead face twisted into a suspicious frown. "What's that?"

The Burgermeister's pickaxe came down on him from behind, burying itself so deep in Dead Guy in Nice Suit's stolen skull that it almost tore his stolen head off.

The body twitched and went still.

"Okay," Dave admitted begrudgingly. "Maybe I *could* get used to this."

Grabbing the deader's limp shoulder, he yanked the axe's curved, pointed blade out. Then, as the Corpse's useless body hit the pavement, Dave made a sour face and started shaking the blood and brains off of what now served as his right hand. Helene came up beside him, saw what he was doing, and turned a little green.

"Not sure *I'm* gonna get used to it," she groaned, covering her mouth.

Unaffected by the Yuck Factor, Sharyn stepped up and searched the Corpse. "Richard Kimble." she said, reading from the dude's wallet.

"Sounds kinda familiar," I said.

The Burgermeister replied, "It's the name of Harrison Ford's character in *The Fugitive.*"

I looked at him.

"We watched it last week," he added. "In our tent in the woods."

"Okay …"

"What's in the duffel?" Helene asked.

I put it down and opened it. Then with a gasp, I closed it again.

"What is it, dude?" Dave asked, suddenly alarmed.

Helene hurried over to me, her nausea forgotten. I showed her.

"Oh God …" she breathed.

"It's *Pelligog*," I said to the others.

According to the Corpses, the *Pelligog* were the only physical creatures capable of crossing the Void. They came from the *Malum* homeworld, were vaguely spider-like, and maybe eight inches long. They lived in a sort of hive made out of their own bodies, dozens of them, all climbing over each other in a weird living sphere.

The Corpses had a very specific use for these little monstrosities. By letting a single *Pelligog* burrow painfully into a person's lower back, the deaders were then able to control that person. Brainwash them. Turn them against their friends. Heck, against humanity.

One downside: the entire sphere was needed to control a single mind. So if a person was unlucky enough to be *implanted*, then they either had to be killed or released—most likely killed—before the *Pelligog* could be used to control a second person.

"Where do you think Kimball was taking them?" Helene asked.

"Toward City Hall," Sharyn replied.

"Why?" Dave asked.

"These things only have one use," I said. Then I looked up at Sharyn and added, "I think maybe we just did somebody a big favor."

"What should we do with them?" Helene wondered.

"Burn it?" Sharyn suggested.

"Maybe." But then I looked over at Richard Kimball. The Corpse lay in a bloody mess in the middle of the dark alley. He wasn't dead, of course, just trapped in a stolen body he could no longer control. By now, he was sending telepathic distress calls out to his deader buddies—though something told me most of them were too busy to respond, at least right away.

"Whatcha thinkin', Will?" the Burgermeister asked.

"I'm wondering if these things work on Corpses like they work on humans," I said.

Beside me, Helene shuddered. Bad memories.

"We don't got time for this, little bro," Sharyn said. "We gotta get to Mifflin."

"I know," I said. Then I met her eyes. "But he was taking these things somewhere. And *not* for any good reason. Don't you think we ought to know where and why?"

The Angel Boss frowned. She glanced at Dead Guy in Nice Suit and then looked back at me. "Okay. Three minutes. Do it."

Easier said than done. Fighting the bile rising in the back of my throat (me and my great ideas!), I went over the fallen Corpse, knelt beside him, and opened the duffle. Inside, the nest of *Pelligog* squirmed and wriggled.

"Um," I said, "could somebody roll him over?"

"I got it," Dave replied. Then he used one end of his pickaxe to tumble the limp body onto its stomach.

I pulled up the deader's jacket and yanked his fancy shirt out of his fancy trousers, exposing the gray dead flesh of his lower back.

Now came the hard part.

Holding my breath, I reached carefully into the duffle, hesitating as the creatures became agitated, as if sensing me. Their bodies were thin and weirdly segmented, and their ten legs seemed to be everywhere at once.

"Be careful, Will," Helene said. Then she put a supportive hand on my shoulder.

I counted to three. Then I grabbed one, managing to catch its tail between my thumb and forefinger.

It didn't like it.

As I pulled, it clung fiercely to its fellow bugs and, for a second, it seemed as if the entire nest was going to jump out of the duffle and—I don't know—eat my face off or something.

But it didn't. So I kept pulling.

Finally, the creature came loose, thrashing and struggling and making me wish to high Heaven that I'd thought to bring gloves.

Carefully, I moved my arm until the *Pelligog* hung over the Corpse's exposed back. Then, after counting to three again, I dropped it.

The creature landed on Kimball's flesh. For a horrible second, I thought it would try to skitter off. But then it stopped, as if sensing an opportunity, and raised its weird, pinch-faced head—

—and plunged it deep under the dead dude's skin.

Helene turned away in disgust.

"Gross," the Burgermeister remarked.

Sharyn said nothing. She just watched.

The *Pelligog* kept going, its legs wriggling as it dug in deeper, until its entire body disappeared into the Corpse's back, leaving behind only an angry checkmark-shaped scar.

I swallowed dryly.

Then I asked the lifeless body, "Can you hear me?"

The response was immediate. *"I. Hear. You."*

Deadspeak, the only language a Corpse in this condition could use.

I said. "Where were you taking the *Pelligog?*"

At first, I didn't think he'd answer, that maybe these nightmare creatures didn't work on the dead after all.

But then: *"To. Queen."*

"And where's she at?"

"Office. Of. Mayor. City. Hall."

We all swapped looks. "Cavanaugh wants to implant the mayor?" I asked.

"No. Governor. Mayor. Already. Cooperating."

Dave asked. "Why would the mayor cooperate with Cavanaugh about anything? Doesn't he think she's dead?"

"Queen. Revealed. Herself. To. Him. Using. Him. To. Lure. Governor. To. City."

"When?" I asked.

"Tonight."

"Figures," Helene muttered.

"She's makin' a power play," Sharyn said. "Now that the gloves are off, she's gonna kill us and grab state-level power, both on the same night."

"Thanks for your help," I told the Corpse.

"It. My. Honor. To. Serve." Then, as if the word was difficult for him to manage in Deadspeak, he added, *"Undertakers."*

"I straightened up, wiping my hand on my pants. Later on, I figured I'd wash it for about an hour, just to get the feel of the *Pelligog* off my skin.

"What should we do?" Helene asked.

"Mifflin's gotta come first," the Angel Boss replied.

She was right. We couldn't spare the time to worry about the governor. But at least, without the *Pelligog*, that piece of Cavanaugh's plan was out the window.

"We should let Tom know," I said.

"Good idea," Dave remarked.

But, before any of us could do that, Dead Guy in Nice Suit's smartphone started playing a Barry Manilow tune.

CHAPTER 37
THE PEP TALK

Lilith

T he Queen of the Dead regarded the Mayor of
Philadelphia.

His Honor sat in his leather chair, his face pale and
his clothes stained with his own vomit. He repeatedly
wiped at his mouth with a trembling hand, trying to
both look—and *not* look—at Lilith.

The governor had agreed to come to Philly, having
responded angrily to the mayor's pleas for "state-level
help during this period of sudden municipal crisis."
The mayor had played his part well; Lilith had to give
him that. He'd stayed vague on the particulars, but
had sounded desperate enough to win the governor's
agreement without specifics.

Of course, most of the mayor's desperation hadn't
been faked.

Unfortunately, the governor wouldn't be able to
arrive in Philadelphia until at least eleven p.m. A longer
wait than the Queen wanted, but better than nothing.

"Just relax, Frank," she told the quivering fool. "You've done well enough. Now, I have a phone call of my own to make. It won't take long."

Lilith took her smart phone from her purse and opened the special app that Richard had given her. This app—the Queen neither knew nor cared what its name was—worked similarly to Skype, except that it opened a one-way link between Lilith's phone and fifteen hundred others.

Her army.

Time to address the troops.

She waited while the app did its work. After several seconds, the screen lit up as her face, Lilith Cavanaugh's unmistakable cover, was fed through the phone's camera and projected out to her minions.

"*Malum*," she said.

She hadn't rehearsed. She hadn't needed to. The words flowed from her like water.

"Tonight, we launch our final campaign to eradicate the human blight from the universe. We begin by striking down their only viable defenders, thus clearing the path for the sweet destruction that will sweep across this world over the next weeks and months.

"Regrettably, our plan to corrupt and destroy this world and its inhabitants by stealth has failed, thanks to the enemy you face tonight. Their constant interference has ruined the *beauty* with which we might have orchestrated their destruction. Instead, we must set aside our art and turn to more direct methods.

"In moments, you will lay siege to the place called Haven. You will tear down every barricade, push through every defense. You will slaughter every human you encounter. You will leave none alive.

"I command you to *enjoy* the coming battle, to revel

in the blood and the carnage. I command you to take lives, as many as you can, to kill and kill and kill until your warrior Selves thrill from the glorious savagery of it. I command you to give all of yourselves to the task, driven by the knowledge that you honor me with each life you destroy.

"So, the word is given.

"Go forth now, and *kill* the Undertakers.

"Kill them *all*."

Lilith broke the connection, pleased.

"What do you think, Frank? Inspirational enough?"

She looked over at the mayor, who seemed to rouse himself from a stupor. Shock, no doubt. "W—what?"

"My speech just now," she cooed. "Weren't you listening? How rude of you."

"I'm ... sorry," he stammered.

"'I'm sorry' *what*, Frank?"

"I'm sorry, ma'am."

She nodded. "Very good, Frank. Just as I taught you. Really, you should try to embrace your new reality. Right now, as we speak, one-and-a-half thousand of my minions are storming the Undertakers' lair."

"The Undertakers ..." he echoed. "You mean that teenage street gang?"

"Oh, they're much more than that. In fact, they're quite capable resistance fighters. You see, while you and your ilk have been blindly going about your business of mismanaging this city and lining your pockets with taxpayer money, these children have been fighting for the security and safety of your entire world.

"However, their fight ends tonight, with their deaths."

"Deaths!" the mayor exclaimed. "My God, no!"

"Almost three hundred children, Frank. All of them torn apart by beings who look ... more or less ... just like me."

Then she grinned with Sarah's dead mouth.

"And all on *your* watch, Mr. Mayor."

His Honor buried his face in his hands.

Delicious.

Lilith's phone rang.

It was still in her hand—Sarah's hand—and she looked at it, momentarily taken aback.

The Caller ID said "Richard."

Annoyed, she put the phone to her ear and demanded, "What is it?"

A voice said cheerfully, *"Your Royal Wormbagginess? Please hold for Mr. William Ritter."*

There was a pause. Lilith heard voices—children's voices. A brief exchange that seemed to consist of: *"I don't want to talk to her. You talk to her. No, you talk to her. No, you talk to her."*

Finally, as the Queen seethed, a familiar voice came on the line.

"Cavanaugh, we caught your speech just now, right on this phone. Nice pep talk."

"Ritter!" Lilith exclaimed. "Where did you get this phone? Where's Richard?"

"Kimball? He's kinda … indisposed."

The Queen exploded. "I will feed you your own entrails, boy! Your meddling—"

"Look. I don't gotta lot of time, so let's skip the part where you threaten to disembowel me. We wasted your errand boy and, as you can see, we got his phone. We also got his Pelligog. In fact, we used one on him just now and he told us all about the governor. So we just phoned the state police and gave them an anonymous tip that the governor's life would be in danger if he went to Philly. I'm guessing that fouls things up for you pretty good."

For a moment, Lilith thought she might crush the phone in her rage. But she held herself in check. "I'm going to find you, Undertaker," she hissed, putting as much hatred and menace as she could behind those words. "And when I do, I'm going to kill you with my bare hands ... slowly!"

"Good for you. Gotta go. Busy night. Things to do. Have a good one."

And, just like that, the connection broke.

He hung up on me! The little brat defeated my assistant, stole my Pelligog, *and now he's hung up on me!*

She glanced over at the mayor, who regarded her with a look of such terror that the Queen wondered how the man's heart didn't stop cold. For a moment, she considered killing the worthless human, ripping him apart or crushing his head between her hands—Sarah's hands—like a rotted melon. After all, what good was he now? The governor had been warned off and, even if he hadn't been, her means of controlling him was lost.

Lilith went as far as to take a single step toward the mayor, who squeaked in fear and tried to bury himself in his office chair.

But then what the Ritter boy had said hit home.

"Gotta go. Busy night."

Obviously, Ritter wasn't in Haven. Yet the Queen's minions had reported *seeing* the boy, along with Jefferson, enter the Love Park garage in a white van, just minutes before her people had closed off that entrance.

There's no way out of that subterranean rat hole. Not anymore.

But, evidently there was, as Ritter and at least one other, the one pretending to be his 'secretary,' had been outside when they'd encountered Richard. Had they abandoned the Undertakers?

No. Ritter was many things, but a coward was not among them.

Then why leave? Where were they going?

"Things to do."

What things?

What had Dillin, the traitor, *told* him?

What *could* he have told the boy that would have caused the most harm?

The Anchor Shard.

No!

"Frank," she said, forcing a calmness into her voice that she definitely didn't feel. "Change of plans. I need to get to Fort Mifflin ... now."

"What?" He looked so blankly, so stupidly at her, that she nearly killed him anyway. But again, with Herculean effort, she restrained herself.

"I need to get to Fort Mifflin," she repeated. "A car won't be fast enough. But, tell me Frank, do you still have mayoral access to that lovely helicopter?"

CHAPTER 38
ENEMY AT THE GATES

Tom

"Undertakers," Tom said into the microphone. "They're coming. I know y'all are scared. I'm scared, too. But we're gonna be strong. We're gonna stand. Right now, some of us … some of our very best … are out on the streets tryin' to finally end this thing. All we gotta do is hang tough and give them the time they need. For ourselves. For our families. For our world.

"So when y'all start seein' Corpses, when they come within strikin' range, remember this: I'm in it with you. I'll be fightin' right beside you. We're Undertakers. And Undertakers are *never* alone."

He flipped off the newly installed PA system and turned to Alex and Steve. "They all heard me? Everywhere?"

"Everywhere," Steve replied. "And we have cameras set up at all three exits." He pointed to three secondhand computer monitors that had been set up.

Alex said, "I've got some of my crew at each site to

shore up any weak spots."

"Then we're as ready as we can be. Get to your positions."

As Steve and Alex left the Infirmary, Tom glanced over at Susan Ritter. Haven's medic was counting inventory for probably the fourth or fifth time in the last hour. Busywork. Something to do—before the wounded started to arrive.

It had been Susan's idea to reserve a corner of the Infirmary for running the siege. To Tom, it made perfect sense. It was a large space, more or less equidistant from each of the exits, and close to the maintenance door into City Hall—just in case they had to start evacuating people.

Alex's crew had set up the cables and cameras last week, before Tom had told anyone about his invasion fears. That meant it had simply been a matter of running the lines into the infirmary and setting up the microphone and monitors atop an old wooden table.

Instant command center.

Tom also had four different sat phones lined up, not counting his own, which was reserved for calls from Sharyn. There was one phone for each of the Angels running each of the defensive fronts, plus a fourth for Ramirez. That would keep the lines of communications open and constant.

Just a minute ago, one of the smart phones that Tom had taken off the Corpses in the park that afternoon had rung. On it, he'd watched Lilith Cavanaugh's "troop address." It had been short and to the point. Commence the siege. Kill everyone.

Now it starts.

And we're ready.

As if such a thing were possible.

**

The Corpses hit Haven's western entrance first, ramming their stolen bodies repeatedly into the steel door leading from the sentry room to the lowest level of the underground parking garage. This door had been shored up from the inside, criss-crossed with thick, heavy planks of wood bolted into the surrounding concrete.

But within minutes, those planks began to tremble.

* * *

They hit the southern entrance next, tearing at the barricade that closed off the mouth of the subway spur. They had almost no light to work with, but instead clawed and ripped at the obstacle blindly with strong, dead hands. The structure, almost twenty feet high and loosely assembled, shuddered from the assault.

* * *

They hit the northern entrance last, coming at the old door from the sewers the only way they could: one at a time. But this door, while also reinforced by Alex's team, was older and far more rusted than the one in the parking garage.

A few of the dead, squeezing in and working together, managed to rip it from its aging hinges within the first few seconds. This earned triumphant growls from the others as the first of their number spilled into the long, dark corridor that now stood between them and Haven.

There they stopped, looking perplexed.

There was music playing. And it was playing *loud*.

***

Burt called in. *"They're through!"*

"I see it," Tom told him, watching the monitor. "You ready?"

The boy laughed. There was eagerness in that laugh. And terror. *"Yeah, we're ready."*

"Wait until as many get in as possible."

"If the inner door holds," Burt said.

"Is Alex with you yet?"

"Yeah."

"What's he say?"

"He says it'll hold ... for a while."

Tom said, "Lemme see if I can slow 'em down a little bit."

"Thanks, Chief."

"Hang tough, Burton."

"You know it. Is my brother okay?"

Steve's voice filled the call, surprising Tom, who hadn't known the Brain Boss was also monitoring communications. *"I'm fine! Now do your job and don't die!"*

"Good advice, big brother," Burt said.

Then he hung up.

***

At the western entrance, the parking garage door trembled violently. As Tom watched, the first of the crossbars gave way, its bolts bent and twisted from the repeated body slams.

Within seconds, another one weakened.

In the door's upper corner, away from its hinges, the steel peeled back, sounding like the shriek of a freight train.

Gray fingers, torn and lifeless but horribly strong, reached through the opening, clawing and grasping at the air.

***

At the southern entrance, the barricade finally surrendered to all of the dead fingers digging away at it. Deliberately built to be top heavy, the two-story structure, bathed in darkness, collapsed, burying dozens of Corpses under a ton of debris.

The others noted this.

Then they began climbing over their fallen comrades.

***

Tom raised the microphone to his lips.

"Attention, deaders!" he announced cheerfully, watching the monitors. As he'd hoped, the Corpses on all three fronts stopped, or at least slowed.

He said, "This is Tom Jefferson, Chief of the Undertakers, and I'd like to welcome y'all to Haven. By now, some of you've already clued in on a few of tonight's festivities. By my count, maybe twenty of y'all just got crushed when that barricade fell. And there's lots more surprises to come!"

Tom paused, studying all three monitors. The western outer door had been breached, and maybe three-dozen Corpses had already flooded the narrow, high-ceiling corridor between the main sewer channel and Haven's entrance. The northern door went next. Half its bolts had been either shaken loose or ripped free. As Tom watched, the final ones gave way and the door tore from its hinges. Corpses, two abreast, stepped into the sentry room.

At the same time, fully a hundred—maybe more—of Cavanaugh's soldiers were spilling over the remains of the barricade and filling the subway spur.

Still coming, but listening, too.

Yes, he had their attention, which was kind of a victory all by itself.

He said, "We've had lots of time to prepare for y'all. We got all kinds of party favors waitin'. And some o' those ain't the 'break my host body so I gotta wait for a new one' kind of favors. They're more like the 'waste me so bad that my Self's got no place to go and I'm history' variety.

"Here's what each of you might take a second to think 'bout. There's three different groups of y'all, each knocking on a different door. Each one's got its own surprises comin'. You don't know what they are, or how bad they'll hit you ... but I promise, you won't dig 'em. Not one bit.

"So now, what y'all have to decide is this: who's first?

"The night's young ... and we ain't goin' noplace."

He put down the microphone and watched the monitors.

At all entrances, the deaders in the back were still coming, spilling in like ants out of their nest.

But the ones in front had stopped moving.

Tom started counting the seconds. He figured that little speech had bought them five minutes, maybe ten.

Hurry up, sis. Will.

Hurry up.

CHAPTER 39
MIFFLIN REVISITED

Fort Mifflin is an old Revolutionary War fort that sits in the marshland southwest of Philly. A museum until the Corpses turned it to their own purposes, it consists of a dozen or so buildings surrounded by high brick ramparts that form a funny star shape when looked at from above.

The last time I was here, I'd been new to the Undertakers and had decided to go "off reservation," leaving Haven without permission. As a result, I'd managed to rescue Amy Filewicz from the deaders, but had nearly lost Helene in the process.

Not my finest hour.

But I was still kind of proud of it. Weird.

Back then, getting here had been tough: a subway train to the airport, then bikes down to the marshes.

Tonight, we had a van, which had been parked right where Sharyn said it would be. The four of us piled in, having left Richard Kimball lying in the alley.

The *Pelligog might* have come in handy. We *might* have used them to control another Corpse, maybe get him or her to waltz into the East Magazine and unplug the shard for us. Problem was: the nest could only control one person at a time. And we'd had no easy way to get to spider-thing I'd stuck into Kimball out of him again.

So, after some heated debate, the *Pelligog* "ball" had come along, but only because we hadn't yet figured out a handy way of destroying it.

With Sharyn driving, we came within a half-mile of Mifflin, which from this distance, looked as lit up as a football stadium.

"Just like last time," Helene remarked.

"Some differences," I said.

"Yeah," Sharyn added. "Like this time you're *allowed* to be here."

"That's one."

Beside me on the back seat, the Burgermeister held up his right arm. In tight quarters, the pickaxe attached to his wrist looked particularly big. "Here's another," he groused.

I'd been watching him carefully since we'd left Haven, looking for signs of trouble. After all, the Anchor Shard may have healed his body. But, as any soldier will tell you, sometimes the mental wounds are worse than the physical. Until this point, he'd been going on momentum, on adrenaline. But now, riding in this van with little to do but think, I could see the weight of his new situation—no pun intended—pressing down on him.

"You okay?" I asked.

"I'm cool," he replied.

I tried to think of something else to say. But nothing came to mind.

I wish it had.

"I'm seein' a lot of cars in the lot," Sharyn said. "We're gonna have to pull over and hoof it from here. I'm guessin' you three know the way?"

We parked partway down a dirt access road and headed into the marshland that surrounded Mifflin. No flashlights. Couldn't risk being seen from the fort. Instead, we used *its* bright lights to guide us along, which isn't as helpful as it sounds when there are brambles, mud pits, and sinkholes all around you, invisible in the dark.

Sharyn was sticking close to Dave, who lumbered along, trying to learn a new rhythm of walking with that extra weight on his right side. His girlfriend kept pace, holding his left hand and talking to him, though in so low a whisper that I couldn't hear what she said.

I looked at Helene.

She looked at me.

Then, almost without thinking, I took her hand as well.

A pretty crazy way to sneak into a fort full of deaders— holding hands, I mean. But you had to be there.

"You brought the *Pelligog*," Sharyn said to me at one point.

"Yeah," I replied.

"Why not just leave it in the van?"

"Because I think I know how to kill the nest."

Helene asked, "How?"

"I'm gonna leave it beside the Anchor Shard when we pull its plug."

Behind me, Dave remarked. "I like it."

"Me, too," Sharyn added.

Helene squeezed my hand.

There's a little-used footbridge that approaches the fort from the east. As the four of us crossed it, single file, my sense of déjà vu felt as thick as soup. A couple of times I caught Helene's eye.

She felt it too. Foreboding.

Last time, things at Mifflin had ended *badly.*

"We gotta get over the wall," Sharyn said, looking up at the ten-foot rampart rising steeply out of the marsh. "How'd you dudes do it before?"

"Dave threw us over it," Helene said. "Then we pulled him up."

The Burgermeister scowled. "That ain't gonna work this time. Step aside."

We stepped aside and he marched up to the dirt wall and *jumped.* He didn't get too high. Jumping wasn't his—specialty, but at the top of the jump he swung his right arm up and jammed the pickaxe deep into the mortared surface of the wall.

For a split second, he hung there. Then, flexing those ridiculously big shoulders of his, he pulled himself high enough to grab a fistful of grass at the top of the wall.

Just like that, he was over.

"Huh," I said.

"Wow," Helene said.

Sharyn grinned. "Hot Dog."

A moment later, he reappeared, lying flat on his belly with his shoulders over the edge the rampart, reaching both his hand and his pickaxe down toward us.

"Well?" he whispered harshly. "The world ain't gonna save itself!"

Sharyn went first, running up the wall and grabbing hold of both the hand and the axe. The Burgermeister swung her up and over the lip of the rampart.

Helene went next and I took up the rear, worried that the duffle of monsters might add too much weight. It didn't. In seconds, I was atop the wall, with Sharyn and

Helene pulling me to my feet.

"Nice," I told Dave, meaning it, as the big kid rose and brushed the dirt and grass off the front of his shirt.

"Yeah," was all he said.

Hidden in the shadows, the four of us faced the interior of Fort Mifflin.

"Oh … crap," Helene whispered.

Corpses.

Well, of course we knew there'd be *some*. I mean, Cavanaugh wasn't dumb enough to leave her Anchor Shard, and its precious Rift, unguarded. So we'd come down here expecting to have to fight our way in. And we'd come prepared—with the weapons and strategies necessary to take out a half-dozen deaders, if we had to.

Except there weren't a half-dozen.

There were twenty.

At least.

"Okay," Sharyn said. "*Now* it's time to phone home."

CHAPTER 40
COLE'S DEAL

Tom

Tom closed his sat phone, the one he'd earmarked for calls from Sharyn.

Barely five minutes had passed since he'd cast his challenge and, so far, the Corpses still seemed confused and wary. None of them had ventured any deeper into any of the entrances.

Yet.

"Who was that?" Susan asked.

"Sharyn." For a moment, he wondered how much he should tell her. But then he decided, at this point, everybody deserved to know all of it. "Seems there're more deaders guarding the Fort Mifflin Anchor Shard than we expected."

"What're they going to do?" Will's mom asked. She tried to sound cool about it, but Tom could read her face. She was worried for her son.

"They don't know yet, but they'll figure it out," he said. "This is *Will*, Susan. He always figures it out."

"I know," she replied.

But figuring it out will slow them down. And time ain't our friend.

A voice from one of the monitors said, *"Chief Jefferson."*

Tom turned. A figure, a deader, stood in the spur, about halfway between the fallen barricade and the door to Haven. While his peeps were all shuffling nervously, this one stood stock-still, his milky eyes fixed on the camera, which was mounted in the high ceiling.

He was a Type One, big and strong.

"Can you hear me, Chief Jefferson?"

Tom picked up the microphone.

"Should you?" Susan asked, putting a gentle hand on his arm. "Maybe it would be better to ignore him."

"Don't think so," he told her.

Then he hit the TALK button and said, "This is Jefferson."

"My name is Cole. I imagine you've heard of me."

"Co-Chief of Police," Tom said. "Parker's brother 'Special.'"

"Imprecise, but adequate. I'm the commander of this assault force. I'd like to offer you a deal."

Tom thought: *A deal? Y'all outnumber us five to one. Your soldiers are faster'n us. Stronger'n us. And they don't even feel pain. You know as well as I do that we can't hold you off for very long. So why deal?*

"I'm listening."

"Surrender now."

"Uh-huh. We do that and you'll … what? Let us walk?"

The Corpse slowly shook his head, pasting a smile on his dead face that might have looked rueful on a living man. *"I wouldn't insult your intelligence. No, Mr. Jefferson.*

You're all going to die tonight. Every last one of you. But there are different ways to die. Surrender now, and I will guarantee that the children under your command will meet death quickly and painlessly."

"That's solid," Tom said dryly.

"Actually, it is. Especially when one considers the alternative. Defy me and I will give orders that every boy and girl in this rathole be slowly broken, torn apart piece by piece, screaming and in agony. Is that what you want?"

Tom didn't reply.

"You've fought a good fight. Better than any we've ever encountered. I have nothing but respect for the Undertakers. But the time has come for this charade to end. You don't have a chance. You never really did. I offer you an honorable, dignified death. I suggest you choose it over the slaughter that's coming."

Tom looked at Susan. She was crying, but she didn't say a word. He turned next to Julie and Amy, who watched from another part of the Infirmary, their faces masks of barely contained terror.

And finally he looked at Emily. Little Emily Ritter.

Who pretended to be asleep.

"Why?" he said into the microphone.

"What?"

"Why be so generous?" he asked thoughtfully. "You dudes live to cause suffering. Why offer us an easy way out?"

"You ask too many questions, boy," Cole growled. *"Just take the deal!"*

Tom stared at the image on the monitor for a few more seconds. Then he raised the microphone to his lips and said, "I'll get back to you on that."

And clicked off.

"What's going on?" Susan asked.

"He knows," Tom said, feeling ice water in his veins.

"Knows what?"

"About the Angels at Fort Mifflin."

"What?" she exclaimed. "How?"

"Not sure. But he's offering to kill us quick and painless because he's worried about what might happen if we keep him and his peeps out for too long. Someone tipped him off. And if *he* knows ..."

He snatched up one of the sat phones and dialed.

After a few rings, Sharyn said, *"Jeez, bro ... remember the whole 'Only call if you gotta' speech?"*

"Cavanaugh knows you're there," Tom said. "It don't matter how, but she does." For a long moment, he hesitated, almost telling his sister to run, to take Will and the rest and disappear. Maybe it would be better if those four survived, even if it meant the rest of them died.

But then he looked again at Emily, sweet fake-sleeping Emily, and thought, *Sharyn'd never go along with it anyhow.*

So he said, "Whatever you're gonna do, do it *now!*"

On the monitor, Cole growled at the nearest of his hesitant underlings, ordering him to advance. When the deader, a Type Four, hesitated, Cole seized him by the arms and ripped him apart.

The act was so abrupt and so savage that Susan, who'd been watching, had to turn away in horror.

But Tom didn't. He just *kept* watching.

The effect on the other Corpses was slow but certain. They moved.

"Time's up, boy!" the Corpse commander roared, looking once again into the camera, his stolen face twisted with hatred and splattered with blood and gore. *"We're coming for you all!"*

CHAPTER 41

THE IDEA MACHINE

"We could blow up their rides out in the lot," Sharyn suggested. "Distract 'em."

"We've done that before," Helene said glumly. "They wouldn't fall for it twice."

"We could cut the power to the stadium lights," Sharyn said. "Sneak past 'em in the dark."

"Done that too," I said.

"Okay ... maybe one of us could run through the fort, draw 'em away from the East Magazine." Then, reading our expressions, she added, "Done that too, huh?

"Twice," Dave replied.

"We're outta moves," Helene said miserably.

We all huddled behind the Artillery Shed, the building nearest to the place where we'd cleared the ramparts. It wasn't far from the spot where, six months and about a lifetime ago, Helene, Dave, and I had listened to Kenny Booth rally his own dead troops.

Like I said: a bad night.

But maybe not as bad as this one.

"No, we're not," the Burgermeister said.

"Not what?" Sharyn asked.

"Outta moves. We just gotta make up a new one."

Then, to my horror, they all looked at *me*.

"What?" I exclaimed.

"Man with the plan, little bro," said Sharyn. She tried to be light about it, but the desperation was plain in her eyes.

"Dude, we need your magic," the Burgermeister added. I noticed that he sidled close to Sharyn, not quite touching her.

Helene said nothing.

I slid down the Artillery Shed wall until I crouched on my haunches in the grass.

This. Was. Not. Fair!

"You can't put this on me," I told them all in a harsh whisper. "I'm no genius! I've got nothing. You hear me? Nothing!"

We had twenty Corpses between us and the Anchor Shard. It was only a few dozen yards away. Yet, it might as well have been on the other side of the planet. No way were we getting to the crystal, at least not in time.

Suddenly, it felt like everything that had happened, all my stupid risks, last-minute rescues, and crazy half-baked schemes, had been for nothing. For here we were, standing on the precipice, and with no way to forge the gap.

We'd need an army to cross the fort and reach the East Magazine in time.

Or a tank.

Or if not a tank, then at least—

My mind came to a screeching halt.

I remember thinking, *Crap. If this works, they'll never*

stop talking about it.

Slowly, wearily, I stood up. The three of them were still looking at me expectantly, as if my collapse and outburst had, in their eyes, simply been part of the inspirational process. Just another cog in the Idea Machine.

And the worst part?

Maybe they were right.

"Okay," I said. "Here's what we'll do."

It took ten minutes—minutes we couldn't spare—to drop back down off the rampart and follow the outer wall of the fort counter-clockwise. The route was risky; it would be *so* easy to get spotted by one of the deaders patrolling the ramparts, but we didn't dare risk the time to re-navigate the marshes.

We made it.

Ahead lay one of only two ways into Mifflin, an arched brick tunnel built through the ramparts called the East Entrance. Straight across from it, a wooden bridge spanned the moat—yeah, it's got a moat, and a pretty one. From there, an access road led north to the employee parking lot.

That's what we were after.

"Look for SUVs or pickup trucks," I said. "Something with four-wheel drive. Not too big, though ... the bridge and tunnel are pretty narrow."

The parking lot stood dark and deserted, the only light coming from the fort. Maybe a dozen cars were in evidence—apparently some of the deaders had either walked or carpooled.

Sharyn and Helene picked a black Ford Escape, a smaller SUV. The Burgermeister and I climbed into a red Toyota Tacoma, a medium-sized pickup.

As part of my Angels training, I'd learned how to hotwire a car. I won't bore with you with the specifics.

Suffice it to say that I used my pocketknife blade to pop the steering column. Then I found the right wires, stripped them, and touched them to each other in just the right way.

Nearby, in the SUV, Helene was doing the same with a small combat knife she liked to carry.

"If this works," Dave said from the passenger seat as I worked, "they'll never stop talking about it!"

"I know," I groaned.

The Tacoma's engine started.

We took it slow at first. While both Helene and I had learned how to drive, neither of us was what you'd call an expert. So we maneuvered our way out of the parking lot and down the access road to the bridge, our Tacoma in the front, their Escape behind us.

The engines sounded loud, *way* louder than I'd counted on. It worried me. Surprise was important. We wouldn't get a second shot at this.

The bridge creaked and moaned as I carefully eased the Tacoma across it. For a second, I thought I heard the wooden boards cracking under the truck's weight. But I kept going, and we made it to the other side.

As we slowly approached Mifflin's East Entrance, I checked the rearview mirror, breathing a sigh of relief when I saw Sharyn and Helene clear the bridge as well.

So far, so good.

Now … if we can just fit through the tunnel.

We did, barely. In fact, there at the end, it sounded like the paint job at the top corners of the truck's cab got scraped down to the metal by jutting bricks.

But then we were through.

I hit the brakes and killed the engine. Then I waited until, behind us, Sharyn and Helene did the same.

I pulled out my pocketknife, letting my thumb hover

over the **8** button.

My pocketknife has a special tool that you won't find in the Boy Scout's catalog. It's able to fire off an electromagnetic pulse, or EMP for short. This burst of energy basically fries every working electronic device within its range.

It would kill the lights, no doubt about it.

"You sure it won't kill these cars, too?" Dave asked.

"Pretty sure," I replied. Steve had once told me that EMPs couldn't fry electronics that weren't actually turned on. This meant that, as long as our stolen cars weren't running, they wouldn't be affected.

At least, I *hoped* that was what it meant.

"Do it," Dave said.

I hit the **8** button.

The lights went out, throwing the entire fort into sudden, perfect darkness.

Then I reached under the steering column and tapped the battery, ignition, and starter wires again.

The moment of truth, I thought.

The truck's engine roared back to life.

"Yes!" the Burgermeister declared, pumping the air with his remaining fist.

I let out the breath I'd been holding. Then I slammed us into drive, flipped on the headlights, and stamped down on the accelerator. The Tacoma leaped out of the tunnel and onto the grounds of Fort Mifflin.

"Okay!" Dave exclaimed, rolling his window all the way down and sticking his right arm, with its pickaxe, out into open air. "Let the Deader Demolition Derby begin!"

Now you know why *I* drove.

CHAPTER 42
PARTY FAVORS

Tom

The northern sentry room filled up as twenty or so Corpses crowded in and went to work on the reinforced door at the far end. They hammered at it, snarling and snapping like a pack of dogs.

Tom watched them for a few moments. Then he called Chuck and said, "Let 'em have it."

Chuck let 'em have it.

The nozzles that had been mounted in the sentry room's ceiling opened up, raining liquid down on the heads of the dead. At first, the Corpses didn't seem to notice the spray. Then, gradually, a few did, turning their stolen eyes upward. They seemed confused, as if they'd expected saltwater and were surprised that it wasn't working on them.

No, not saltwater. At least, not yet.

Tom said into the sat phone, "Light 'em up."

Chuck lit 'em up.

The electrical wire that he'd run into the sentry room

fed into a small square box mounted near the floor. The box was Steve's brainchild, and it did just one, very simple thing.

It generated a spark.

The gasoline that rained down from the ceiling erupted into flame, engulfing every Corpse in the hallway and at least a dozen more in the parking lot beyond the open door. Tom watched as the creatures moaned in panic, throwing themselves against the walls and each other as the flames consumed their stolen bodies.

Within seconds, half of them were incinerated to the point where they could no longer stand. Seconds after that, the hallway floor was littered with twitching, fiery bodies.

And seconds after *that*, the dark energy started appearing.

Fascinated, Tom saw indistinct, man-sized shapes emerge from disintegrating bodies that could no longer protect them. These figures had no physical form—the *Malums'* Selves, the part of them that had crossed the Rift.

Fear and hatred radiated from them as, one by one, each of them died.

The hallway went quiet.

"Cool!" Chuck exclaimed over the phone.

***

In the subway spur, three hundred Corpses, Cole included, rushed for the door to Haven's southern entrance. As they neared it, Tom lifted the sat phone and dialed Jillian.

"Step One," he told her.

On the monitor, the Corpses hesitated a second time

as four small sections of the wall on either side of Haven's southern entrance popped open. The newly revealed gaps were only nine inches square, just wide enough to let the business end of four air cannons emerge.

Air cannons were actually easy to get. Stadiums used them all over the country to launch T-shirts and other soft, harmless projectiles into gimmick-hungry crowds. Powered by compressed air, they could shoot hundreds of feet.

But, for their purposes, the Undertakers only needed dozens of feet.

The first cannon fired, not with a *boom* but more of *thwump*, its load overshooting the stolen heads of hundreds of deaders before smashing into the ceiling of the spur. There the projectile burst in an expanding cloud of falling crystals.

Salt crystals.

The second cannon fired. Then the third.

Each projectile weighed less than three pounds, but its packaging had been constructed to send the salt in a hundred different directions on impact.

The fourth cannon fired. Then the first fired its second volley.

From somewhere within the horde of snarling, moaning dead, Tom heard Cole's voice. "Forward! Attack now! Quickly!

As the cannons continued to fire, and as more and more salt peppered—pun intended—the faces and shoulders of every deader in the subway spur, Tom raised another sat phone to his lips.

This time, he was talking to Hugo Ramirez. "Step Two, Hugo."

"My pleasure," the agent replied.

There came a rumble from the ceiling above the spur.

Ramirez had planted a small explosive charge in the sewer system just above the subway tunnel. Nothing disastrous—all it did was rupture the right pipe.

The ceiling collapsed as toilet water, lots of it, spilled down.

The Corpses flew into a panic.

The cannons kept firing, this time lower, their contents slamming into heads of fleeing dead people and bursting all over adjacent dead people. Meanwhile, Cole's voice roared over the general chaos. "Attack! You cowards! Attack!"

But even as he said this, the sewage and the salt mixed, and more and more of his soldiers fell. At first they convulsed, writhing in the mud. Then, as the mud thickened and the exposure to saltwater increased, their control over their stolen nervous systems collapsed completely.

Not dead. Just trapped.

I'll take it, Tom thought.

***

Meanwhile, at the northern entrance, where the narrow corridor led from the sewer door right to Haven's threshold, Corpses were crowding through single file. They didn't seem to appreciate the deafening heavy metal music being piped in all around them.

Then again, it wasn't for their entertainment.

A dozen deaders filled the confined space. Then two dozen.

Enough.

Tom picked up the third phone and dialed. "Burt," he said. "Do it."

"You got it, Chief."

Mounted high in the shadows at the top of the long corridor were dozens of cages, the noise coming from within them drowned out by the roaring music. At the press of a button, these cages popped open and their contents tumbled down onto the unsuspecting dead.

Cats.

Since moving into Haven, the Undertakers had been dealing with the cat problem. A century ago, in an effort to fight the rat infestation in City Hall's cellars, cats had been introduced. But they'd done more than just clear out the rats—they'd replaced them. Now, after generations born without daylight or human contact, these animals were feral and, when cornered, *very* aggressive.

Since moving in, the Monkeys had set up humane traps to capture these noisy, dangerous pests. The original policy had been to release them somewhere away from people. Then, about a month ago, Tom had instituted a *new* policy.

Now, they trapped and *kept* them.

The creatures that rained onto the heads of the Corpses bore little resemblance to "kitties." They were scrawny, muscular, bad-tempered biting and clawing machines.

The loud music didn't help matters.

Their captivity hadn't helped either.

Neither did the fact that the corridor stank of rotting flesh.

These cats *loved* rotting flesh.

The chaos caused by angry, hungry cats shredding the faces of the startled dead was perhaps the most satisfying of all the party favors. While they could feel no pain, the *Malum* nevertheless recoiled in terror as their eyes were torn out by creatures that seemed to be everywhere at once.

Then, in the midst of such chaos, Burt killed the lights.

***

Tom said into all three phones, "Solid work, everyone. Get ready for the next wave."

Susan Ritter was at his side again. "Think they'll give up?"

He looked at her. "Do *you?*"

Before she could answer, another voice sounded through one of the monitor's speakers.

"Chief Jefferson ..."

Cole.

Tom studied the image of the Corpse commander, who stood amongst his fallen peeps. Around him the air cannons had gone silent, the rainfall of filthy water having dropped to a trickle.

That particular game was over.

And, somehow, Cole had avoided the saltwater mud bath.

Tom watched the deader commander move easily from rare dry patch to rarer dry patch, often treading on the backs of his convulsing soldiers. Will had warned him about Specials—how their strength and speed was unique, even among Corpses.

Well, here it was in action.

"I commend you. You understand the principles behind siege warfare. I am receiving reports from our other attack points of different but equally effective measures. Well-played, Chief."

Tom offered no reply and Cole didn't seem to require one.

He said, *"But we are legion, Chief Jefferson. Kill twenty of us, and forty replace them. How much salt do you have? How much gasoline? How many cats? We will outlast you, overrun you, and kill you all.*

"*But I couldn't let you die without expressing my admiration.*"

As Tom watched, the Corpse reached down, grabbed one of his fallen soldiers, and blithely tore the deader's head from his shoulders. Then, with a furious gleam in his milky eyes, he *threw* the head at the camera.

The monitor winked out.

"Get ready, Susan," Tom told Haven's medic. "From here on, kids are gonna start gettin' hurt."

CHAPTER 43
DERBY

The Corpses spotted us almost immediately, which wasn't surprising, since ours were the only lights left on in the fort.

Three of them, a couple of Type Twos and a really gamy-looking Type Four, headed our way immediately. The Twos were fast, bounding across the grass like gazelles. The Four moved more stiffly, making me wonder what he was doing on guard duty anyhow.

"Ready?" I asked Dave.

"Oh, yeah!" he replied, a stupid grin on his face.

I turned the Tacoma toward the advancing deaders. The four-wheel-drive truck bounced crazily over the uneven ground, but it stayed upright and kept going.

The Type Twos split up at the last minute, probably hoping to jump onto the sides of the cab or maybe into the truck bed. The Four, for reasons I can still only guess at, kept to the middle.

The Type Two on the left lunged at the Burgermeister,

who swung his pickaxe, slamming it into the dude's chest with enough force to knock him completely off his feet and send him flying.

"Nailed him!" he exclaimed.

The one on the right made a grab for my door, his face—a Halloween mask of death and animal fury—suddenly filling the driver's side window.

I slammed on the brakes and watched him get torn off and go tumbling over the hood. The moment his body hit the grass, I gunned it and squashed his head under one wheel. I felt the bump.

A moment later, the Type Four hit our grill, and got splattered across the windshield for his trouble.

Three down.

I had no idea how well the girls were doing, and didn't have anything like the time to look for them.

Six more deaders were coming.

"Floor it!" Dave yelled.

I floored it.

The Tacoma sprang forward, churning up the grass. To our left stood the Arsenal, a small, one-story building of yellow brick. To our right was the Quartermaster's House. We were steering for the central building, the Commandant's House, which was where maybe half of the Corpse contingent seemed to be hanging out.

Why not steer straight for the Magazine? Because to pull this off, we had to take out as many deaders as we could first.

The truck's speedometer hovered around forty, not bad, given the uneven parade grounds. The steering wheel bounced in my hands like a living thing, while each new jolt dug my seatbelt painfully into my midsection.

Nevertheless, I pushed the accelerator pedal a little harder.

Forty-five.

We hit a circle of deaders, a half-dozen of them, all of whom scrambled to get out of our way. I clipped one with the front fender and managed to rip his leg clean off. Another stumbled and went head first into one of the headlights, breaking it. A third tried to jump onto the hood, but mistimed it and instead bounced over the roof. A fourth took Dave's pickaxe in the face. His head came clean off.

The other two, however, managed to make it into the truck bed.

"Crap!" I yelled.

Then I hit the brakes again.

They both flew forward, slamming into the back of the cab.

I hammered the gas—*hard*.

One tumbled backward and fell out over the tailgate. The other grabbed onto the edges of the cab roof, hanging on like grim—well—death.

"Crap!" I yelled again.

A dead fist shattered the cab's rear window; grasping dead fingers reaching for my throat.

I took one hand off the wheel—not a good idea—and fished out my pocketknife. Activating its Taser, I reached back and blindly stabbed with it, hoping to connect.

I did.

The electricity passed through the Corpse and into the truck bed. It didn't quite zap Dave and me, but we felt it, and it almost caused me to lose control of the wheel completely.

The deader however, stiffened and fell back into the empty bed, did a crazy sort of momentum-driven backward somersault, and then went the same way as his bud, out over the tailgate.

I cut the wheel hard, brought us around, and, before either deader could regain his feet, flattened them both.

Nine down.

"Dude," the Burgermeister said. "Watch it with that Taser, will ya?"

"Sorry," I told him.

We spotted the girls.

The Escape had gone around the back of the Arsenal, hammered two deaders, and was cutting across the parade grounds behind us, straight into a mass of four more Corpses.

Helene drove and Sharyn, like Dave, was leaning out the passenger window. In her hand she wielded Vader, which was working at least as well as Dave's pickaxe. Heads went flying. Three of the four Corpses were decapitated as Helene spun the wheel, bringing the SUV around in a tight circle.

The fourth managed to jump onto the hood, hanging on fiercely as the Escape neared the Officers Quarters.

For a terrible moment, I thought Helene meant to drive right through the building's wooden frontage. But instead, just before she hit the porch, she slammed on her brakes. The deader clinging to the hood went flying into one of the vertical posts holding up the porch roof. The post snapped in half.

So did his spine.

So far, so good.

I spun the wheel again and brought the Tacoma back around. With the Escape following, we headed for the East Magazine.

This wasn't a normal building, but instead more like a big grassy mound. Around its front was a narrow brick entranceway that led into a tight left turn and then a tight right turn before spilling into a large windowless space with an arched brick ceiling. This was where, once upon a time, the fort had stored gunpowder.

When I'd visited it as sixth grader, the East Magazine had stood empty and eerily quiet, since no sound could penetrate the layers of brick and dirt.

Now, according to Dillin, there was a door in there, big and steel and built very recently. And beyond that, the Anchor Shard.

That was the good news.

The *bad* news was that I'd lost sight of the rest of the Corpses. They'd run off somewhere, probably into one of the buildings to regroup.

On top of that, a new light now illuminated the darkened fort.

A helicopter was approaching, flying low over the northern ramparts.

And I knew who had to be onboard.

CHAPTER 44
BREACH

Tom

"*They're through!*" Chuck reported from the western entrance. He was trying to be cool about it, but there was no missing the edge of terror in his words. *"We cooked maybe sixty of 'em before we ran out of gas! Then they just climbed over their charred buds and hit the door!"*

"Where you at now?" Tom asked urgently.

"Back at the first barricade, about forty of us. We're hosing 'em with Super Soakers, but they just keep coming!"

"On my way. Pull back more if you gotta." He broke the connection and yelled, "Susan!"

Will's mom came running, her face going pale. "Tom?"

"The Corpses broke through the west entrance. I'm headin' there. If ... *when* you get calls from Burt or Jillian, put 'em through to me. Can you do that?"

"Of course." Then: "Tom, what if—"

He fixed her with as hard a look as he could muster.

"Even if they get through the western entrance, we might be able to hold the line a bit longer. But if the southern one falls, with the numbers they got in that subway spur ... Susan, if that happens, grab the girls and go out the through the maintenance door into City Hall."

She shook her head. "I can't. I told you, I'm not—"

He took her shoulders. "I'm your chief. And I'm asking you to make sure those girls get out of here alive. You hear me?"

"The wounded ..."

So he told her what he'd really hoped he wouldn't have to. "Susan, if Haven gets overrun, there won't be nothin' you can do for the wounded."

A single tear rolled down her cheek. But she nodded. "If we do get out ... what then?"

"You run," he told her. "And you keep running, as fast and far as you can. Change your name. Disappear. And pray."

She nodded again.

Tom turned and did his own running.

As he tore through the empty, dimly-lit corridors, the only sound at first was his own ragged breathing. But then he picked up cries, fearful and desperate, and he hastened his pace. Past the cafeteria. Past the Brain Factory. Almost to his own office.

Then, in the corridor ahead, he saw.

Corpses were *throwing* kids, slamming them up against walls.

They'd breached the hallway barricade. Tom didn't look at the bodies on the floor. He didn't dare. He simply pulled out his pocketknife, popped the **2** and **3** buttons together, and leaped into the fray. His Taser zapped, and his knife sliced. A Corpse went down, his brain stem severed. Another fell, his eye pierced all the way to the frontal lobe.

More came.

"Chuck!" he called.

"He's down," someone answered. A girl holding a Dillin Dagger. One of the newer recruits. Tom didn't even know her name.

"Soaker!" he yelled.

Someone threw him one. It was pretty full and he started firing, crippling one deader after another.

More came.

"Back!" he cried. "Everybody back!"

Kids darted past him, blurs of frantic movement. Corpses tried to follow, but Tom hosed them, moving in careful rearward steps, his eyes locked on the advancing enemy.

His sat phone rang.

Oh God!

"Get down, Chief!" someone yelled.

Tom didn't question the command. He didn't turn to see who'd said it. He just dropped to the hallway floor.

An instant later, a flash of white light lanced the air above him, so heavy with power that the hairs on the back of his neck stood on end. Lifting his head, he saw the white light hit the first two Corpses. They disintegrated before his eyes, turning to dust in a split second.

A moment later, a second flash lasered out, cutting down another three deaders. Then a third, which turned two more of Cole's soldiers to ash.

Finally, the rest clued in and either turned and fled or ducked into nearby rooms for cover.

Tom rolled over and sat up.

Steve Moscova stood maybe ten feet behind him. He wore some kind of contraption on his back that it took Tom a moment to identify: a car battery. The battery was wired to the anchor shard, held in place with thickly applied electrical tape. Steve clutched the alien crystal in his right hand, on which he wore a heavy gauge rubber glove.

"Answer your phone," the Brain Boss told him.

Tom stood up and did just that.

A moment later, Burt's voice was in his ear. *"Outta cats, Chief! They're at the door. They'll be in any second."*

"Fall back!" Tom told them. "I'm on my way."

He went to Steve. "What is that thing?"

The boy shrugged. "Haven't had time to name it. It just occurred to me that maybe the Shard's effect on organic matter had … military applications. Looks like I was right. Was that my brother?"

Tom nodded.

"Is he okay?"

"Yeah." Tom turned to the kids filling the hallway, the remainder of Chuck's contingent. "Listen up!" He called. "Work with Steve. Some o' y'all get the wounded to the Infirmary. I want the rest to pull back as far as the first intersection and hold the line as long as you can."

"Where's Chuck?" Steve asked nervously.

"Don't know," Tom told him. "Wounded … I hope."

The boy's face lost some of its color. But his grip on the Anchor Shard remained steady.

Tom said, "I gotta get to the northern entrance."

"Take this," the boy replied, motioning to the crossbow at his hip. "I spent some time with it after Will and the rest got back with his Dillin Dagger idea. I've replaced the Ritterbolts with Dillinbolts … regular crossbow bolts coated with Corpse-killing poison. They're rapid fire, so no reloading. But I only had time to make six of them."

Tom leaned in and detached Aunt Sally from Steve's belt. "Since when are you Rambo?" he asked the boy.

"Since Ian died. Now get going. I got this."

Tom got going, once again navigating Haven's warren of corridors. He passed the Monkey Barrel. He passed Sharyn's room, and Helene's, and Will and Dave's. What were they up to now? Were they even still alive?

He couldn't spare the time to worry about it.

Maybe thirty Undertakers filled the chambers just inside the northern entrance. As Tom arrived, Burt ran up to meet him. "Alex did something to the door that seems to be holding them off ... for now."

Tom sidestepped him and ran to the small room that marked the edge of Haven's border. There was the old sewer door, barred and bolted as its western counterpart had been, shaking and trembling with the weight of the dead behind it.

But, he noticed, it *wasn't* giving way.

A three foot steel bar had been hammered into the floor about two feet from the exit. Then the bar had been tilted forward, until its opposite end rammed firmly up against the door.

"It's a buttress," Alex said. "The same thing they used to use to hold up cathedral roofs."

"They can't break it down?" Tom asked him.

"The buttress? Not a chance. But Chief ... they *will* eventually split the wood enough to tear the door away from the other side. Then we're toast."

Tom turned to Burt, who'd come up behind him. "Start moving your Undertakers back to the first intersection. Once the Corpses get through, pick a few kids and make their only duty grabbing any wounded and getting them to the Infirmary."

"Gotcha, Chief," Steve's little brother said. Then: "Is my brother okay?"

Despite everything, Tom smiled at that. "He's cool. In fact, he's awesome. He's holding 'em back at the western entrance with the Anchor Shard ... and a bucket o' guts."

Burt's grinned. "That's my bro. How about Chuck?"

Tom's smile died. "I don't know."

The boy's grin vanished. "K," was all he said.

"One thing at a time," Tom told him.

Then he handed Alex the Super Soaker. "Use this when they bust through. Might buy y'all a chance to pull back."

Alex took it. "Chief," he said, with an odd, completely uncharacteristic look on his face. "I'm scared out of my mind."

"I know it, man. Me, too."

His sat phone rang again. Even before he answered it, he knew what the news would be.

The southern entrance is falling. We're down to minutes. Will. Hurry up.

CHAPTER 45
THE MAGAZINE

We were almost at the East Magazine when the rest of the Corpses, having recovered themselves and reorganized, attacked.

They rushed out of the Commandant's House, maybe a dozen of them. A few targeted our flank while the rest charged the Escape, their stolen legs carrying them across the uneven ground like loping tigers.

A Type Three lunged at our open passenger window, but the Burgermeister gave him a mouthful of pickaxe, with enough force to snap the deader's neck like a dry twig. At the same time, two more Type Twos slammed into the Tacoma's side and hung on as I gunned it. A head appeared in the corner of Dave's window, teeth snapping, trying to take a bite out of the boy's thick biceps.

I spun the wheel and he went flying.

The last one scrambled up onto our hood, so I took a page from Helene's book and made for the Commandant's House, slamming on my brakes at the last second. The deader flew forward and slammed, head first, into the side of the big building's red brick porch.

Nearby, the helicopter was settling in over an empty patch of parade ground, the wash of its blades throwing up dust and grass clippings. It was a small chopper, and it bore the City of Philadelphia's official seal on its sides.

I could throw another EMP, I thought feverishly. *Make it crash.*

But no. If I did that, then both the SUV and the Tacoma would get fried as well, leaving us stranded in the dark with Corpses all around.

So instead, I threw the truck into reverse, spun the wheel, and looked for the girls.

I found them.

The Escape was in trouble.

Most of the remaining Corpses seemed to have focused on the small SUV, hammering at it and rocking it back and forth. Amidst their bodies, I could see Vader flashing out, again and again. One head went flying. Then two. A third dead dude got stabbed right through the eye, Sharyn's blade popping out the back of his rotting skull.

It wasn't enough.

As the Burgermeister and I watched, the Corpses gave a final heave and rolled the struggling SUV onto its side.

"Will!" Dave yelled.

"I see it!" I slammed my foot down on the gas pedal. "Get ready!"

Our Tacoma reached the Escape within seconds, its engine noise masked by that of the SUV, which roared like a toppled elephant. Though the windshield hadn't broken, I still couldn't see the girls. It was just too dark.

"Now!" I told Dave.

He extended his right arm, axe-point horizontal against the slipstream.

I drove past the Escape at high speed, having picked an angle that would put most of the Corpses between us and them.

Their heads exploded as the pickaxe hit them. The impacts would probably have torn my arm off. But Dave's arm wasn't mine and, though he gritted his teeth, he kept steady.

Three heads. Four. Five.

Not bad.

Then the rest scattered.

"Helene!" I yelled.

"Sharyn!" he yelled.

No answers.

I slammed on the brakes, put the truck in park, and we both climbed out. I jumped up onto the Escape's upended flank and grabbed the passenger side door handle. At the same time, the Burgermeister came around the front of the SUV, leaning over to peer through the windshield.

I'd expected the car door to be locked. It wasn't, but instead opened so wide that I almost toppled backward off the Escape's slippery side and down to the grass. Luckily, I managed to grab onto the doorframe and steady myself.

"We're okay!" came a voice from inside the car. It sounded weak.

"Helene?"

"I'm here!"

"I'm here too, little bro!" Sharyn added. "Thanks for asking!"

"Dave, they're okay!"

The Burgermeister let out a sound halfway between a grunt and a cheer. "So, get 'em out!" he yelled.

I reached my hand down to Sharyn, but she shook her head. "Can't do it. My leg's pinned under the seat and Helene's belt buckle's jammed. We'll need a couple minutes."

Dave exclaimed, "Get clear. I'll break the glass!"

"Don't!" Sharyn yelled. "You'll cut us both up!"

"Will," Helene told me. I could just see her now, little more than a shape among shadows. "Go! We're fine!"

"I'm not leaving you! There's more of them! And a helicopter!"

"Listen to me, Ritter!" the girl called back. "Haven's in trouble. Your mom. Your sister. *My* sister. We don't know how much time they've got. It might already be too late. Go!"

She was right. As horrible as it was, she was absolutely, one hundred percent right.

Maybe *dead* right.

That was when I glanced over at the helicopter, and my heart stopped beating.

It did. I swear it did.

A Corpse was climbing out.

A female Corpse. A Type One.

I exclaimed, "Cavanaugh's here!"

"Red," Sharyn told me, her tone totally calm, totally in control. "You gotta get to that Anchor Shard. This ain't 'bout us. It ain't even 'bout Haven. It's 'bout everything, all of it. You gotta leave us. Now."

The Queen was scanning the battleground. We had maybe five seconds before she spotted the toppled SUV. After that, she'd be on us like a hungry cheetah.

Hating it, and hating myself for doing it, I jumped off the SUV. "Come on, Dave," I said flatly as I pulled his backpack and Kimball's duffel out of the Tacoma.

The big kid looked from me to Sharyn, and then back to me. "But, Will—"

"Hot Dog!" Sharyn yelled through the windshield.

"Get it done. It's cool!" Then, after a beat she added, "I love you."

For a moment, I didn't think he'd come. And I don't think I would have blamed him. But then, with more pain on his face than I'd ever seen there, he followed after me and we ran for the East Magazine.

We reached the brick entranceway, staying low, trying to keep the truck and the toppled SUV between us and the helicopter—

—staying out of Cavanuagh's line of sight.

We almost made it.

"Ritter!" I heard just as we ducked into the entranceway.

"Run!" I told Dave, handing him his backpack and pushing him ahead of me.

A tight left turn, followed by a tight right turn.

Then came the large chamber lit by a single arc lamp. Brick walls. High arched ceiling. And a newly constructed cinderblock wall, cutting the room's length in half, broken by a single door.

A heavy metal door.

Like a freaking *submarine* door. You know: the kind with a big wheel in the center instead of a doorknob.

And a thick chain and combination lock holding the wheel in place.

The Burgermeister uttered some words I didn't think *anyone* would approve of. Then he turned to me, sweat glistening on his brow. "You gotta pick the lock, dude."

"I can't," I said, holding up my pocketknife. "This only works on keyholes, not combo locks."

It was *totally* Cavanaugh. Keys could be lost or stolen, but combinations were numbers that stayed safe in her head.

"We gotta get in there!" Dave exclaimed.

"So *get* us in there!" I yelled back.

He held up his right arm. "Oh."

"I'll guard your six."

I turned toward the Magazine's narrow entrance, my Taser and knife in one hand, a water pistol in the other.

Behind me, I heard the Burgermeister's pickaxe strike the chain. A loud *clank*. Metal on metal.

"Damn!" he cried.

"Keep trying!" I told him.

"Mr. Ritter?"

I leveled my pistol, but the voice had come from around the bend—just out of sight.

"What are you up to in there, Mr. Ritter?"

Answer or not answer?

I decided to answer.

"Nothing," I called back. "Never mind us. Just sightseeing."

"I rather doubt it," she said. "What did that traitor Dillin tell you?"

Behind me, the pickaxe came down a second time. Loud. Dave cursed again.

"Who?" I asked.

She chuckled—an awful sound. But, behind it, I thought maybe I heard a little fear. "I'm prepared to be generous with you, Mr. Ritter," she said. "Just walk out of there and I'll let you go."

I waited ten seconds. Stalling.

Dave struck again. "Crap."

"Mr. Ritter?" the Queen cooed. "This is a limited-time offer, and the clock is ticking."

I looked at the Burgermeister. He looked at me, his right arm raised for another blow.

I nodded.

The pickaxe came down. The lock shattered. The

chain rattled as it fell to the floor.

I turned back to the entrance.

"Nice offer," I told the shadows beyond the turn in the entranceway. "Thing is: there's something I've always wanted to say to you, and now seems like the right time."

"Ritter … I'm *warning* you …"

I grinned and raised my pistol higher.

"Drop dead."

Behind me, the Burgermeister remarked, "Good line." Then he spun the wheel and pulled the heavy door open.

"No!" the Queen of the Dead roared in Deadspeak, the single telepathic word drilling into my brain.

Then she appeared.

I fired, but I wasn't even close to fast enough. Cavanaugh moved in a blur, knocking me over as she exploded past me.

Dave stood in the open doorway, his attention fixed on something that I couldn't see.

He'd just started to turn when the Queen hit him, slamming him up against the wall, nearly lifting the huge kid off his feet. His backpack crunched loudly with the impact. Dave tried to swing his pickaxe, but she caught his forearm in an iron grip, her other hand on his throat.

"Clever little attachment you've got there, child," she said through clenched teeth. "Had a little accident, did we?"

Then she let go of his forearm and grabbed the head of the axe, giving it a savage tug.

The Burgermeister cried out in pain as the leather straps snapped.

I climbed to my feet in time to see her throw the boy to the ground, toss the pickaxe across the room, and then turn to face me.

I fired my pistol.

Cavanaugh tried to dodge, but the saltwater caught her on one arm. I watched it go limp.

Snarling, she came at me, all power and menace.

But, lying on the ground at her feet, Dave caught her ankle with his only remaining hand, tripping her up.

She landed hard, losing several teeth on the Magazine's floor.

I fired again, this time catching her in the back of the head with my final squirt. She started to convulse.

"You okay?" I called to the Burgermeister.

"Yeah," he said, struggling to his feet, no easy task with only a stump for a right hand. He looked dazed.

I ran up and slammed my Taser into Cavanaugh's back, giving her a good long zap. I wanted to keep it there—a minute, maybe more—which would cost her that nice host body she was wearing.

But we didn't have time.

Straightening, I stared through the open door.

The Rift.

It was much like the hole in the world that Steve had made, only bigger—a shimmering, jagged black *nothing* that floated in mid-air, almost right up against the East Magazine's back wall.

This was it. The source of the invasion. The door that the *Malum* used to enter our world. Close it and it was over. No more would come. And the ones already here would die. Finally and forever die.

Including this monstrosity on the floor.

I ducked my head in and turned to the right. There, fitted into a niche beside the door, sat the Anchor Shard. The crystal was about the same size as ours, though shaped a little differently. And it was connected to six—count 'em—*six* car batteries.

Cavanaugh, knowing the stakes, had taken no chances.

"Um … dude?"

Something in Dave's voice made me turn.

In his hand, he held the MacDonald, the guillotine-like gadget that we were going to use to "time-delay cut" the cables powering the Shard.

Well, he held *part* of it, anyway.

The gadget had been in the Burgermeister's backpack when Cavanaugh had slammed him against the wall.

Now Dave stared down at its broken pieces, which had tumbled to the floor at his feet. On his face was a look of absolute, hopeless despair.

Oh God.

CHAPTER 46
KILLING FLOOR

Tom

When Tom reached the southern entrance, he found it a war zone.

The Corpses, after taking losses in the hundreds, had eventually reached the old service door, climbing over the bodies of their peeps to do it. Fueled by rage and Cole's ferocious discipline, they'd hammered at the door until, finally, it was torn away.

Then they'd come in.

Tom counted maybe a dozen of them, mostly Types Threes and Fours. Not the crack warriors—most of *those* probably had gone down in the sewer-saltwater.

But bad enough.

And worse, they were just the beginning. Beyond the open doorway, he could see dozens, maybe hundreds more. The only thing keeping them out, keeping Haven from being completely overwhelmed, was the fact that most of the combat was going on right here, at the threshold, stopping up the works.

The Undertakers were fighting as best they could with whatever weapons remained at hand. The air cannons were out of ammo—useless. The Super Soakers were all empty. They were down to water pistols, Dillin Daggers, and clubs of one kind or another.

And they were losing.

Turning the corner, Tom took all this in within seconds. Then, cupping his hands around his mouth, he yelled at the top of his voice, "Fall back! Undertakers! Fall back!"

But combat was noisy, and not all of them heard.

Those who *did* hear started the retreat. And those who heard but weren't in a position to do anything about it kept fighting. Kid after kid went down, until the floor was littered with small human bodies.

Tom felt his stomach flip-flop, but not with nausea.

With guilt.

I blew it. I've killed them all.

But then that unhelpful thought buried itself in the back of his mind. It would stay there until later when, if he survived, he could pull it out again and decide for himself if it was true.

He had other priorities.

Aunt Sally was hooked to his belt. For now, he left it there. He only had six Dillinbolts, and something told him he would need them.

So instead, with his pocketknife in one hand, he snatched up a length of lead pipe that one of the fighters had dropped.

Then he waded in.

He spotted Katie. The girl was pressed up against the wall, just inside the shattered entrance. Two Corpses were on her, their arms swinging and their teeth snapping.

Tom went to her rescue, bashing deaders to his left and right. When one got close, Tom gave him a zap in the eye and he went down. When another leaped up and grabbed him by the throat with rotting hands, Tom rammed the pipe into his gaping mouth with such force that it exploded out the back of the Corpse's skull.

He reached the two who were attacking Katie, hammered one with the pipe and rammed his knife blade into the other's brain stem. Both dropped like sacks of sand. Katie looked up at him, her face cut and bruised, her eyes glassy with fear.

"You solid?"

She blinked. Then, she said in a shaky voice, "I think so. But Tom ... there's so *many*!"

"I know."

Tom spun in a circle, beating down two more deaders in the process. One of them dropped, but then latched onto his ankle, biting deeply into the flesh of his calf. Pain lanced up his leg, making him cry out.

Then Tom pivoted and slammed his other foot down against the Corpse's temple. The dead dude's skull caved in.

"Get everyone back," he told Katie. "Toward the Infirmary. Grab the wounded. Bring 'em along."

"But they'll be on us, Chief! Every step of the way!"

"No, they won't. Go!"

She nodded and started yelling at the others to fall back.

Meanwhile, Tom pulled Aunt Sally off his belt.

It wasn't a practical weapon, not against these numbers. But right now his priority was to give Katie and her crew time to retreat and regroup.

But ... where's Jillian?

As three more Corpses piled through the ruined doorway, he kicked one hard in the chest, knocking him back into his friends. Then he took aim and fired a

Dillinbolt into another's midsection.

The deader squealed in terror as the salted metal bolt perforated his stomach.

At the same time, two more Corpses came at Tom from behind. Sensing them, he ducked under a swinging arm and came up with his knife, planting it in the first one's forehead. The second one he tripped, caught it in a one-armed headlock, and *twisted*.

The Corpse's neck snapped.

At the same instant, the deader he'd "Dillined" exploded.

"Keep going!" Katie yelled to the other Undertakers.

How many more were behind him? Three? Four? With hundreds in front?

This was beginning to seem like a really bad idea.

So he backed himself up against the side wall and fired his next bolt into the chest of the freshest-looking cadaver. The creature groaned and spun around, grabbing onto one of his buds, as if that would help.

The Corpse exploded. Parts rained everywhere. As with the first, a vague man-sized shape appeared where the monster had been. It was already dying.

For a moment, the deaders all stopped, looking at the apparition with what seemed to be genuine horror.

"We call 'em Dillinbolts!" Tom announced. "And *that's* what happens when I stick you with one. No new host. No rising to fight again. Just dead. Real, solid, permanent dead."

A nearby Corpse hissed, "You can't kill us all, boy!"

Tom shot him in the gut.

Then as the third one popped like a meat balloon, he took aim again.

"Nope," he admitted. "But I can kill whoever takes the next step!"

Then, focusing Aunt Sally's attention over all of them at once, he slowly maneuvered himself until he stood at the mouth of the corridor, with all of the Corpses in front and the fleeing Undertakers at his back.

The deaders watched him, hissing and snarling.

But none of them moved.

Standoff.

Then a voice said, "Chief Jefferson."

Cole appeared in the doorway, throwing hesitant Corpses aside like rag dolls. He was still in his Type One body, fresh and strong and fast. He grinned as he stood there, unafraid and in total control.

"Look at me, boy," he said, emerging into the corridor, into Haven. "I took a step!"

"Yeah, you did," Tom muttered.

Then he fired.

Cole's hand shot up and caught the bolt.

Still smiling, he dropped it to the floor.

And took another step forward.

"You have courage, Undertaker," he said. "And you've managed to instill that courage in your people. My compliments."

Tom took aim and fired.

Cole grabbed a nearby Corpse and, to the deader's horror, used him as an *inhuman* shield. The Dillinbolt caught the dead guy in his chest. Laughing, Cole tossed him aside, where he exploded.

Tom had one shot left.

"Better make it count, Chief," the Corpse commander told him, sidestepping two more of his soldiers, who skittered nervously away. They'd seen what he'd done to the last dude who'd come within reach. "A child general," Cole remarked, sounding amused. "I'm amazed it's taken the Queen this long to exterminate you, despite your obvious talents."

Tom raised Aunt Sally and leveled it at the deader's torso.

One last shot.

Cole grinned, showing loose yellow teeth. "Fire when ready, Chief. But first, any last words?"

"Watch out for the girl," Tom said.

The Corpse's smile faded. "What girl?"

Jillian rose up from among the fallen bodies, both human and *Malum*, that littered the floor. She was covered in cuts, and half her face was swollen from a blow she'd evidently taken. But her eyes were clear as she slipped past the two remaining Corpses in the hallway, turned, and ran right up the left-hand wall.

Then using the momentum and added height, she executed a perfect back flip and landed smoothly on Cole's shoulders.

"*This* girl," she said.

Throwing all her weight backward, she toppled the stunned Corpse commander, pulling him down onto his back before rolling clear.

Tom stepped up and fired.

His last Dillinbolt hit Cole in the chest. The deader stared at it as if not quite able to believe it was there.

Then, in Deadspeak he said, *"You. Will. Die. Anyway."*

"Everybody does," Tom told him.

As Jillian regained her feet and ran to Tom's side, the Corpse commander exploded. For a few seconds, his Self floated in the air, not panicked, but oddly calm.

Until, with a funny *pop,* it vanished.

As if on cue, the rest of them charged, pouring through the door and rushing at the boy and girl like a stampede, like a tidal wave—

—like a horde of the living dead.

CHAPTER 47
THE END

"What do we do?" the Burgermeister asked, looking at me.

My mind reeled.

We've made it so far!

Faces flashed through my memory. They started with my father, who'd been murdered by the Corpses. Then came Tara Monroe, who'd died so that I and a bunch of Undertaker recruits could escape. After that was Ian MacDonald, Haven's medic, killed in a freak accident while experimenting with the Anchor Shard. And others, so many others. Too many others. Charles O'Mally. Lindsay Micha. The nameless people along the river today, whose only crime had been being in the wrong place at the wrong time.

Principal Bob Dillin.

He'd been a Corpse, and yet he'd given his life to get us to this very point.

And we'd gone and blown it.

"I don't know," I said.

"Will," he pressed. "You *gotta* know!"

But I didn't. Looking down at the broken pieces of Steve's latest brainchild, I found myself empty. Zip. Zilch. The Idea Machine was down for the count.

Well, not entirely.

Sometimes dying well is its own reward.

"Dave," I said.

"Yeah?"

"I need you to do something."

"What?" he asked, his eyes as eager as a child's.

But, of course, he *was* a child. So was I. We all were.

"Get your pickaxe and use it to make sure Cavanaugh doesn't get up again." It was a legitimate concern, since the Queen's convulsions, brought on by my Taser, seemed to have slowed.

"Um ... sure. But what good will it do?"

I didn't reply. I just looked at him.

Then, as my friend turned and marched across the room to where Cavanaugh had thrown his new "hand," I eased through the doorway and into the Rift Room. Then, I carefully began to close the submarine door behind me.

Sorry, Dave.

At the last second, a hand darted through the shrinking gap between door and jamb, catching the metal's edge and holding it fast.

"I don't think so, Ritter," the Queen hissed, her dead face partially visible through the narrow gap.

Then she ripped the door all the way open and lunged at me.

We both tumbled back into the Rift Room. She was crazily, impossibly strong—yet not as strong as she *could* have been. Apparently, she hadn't completely recovered from the zap, which was the only thing keeping her from snapping my neck.

Fingers laced around my throat. I kicked upward, but she held on fast, her face a twisted mask of fury and hatred.

An instant later, she was off me, lifted up from behind and thrown out the open door and back into the front room. The Burgermeister lingered for a second. His gaze met mine, and I could see that he knew what I'd been planning to do.

And he didn't like it.

Not one bit.

But then he turned and charged Cavanaugh, who'd already regained her feet.

I struggled up and went after them, readying my pocketknife.

The Burgermeister body slammed the Queen, driving her back against the wall. But, as he tried to shove his huge forearm under her neck, she pushed him off with ridiculous strength and backhanded him to the floor.

Then, as I lunged with my Taser, she caught my wrist and threw me across the room, where I landed beside the pickaxe—

—and Kimball's duffle.

She didn't gloat. She didn't mock. She was past all that. All she did was come at me in slow, staggering steps, her stolen body badly damaged in the struggle. I rose to my feet, my head spinning.

My hand reached down. I'd hoped to come up with the axe.

Instead, I came up with the duffle.

For some reason, *The Wizard of Oz* flashed through my mind.

"Kill you ..." Cavanaugh murmured, reaching for

me with her cold, dead fingers. "Finally, kill you."

"Funny," I replied. "I was thinking the same thing."

Then I threw the contents of the duffle into her face.

The *Pelligog* nest exploded against her, the critters immediately latching on and boring in. Two dug out her eyes before disappearing into her skull. Another ate through one cheek. Two more wormed into her neck.

The Queen wailed and stumbled backward, pulling at them. Though I knew she couldn't feel pain, *something* that the creatures did was obviously hurting her. She spun in blind, crazy circles, bouncing off the newly constructed wall.

Then she fell to her knees.

As she did, I reached down again.

And *this* time I came up with the axe, holding it by one of its blades.

It was heavy. Really heavy. But I didn't mind.

Cavanaugh managed to pull one of the *Pelligog* off of her and crushed it in her fist. She tried to stand, but lost her balance and toppled over again, landing on her back in the dirt. Though her eyes were gone, she seemed to sense that I was there, because she suddenly went very still.

"I'm the Queen of the *Malum!*" she croaked, her cheek flapping hideously where one of the *Pelligog* had chewed through it. "What are you? What are you ... *boy* ... that you can do this to me?"

I stood over her and raised the pickaxe high.

"Ain't you heard?" I told her. "I'm the boogeyman."

Then I planted the axe in her forehead, turning her stolen brain to mush and pinning her to the floor.

Down.

Down but not out.

Not unless I could pull the plug on the Anchor Shard.

And that's when I heard the *clank*.

Loud. Metallic. Unmistakable.

I whirled around in time to see the wheel on the submarine door spin shut.

"Dave!" I screamed, throwing myself forward. I grabbed the wheel with frantic fingers and pulled. But it wouldn't budge. Had he somehow locked it? I didn't think it *had* a lock. Otherwise, what would've been the point of the chain and combo?

He *had* to be holding it.

"Dave!" I screamed again, though I wasn't even sure if he could hear me.

Then a muffled voice replied, "Yeah, dude."

"Open the door!"

"Can't do it. Got my stump wedged in real tight. Damn thing's good enough for that much at least. And it frees up my other hand, so that I can just reach the battery cables."

"No, Dave! Don't do it! We'll find another way!"

"Ain't no other way, dude. You know it as well as I do. You were gonna do it yourself, until the royal wormbag stopped you."

I considered lying, considered saying anything to get him to open the door. But the words wouldn't pass my lips.

So I said nothing.

There was a long pause. Then: "Will, you there?"

"I'm here," I replied. "Please ... open the door."

"Shut up and listen, will ya?"

I swallowed. It didn't help. My throat felt like the Sahara. My hands on the wheel were slick with sweat, and I could hear my heart hammering behind my ears.

Dave said, "I got something to tell you. And we both know I gotta be quick. So don't interrupt."

"I'm listening." I fought to keep my voice steady.

"Back in the old days..." He sounded like his lips were right against the door. "Before all this started ... I was a bully. A jerk. I know that. I picked on kids smaller'n me and thought it made me tough. But I didn't know what tough was ... not until I met you."

"Burgermeister—"

But he rolled right over me. "This skinny redheaded kid with more brains and guts than anyone I'd ever met. You *taught* me. You showed me what it means to be a hero. And now, finally, I get to pay you back."

Terrified, I beat on the door with my fists. Stupid. Useless.

He said, "Do me a favor? Tell Sharyn I'm sorry? Tell her ... aw, hell ... tell her I love her too, okay? I know it's cheesy. But, in return, I'll tell your dad you said hi."

"Dave, please!" I begged, openly sobbing now.

"You know," he said, "there's something from the movies, those war movies. Something they sometimes say. Always thought it was lame. But now ... now, I think I get it."

"Burgermeister ..."

"Will?"

I slid down the door, clutching the wheel, beaten. "Yeah. Yeah, Burgermeister?"

"It was an honor serving with you."

"No..." I whispered.

Then my friend, Dave "The Burgermeister" Burger, saved the world.

I didn't see the wave of released energy. The walls and the heavy door blocked it. But I saw the Queen's host, already limp, go completely and finally still. And I saw the *Pelligog* that were ravaging her body die. Every last one of them. I didn't know why or how, but closing the

Rift had killed them, too.

Lilith Cavanaugh managed a single, silent scream. Not Deadspeak exactly. But definitely telepathic. A shriek in my head that had a lot behind it.

Terror. Disbelief. Defeat.

And I knew that she'd been destroyed.

The rest I didn't find out about until later.

The effect of the closed Rift moved outward, like ripples in a pond.

It hit the parade grounds first. The last half-dozen of Cavanaugh's guard force were just about to break in on Sharyn and Helene inside the SUV when all of them just dropped dead.

The girls swapped incredulous looks.

"They did it …" Helene whispered.

After that, the ripples reached outward, away from Fort Mifflin and up into the city, where people of all walks of life—plumbers, teachers, doctors, taxi drivers, even a couple of priests—suddenly collapsed. Not hundreds of them. Not even thousands. *Tens* of thousands.

Every Corpse.

Everywhere.

People, human people, screamed as the Masks of their colleagues, bosses, or friends vanished, revealing the rotting cadavers beneath. Then these stolen bodies dropped where they stood, many breaking apart, some exploding in a rattling symphony of bones.

And in Haven, just as an army of the dead descended on Tom and Jillian, the whole of their attack force went limp and died, tumbling over one another. No man-sized lumps of dark energy. No final curses or groans.

It.

Was.

Over.

But, as I said, I didn't find out about all that until later.

For now, I just leaned against the submarine door, sobbing. Then, while trying to stand, I discovered that the wheel would turn. Moving as if in a trace, I spun it and pulled the door wide open.

The Rift was gone.

The Anchor Shard lay on the floor, a floor that looked as if it had been excavated down at least two inches. The walls were weirdly clean, though the bricks and mortar remained old and somewhat crumbly.

All organic matter ... I thought.

Dave was gone.

I spotted parts of a watch, his sat phone, and a few other trinkets shiny enough to catch the light bleeding in from the other room.

But that was it.

While I stood there, too stunned to move or speak—good old-fashioned shock, I guess—I heard tentative footsteps behind me. A hand touched my shoulder. It turned me around and I gazed down into a pair of hazel eyes.

Helene asked no questions.

She just put her arms around me, gently at first, and then fiercely.

It felt good.

"Hot Dog?" a quavering voice asked.

I looked up to see Sharyn standing in the doorway. As she came forward, I saw that she was limping a little. A twisted ankle maybe. Vader was still in her hand. She clutched it tightly as her gaze floated around the room, taking in everything before settling on me.

"Hot Dog?" she asked again.

Slowly, *very* reluctantly, I pulled away from Helene,

whose eyes had blurred with tears. Then, on legs that felt stiff as tree trunks, I went to Sharyn.

Seeing something in my face, she said, "No."

I came closer.

"No," she repeated, her voice breaking.

Then she fell into my arms.

So I held her. I held her as Helene had held me.

I held her while she grieved.

CHAPTER 48
AWAKENINGS

Over the next few days, the truth started to come out. It does that.

Sometimes.

It started with the "incredible" news from Philly that not only had thousands of people dropped dead all at once, but most of them seemed to have instantly decomposed. Some folks, through blind 21st-century luck, had even managed to catch this on their smart phones.

Pretty quickly, crazy theories popped up: terrorists, aliens, zombies, government conspiracies.

Okay, maybe they weren't so crazy.

Since fully half of the police force "died" on the same night, the governor declared martial law in Philadelphia. The mayor was no help; he'd suffered some kind of mental breakdown and was blubbering to anyone who would listen about being visited by the walking dead.

Apparently, he'd even loaned one of them his

helicopter.

Then, in the midst of all that chaos, who should step up to the microphone but Senator James Mitchum.

He talked about alien invaders who animated the dead. He talked about how they'd disguised themselves, faked their backgrounds, and secured key positions, first at the city level, then at the state level, and then at the national level. He talked about Kenny Booth, Lilith Cavanaugh, and Lindsay Micha. He talked about Hugo Ramirez coming to him, and about the unmasking of Gregory Gardner.

And he talked about the Undertakers.

He talked a *lot* about the Undertakers.

But all of that came much later.

Today wasn't over yet.

The three of us left the East Magazine, emerging into an empty fort. There were bodies everywhere, just normal dead folks, all of whom were left behind when the *Malum* inside them—departed. They would need proper burials, of course. And they wouldn't be the only ones.

But that was somebody else's problem.

We checked the helicopter. In there, we found the body of the pilot. His neck was broken. Apparently, Cavanaugh had killed him the moment they'd landed, probably because he was human and she didn't want him getting in the way. Sounded like her style.

We headed back to Philly.

Center City was alive with activity, even this late at night. People crowded the streets. Emergency vehicles were everywhere.

A lot had happened and no one understood it.

We reached Haven, parked in the underground garage, and went in through the western entrance. The sentry room was crammed with cooked dead bodies. Not

Corpses—not anymore. Just dead people. You wouldn't think there'd be a difference.

But there is.

Getting past them wasn't easy, and it wasn't fun. But we did it, and made our way through the darkened corridors. No one was around.

We passed the northern entrance. Like the western one, it had been ripped open, the rooms just inside it littered with bodies.

None of us spoke. None of us had really spoken since leaving the fort. There just didn't seem to be anything to say. Now, in the wake of this destruction, all we could do was swap looks that mixed worry with exhaustion.

So far, as near as we could tell, none of the bodies were kids.

None of them were Undertakers.

The southern entrance, the one closest to the Infirmary, was the worst.

There had to be hundreds of now empty deaders piled into the corridor, all spilling through the ruined doorway that led into the subway spur. Getting to the doorway was impossible; there were too many bodies. But we could see through it a little bit, and what we saw chilled my blood.

Hundreds more were out there.

Haven had become a crypt.

But still, no kids.

We finally found them in and near the Infirmary.

The sounds reached us before anything else, floating up the corridor and around the bend. Voices. Lots and lots of voices.

We started running.

And that's where we came upon the Undertakers.

They were crammed into the Infirmary and the

various storerooms and bedrooms that lined the same corridor. Apparently, they'd all retreated here when the entrances were breached, and here they'd stayed, even though it was obvious to everyone that the danger had passed.

I saw Nick Rooney, the Moms' Boss. He was doing his thing: passing out bottled water and cookies to the kids who lined the hallway. A few were sleeping. Others were crying. Others just sat and stared into space.

But they were alive.

"Where's Tom?" I asked Nick.

He looked at me wearily, with neither surprise nor relief. Then he pointed to the Infirmary's entrance.

We went in.

The place was crammed. All the gurneys were full, and bedrolls had been set up all over the floor with more kids on them. Blood and broken bones, cuts and bruises. My mother moved among them, with Amy and Julie close behind, tending to the wounded while, off in a corner, Emily sat sucking her thumb.

"Will!" my little sister exclaimed, jumping up and running to me, throwing her arms around my legs, as was her way.

For a moment, my mom stopped and looked at me. Our gazes locked.

She smiled wearily.

Then she went back to work.

I understood.

Tom and Jillian came over.

Sharyn saw her brother and started crying again.

The chief wrapped her up in his arms and held her, much as I had back at Mifflin, but maybe more confidently. He didn't ask about Dave. He didn't have to. The Burgermeister wasn't with us, and that seemed to say everything that needed saying.

Tom told us that Chuck Binelli's body had been found at the western entrance, buried under a half-dozen deaders, most of which he'd taken out with his poisoned knife before they'd broken his neck. Steve, who'd taken charge of the crew, had pulled him and the rest of the fallen Undertakers out.

Their bodies now lay on cots that had been set up in the Brain Factory, with blankets draped over them.

All together, fourteen kids were known to be dead.

Fourteen.

At least, so far.

Dozens more were badly injured. The worst had already been taken to local hospitals, something that was no longer a death sentence.

Tom told us to get some rest, told us that pretty soon *people* would start coming. "Cops are stretched thin right now, since only the human ones are left. But pretty soon they'll find us and then the questions'll start. Once they do, they likely won't stop, not for a long time. So, if you can sleep, sleep. Y'all earned it."

He didn't thank us.

We didn't mind.

We were Undertakers.

And we'd *won*.

CHAPTER 49
NEXT

I tried to sleep. I really did. But it just wasn't happening. I hadn't slept in this cot for more than a month, having spent all that time in a tent with Dave up in Allentown. Now the tent was gone, and so was Dave, and nothing in this room felt familiar or in any way "right."

So I finally gave up.

And went to see Sharyn.

She was in her room, alone. Sharyn didn't have a roommate. She'd never had one, and, as co-chief, one had never been forced on her. She sat on her bunk, staring at nothing, much the same way Dave had been when he'd lost his hand.

For a long time, I just stood in the doorway and looked at her. I'd heard the term "heartsick" before, but until today I hadn't known what it meant.

Finally, I cleared my throat and said, "It should've been me."

She looked up, her eyes puffy from crying.

"I mean it," I told her. "It was *going* to be me, but Cavanaugh stopped me before I could shut the door. That's what gave him the idea. If I hadn't decided to 'take one for the team' or 'throw myself on the grenade' or whatever, then he might still be here."

"And Haven wouldn't be," she said.

I didn't reply; she was right.

"He was a *hero*, little bro," Sharyn told me, rising slowly to her feet. "And he did what heroes do. He did it for you and me ... and, I guess, for the whole world. But that don't keep it from hurtin'."

"He told me ..." I began, but the words stuck in my throat. So I swallowed and tried again. "He told me to tell you that he loves you, too."

She nodded, fresh tears falling freely.

"I'm sorry, Sharyn," I said.

"Me too, Red." Then: "Would it be cool if I went to your room later and ... I dunno ... packed his things? I guess his grandma should have them. His folks've been dead for years. I'd kinda like to be the one to take 'em to her ... just to meet her, you know?" Then she added hastily, "Unless *you* want to, I mean. He *was* your best friend."

"I think maybe we should both do it," I suggested.

"That'd be cool."

I left her alone.

Helene was in her room as well, lying on her back and staring at the ceiling. When she saw me, she jumped up and ran to me. We swapped a hug, and then a long, sad kiss. Might sound weird but, at the time, it seemed like the most natural thing in the world. I didn't ask her if she was okay and she didn't ask me. That would have been stupid.

So, instead, I said, "Um ... I love you."

"Me, too."

And that seemed like the most natural thing in the world, too.

I stayed with her for a while, until she fell asleep on her cot. Then I spent some time wandering Haven. I found Steve and Burt in the Brain Factory and hugged them both. I ran into Alex in the Monkey Barrel and shook his hand—a hug with that guy was just a bridge too far, if you know what I mean. I went by the cafeteria and spotted Katie. She was holding a pair of sunglasses and crying softly.

I let her be.

Finally, my feet led me back to my room. Walking in, I half expected to find the Burgermeister there, sprawled across his bunk like a gorilla in a hammock, snoring crazily. When I didn't, the sadness that crashed down on me was like a ten-ton weight.

Victory.

Except it didn't *feel* like victory.

I dropped onto my bunk, even though I had no intention of trying to sleep. That was just as well, since almost the moment I sat down, a Rift opened.

I blinked at it, too surprised to be scared.

Unlike the jagged hole that Steve had created in the Brain Factory, or the bigger one at Fort Mifflin, *this* Rift was a rectangle. A perfectly-shaped, faintly shimmering black doorway. It floated in the air beside Dave's cot, motionless.

I could see nothing through it.

Then a figure emerged, just stepped out of the nothing between here and whatever was *there*.

It was a woman.

Tall. Blond hair. Soft, angelic features.

"Hello, William," she said. For once, her voice didn't

sound like it was down a tunnel.

"Hello, Amy," I replied.

The woman smiled. There was a lot in that smile: sadness, regret, gratitude, sympathy. She wore a white "gown" that, for the first time, I understood to be some kind of lab coat, like they wear in hospitals.

She said, "So ... you figured it out."

I shrugged, lowering my gaze to my shoes. "Some of it. You've always looked familiar, but I could never place you, until this last time ... when you saved Julie and me from drowning. You always call me William, and the only people who ever did that were Ian, as a joke, and Amy, because Ian did it.

"I know you're Amy Filewicz ... grown up. And I know that you've somehow been reaching back in time, pulling me out when I got hurt or when you had something to tell me. I know that you haven't healed me, exactly, so much as cleaned my wounds and kept me with you, asleep, until my body healed itself. I know that at least a full year of my life has been spent in that 'white room' of yours.

"I know you've been trying to help me ... to help *us*. But that there were some things you couldn't tell me."

I looked up at her. "How'm I doin'?"

She replied, "Very well." Then she went to Dave's cot and sat down. It occurred to me, weirdly, that I'd never seen her sit before. "I'm so sorry about the Burgermeister. I wish ..." her words trailed off.

"And Chuck," I said.

She nodded. "Yes. And Chuck. And the others. Especially Ian." At the mention of his name, the woman's face fell. "I still think about him almost every day, even after all these years."

"We won, Amy," I said.

"Yes, you did."

"So why doesn't it feel that way?"

She said, "That's … a complicated question."

"And you're done answering my questions?"

Her smile was back, knowing but also slightly sad. "Actually, I came to see if you wanted me to answer *all* your questions."

That caught my attention. I sat up a little straighter. "Yeah," I told her. "I'd like that."

"But there's a catch," she said.

"Always is," I said.

She stood up and held out her hand. "Come with me."

I stared at her. "What?"

She motioned back at the Rift.

"I've seen the white room," I said dryly.

"There's a lot more than that. A *whole* lot more."

"I don't know if I've got the energy for a tour of the future."

Her smile vanished. "This isn't a tour. This is the *reason*."

"The reason? The reason for what? I don't get it."

"I know you don't, and it's too complicated to explain. But there are things you need to understand, things *we* need you to understand. Everything we've done for you up until this point has been part of a plan … a part that's now over. It ended the moment the Burgermeister pulled out that battery cable. But now there's the *next* part, one that's just as important, maybe even more so. And we need your help."

Great, I thought. *The future needs my help. Who doesn't?*

"To do what?"

She seemed to consider her words before answering.

"To make sure that the Burgermeister didn't die in vain."

I looked at her. "You'll show me everything?"

"Yes."

"And you'll bring me back?"

Did I see hesitation in her eyes? Apprehension? I wasn't sure. "Yes."

"Is it dangerous?"

A pau*se. "Yes. Very."*

*"Is it import*ant?"

"It's the most important thing in the world."

Great, I thought again.

I almost said no. In fact, I almost suggested she smooch my butt. Future Amy. The Queen of Secrets. *She* might have given me the knowledge I'd have needed to save so many people. But she hadn't. She'd been sick about it, that much I believed. But she still hadn't.

What kind of future is this?

So, I almost said no. Except for one thing.

She'd called him "Burgermeister." Not Dave. Not Burger. "Burgermeister."

And that told m*e something that made all the* difference.

I was looking at an Undertaker.

So I got up and put my hand in hers.

She sighed and smiled again, almost laughed.

"What's so funny?" I demanded.

"Nothing," she replied. "I ... just lost a bet."

Then she turned and, still holding my hand, led me into the Rift. As that weird shimmering darkness enveloped me, I remember thinking: So ... it's not over after all.

And it wasn't.

Not by a long shot ...

TY DRAGO

Ty Drago does his writing just across the river from Philadelphia, where the *Undertakers* novels take place. In addition to *The Undertakers: Rise of the Corpses, The Undertakers: Queen of the Dead,* and *The Undertakers: Secret of the Corpse Eater,* he is the author of *The Franklin Affair* and *Phobos,* as well as short stories and articles that have appeared in numerous publications, including *Writer's Digest.* He currently lives in southern New Jersey with his wife and best friend, the *real* Helene Drago née Boettcher.

OTHER MONTH9BOOKS TITLES YOU MIGHT LIKE

THE UNDERTAKERS: SECRET OF THE CORPSE EATER

FINGERS IN THE MIST

FLEDGLING

AVIAN

THE BROTHERHOOD AND THE SHIELD: THE THREE THORNS

Find more awesome Teen books at
Month9Books.com

Connect with Month9Books online:

Facebook: www.Facebook.com/Month9Books

Twitter: https://twitter.com/Month9Books

You Tube: www.youtube.com/user/Month9Books

Blog: www.month9booksblog.com

Request review copies via publicity@month9books.com

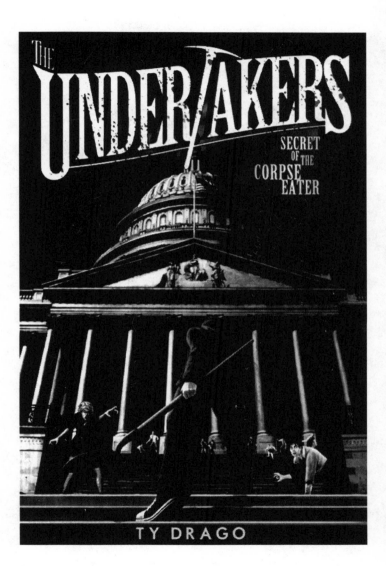

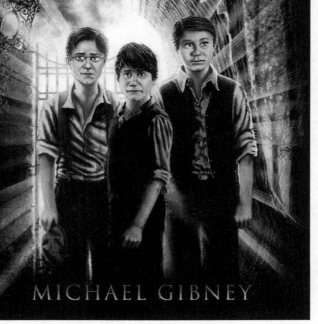

The
BROTHERHOOD
AND THE
SHIELD
THE THREE THORNS

MICHAEL GIBNEY